MW00911130

FROM THIS DISTANCE

FROM THIS DISTANCE

KAREN McLAUGHLIN

A novel

Cormorant Books

This is a first edition.

Canada Council for the Arts Conseil des Arts du Canada

The publisher gratefully acknowledges the support of the Canada Council for the Arts and the Ontario Arts Council for its publishing program. We acknowledge the financial support of the Government of Canada through the Book Publishing Industry Development Program (BPIDP) for our publishing activities.

Printed and bound in Canada

LIBRARY AND ARCHIVES CANADA CATALOGUING IN PUBLICATION

McLaughlin, Karen, 1954–

From this distance / Karen McLaughlin.

ISBN 978-1-897151-40-2

I. Title.

PS8575.L357 F76 2009 C813'.54 C2009-900668-5

Cover image and design: Angel Guerra/Archetype
Text design: Tannice Goddard, Soul Oasis Networking
Printer: Friesens

CORMORANT BOOKS INC.
215 SPADINA AVENUE, STUDIO 230, TORONTO, ON CANADA M5T 2C7
WWW.CORMORANTBOOKS.COM

For
Sara Juel and Jennifer Morain
with love and gratitude

ONE

THIS MORNING THE headlands of Nova Scotia are shrouded in fog. Boundaries of sea, sky, and land are smudged. I can't tell if the tide is halfway in or halfway out; I haven't been paying attention these last ten days. Nor have I checked the tide predictions for many years. It doesn't matter anymore. I am headed west in this two-tone Buick Skylark that has been willed to me by Muriel, a woman who complained endlessly that she had lived her life according to the will of others. I have stopped here on the gravel verge across from the entrance to Fundy National Park to breathe in salt marsh and think about the young slim girl who stood at this same edge, twenty years ago.

Behind me now is the Village of Alma. I have crossed the bridge that spans the millpond and mouth of the Salmon River that connects the park to the village. To the left is the great sweep of Alma beach — cut in two by a deep channel created by run-off from the river. A fishing wharf juts out into the channel between the Irving Gas Station and the once-grand Parkland Hotel. To the east, on the village side, the beach is bound by the headlands of Owl's Head and to the west, just ahead, winding up into the park, by Church Hill, steep and stately with its columns of Aspen trees that are just beginning to leaf out on this warm spring day.

A massive breakwater protects the sand dunes, marsh, and road. Out on the beach, long slicks of red-brick mud gleam up against the gravel flats. Springs trickle around sandbars. The channel winds through in a slate blue rush and, scattered all about are rocks, large and small. At the water's edge, even in this smudged, silvery light, the water is streaked with bands of mauve.

If the tide is on its way out, then in a few hours the whole bay will be emptied, exposing the bottom of the sea for a short time until the current begins to build speed and reverse direction. Even if the pace of the rising water appears leisurely and the tide is on its way in, then momentum is already present. Here, the largest tides in the world occur. Two monumental highs and lows power in and out, like sorrow in a family, every twenty-four hours and fifty minutes. A person could set her watch on the rhythm. In the summer of 1971, I set my heart by it.

Looking out I feel myself as that young woman, a girl really. Seventeen, with an open heart. I am standing ankle deep in slack water on the flood tide. Sand and pebbles sift under my toes. A small breeze stirs, dispersing the mingled smells of red mud and salt marsh freshly awash in tidewater.

My senses tingle. Before I know it, that slim young body slips right through me like a soft white light. I shiver. A deep resonant *unh* escapes my belly and mouth as I lurch for something elusive. That old longing of mine.

My eyes close. Transported, I feel the water rocking gently as I wade up to knees. Sun warms my shoulders. Small trenches of sand begin to fill in as soon as I lift my heel. In the shimmering light inside my head I scan the expanse of Chignecto Bay, its surface undulates in oily patches of light blue and dark blue, as if draped over a giant body, briefly at rest, with nowhere to go. On days like this, when a layer of cool air pools just above the water, distance seems to shorten.

The cliffs of Nova Scotia loom tall and close. Ile Haute hovers in the still air. Sound carries clearly. Cold water penetrates my bones. My ankles ache. Shins sting. That deep chilling sensation.

My eyes fly open. Cold streaks right up into this heart of mine. It is not so open as it was twenty years ago. It has bulked up like my belly that has begun to fold over the tops of my legs when I sit down if I don't remember to hold it in. That belly that seems to be mine, and not to be mine. That won't go away no matter how many miles I cycle along the interconnecting pathways and parks in the sprawling prairie city of Calgary where I live with my daughters and — until a few months ago, before he went away — with Muriel's beloved, though bewildering son, Jamie.

The husband who seems to be mine and not to be mine.

The summer I pose ankle deep in slack water, I feel his eyes on me before I even see his face. He is brazing up and down Church Hill in a shiny blue Triumph Spitfire. The sound scatters my concentration. There's been a buzz about that neat little wind-in-your-face car in the coffee shop in the park where I work, ever since Jamie's father Donny, one of the wardens, won it in a poker game at the Legion. I have not noticed Jamie before at the weekend parties but a high school friend who came here with me talks about him all the time. So I have this image of him.

I wouldn't mind a ride in that car that is somehow above the crowd, and below the crowd, at the same time. I could use a diversion, though that's a word I don't know at the time. I am searching. Restless. The mystique of spending the summer in a National Park is beginning to wear off. Cat Stevens was rumoured to have camped here in late spring but nobody remotely like him has materialized in the crowds of people who flock here from all over to experience the highest tides in the world. And the parties aren't what they're cracked up to be if all you do is end up on the sidelines observing everyone getting stoned. Last year in math class I read *Valley of the Dolls* twice and saw it as a morality tale. So I don't smoke dope or drop acid, and in answer to Gordie-the-campground-attendant's question the night of our first date, I don't *ball* either. At least not with guys like him.

By August, to relieve disappointment I let myself get caught in a spell by the monumental rhythm of the bay. I pace the shore along the sand dunes and watch the oscillating patterns of tide and current. The way waves come in. Waves within waves, Chignecto Bay within the Bay of Fundy. The pattern constantly changing. Somehow I have it in my head that if I try hard enough, my body can be a measuring stick to detect the exact moment when the tide turns. I believe that the shift must happen in a moment that is as precise as the centre part in my dark brown hair. There's something I want but I'm not sure what it is. Something bigger than myself and at the same time, something more naked than naked. Something of essence. I'm not sure. Perhaps all I'm saying is *Here I am. I feel you. Do you feel me? Let me know.*

With the sound of the Triumph behind me, I edge further out into the water and hold my body still, trying with all my might to detect the shifting tide. When the cold water laps my thighs and stains the hem of my short skirt, I look down, heart sinking. The water has turned a milky silted blue, saturated with mud particles stirred up by tidal currents. Sea, sand, and pebbles sieve through my toes. Water sloshes behind me. I turn toward shore to witness white foam ruffling the beach in its wake. Though the surface is calm, the water has started to reverse direction, building power to shift away. A smooth rolling swell drenches my skirt. Soaks my panties. Leaving me agitated as it starts to pull out.

The tide has turned and I have missed the moment again.

AS I SCRUNCH up through the tidal trash, the Triumph idles by the side of the road. I lean against a ledge of sandstone riprap to clean off curly black strings of seaweed and tiny, rosy, fragments of clamshell and sticks and tide-tumbled stones plastered to my cold red feet. Jamie and his buddy sip lukewarm beer and watch me from the car. When he pushes in the clutch and slips into first, pulling away, he looks over to me and nods to his buddy *She's the one*. I know this because his utterance is the first line in the enduring story we tell about our marriage. *She's the one*.

We have been together for more than half our lives.

As I leave this place where I once felt at home, but am now casting off, I feel like a crab shedding its shell. For the first time in several years, I feel raw and exposed. Not defenceless and naive like the girl on the beach, but aware and tender. Because for one split second — a few days ago on that cataclysmic afternoon when the ground was opened up to take Muriel — where we stood in disbelief in front of the crushed marble fireplace in that bilious living room of hers, Jamie collapsed into me with a sob that will crack me open forever.

And into that crack flooded images and smells and tastes and sounds, and in an instant, feelings and sensations that had long been buried detonated into the present. I can no more ignore these memories — they seem more real to me than recent events — than I can ignore the simple fact that I am rolling down the car window. I don't need to get out. I only need a little air. A few minutes to shake off some of the dander from two funerals before I hit the road.

As I adjust the seat, pulling the seatbelt across chest and hips, I feel a flutter of relief and a flutter of regret start to duke it out in the corridors between my belly and heart.

I will miss this landscape. But will I miss this place? Back then, I felt attuned to the natural world and was filled with possibility. Now I live by demands or expectations, and desire only to build on my hard-won successes. I don't even know if I live for myself.

Wedged between my purse and file folder of maps on the passenger's seat there is a picnic basket, like a nest, heaped with the remnants of funeral food Muriel's sister Agatha thrust into my hands just a few moments ago. *Waste not want not* was on her lips, but I think she recognized that the nature of our relationship has shifted. In the last few years I have outgrown the schoolgirl crush I had on her. For our farewell, she silently wobbled as I hugged her ancient corseted body. An armful of feathers after eight months in the role of nursemaid and warden. Instead of thinking this might be the last time I hug Agatha, I fill my head with an image of her kitchen-sitting-room layered with accumulated books and newspaper clippings, postcards and string, or her floor-to-ceiling pantry, chock-a-block with festering jars of preserves left over from her mother Philomena's days. The antiquated, almost-used-up bottles of Kraft salad dressing lined up next to faded packets of Jell-O with logos from my childhood era. I don't buy that Depression, *we-had-to-do-without-stuck-down-here-in-the-woods-so-we-don't-throw-anything-away* argument anymore. Or that she's far too busy with local politics to bother concerning herself with the triflings of domesticity. That's too easy for Agatha. I am finally figuring out the difference between excuses and reasons. Agatha is a hoarder by heart. Something inside her makes it impossible to make decisions about what to do with the mess; she simply can't part with anything — even family secrets. Until she spilled her guts to me on the Veteran's Ward up at the Georges Dumont Hospital in Moncton just after Muriel's funeral.

If Muriel had been quietly laid to rest without being upstaged at her own funeral, I would have told a different story than the one that's bursting in my heart today. Funny how you think a person's story is over when they die. Then something happens. Someone gives you new information. The story takes on another life and the dead cultivate a new beginning — inside the garden of your head.

Too many things live on. Like the spite and jealousy between Muriel and Agatha. "I can't believe," Muriel told me in suppressed rage after her diagnosis last summer, "that Agatha will get to go to Andrea's wedding and I won't."

When I hug Agatha to say goodbye, I feel her X-ray vision penetrating my body and tabulating all the stuff I've got stashed in the car. I almost hope she sees that hideous tapestry handbag that used to belong to Philomena, thrown so carelessly on top of my suitcases in the back. "I'll let you have this bag," she told Muriel a few years ago, "as long as you promise to never let it fall into Robyn's hands."

My motives aren't as squeaky clean as my new-found reasoning or understanding of family events. I wouldn't let her take back the antique chocolate set she gave Muriel for her birthday the year we all met, either.

I don't know what I feel as I hug this eighty-year-old body. Something real passes between us.

She kept the ring. She kept everything. Muriel's voice from the Great Beyond intrudes. An old complaint, thinly veiled as they all were: *Don't love her. Love me.*

When well out of sight, I'm going to dump Agatha's offerings. What really interests me is the booty in the bottom. The photograph in the silver frame of Muriel and Agatha when they were four and five that I snitched from the whatnot upstairs. A blue velvet Birks box with two identical tiny gold lockets that was left on top of the clock on Muriel's nightstand. A packet of letters with no postmark that I found nestled in a hatbox at the top of the attic stairs along with Muriel's stripeless nursing cap and a shiny muskrat stole with little feet, empty eyes, and a scrunched up nose with a fastener embedded in the mouth that grasped its tail. Stashed in Muriel's underwear drawer was a heart-shaped chocolate box fringed with white lace that held two folded notes Jamie wrote to her when he was little and home sick from school.

Between the funeral food and all that stuff of Muriel's is a floppy goose down pillow that I take on my travels and the black velvet bibbed hot pants I wore the first Christmas Jamie and I spent with Donny and Muriel. Finding them shocked me almost as much as donning my black suit and sling-back Bally heels to attend a second funeral in four days.

My hot pants, Muriel? What were you doing with my hot pants in your cedar chest? So small they almost look like doll's clothes. I always knew you took an interest in what I wore and you bought me some pretty nice duds over the years. But finding my hot pants in your cedar chest makes me feel sort of creepy. It suggests a kind of collusion I find hard to stomach. As if I have something to be ashamed of. As if you were there from the very beginning, before I even knew. My black velvet hot pants you squirreled away makes me wonder. What was being played out when Jamie watched me from the side of the road? Or later that night when we eyed each other at a party up at Shadow Lake?

MOST OF THE summer park crowd is stoned or drinking *goof*, listening to Jimmy Hendrix. Still agitated, but straight, I dance around the edges of the room all alone. Wearing a bubble shirt. Skin-tight. Pale pink like my pale skin. A pair of hip huggers, bell-bottomed GWGs, and a wide belt. My high school friend is sitting on Jamie's lap on the sofa but he can't keep his eyes off me. (He thinks I'm topless. This is the second line in our story.) Swivelling my hips like a go-go girl, I have all the moves, but anxious and unsure, split that scene before I steal my girlfriend's date.

All the next week, even though he's gone back to his surveyor's job in Kouch up on the North Shore, Jamie's gaze hovers around me. Days before I had hardly been aware of his existence, but all of a sudden I am living in a bubble that is somehow about him. The feeling is seductive although I don't truly know the meaning of that word yet. I am being chosen. This feels good since I arrived here so heart-sore. And better than being all-keyed up wondering if Gordie or one of the other camping lot attendants (never a naturalist) was going to come along and get me into the Parkland Bar where I'd nurse a rum and coke, thrilled to be included with the fast crowd.

That gaze has me stymied. Even the tides and the beach don't draw me in. By the weekend I drift off with the coffee shop girls over to the bunkhouse with a bunch of guys who came down from Montreal. I finally give in and take my turn nibbling a lump of hash the size of an Easter egg as it makes the rounds. Someone gets the bright idea to break into the saltwater pool over by the golf course. The guys strip off. I'm the only girl who dares to jump into the black water in my underwear. When we stumble back to the boarding house it's past curfew, we're locked out, and end up sleeping on the porch. The deep creeping chill of fog permeates my wet underwear and hundred and ten pound body. This big handsome guy with a Lebanese name cuddles and necks with me all night to keep me warm but neither he nor the stupor of my body-stone dispels the bubble of Jamie's gaze. In the morning I come down with a sore throat.

That's the last time I went out with anybody else but Jamie and if I'd had even an inkling that in a year I'd be married, perhaps I would have tried a little harder to remember the guy's name, or at least his face. As it is, all I have is this impression of him: large, older, comfortable. In some ways, during the last few years, everywhere I go, I'm hoping to bump into him.

Does this shock you, Muriel? Somehow it feels like you have slipped out of my head and have settled into the seat beside me. (A passenger as always. Even in death.) I see entitlement has survived internment. Oh well, make yourself comfortable, it's not like I'm not used to having you around. And I feel a little entitlement of my own after sorting through all your earthly possessions. I can ask you anything now that you're on the other side. Is that how you felt about young Dr. Moore when you left him behind in Montreal in 1937? Were you always on the lookout for him too? His name was still on your lips more than thirty years after your nursing school misadventure, although in reality I doubt somehow that his lips ever got anywhere near yours.

Oh god Muriel. The things we remember.

IT WOULDN'T BE too long before I abandoned all desire to measure the exact moment when the tide turns. You had your hand in that. You wanted me for something else. How could I have predicted that? Or predict that I would tail the last generation of North American women who followed their pioneering men unquestioningly from east to west, north to south, back and forth again as they plundered and manipulated the continent's natural resources. Let alone predict that in the last two years of your life you would act so out of character, and besmirch, as Agatha — that repository of authority — charged. Besmirch your good family name. (Of course she meant the name the two of you shared, your maiden name, Steadman. The Gallagher name, she divulged last week, had been ruined in 1927.)

Thinking of pioneers, you, in your own way, Muriel, were a pioneer of sorts too, weren't you? You held your ground in the fifties and sixties (it was too late by the seventies) in favour of your own profession. You would not budge. Even when it cost Donny all chance of promotion. What gave you that power over him? Did you always feel superior? Was it your Methodist and Baptist upbringing? Or was it that you had such an abiding historical sense of yourself? The big moments. Think about it Muriel, you were born the month the Great War was declared. You remember sitting on your father's shoulders the night four years later when the whole village turned out on the beach to burn the Kaiser in effigy. (Even though Agatha always harrumphed that you couldn't possibly remember that event because she can't, and she's older — though not by much.) You remember the fire that swept through the village burning eleven houses (one of which was your family home), four stores (including your father's general store), the Alma Superior School, the Orange Hall, the United Church, and all the mature maple trees that had adorned the main street. You remember your father burning his Depression ledger in a rusted oil barrel out in the backfield because he knew there was no money in the village to pay him. *I can't even talk about it*, you'd say whenever the Hungry Thirties were brought up (and they were always brought up at some family dinner in regard to somebody's thanklessness) and you'd throw your hand out in front of yourself as if to brace against the whole weight of the Depression.

I always wanted to ask what couldn't you talk about, Muriel? Last week Agatha gave me a clue. Mentioned a detail that never passed your lips. Tell me, what else did your father burn in that barrel? I want to hear it from you.

You went to university during the thirties for four years. (Five. I now have to correct myself since Agatha tattled on you that it was five years because you dragged your heels for a year. *And father had to pay.*) Mount Allison no less. That august institute of higher learning tucked away in Sackville that has the richest alumni in the country because that's where so many daughters and sons of the high and mighty were shipped off to for decades. It was the place to get into. Still is. Though I have yet to fathom what you learned there. You never talked about those years except to complain that Agatha told on you for going to dances, playing tennis, and wearing nail polish — all unladylike activities in the eyes of Perley and Philomena, those self-consciously Victorian parents of yours. (Not that I ever met them, but they were always so damned present.) What subjects did you like? What books did you read? Two biographies, one of Jacqueline Kennedy and the other of Jennie Churchill, are the only books I've known you to read. You were a magazine thumber. Constantly clearing your throat while you flipped the pages. The *Moncton Times* got a casual perusal, though in the evening you usually fidgeted with the crossword puzzle while you listened to television. Something always had to be on the go.

(Did you ever notice that you were faithful to the clothes and convolutions of your afternoon soap? Do we ever see those things about ourselves?)

Just what did you get out of your education except an achievement, a degree, a teaching profession?

The only tangible trace of those five years is the Limoges china you hand-painted in an elective. I've got the big vase and two plates wrapped in those monogrammed towels you never used tucked away in the trunk. Alexis took the rest. Jamie was indifferent to the china, but he kept your graduation portrait we found in the linen closet. In that portrait, except for the tilt of your head, you are almost unrecognizable. Smooth, sweet, and dewy. Hopeful. Only the silenced part of you looks familiar.

What I remember you saying about university is that it's not what it's cracked up to be. All your suffocating talk those first years was family politics, loaded with defences and excuses and *What Ifs* and *If Onlys*. Full of the *Great War*, the *Hungry Thirties*, and then *The War* and *The Sacrifice* — all that collective suffering that gave you moral authority over us — and the knitting of socks for six years while your heart burned for Donny (or his cousin) to come home.

ALL THAT WEIGHT on you, Muriel. You knew exactly where you stood.

I suppose you detect a tone from me. You're right. If you knew yourself historically, then I must confess from the start of this trip that I, as one of the late Canadian Boomers (the ones too late for Woodstock), aim to know myself psychologically. We Boomers are fascinated with our bodies and our minds. We analyze everything. We can't get no satisfaction. We don't have the privilege of history anymore; you old folks stopped it dead in its tracks when you saved us from evil. (Well obviously that's a bit of an overstatement but that's how it feels.) If we've heard it once we've heard it a thousand times. *You have no idea* ... And it's true. We have been largely protected from the great horrific moments of the exterior world. So some of us journey inward, away from the tribe, into the defining moments of our own lives. These moments are scary places, Muriel. They make us shake and tremble, but we try to stick with them and see what they're all about.

Here's one, Muriel. *Don't go near the water.* Your mother's hysteria. That's why you never learned to swim until you were well over sixty. You blamed Philomena for that until the day you died. Even when you had conquered some of your fears and paddled about, your short fat arms whirling frantically while you strained to keep your thin, brittle hair dry, you would never go out over your head. In your heart, you were always afraid of the water, but you had such longing. I was proud of you for learning to swim. Hell's bells, I was proud of you for pouring yourself into spandex and risking those heavy dimpled thighs to public view. Inspired. Ever believing that you'd somehow confront the other disappointments and failures of your ponderous life with the same determination. In so many ways you became my role model.

A mother that seemed to be mine and not to be mine.

That coy voice of yours calling from your bedroom, "Is that you sweetheart?" to Jamie the night of our enchantment. Your voice was so reassuring. After all, I had been expecting, "Who the hell is making all that noise?" in a voice like my mother's, when we landed at your house to make a pizza at two in the morning.

"Won't they mind?" I asked.

"Nah, the Old Lady won't mind. And the Old Man sleeps like a log."

Your kitchen smelled like biscuits and jam with a faint hum of Javex from the dishcloth wafting over everything. There was a clutter of crockery and jars on the counters. With one eye I spy a Friendly Village bowl, surprised to see you had the same hideous, nostalgic set of dishes as my mother, thinking you wouldn't catch anyone making a pizza at my place at two in the morning. Not on your life. With the other eye I took in Jamie, weight on one foot, leaning halfway out the kitchen door that connected with the hallway, his wide shoulders and rugby-playing backside.

"Don't forget there's lots of cake left," you sang out softly.

"It's her birthday," he whispered to me. "That's why I was so late coming over to the boarding house tonight."

"Did you have a party?"

"Nah, the Old Lady doesn't take a shine to a lot of people."

I didn't think to question what he meant by that. I don't question at all. I marvelled that only a couple of hours earlier, sometime around midnight, Jamie had come over to the boarding house to claim me.

I see myself perched on a tall stool wrapped in an old green blanket in the middle of the kitchen feeling sorry for myself because I have greasy hair and everyone is getting ready for the big end-of-the-summer party out at Waterside. I'm not going anywhere. My throat is still sore. I'm flapping my friend and her date — she'd given up on Jamie at this point — out the door when he knocks and walks in, brushing past her.

Aw fuck, she turns and mouths to me.

But I knew, Muriel, I just knew that Jamie had not come for her.

"Are you going to the party, sad sack?"

(This is the third line in our story.)

"Can't. Sore throat."

"Okay." He closes the door.

Subdued by languid thoughts I eyeball the dingy wallpaper peeling around the scratched and worn wainscoting, contemplating the oily patches of light blue and dark blue that reappear here and there from previous patterns layered over the years. The summer is almost over and soon I'll have to go back home. I don't know what to do. The thought of going back to those dull-eyed teachers in the high school in Sussex makes me intolerably restless. I didn't even stick it out for grade eleven. Its smell makes me sick. All my friends are older and have graduated and are moving on to bigger things. I have no encouragement from home. My stepfather is a self-made man and has no use for higher learning. Mum wants me to be a nurse but that's her old dream. I have this half-assed idea about becoming a hairdresser. You only need grade ten to get in and I'm pretty good with my hands.

The door opens a crack.

"Are you sure?"

That's when I look Jamie full in the face. Shaggy sandy hair, olive green eyes, smooth tanned skin. I get all shivery. Run my cold hands through my long layered hair. "Okay, what the hell," I shrug as if this statement isn't going to change the whole course of my life. Up the broad oak stairs I run two at a time, brush my teeth, decide it's too late to bother with make-up, and throw this loopy black-and-white crochet hat over my head to hide my greasy hair. All night I don't dare take it off, especially in the Javexy glare of your kitchen.

After the pizza, we vamoosed in Donny's Spitfire, roaring over hell and hackety all night long, hugging the winding roads, pounding over potholes, in and out of fog banks, up and over hills, always on the lookout for deer or moose. In no time we establish that Jamie hates school as much as I do and cautiously confesses that he's on probation in engineering down at Saint Mary's in Halifax. I don't give a shit about his marks. Achievements are not on my mind. My body thrums with the car's vibration on the pebbly surfaces. We are so low to the ground.

I AM ABOUT to enter the magical kingdom of Jamie's childhood, Muriel. Two hundred and six square kilometres of the great beauty of the Maritime Acadian Highlands, an extension of the ancient Appalachian Mountains. Fundy National Park, created in 1948, preserved and protected by the Government of Canada and patrolled by Jamie's father, your war-worn husband. There was nothing Donny liked better than tramping through the deep spongy woods or wading across the park's system of streams and rivers counting trees and marking deer in the deep valleys; sitting by a milky-white waterfall eating the hearty lunch you had so lovingly prepared; or pounding along the thirteen kilometres of coastline in an open power boat scouting the sandstone cliffs and beaches in the name of his father, and for his son, and the holy ghost of lost opportunities and misplaced memories. Trying to forget the six years spent as an armourer in England loading Lancaster bombers with deadly payloads. Or worse yet, running toward a bomb with his tiny set of tools, to diffuse what had not been dumped over Europe, as the pilots and crew ran from their aircraft when they came back from their missions with altimeter bombs that had not disengaged. (Bombs, bombs, bombs. They riddled Donny's brain.)

Our first stop in the magical kingdom is the warden's bungalow way up the back logging road that cuts into the steep hill by the radar station on the park's eastern boundary. This is where you moved in the early fifties from the house that you and Donny built in the village after you first got married in 1947. And this is where Jamie begins to speak from a place so deep inside him, from a well of such depth, tenderness, and piety, that there is no space between him and me.

The enchantment begins.

"Dad used to let me sit on his lap and steer the old International Jeep he drove on patrol. There were no other kids around to play with so Mom let me hide her old pearl and rhinestone jewellery in treasure boxes out in the yard. I never got tired of digging it up. In the winter she'd take me tobogganing. In the summer Dad taught Alexis and me how to swim out at Broad River. They even bought us ponies that we kept in a pen out back."

The ponies really got to me, Muriel. I would have died for one when I was a kid. And you know what? Jamie's real feeling about those ponies didn't come out until a few months ago, when his anger about them seem to boil up out of nowhere one morning. But that night he told me the stories he lived by. He gave me snapshot versions of *the curtains, the cake, the kick in the ass* when you were going through *the change*. He made these legends out to be funny and charming. But how could he have left out all that rage of yours? How could I have understood that by making these stories harmless they set you in irons on a hormonal sea? I couldn't. Not then. Completely hoodwinked, I was convinced that you and Jamie and Donny and Alexis made the ideal family.

As we lean against the Spitfire watching the distant lights at Apple River over in Nova Scotia hover like tiny blobs of stars through the patchy fog, which is beginning to dissipate, it dawns on me that this is the site of one of the radar stations that was lit up on a giant painted plywood map of the Maritimes mounted on the wall at the radar station in Chester on the south shore of Nova Scotia where my English stepfather worked as the station manager just after he and Mum got married. She was pregnant with my brother and sometimes we used to sleep there when Dad was on the back shift. Those nights were always magical to me. The dials and switches on the banks of equipment. All the beeps and squeaks. The alien, burning-dust smell of electronics. *Mind those little fingers. Don't touch.* Lying on a mattress on the floor in an electronic fortress that sent and received signals out into the ether, wondering about the people in the other places lit up on the map with light bulbs. Wondering if I would ever go anywhere. Thinking this map encompassed my world of possibilities. Knowing I could never go to England because *all English children are naturally good and all Canadian children are naturally bad.*

"You were in this house, right here, next to the radar station when I used to stare at the lights on the map," I say to Jamie, getting my stepfather's voice out of my head, as a wave of something I think must be fate plunges through me. I feel a little dizzy. Hooked.

"Is that where you lived before you moved to Sussex?"

"Oh god no. We were out of Chester by the time I was six. I've always wanted to go back there though. We moved all the time until Dad finally took the leap and opened his photography shop in Sussex three years ago. But I hate that valley town. Every square inch. If I ever get out of there I'm never going back."

I try to think of a funny mother story in return for *the curtains, the cake, the kick in the ass* stories, but my parents are always getting mad at each other, and during the last couple of years, especially since my aunts were killed in a car crash, my mother goes off the deep end and disappears from time-to-time. I keep most of this to myself. For now I tell Jamie about the heat wave last summer and my mother with her feet stuck in a lasagna pan of cold water the day she gave up painting the house, fanning her face with a copy of *Mandingo* muttering to no one in particular (because nobody listened to her either, Muriel), *I can't believe this Christless heat.*

"I'm not a women's libber," I declare, after this useless information. "Someone has to keep the peace in the family." (This is the fifth line in our story.)

"I want a job in the National Parks like my dad," Jamie beats the big drum. "Play golf on Friday afternoons and not work too hard. Take my kids out on picnics. Buy furniture on credit. Carry on the family name." (This is the sixth.)

At the park headquarters we drive by the bungalow where you lived when he was in elementary school. According to Jamie, this was the greatest place in the world to grow up. Close to the ballpark. The woods. The beach. Just up the hill from the village and his grandparents who treated him like gold.

"I was never in, always out. Always on the tear except when playing in the sandbox with my trucks. I remember the day Dad came home from work and towering above me in his warden uniform and felt hat said, 'Boy, when you grow up you're going to be an engineer and build a big road. A real one.' He made me feel so important."

Out at Wolfe Lake on the northern boundary of the park, twelve miles from Alma and thirty miles from Sussex (as you so often complained), we tumble out of the Triumph and stand on the shore of Lake View, so pretty with its fringe of forest and hills that recede into the depths of the park. Through the trees he points out the white bungalow where you and Donny and he and Alexis lived when he was in his teens. Here his voice gets a little boggy. Distance creeps in but he holds it at bay.

"Al and I had to go to private school when we moved out here. There's no high school in Alma. We would've had to take the bus all the way up to Hillsborough, and in the winter the roads are real bad. The Old Lady said it would've been too much going back and forth. So she started teaching again to pay Alexis's tuition down at Netherwood and for a while there was just the three of us. I drove into Alma with her to school every day. Then I got the boot. But it was great when I came home for Christmas. Dad took us out on the park snowmobiles and we'd make a fire and boil up tea. In the summer I had a canoe I rigged up with a sail and spent whole days out on the lake alone. Then Alexis started going out with Ed and he'd come for all the holidays. I had the best days of my life with Ed out on the water, or up in the loft over the garage where we used to sleep."

I should have paid attention to the fact that I was about to hitch my star to someone who already thought he'd had the best days of his life. But instead I was fixated on Netherwood. How I had longed to go to Netherwood down in Rothesay. I bet it didn't stink down there. I bet the teachers were more on the ball. I bet they had horses and art classes. Piano lessons. Lucky Alexis. With that princess name I am in awe of her already. She is three years, two months, and seventeen days older than Jamie is. She never lets him forget it.

"Did you go to Rothesay Collegiate?"

"Nope. They shipped me off to King's down in Nova Scotia."

"How was it?"

"The first term was the pits. When I wasn't looking, Al stashed my teddy bear on top of the stuff in my trunk and everyone saw, so I started off with a lot of ribbing. *Teddy*, they called me, but eventually I muscled out of that one on the rugby field and the hockey team. Then I got to be the Regimental Sergeant Major in the cadets. But shit, it was hard, you know? Sleeping in a strange place with a lot of rich kids. By the first Christmas I was pretty much toughened up. The food was never like home food though."

It's hard for me to imagine that he missed your cooking, Muriel. But he did. And what's alarming for me these last couple of years is that he has begun to prefer his steaks well done. Potatoes lumpy and watery. Pasta mashable. Turnips with everything. Not a green veg in sight.

The enchantment is almost complete. On the way to Point Wolfe we drive past your bungalow snuggled in the woods on a rise down near the Herring Cove turn-off where, a few hours earlier, we had made pizza and listened to Cat Stevens straining from the middle of his throat that he's old and happy while Donny sawed logs. (And you, Muriel, probably laid on your back with your legs crossed on the cheap twin beds that you and Donny had bought in an effort to be together but apart while you struggled to hear what we were talking about.) To my young mind all these isolated outposts look like havens of peace and are abstractly comforting. Romantic even. Ideal places to raise a couple of kids. Not that I think of having kids in any real kind of way. (Only years later does it occur to me that in reality, these are the ideal places in which to incubate anger and despair.)

Jamie toots the horn for good luck when we pass through the red covered bridge by the old damn at Point Wolfe. A wave of pleasure surges through me when we park and he clutches my hand as we climb up on the rocks beside the covered bridge. While we listen to the water from the Point Wolfe River spilling over the remnants of the old damn down into the estuary that winds its way out into the bay, Jamie stands behind me with his arms folded loosely around my waist. Fog clings to the cliffs and treetops. The smell of fir and moss and salt mingle in the mizzling rain. I bide my time waiting nervously for a kiss. He tells me how the long-gone mill here used to supply electricity to Alma from early in the morning until 9 pm, when the lights would blink as a warning that they were shutting down for the night.

Then he tells me proudly how his father's father made enough bonus money during the First World War when demand for timber was acute, to buy his own portable sawmill, and set himself up as a businessman. Making the Gallaghers sound like a dynasty, he goes on to claim, "I was named after him and my son will be named after my father. That's the way it is in my family." (This is the seventh line. The fault line.)

I have this image of myself as a little girl down in Nova Scotia the year of the crib death, in the last light of a damp winter day, opening the front door a crack looking into the living room where I know my mother will be rousing herself from the couch, lighting a cigarette with one hand while pushing the back of her other hand across her groggy Snow White face, getting up the energy to go into the kitchen and start supper. Little balls of ice rim the edge of my sleeves, orbiting my skinny wrists, leaving smeared red stinging slashes in their wake. My mitts are soaked and the wet woolly snow pants I hate with a passion are itching like crazy. "Can I please come in now?" I whisper through hot chapped lips.

This image persists until we scoot past the golf course on the way back down to my boarding house in the village and Jamie tells me about the farmhouses that were expropriated and torn down to build it. "The Old Man inherited a couple of them from his father but when he got back from the war, he just gave them to the people who were living in them. From time-to-time, the Old Lady still seethes about him giving away his inheritance. There was good money to be made from the expropriation."

"Well, people are funny about things. Too bad about the houses though."

"No way. This golf course was designed by one of the best and I know every square inch of it. Do you like to golf?"

"Can't say I've ever given it a try." My opinion of golf is informed by my stepfather who holds a geek's disdain for the game, and my mother who dreams only of golf courses where she could be taken to dance.

"They say I could have been a pro. But the folks are dead set against it. Not very practical, I guess."

(Practical, I will come to learn, is one of the most important words in the family vocabulary.)

By the time we get back to Alma, fog has followed the tide out the bay. Light land breezes skither thin clouds across the stars and full moon. Jamie bumpety-bumps Donny's Spitfire out onto the fishing wharf. He opens my door and gives me a hand out, tucking it under the cable-knit sweater you made for his birthday. In the chilly air we look down at the lobster boats resting on their bellies in the muddy sand and gravel. The air is heavy with the smells of sea, marsh, and creosote; old wood and rough rope; well-mended lobster traps. Diesel fuel and motor oil.

Jamie reveals to me the two types of flying dreams he had as a kid. How they always took place in the olden days. In one it's daytime. He's flying toward the cemeteries up Bucket Hill on the way to Moncton, but when he gets to the point where the road disappears around the bend he's caught in an updraft. He flies down the main rutted street that parts the houses in the village and tries to follow the road out to Sussex, but the wind keeps him back and he hovers over the marsh and millpond. He glances upstream to the mill. There is a constant thunder of noise: water rushing through the turbines, the whining rasp of saws, the muffled sound of heavy boots and lumber being stacked, men shouting back and forth and the clanging beat from the blacksmith shop. He smells the marsh and the mud and the freshly sawn lumber. Smoke from the slash at the mill feathers out over Church Hill. When he tries to swoop down the road past the farms that used to be on the golf course he gets pushed back and all he can do is drift back over the bay. There are waves of hills and trees as far as he can see. He can't get anywhere.

The other dream is just about the same except it's night. The tide is all the way in. The moon is out and the bay looks as if it has been draped with a thin luminous sheet. Fresh stacks of lumber gleam against the dark pilings of the wharf. There's a scow tied up ready to take the deal out to a four-masted schooner anchored out in the bay. He longs to stow away, but it's the same as the daytime dream. He can't get anywhere. He looks down into the water and a thin porridge of sawdust debris from the mill that looks a peculiar green under the water that swills up against the wharf.

The next thing he knows he's in the dining room at his grandparent's doing his homework and the lights blink. He thinks he can put his books away and go to bed, he's so tired from playing ball all day, but you, Muriel, appear with an oil lamp and say, we never had it as good as you, and make him keep adding up columns of numbers that grow longer and longer, all night long.

These dreams are so intimate I feel shy for a few moments and don't know what to say. Then I reveal to Jamie that I have been trying to discover the exact moment when the tide turns.

"Have you ever tried it out at low tide?"

"Only on the highs. The naturalists warned me that it's dangerous to go out there alone because you never know when the tide will turn wrong on you."

"Forget them. I know this bay like the back of my hand. Come on. Let's go. The tide will be all the way out by the time we get there."

I am relieved that he doesn't think my endeavour is weird. "Okay," I whisper.

"Village side or park side?" he asks.

"Park side. No street lights. No one watching."

We scramble over the breakwater. There lies the crescent of beach that wraps the village — completely drained of water. Moonlight plays on the purplish outwash of mudflats and sandbars as clouds floss past. Puddles and rivulets wink against the dark forms of rocks and gravel that have been tossed and scattered by retreating waters.

We shuck our sneakers, roll up our jeans a few inches, and set out for a middle-of-the-night walk on the bottom of the sea, following the channel until it dwindles to a ribbon, criss-crossing here and there as it meets ridges and shallows cut by the tide. An hour later at the shore's edge we turn and look back at Alma. Except for a few streetlights, and a handful of cottage porch lights nestled here and there in the wave of forested hills that loom out behind the village, there is no sign of life. Down on Main Street, old clapboard houses with broad sun porches stand out against the newer, flat-roofed buildings that have been wedged between them. Jamie points out his grandparent's house with the wraparound, glassed-in sun porch next to the squat, charmless post office.

"My grandfathers were the two biggest businessmen in Alma," he says with such reverence.

(A bit grandiose, wouldn't you say Muriel? Where did he get that from?)

When we reach the tide line, we inch into the dark cold water. Jamie curls his arm across my shoulders. I snuggle into his side. His body is hard and muscular with a nice, soft top layer. Resting his cheek on the top of my head, we rock gently, lulled into a half-sleep.

For an indeterminate amount of time, the world stands still. With a start, I glance up. The sky is beginning to lighten over Owl's Head. I suddenly realize that the tide has crept past my ankles. Water gurgles as clam holes start to fill in.

"Shit! I can't believe it," I push away from him. "The tide's gone and done it again."

"It doesn't matter," he says, and pulls me back. Then, scrunching the loopy crochet hat into his pocket he cradles my head in his hands and kisses me. Gently. Deeply. Harder. Christ almighty. He slides his hand over my right breast. The top of my head nearly blows off.

"We can come another time."

A FEMALE WHITETAIL deer nudges her speckled fawn away from the side of the road as I skid to a near stop. What the hell are they doing out here at this time of the day? I wonder. The mother takes an appraising look at the car as if she knows who the real owner is, then in two seconds flat she and the fawn spring up and away, disappearing into the bush.

Jesus, Muriel. That was close. Have you got your seatbelt on?

My heart is racing. Where were we? Oh yes, another time. How could I forget? Another time! We must have walked that tide out a hundred times but we never *made* the time again for my endeavour. There was always a family crisis to attend to or occupy our thoughts. Either your family or mine. At some point I must have stopped thinking about measuring the exact moment when the tide turns. I have no idea when. Somehow, like water seeping into clam holes, duty and responsibility began to fill in the parts of my mind that used to breathe imagination.

When I think about myself, Muriel, sitting on that stool, miserable with a sore throat, wrapped in a green blanket, inert, like the beach waiting for the tide to roll in and change its shape, I have to wonder what happened to the girl who had once turned over every rock, skipped along the railroad tracks, swum across the lake by herself. The girl who was never afraid of the outside world, only the world inside the house. Who had Jamie come back to the boarding house for that night?

The girl who stood ankle deep in cold water on the flood tide. He didn't see my mind working; he was looking at my legs. He found beauty in what he thought was my stillness. He thought he saw something of you in me. What was that? (You have no idea how much this troubles me.) He would have followed me anywhere that night. I had no idea. I was afraid he'd laugh at me. But he wasn't really paying attention. I'll bet he shrugged my endeavour off as an idiosyncrasy. And now that's all I've become to him. A clutch of idiosyncrasies he can't get a grip on. Do you know what he said one evening last year when he came home from the construction site on a turnaround?

"You're weird, Robyn."

"What?" I asked. Surprised and hurt. (Still cringing after twenty years about my loopy crochet hat. *I thought it was a tea cozy*, he confessed, months or years later. That is the last line in our story.) But what good would it do to provoke him? He'd only leave the house to get some distance between us then come back later in martyred silence. (Like one of your great silences, Muriel. You taught him so well.) Then, both gutless, when eventually neither of us could stand it anymore, one of us, almost always me, would start talking about something banal to break the ice.

"Weird?" I asked, from my spot on the love seat. "You mean since I went to art school?"

"No," he answered flatly. Fully. From his spot in the corner by the wall unit. As if he had been pondering this for twenty years and a light bulb he didn't want to look at just went on. "You've always been weird." Then he turned back to his pipe and his scotch, adjusted the headphones, closed his eyes, and cranked up Howlin' Wolf.

As I speed all the way up Church Hill, past the park headquarters and the clump of red spruce where Sid's Coffee shop once stood, gunning up the hairpin turns of Hasting Hills, fishtailing for a moment as I hit the remnants of sand and gravel pooled in pockets where the road freezes and heaves during the winter, I try to push our recent grievances away and bask in the extravagance of these first date memories. I wonder if they would have remained so strong if it hadn't been your birthday, Muriel. If we hadn't been trotting out these memories on the 14th of August for over twenty years.

Thinking of you, those first date feelings subside. Though here's what's really strange, when I remember now — that walk out onto the bottom of the sea — it's as if you're already with us, even though I really didn't meet you until a couple of weeks later. But somehow your presence was there. This is one thing I've learned: how the heart remembers things is not necessarily the order in which things happen. At first you took a shine to me. Maybe you were the moon, Muriel, eyeballing us as young lovers — jealous? disconnected? — and forever following us wherever we went. Sometimes shining brightly on us, sometimes casting shadows. Always present and not present. Always waxing and waning. Because really, when you come to think of it, how can you look up into the sky on a moonless night and not evoke the idea of the moon?

In the end, those hard eight months you lingered when the doctors gave you three weeks completely eclipsed anything we had that was left of us. I hate you for this, Muriel.

Pulling over at the viewpoint at the top of the hills to take one last look at the bay and the headlands, I clutch jacket lapels close to my chest with both hands and roll them in as I step out of the car. All that's visible below is a bowl of low clouds and fog feathering up over the treetops. It's really socked in down in the village. I'm well out of here, I think, grabbing for the door handle. Already the air has condensed and laid a thin film of moisture over the entire car, taking a little of the shine off.

I wonder why the hell you have willed me this car, Muriel. This 1988 two-tone burgundy Buick Skylark. Surely it is a strange bequest from a mother-in-law to a daughter-in-law. It was the only car that was ever just your car. When Donny was carted off to the Georges Dumont, you were hot to get that second-hand Ford Jamie had talked Donny into buying out of your long paved driveway. Not that you'd open your mouth at the time, you just slapped that helpless they're-doing-it-to-me-again look on your wrinkled old face. You chose this car, but I don't think you ever loved it. This poor little Buick was merely a conveyance and a bit of a status symbol. It got you down to Agatha's and the post office — a stroll from your front porch but you always drove — and over to the park for a turn past the golf course on warm evenings to count the deer under the apple trees. It's true you risked driving out to Sussex now and then — I could hear the fear in your voice when you announced this on those dreaded weekly Sunday calls — but you always got Bob-next-door to drive when it was your turn for a shopping jaunt up to Moncton. Driving in a city, even one you had known all your life, scared the pants off you.

How could you have loved this car? You never got the feel for it. Never tested it, pushed it, trusted it to get you out of a tight corner. You babied it. Kept it all spiffed up. Maintained the appearance of being looked after. You took pride in it.

I wonder now if pride was not the motivating emotion your in life. (I wonder what my motivating emotion is.) That air of superiority that hovered around you. God, Muriel. Superiority and fear. What was the potential of that admixture? No wonder you could not walk down the main road in the village where you were born and lived for seventy-eight years. The hinges of your life. Like your reverence for men and privileging their stories over your own. Yet you always had your own bank account. You kept your finances separate from Donny. I thought it so strange the way you divvied up your financial obligations: you paid for Alexis to go to Netherwood and Mount A because she was the girl, and Donny paid for Jamie to go to King's and Saint Mary's because he was the boy. How well did that work out? Hmmm? How come nobody noticed, that crucial year we met, when everything was in upheaval in both our families, that while you were losing your mind, and Donny was losing his marbles, that Jamie was losing weight? He couldn't bring himself to tell anyone but me that Donny forgot to pay his tuition. He couldn't bring himself to remind his father. And he couldn't tell you because he was not your responsibility. Jamie had a different kind of pride. That was one of the reasons we got married. So Jamie could apply for a student loan. What kind of a solution was that?

Our ignorance was staggering. That night when I was seventeen and walked through the door on your fifty-seventh birthday the world was in flux and everything was shifting but I denied it. *I am not a woman's libber* I said. And Jamie upped the ante by saying *I want to be just like my dad.* We revealed so much that night. How Jamie saw the world as reliable and protective. How I saw the world as a trap, hurtful and unpredictable.

I thought I had nothing to lose so I followed him and allowed myself to be coddled in some of the godforsaken corners of this great big country for twenty years and didn't see how things were changing until the women's movement surged into my consciousness the night the dream came to me with that perfect, elusive word, embedded in a crystalline, glass box that I fashioned with my own bare hands. Suddenly I was awakened, not just from a dream, but a lifetime, and transformed into a woman who saw herself both psychologically and historically and then, then there was hell to pay.

There is always choice and therefore personal responsibility.

All this shifting ground, Muriel. I'm not sure where I've been but now I am going home. To my daughters, and my own truth. And I am going to find the elusive word that disappeared the morning I woke from the dream. Somehow I just know it's the key to the whole story.

As I dip down into the curve past Bennett Lake, humming "I'm Being Followed By a Moonshadow" under my breath, your image hovers before me, heavy and wrinkled in a bathing suit at the Banff Hot Springs outdoor pool in Alberta the Christmas before last, when lonesomeness forced you back to visit, though you had been brooding about us for quite a while. It is late in the afternoon, the sun almost faded, and everything is a uniform shade of grey with no shadows. Fat snowflakes, white and aimless, burst from the featureless sky, melting in the halo of vapour surrounding our heads and shoulders. When Jamie and I sit on a shelf that hugs the walls of the pool, and you try to wedge between us, you keep willowing up in the hot mineral water like a tall clarinet note, buoyant and laughing. The density of your old bones no match for the soft folds of flesh. Jamie and I are on each side, holding you down by the elbows and the second we let go you're off again on your involuntary ascent, squealing, "Don't let me go. Don't let me go."

TWO

OH JESUS, MURIEL, if only it was that easy. Believe me, I'd let you go in a heartbeat. You have no idea what I'd let go of. You have no idea what you've left me. It's not the car and the stuff in the trunk. It's the junk left over in my head: affectations and strange associations and imaginings that you'd be horrified to know exist. From day one, you drew me in with your neediness and your contradictions.

The dinner you cook for us the first time Jamie takes me home to meet you, the Sunday before he goes back down to his banishment in Halifax where he is hovering somewhere between second and third year of engineering. You serve us roast chicken, mashed potatoes (not creamy like my mother's, more like pounded potatoes), carrots, and squash. Donny is working the evening shift. You explain there is no gravy because he is not there and you are on a diet. The supper is dry and mealy. I have a hard time getting it down. Especially the squash, which I have never tasted before. I can't figure out why you couldn't have made gravy since you aren't eating anyway. This is before I'd had your Bisto gravy, otherwise I wouldn't have wished for it. I also think it's strange to have two yellow vegetables. Where is the green vegetable? How about some cranberry sauce? All this is going through my head as you watch us eat. Each bite gets harder and harder to swallow under such surveillance.

But there you sit, all five feet of you, in lime green pants and avocado and orange blouse looking all puffed up, smelling of Cinnabar perfume and stale laundry, taking me in. I have been taught to keep eye contact when talking with someone so I look right back. You are awfully wrinkled — like a puzzle swept to the floor in a rage then put back together in haste — and very self-conscious about this facial erosion. Your hair is a bronzy semi-blond, *Donny likes it better this way*, done up in a tight prim perm. You are waxily tanned and wear cat's-eye glasses but no make-up. Still, beyond your get-up — and that enormous rump, Muriel, I can't help but notice how it ripples in those polyester pull-up pants when you run up the stairs — and the weirdness of you watching us eat, there is something appealing about you. Youthful, even. Perhaps your smile. I'm not sure. Don't really care. You are forty years older than me and twenty years older than my beautiful, tragically consumed, mini-skirt-wearing mother, and I am looking for wisdom and guidance.

I guess that you are looking for a nice girl and so I display my English stepfather's table manners that I have learned the hard way. I couldn't have guessed that table manners are not a big deal in a country family, even a well-educated country family. And I sure as hell couldn't have guessed what you were really looking for. Or what the things you say might really mean.

I don't think I'll see Jamie again until Thanksgiving but he calls me at my house in Sussex the first week he's back at school. It's the middle of the night and he's been out on a tear with the boys but I can forgive all that because he misses me. He wants to hitchhike up on the weekend. I ditch my plans in an instant, overjoyed. He really, really misses me! That's the beginning of him arriving at my door in Sussex hungry and horny (or horny and hungry, it's all the same when a young man is twenty) every Friday night. My mother feeds him roast beef or spareribs then we make out on the couch in the rec room.

After Christmas, you move out of the park forever into the big yellow retirement house you bought in Alma. The house with no garage so Donny's blue Triumph Spitfire gets put up on blocks down at his sister's. Jamie and I start driving out there to help with the move, because you are all alone, and you let us feed on love.

Love is the only thing I have any appetite for. The whole feast of love. Another body wrapped up in mine for the night. I am obsessed. The idea gnaws away at me. In school, I hunch down with half a mind and half a heart, the lessons like static in my brain. Home isn't much better. Sunday night to Thursday night my stereo cranks out Carole King, the only consolation, waiting for the weekend. Finally my mother yells, "Are you going to play that goddamn record again?" So I trot down to the Met, oozing my longing, and buy the soundtrack to *Love Story* and listen non-stop. Scribblers and textbooks stacked and uncracked on my desk. I want to be a grown-up so bad I could scream.

During reading week, as we unpack boxes and after Donny is tucked down at the DVA in Lancaster damping down his ulcer, you appear like the fairy godmother, and my scream dissipates like morning fog.

"Don't rumple up your covers in the morning, sweetheart," you say to Jamie. Coy. Almost flirting. "It only makes work for me."

With a little squeeze of his arm, you artfully pass on to Jamie that you are aware that he messes up his bedclothes in the morning to make it look as if he spent the night there, instead of with me in Alexis's old bed. I can hardly believe that a mother, from such a respectable family, an elementary school teacher no less, could be so understanding.

Snuggling down into the covers that night is like crossing over the Milky Way. Jamie and I spiral into each other at the speed of light. As I hover near sleep, I am so aware of his skin, velvety as a rose petal, and his whole body, strong and warm, wrapping mine, head-to-toe. I want to hold this moment in my heart forever and ever. I have never felt so safe in my life. The concerns of everyday existence have receded into nothingness. I feel weightlessly encased. Grateful. Prayerful even, as sleep rolls up the boundaries of consciousness and I fall far, far away from adolescence into the black unknown of adulthood.

Sometimes I wonder, Muriel, if you had left us there rolled up together a little longer could we have created a salve from the sticky substance of our sex to dress our childhood wounds, instead of you hustling us along with your urgent agenda. Would that have been possible given Jamie's magical kingdom childhood? Not that I made a big case for my own wounding. At seventeen, I considered myself whole. It was the only way to proceed, undaunted by the tumultuous events of my past, which I assigned to my mother. (She was the gatekeeper of my sorrows. My date with her was in the future and somehow I think we both knew that.)

This ambivalence toward my mother and stepfather was something Jamie could never understand or tolerate. He was bewildered as over the years I tacked and jibed across the ocean of my unconsciousness trying to chart some kind of real awareness. There was no room for ambivalence in Jamie's mind. There was only loyalty equals love, love equals loyalty all bound up in a body bag of duty. Somehow I mistake loyalty for fidelity. So I don't know, perhaps leaving us in our bliss would only have delayed what was going to be played out anyway.

But still, Muriel, it wouldn't have hurt to let us linger in the heat as we made love upstairs in the frigid room with your discarded rock-hard colonial furniture, up there in a corner of our own in your new two-storey house where the thermostat was never turned on because nobody heated their second floors in the olden days when you grew up.

How could I have guessed that when we emerge from our cosmic cocoon the next morning that sometime in the future I would have this date with you to pick it all apart. Certainly not that morning, when I am starry-assed, and you look so pleased with yourself that I think you're going to pat Jamie on the bum.

"We'll keep this our little secret for now," you say. And I understand that your permissiveness will not extend into Donny's confidence. He will be kept in the dark. In fact, when he comes home from the DVA he will be kept in the bedroom across the hall from yours because the doctors may be able to dry him out and sooth his ulcers for the moment, but nothing can be done about that snoring of his. I don't give this sideways shift of Donny much of a thought. I give you my complete sympathy. Donny's snoring can be heard all over the house.

Only years later will I understand how hard it is to lie next to the body of someone who has been so deceiving. How hard it is to let yourself fall into sleep when the invisible, soundless, build-up of lies and disrespect invades your body. But back then, in my innocence, I take in everything you say at face value. In no time, you move in on me, taking me aside for little chats, fast-tracking our relationship.

"I assume you're taking precautions."

"Uh-huh," I don't know where to look. My mother would shit if she knew I was on the pill. She wants the whole white wedding shebang for me. Something she didn't have.

"Don't worry dear," you beam, bestowing permission. "I understand. Boys have needs."

After this revelation, our relationship reaches a whole new level. You confide in me that women of a certain age — say fifty-seven, fifty-eight — have needs too. And in a very small voice, very late at night, sitting in your cluttered kitchen, you begin to talk in parentheses. (I conceived Alexis on my wedding night.) (I had no idea that Donny had a problem.) You pause to assume a look of martyrdom. (He drinks.) You vent a little backward hiss. He drinks to forget *the dead mother, the missed funeral, and The War*. Now you look at your grandmother's serving dishes displayed on the shelf above the stove. (So there's this other problem.) (He can't get it up, which is a consequence of his drinking that's not his fault, but nevertheless causes you to walk the floors at night, and moan.)

"I just ache."

"Ah, yes. I can understand why," I commiserate, wise for my seventeen years. Sympathetic. Understanding. Opening my heart for the woman who will become my mother-in-law. There's no doubt about it now. Proud to be privy to your deepest secrets. Certainly not understanding what it means when sex has vanished from a marriage. Least of all understanding how hard you tried to justify everything to make it right.

"You have no idea what I have endured with that man. But what can I do? I was only six years old, on our store wagon with Dad when he stopped as we passed Donny on the road. 'Do you want to come for a ride young man?' Dad asked. And as soon as Donny climbed up on the wagon and sat beside me, I knew that he was the one."

How hard you tried to make him fit your standards.

I lock onto you in that instant. *The one.* Someone else knows this feeling. My mother asks *What the hell do you think you know about love* but you don't even question it. You are on my side. So I faithfully absorb whatever you tell me.

With all those grey roots showing, you played your helpless card — *I'm too nervous to drive all the way down to Saint John by myself* — so Jamie and I spend the rest of reading week pacifying you. Escorting you down to Lancaster to visit Donny now that it's finally out of the bag that he's tucked down there (to dry out) because his ulcer is acting up again (because of his binge drinking). The four of us play cards in the visitors' lounge guzzling pop and eating chips, with never so much as a peep as to why Donny is there, or how you got us on your side.

And then the paint. The glossy paint Jamie and I choose at Moffett's Hardware Store in Sussex to absolve you of all prior misery. Covering your dining room and kitchen in a thin coat of aqua before Jamie goes back to Saint Mary's.

Oh the distractions, Muriel. The great big new house and the custom-made drapes and wool carpets and colonial dining room set and the way you decked out your bedroom in hot pink fluff to go with the French provincial bedroom suite. All bought with the little inheritance you got from Philomena. And all that lovemaking. Jamie and I never even stopped to ask what the crisis was because you just played all those old tapes Muriel, the nocturnal recitals that never changed, word-for-word. *The dead mother, the missed funeral, and The War*.

So with all this potential mother-in-law approval under my belt, in no time I give up all pretence of going to school and start working for Dad in his store so I can save enough money to pay for gas because you flip out about Jamie hitchhiking and threaten to take your ugly old Maverick back that you gave him to use for the year. In no time, Jamie and I and you look at engagement rings in a mail-order catalogue, though much to my great disappointment you never cough up on that one. Still, in no time at all my heart defects from my noisy home where everything seems wide-open, blown, and treacherous into what I mistake for the quiet of yours.

No doubt Donny is an afflicted man, but even so, he is clearly considered the head of the household, to be deferred to in matters of serving spinach, picking out a roast of beef, or putting in new windows. In fact, it seems he is to be deferred to in all matters (except his drinking). No one dares to argue with him. He will not be accused. The family always talks about him with reverence. He is supposed to be the best guy in the world. You knew from the age of six that he was *the one*. Presumably you love him. And yet, you ache.

"If I could, I'd take all the alcohol in the world and throw it into the ocean," I declare in support.

"Oh me too," you agree. "Me too." So carried away with your own misfortunes that you don't even stop to ask why I would say such a thing.

"I'll tell you a little secret," I offer.

Isn't that what female solidarity is all about? Sitting around the table sharing secrets. Complaining about men. That's what my mother and her sisters used to do before my aunts were killed in a car accident. Sit around smoking their brains out, all beered up, hooting *this bastard this* and *that bastard that*. "Muriel, I know why Donny causes so much trouble."

"Yes, dear?"

"My mother goes on a bender sometimes too."

Your old puzzle face percolates for a second then smoothes into place. You pat my hand. Rise from your chair. Oh shit, I panic, I haven't shared enough, I have to let it all hang out.

"Sometimes my mother gets drunk as a skunk and takes off."

"Takes off?"

"Yeah, for weeks or months at a time."

Uh-oh. I watch your face erupt, and hear a long strange hiss vent through pursed lips. "Women don't drink."

Ohohoh. I know right away that I have made a Big Mistake. I should have realized that a drinking man is one thing, but a drinking woman is another. It's as plain as the nose on my face that I should have kept my mouth shut. That I should have thought it out. But have you ever noticed how hard it is to see your nose unless you close one eye?

There's a lot you can miss with one eye closed.

You compose your face, allow one more little hiss to escape, draw in a deep breath, make yourself look holy, and say, "Well, Robyn. Dear. This is not what I expected." You rise from the table like a dowager queen who has seen better days and pad up the staircase to close yourself off in your room while a foreboding phrase pops into my swizzling head. *Guilty by association*.

Now that you're gone, I was hoping we'd instantly detangle but your presence is still palpable and I might just as well face up to the fact that you're coming with me on this journey. Our history stretches from Newfoundland and Labrador all the way out to Calgary where I slammed into that godawful truth two years ago when you came out west for the last time, turning the tables. Escorted by your paramour, Charlie Dixon, seeking our approval for your relationship with him.

Remember that afternoon of shopping — you opened that fat pink wallet of yours and showed me the $1000 you had "saved" up for "a little treat" — and we stopped first for lunch. I can still feel those cagey fingers of yours resting on my arm with the familiarity of an old conspirator. Did you feel me recoil? I don't think so. Your mission was over and you were already looking at the dessert cart while I let the words *she's better off he's dead you know* sink in. My feelings for you would have remained less confused if I had simply stuck to your agenda that day, if I had not been trying to blot out the image of you and Charlie humped up in your great aunt's spool bed when you put me on the spot.

"I suppose you're wondering about me and Charlie," you say. And before I can even answer, you give that underwater smile of yours. "We've had sex."

Oh god, Muriel. The favour had been called in and I didn't see it coming. And then you just had to tell me how we had interrupted the two of you on a Sunday evening phone call and after that, poor Charlie couldn't get it up again that night. You were only telling me so that I would tell Jamie and get his absolution for you. Worse yet, it was finally dawning on me that all I had ever done was encourage you. Now I didn't want to do that anymore. I couldn't hold up either.

So I diverted you with a simple question, *What's new in the village of Alma*? And you replied in such an off-hand way, as if it was idle gossip, that Donny's nephew had been killed in a bicycle accident. Then you leaned your old lizard face into me and spit *His mother is better off he's dead you know, he stole that bicycle. People only get what they deserve.* As if I would agree. I understood from that moment that you did not know me or else you would have known better than to say that.

Today I can think of all kinds of ways a son might be better off with his mother dead, but I can't think of one good reason a mother would be better off with her own son dead. You are going to hear me out Muriel. This is your last chance to get to know me.

How does that rattle your old bones? Are you wearing your good white shoes? I couldn't find them anywhere.

We haven't travelled very far, but it seems already that I have donned your Buick Skylark like a crab grows a new shell. I judged you that day. That was my role. You inundated me with your testimony from the beginning and of course I was supposed to find you not guilty. And for years it played your way. Until then. Now I'm going to ask some tough questions. I thought that you were inside of my head but now it occurs to me that in so many ways, I am inside of you.

THREE

GOD IT FEELS good to laugh. I can't remember if we laughed during the last ten days or not. We must have.

Is any of this tickling your funny bone, Muriel? No? I'll try to think of something.

Oh I remember. Last week when I'm fingering through your stuff, getting up the courage to attack your walk-in closet, I hear Jamie and Alexis break out in childish belly laughter. I fly down the hall to find them huddled over a pile of papers from your desk. Alexis passes me your little blue book for recording birthdays. Across the entry for Dr. Edwin Conrad is a dark angry slash with the word KAPUT printed firmly in block letters. You're not even six feet under, yet I mock you from back in '78, hands on my hips, eyebrows raised over pretend glasses (I wish I could have got the red streak to appear between my brows) and say, *I bought him his suit for his graduation from medical school. I don't know how he and Alexis can even think of getting divorced.* And then I hiss your hiss. You know that funny little sound you always made when things weren't going your way but the wheels were grinding in your head. I'm not exactly sure how you did it but I kind of roll a bit of spit around in my mouth and then suck it backwards. It's the best I can do on such short notice. We roll on the floor. Although maybe if we'd known Ed is going to show up like an apparition in the next couple of days we might not find it so funny. But honestly, at the time, we laugh our asses off.

Oh come on, Muriel, you know I swear like a trooper. Ed was such a thorn in your heart. You blamed him for the migraines Alexis suffered, and the bouts of acne that erupted on her beautiful face from time-to-time. Deep in your heart, you knew he was no good for her though there was this one thing about him that you hung on to. Ed was going to be a doctor, a surgeon no less. All this desirable potential almost made you forgive his black-bearded Fidel Castro looks and cocksure bullying behaviour. Though oddly enough, the thing that you seemed to fear the most about him was his influence on Jamie. Honestly, sometimes the way you talked it seemed to me that you or Donny didn't think that Jamie had a thought to call his own. When the laughter stops, I fall away from Jamie and Alexis as they lock themselves back into their task. You were their mother. I can't slip into the sleeve of their grief. Things have been tense between them the past few years since they had the big argument about you in our backyard, but they seem to have put their differences away.

How did that story go? One of the suppertime favourites, about Jamie not talking until he was two years old — then one day, driving down the hill from the Radar Station, he blurted out *ere de duck* and pointed out the window to the duck along the side of the road. You always rounded off that story by explaining, Jamie didn't need to talk, Alexis always did all the talking for him.

I slump back into your bedroom, feeling abandoned with the contents of your intimate life, knowing that neither one of them will step across the threshold of your doorway. I've lost my place and don't know where to start again, so I pick up the little teddies sitting on your night table and hold them to my nose. They're brand new and compared to the rest of the place I have no attachment to their smell. It is store-ish. They haven't been around long enough for their polyester fibres to attract the odours from your room. Funny looking little things. Sad little things. A larger bear with its Velcroed arms encircling a smaller bear, holding fast. A pink heart tied to its neck that says *I Love You*.

I feel so abandoned here in your room, Muriel. Uneasy. Cut off. Out of the blue, I remember a cool foggy afternoon in August just before Jamie and I got married when we took Alexis up to Dennis's beach because she wanted to go for a swim and then jog the five miles home. Jamie made fun of her Spartan nature but when we watch her walk away from the car in her Speedo, old brown towel thrown over her arm, army surplus knapsack on her shoulder, Jamie looked over at me and said, "Don't you think Alexis has just about the nicest bum you've ever seen?"

I can't tell you how weird that comment made me feel, Muriel. I squirmed in my seat. What do you think? Do you think what Jamie said is the least bit odd? Or do you just think it's a more or less truthful comment. Alexis did have a nice bum. You once told me that you wished Alexis would give up teaching and science altogether and become a model. Ha! A model of what? A model of your unlived life? Not a chance. Not Alexis. If she were to use anyone as a model, Agatha would be my bet. *Don't love her, love me*! I know, I know. I shouldn't heap anguish on you now that you've got six feet of soil pressing down on you. But really Muriel, what am I supposed to do with all these fragments of conversation wrapping around my head like a Mayday pole. Put them out of my mind? That's what you taught me and for the most part, that's what I did. Put comments that caused me to squirm in my seat out of my mind. But going through the pockets of your suit jackets I keep finding old wads of Kleenex or empty after-dinner mint wrappers and to tell you the truth it's downright impossible to keep things out of my mind.

With that thought, I bolted downstairs to sort through your proud collection of cups and saucers for Andrea and Caitlin. I am well aware that the Mikado is more valuable than the rest because you showed it to me and asked to make sure it went to your first grandchild.

You didn't say Andrea, you said first grandchild. You made that distinction and I hated you for it. You should have known better, it was one of the great complaints of your life. I'm sorry to tell you, Muriel, it got broken into a thousand pieces.

All the mess we made in those first few days would appal you. You'd be more appalled by how quickly we manage to dismantle your household. But it would have done your old heart good to see Agatha's jaw quiver when we donated your good lamp with the solid brass base and the antique-looking globe to the Senior Citizen's Club white elephant sale. You would have got a laugh at your old sister because she wanted that lamp for herself. But you would have been cross that we hadn't kept it. Perhaps we try to replace your absence with what is familiar: hard labour. With your lot, family was everything, and work was sacred. So we sort and sweat and cart from the upstairs, the downstairs, and the basement. All manner of things shifted or booted out the back door in boxes and bulging green garbage bags. Some were simply propped up in the hallway. Every single item has to be appraised. Did you ever think how it would be for us rummaging around in all your stuff? It's not just the heirlooms and legal shit we had to deal with, it's the dozens of mason jars in the basement, packages of nylons from the sixties in your dresser, the tubes of toothpaste, and leftover morphine. Alexis and Jamie work with demonic speed. Agatha turns her face from the violence. And for once in my life, I keep my trap shut. Or mostly. The night before your funeral, I wander into the kitchen and spy that pink leather wallet at the top of a heap of trash in a brown paper bag. I filch it out.

"That's garbage," Jamie says.

"No it's not," I snap. "I gave your mother this wallet for her birthday a few years ago. It's in perfectly good condition."

"Put it back. It's just an old wallet."

"No."

I see the kind of anger build in him that frightens me. The kind of anger that boils up beneath his skin and makes his face go squashy.

"I want it." There is something at stake I can't figure out.

"It's garbage." Jamie struggles to control his voice.

"I'm keeping it," I say with such finality that his whole body goes flaccid. Momentarily his face resumes its normal shape.

I kept your wallet and now I've got your car. I can't figure it out. I always thought I'd get the mink coat. After all, I was the one who escorted you to the furrier the week after Donny got his diagnosis and you thought your life was over. Humph, I said to myself, when Alexis took it back with her on the plane in the summer after that last, awful week we spent with you in August. I couldn't complain though, you'd palmed me one of your diamond rings (not the good one) after I'd promised to make sure you got a nice, tasteful (meaning expensive) casket. You might have adored your children, but you never trusted them in matters of taste. At least you trusted my good will, because I hadn't let on — wouldn't let on, under the circumstances — that since our lunch that day I didn't know if I loved you anymore.

TEN DAYS AGO Jamie and Alexis and I converged in Toronto for our connector to Moncton suspended in the agony of not knowing, after the long hard months of your unbelievable remission, if you are still hanging on. Bob-next-door meets us by the baggage carousel and I beat it to the washroom, surprised, because as you very well know, we had never been chummy, when Alexis sucks in right behind me.

"Oh Christ," I say as I examine my face in the fluorescent lighting. Greenish skin drowning in a sea of red bumps like I'm pickled in years of guilt and bad memories. "I can't believe she hung on for so long."

For just a second another arrival in this airport, in this washroom when you and I brought Andrea home from the hospital lights up in my head, but before the image congeals, Alexis surprises me again.

"Unbelievable," she says, so uncharacteristically, tossing the paper towel into the garbage like a basketball, her other hand on the washroom door. "But what I want to know now is, like, is she day-ead?"

And with that, the door flings open and there is Jamie, oscillating head-to-toe, Bob-next-door right behind him. "She's gone, Al," he cries, lunging into her arms, half-in, half-out of the women's washroom at the Moncton Airport.

"This morning at about eleven o'clock," Bob-next-door tells me over the huddled form of your two children. That's how we found out, Muriel. It kind of fits, don't you think? I almost died in here and you didn't notice. And then we found out you had died before we could get to your deathbed and it was all so ordinary. Weird. But ordinary. One moment just passed to another.

So we stopped at the funcral home on the way down to the village and made the arrangements. Then arrived in the village without a word that Jamie and I had been living separately since Christmas. We didn't want to make waves any more than we had to. Things were bad enough as it was. Donny tucked away at the Georges Dumont. Charlie had either deserted you or been shown the door, it doesn't matter; the thing was he didn't wait for you to draw your last breath to take up with that mousy cousin of yours. And you knew it. The humiliation you must have suffered on top of acute physical pain. So we kept tight-lipped and slept in our old room — thankful the twin beds had been moved in to accommodate the night nurse in the room across the hall from you — our backs turned as if we were complete strangers.

Last night in the dark, in that same room, the room of Milky Way nights, after we checked the rooms, starkly nude of all heirlooms and bric-a-brac, before we closed up our suitcases, a question pooled between us that I could not answer. Not in that goddamn yellow house of yours with the dinnertime prattle still ringing off the walls: Philomena and Perley and Donny the good, Agatha the old maid, Alexis the reluctant bohemian, and sweet little "ere de duck" Jamie, who did not utter a word until he was over two years old. I couldn't answer, with the ghosts of nighttime sob stories still swelling in the kitchen packing a fury like the wind blowing up the great big bay, shaking and rattling the bedroom windows. I'd thrust too many balled up socks between the panes over the past two decades and ended up barefoot before the whole bloody bunch of you one too many times. No, I couldn't answer a question like that last night with the past mounted up like thunderclouds.

I need to be clear. I need time and space. I need to mull over the momentous, unpredictable event of this journey home — the event that changes the way I tell the story — and has pulled me back into this family's influence when I thought that all of us were finally out of seiche forever. What am I feeling this morning? Is it loyalty? Nostalgia? Grief? Fear? Is there love?

Tell me Muriel, is this your story or mine?

Looking over my shoulder as I blow past the Fundy National Park boundary I think how fog forms along the tide line. Eyes back on the road, the idea of thousands of miles and a couple of weeks to myself spreads out in my mind like the warmth of hot sun on a stretch of wet beach. I am in the driver's seat.

Where are you, Muriel? You seem to be here and not to be here, in this car that was yours and now belongs to me.

It was so odd in the big yellow house without you, although after a few days your huge absence somehow made you weirdly present. But in the church and up the hill at the graveyard you simply were not in the here and now, not one bit. I have rarely felt so unlike myself as people line up to utter their condolences. The women take care their high heels don't sink into the spongy, fusty earth. I first notice this when one of my own slim heels sinks to the sole with a slurp that echoes above the sound of my snuffling and nose blowing. Then I realize that all the women in heels are leaning forward on their toes, making them appear as if they are expecting something to happen.

Two old hands close over one of mine. A trembling little voice utters, "I'm so sorry, your mother was such a ..." Unrehearsed in funeral matters we'd got the reception line by your casket all fouled-up. "I'm the daughter-in-law, she's the daughter," I say, pointing to

Alexis who is out-of-place, staring at the trees, not much more present than you. Jamie beat it over to a corner with the pallbearers to light up a smoke the moment the prayers were over. I try to get Jamie's attention as the procession toddles toward me with their earnest expressions of sorrow and curiosity, decked out in their best but looking comfortable. After all, the three hundred souls of the Village of Alma attend funerals with a greater regularity than weddings. Finally Agatha guides Jamie to my side at a pace to accompany her hip replacements and respectable sense of grief and slides Alexis into place to correct the error, and let me off the hook.

Driving down the hill I think about Jamie's old dreams and catch a glimpse of the bay, wondering how you like your new address: the United Church Cemetery, overlooking the back road on Bucket Hill, not far from the wild Bay of Fundy, not that far from your old address — the seventh house down from the Baptist Church, on the rise, yellow, two-storey, four bedrooms.

I remember the afternoon when Andrea and Caitlin were little and we all trooped up to look at your plot, how curious they were with this cemetery adventure.

"Where are all our relatives?" they asked, wide-eyed.

"Down at the Baptist Cemetery," you replied, as if they should have known.

"Well how come you and Grandpa are going to be up here and our relatives are someplace else?" Andrea asked.

"We changed, didn't we Donny? Donny. DonnyDonnyDonny."

When Donny realized he was being addressed, he answered up smartly before he even knew what the question was. "Oh yes, Yesyesyes." He never missed a beat did he? That's why I had so much trouble convincing anyone that something was wrong.

You changed. Well, you could put it that way. It wasn't the first time either. With your places in heaven dutifully secured by your forefathers it was almost mindless to migrate from Baptist to United, and then sometime in the late 1960s you both had another spontaneous change of faith from the United Church of Canada (around the same time you shook off church-going in favour of taking your travel trailer up to Shediac on weekends) to the Benevolent Government of Canada, which was just as well since you were both practising holy civil servants. And by the 1970s your tenets of faith such as the Canada Pension Plan, Old Age Security, and unbridled Medicare were as entrenched as the Ten Commandments and, never questioning where your new faith spawned, you both voted Conservative in every election, provincial or federal, as did your parents and their parents before them, thus ensuring, like spots in heaven, the continuance of candidates best suited to those long gone. You were a devout lot all right — to one another.

But that wasn't the only change that took place over your century was it? It wasn't just a matter of going from Baptist to Government. It was the whole ethos from two millennia that was discarded. You fell for the Holy Grail of Romance as the great motivator and influence of happy endings the same way you fell for tanning as a sign of good health and the nuclear family as the measure of all things good. It's all so ordinary, isn't it Muriel. So banal. Uninspiring. Do you have any idea how much more I was hoping to learn from your death? Can you see how disappointed I am?

Why don't I feel more?

Dreading the social after the burial, I am surprised by the waves of relief that wash over me when we sit down to a cup of tea at the Seniors' Centre. A feeling of empty-headedness. Not having to think about going up to Moncton the next day to visit Donny. Not having to think how he looked like a prisoner of war last summer when we saw him. Surprised by my fiendish appetite, I wolf down all that funeral food: dainty little sandwiches rolled and cubed and laden with butter and Miracle Whip. Brownies, date squares, some kind of Jell-O thingies that I'm not sure how to eat but manage without too many crumbs landing on my black, art-opening suit. Although I'm sure I only look swish from the neck down, my face feels bloated and blotchy from trying not to cry. Knowing you would have approved of my mixture of style and stifled grief. I keep wondering if you were buried in that pink dress with the cream and silver polka dots you showed me last summer. It isn't in your closet. I know you made your wishes known to Agatha as well, so I am assuming you're wearing it now, but honestly, Muriel, after taking a good look at the picture of you at Christmas looking like a small thing in a bony cage, I can't help but think the dress must have been miles too big. And not warm at all.

I'm tempted to ask Agatha about it when she leans over to tell us to *circulate, circulate*. The villagers refrain *He must have known. He must have known.*

Everything? How could he have possibly known everything?

I chase outside after Jamie and am stunned by the image of Charlie Dixon, of all people, twisting his foot in the dirt. His hand on Jamie's shoulder. All the friendly village there to witness.

Driving up here in the hills, I catch glimpses of the remnants of dirty snow crusted woods and wonder how it is that for years I've had this persistent image of you and Donny. Why I always see the two of you spending your wedding night out in the travel trailer left abandoned for a decade on your blacktop driveway. Hard to say. Could be because of the underwater smile in your wedding photo. Could be because you told me more times than I cared to hear how you conceived Alexis on your wedding night. Could be because it's so hard to imagine you anywhere else. Or perhaps because over a period of twenty years you revealed so much about the sad, small sex life you shared with Donny, that a dream home on wheels, with a bed constructed from collapsing the kitchen table and folding down the sitting area, where you had to stroke yourself to sleep, is as good a site as any for foiled desire.

FOUR

THE AIR IS different here in the valley. Funny about smells. I'm aware of them and then not aware of them, but rarely mark their passage. My heart squeezes at the loss of salt and marsh. Alberta smells different. When I get there, I hope there is a wind off the mountains to fill my arrival with a clear, light scent.

I feel guilty breezing past the Sussex turn-off on my way north via Fredericton, even though I called my stepfather last night to tell him I won't be stopping in on my journey west. Jamie and I had dinner with him and his partner one evening between the funerals and caught up on all the news. Well, all the news that we share. I haven't told them yet that Jamie and I are on the skids. We mostly stick to the surface stuff: how Andrea and Caitlin are doing at school, my new job at the Glenbow, Jamie's latest construction project. Still, after a few glasses of wine and the drama of what had happened at Muriel's funeral, I felt a little reckless, and got up the nerve to ask my stepfather a question that had been on mind for so long.

"Why did you stay with Mum all those years, with the ups and downs and the comings and goings?"

My stepfather twirled red wine around in the bottom of his glass. "For you and your brother, I suppose."

What had I been hoping for? Had I been hoping he'd say *Because deep down I always loved your mother, no matter what*. This is what I wanted to hear. Even at the age of thirty-nine, I wanted to hear that my parents had loved each other. I suppose they did, in the beginning. I remember my stepfather never failed to kiss my mother goodbye when he left the house for work. I remember laughter and cuddling. Not just kegs of ketchup whizzing through the air in the general vicinity of my stepfather's head.

For you and your brother, I suppose. It's a humble, honest answer.

"Don't feel guilty," my stepfather said, looking me in the eye.

Did I feel guilty? I think I did. I would have done anything to protect my parents from their shame.

"There's another thing I want you to know," he said without a prompt. "I was never unfaithful to your mother."

This was so out-of-the-blue that I was silenced. I felt tender toward him. His face revealed pain. I realized that he probably could have prefaced his statement with *unlike your mother*.

I called Mum last week. Your death, Muriel, being a good excuse to get in touch. She's been fuming since we arrived at her place with you in tow the last time we all came back, almost three years ago. Then at Christmas, I hung up on her because she still wouldn't let it go. Some holiday that was. If you can call one muggy week drenched in guilt, stuffed with lobster and scallops, crammed with everybody who loved us a holiday. What had I been hoping for? It was doomed from the get-go. Jamie didn't want to come.

I talked him into using up all his Aeroplan points because I needed to get away. He was always going away and was always worrying about money, so we ended with a compromise that suited no one: one week back east because going home was free. Can you hear me laugh? I knew it wasn't going to work the minute I stepped through your door. I was hit with the heavy, volatile, damp-sea-air permeated with firewood-stacked-in-the-musty-basement smell finished off with a top note of Hawes Lemon Oil, and an astounding thought popped into my head. *I can't do this anymore*. Like walking into a screen door.

The day before we left, you treated us to a show of the new headstone you'd just bought. A big black shiny double, sun glinting off its polished surface. *Gallagher* sandblasted across the top and below two columns. *Donald J, 1915 — Muriel C, 1914.*

"Perhaps you and Robyn would like to get your plot now, while there are still some nice and handy," you said ever so sweetly.

Bad timing, Muriel. I was in the early flush of my Big Awakening. The thought of getting swallowed up, once and for all, by you made me revolt. Then I threw you a look Muriel, and thought, *What does that old frump need a monument for? She's got a living, breathing one standing right next to her. And I'm married to the poor bugger.* You can see how I was beginning to change. Before then, I was all ears and eyes. That summer, after exercising my intellect for a few years, I began to develop a mouth, but it was still in my head.

Oh why, oh why, oh why did we try to do what was best for you two instead of what was best for us? Why didn't we just drive out to Vancouver Island for a week? We would have had to pay for motel rooms, but then it would only have cost us money. We might even have had fun.

Why did we think this holiday would work? You lived in fear of doubling a banana bread recipe in case it wouldn't turn out, and my mother might get up in the middle of the night and dismantle the couch to draw up a pattern for new upholstery — even if she had never done it before. You thought my mother had what in your day was called "bad nerves," and bad nerves were attributed to a lack of moral fibre.

Still though, when I talked to her the other day, the first question she asked was, "Have you seen your father? How does he look?" Even after fifteen years, there is still an attachment. My stepfather never asks about her. I think he's grown indifferent. I don't blame him, but his indifference bothers me. Poor Mum, she never made anything easy for herself. I don't think she looks for happy endings. What she craves are moments of stillness. She thinks she has managed to position herself in a place where she has a chance of finding them. Not a sound but the cattle in the lower field.

But you, Muriel, held a child-like faith in happy endings; the present was a means to get there.

Did you ever really love me, Muriel?

I'm not sure if my own mother loved me, or even the idea of me. What do you think? Now that you have an elevated view, so to speak. She's supposed to be mentally ill and you're supposed to be normal — if you can be normal when you're dead. If it's normal for a mother to secure a sex life for her son.

Boys have needs!

And a girl can go on the pill!

When I think back now, it makes my blood boil. I'd better stop this car before I blow a gasket. There. It feels so good to slam your door.

Boys have needs! As if I didn't know the troubles you and Donny had had with Jamie. *Boys have needs* indeed. Now I know what you were saying.

The mother of a boy has needs. The mother needs no further trips to Halifax to plead her son's case with the Dean, to promise her son will never piss on the Don's door again. He has a private school education, it's not his fault, it's the company he keeps. The mother needs no more skipping of classes, no more rowdiness in the taverns, no more messing around with a certain second cousin and the infamous Miss Murphy, who has had a baby and has been heard to say, "C'mon Gordie, you know I don't fuck on an empty stomach." No, no and no. The mother needs no more failed grades and no more slacking off. It's bad enough that he goes to a Catholic University and not Mount Allison like the rest of the family — hers, not Donny's. *My marks were too low, Mom. Nonsense, sweetheart. Nonsense.*

But a boy has needs and a mother recognizes these needs. She has a need to save her boy from unfortunate affiliation, undesirable incrimination, unjustifiable jaunts into the bewildering bowels of boyhood mania, the hormone-rocketed reverence for fast cars and pointed tits. A mother understands a boy's needs and she wants to control them. With a nice girl from Sussex, Queen of the Fall Fair, whose father owns a store and fixes movie cameras. With a girl who's smart enough to go on the pill.

Or better yet, with a young wife who wants to please. Pleasant as rain. What a shame Jamie and I grew out of the stories we told each other the night of our first date.

"I want a job in the National Parks like my father," that young man said. "Play golf on Friday afternoons and not work too hard. Take my kids out on picnics. Buy furniture on credit. Carry on the family name."

"I'm not a women's libber, someone has to keep the peace in the family," that seventeen-year-old said in return.

All this passive resistance you understood in your old flesh. Did you see me coming? I'll bet Jamie wasn't the only one who said *She's the one*. You bore down on me, Muriel, and I opened myself like a funnel, figuring that if you trusted me well enough to confide your frustration with Donny's-not-getting-it-up, and to appeal to me to have pity for the life you had led with *that man*, then I had it made. I knew marriage to Jamie would be a package deal. That he came with his family all wrapped and tied up with a cord of respectability and there was nothing I wanted more than to cozy up with you under the smooth brown paper. It never would have occurred to me that what was under there was fear. It takes half a lifetime to figure those things out.

"What the hell do you want to get married for?" my mother ranted.

"I'm in love!" I shouted.

"Love! Love! What could you possibly know about love? Don't fool yourself."

"You can't stop me."

"Why would a boy his age want to get married anyway?"

"Because he's been living in a dorm for almost eight years. He wants a home."

"What about you? You've got a home."

This is where my mother and I locked eyes in silence. I wouldn't back down.

"Go on. Get married," she spat, and lit up an Export A, the smoke veiling her face. "Find out for yourself."

The two of you, Muriel. She always pushing me away, you always pulling me in. How passive was I?

Isn't that exactly what Alexis accused you of being? Passive. Just over a week ago when the minister came to the house the day before your funeral and asked the four of us, Agatha, Alexis, and Jamie and me, to talk about the kind of person you had been. There we sat, five points of a star struggling toward some truth about a seventy-eight year old woman, but we couldn't find the words. When the silence got too big for me to bear I finally said, "She liked to go shopping." Then thought better of it and added, "She was a really good grandmother." We all nodded in agreement.

"Have you any regrets?" the minister asked.

Alexis piped up.

"I regret that all of her life, my mother was so passive."

"I regret my mother never got to do what she wanted," Jamie said.

"What she wanted?" Alexis snapped. "How about Daddy? He never got to buy a boat and never got to go back to Europe because she wouldn't let him."

"Well Mom always wanted to be a nurse," Jamie fairly shouted.

Your children, Muriel, like pillars of faith holding up the lintel of a broken marriage and its broken dreams. The weight of the unlived life. Jamie had bonded with you and kept the big sorrow of your life in the past, so he wouldn't have to think about what was going on in the present. Alexis bonded with Donny and carried the sorrows of his life fully in the future that couldn't happen, to avoid thinking about the present.

Agatha sat stone-faced. She would reveal nothing in this conversation. Only someone who knew her well would notice the tiny tremors in her clenched jaw. Who knew if in her old Baptist heart she had forgiven Muriel for that business with Charlie Dixon?

The minister was clearly offended by this turn of conversation. He had meant *Have you any regrets about your relationship with your mother, sister, mother-in-law? Is there anything you have left undone, or left unsaid?* We should have come up with something better than "shopping" and "passive." We should have done better than that.

I pace the length of the burgundy Buick Skylark. Scuff my toes in the dirt. Open the door, remove the funeral food, and slam it again. Toss the food into a dumpster. What else I could have come up with? Crafty? How about crafty? The old girl was crafty.

Why did I get into this mess? Because I wanted to be all grown up? What a laugh. Now I wonder why I thought being a grown-up was the be-all and end-all. The conceit of youth. The power of believing I would make a better job of it than my mother and her mother. All I had to do was be careful, I thought. Trouble was I didn't know what to be careful about. All I knew was my own circumstance, the code of home. I didn't know how to judge the appearance of the outside world. That's why I'm barrelling across the Trans-Canada in the belly of my mother-in-law's car — deceased mother-in-law that is, it's so hard to get used to thinking of you as dead — wondering how I got to be so pissed-off at the world. This morning I started out feeling sad, but now the anger and resentment that attached itself to me over the last ten years is simmering below the grief and shock of the past few days.

I'll tell you this much, Muriel, I don't plan to turn forty and get led around by the nose only to be angry and frustrated the rest of my life the way my mother is, the way you were. There has to be a way out of these patterns. I don't want to live my life in a circle of *What Ifs* and *If Onlys*.

And there's another thing: I wish I hadn't been in such a hurry to let sex and desire lead me around.

I'm tuckered right out. Here I thought I'd get all the way to Edmundsten today, but my legs and arms are dead weight. I try to focus on the landscape gliding past me, the trees along the Saint John River are brushed with hazy green, almost ready to burst into leaf, but I find myself keeping an eye out for the ferry that I used to take with Mum and my stepfather when we went to visit my aunt and her family up in Oromocto. The water is still high in the river. I wonder if there were any floods when the ice broke up. I'm glad the day is warm and dry; this road can be so treacherous in bad weather.

I'm going to stop at the next motel. The smell in this car is getting to me. It reminds me of your closet, Muriel.

The day you died, we arrived in Alma around midnight. I slipped upstairs while Jamie and Alexis poked in cupboards and opened drawers like naughty children, as if they were looking for you in the smallest places. I stood at your bedroom doorway not knowing if I was relieved you had passed away before we arrived, or sorry that we didn't have one final goodbye.

Wherever you were, I was hoping you'd feel at home, because you sure as hell never seemed to feel at home here in Alma.

Agatha must have made herself busy before she retreated back to the old house. Your bed was neat and tidy. I peeked under the spread but there was nothing there, just the naked mattress and box spring. I thrust my fingers between them, looked under the bed, sniffed the spread. Freshly laundered. Agatha was fast, you had died on that bed just twelve hours before, and I couldn't detect a smell at all. I ran my hand along the wooden spools of the bedstead.

Fingering the ruffles of your pillow shams, I thought I'd feel queer, but I didn't. A kind of blankness overcame me and I noticed for the first time how worn your hot pink carpet was. It looked grubby. I suppose you hadn't had it cleaned in twenty years. Skin ash, I thought. Skin ash rubbed into everything. I was with you when the vacuum salesman demonstrated how much skin ash lay around the average house and you bought that hulking silver vacuum cleaner lickety-split. A person would think skin ash from people as white as us would be whiter but it isn't. It's a dirty grey, like old snow.

It wasn't until I opened your closet that I was overwhelmed with the feeling of trespassing, because that's when I was hit by your smell. Your almost-smell. Stale perfume and locked-up body odour. Traces of fried food and hair spray. Vestiges of cigarette smell from parties held long, long ago. I backed off and went into your bathroom. Surveyed the medicine chest. Stood on your scales.

Funny. I thought I'd weigh a lot less with you dead.

FIVE

WHEN DID NIGHT fall? Somewhere between my mother's hoots and your closet, Muriel; somewhere between when that flutter of relief became a flutter of regret. There's nothing but trees to keep me company on this cracked and pot-holed road through flatland central New Brunswick. The goddamned spindly second or third growth of fir and spruce that has been ravaged in decades past by the spruce budworm and doesn't even make the grade for pulpwood. In the dark, the trees look ghostly. I feel isolated. Most of that warmth I felt earlier today starting out has dissipated into a general feeling of unease. I don't feel you sitting beside me anymore, Muriel. What am I doing with this car? Where do I think I am going all by myself? Home. Sure. But home is so far away now. Am I really up to days and nights alone in the wake of so much sorrow? Do I have the strength?

What if I am nothing but this string of thoughts in my head? The sound of my own voice no one can hear. What if this elaborate narrative simply collapses? Who will I be then? I'm frightened, Muriel. This is our final act. What if I'm not up to it?

Would you tell me — if you know now — what becomes of us

when we can no longer be the person someone else wants us to be? Do we become a wasteland?

What's that in the mirror? The moon? No, it's moving. Jiggling up and down. It's bearing down on me. What the hell? I touch my brakes. A logging truck hurls past, blaring its horn in a great thunder, flashing its lights. The force lifts the body of the Buick up and I have to hold steady not to get sucked into the truck's path. What is the matter with that asshole? Didn't he see me? Why all the noise and flashing lights? I'm shaking all over, holding fast to the steering wheel. I become dimly aware there are no dashboard lights on. I can't tell how fast I'm going. I'm driving with only the running lights on. The truck didn't even know I was here till I touched the brakes. Somewhere back there I should have turned my headlights on. Why didn't I see his lights coming up behind me? My hand fumbles around the dash and the steering column. I'll bet he only had one headlight, that's why I thought it was the moon at first. He's just as stupid as I am. Where's the knob, Muriel? Flip-flop — wipers. Spshhhhhh. Wiper fluid. Click. Lights. My pulse is in overdrive. You don't often get two chances with a logging truck. You don't get two takes with anything. My heart is rattled. Are you still out there somewhere, Muriel? Do I hear another rattle? Your old bones, perhaps, re-igniting your rage? Do I hear a rustle, the *fissht* of your good dress quivering against the ivory satin of your casket? All those polka dots letting loose. Are we going to take your unexpressed rage on this trip, too?

I wonder what's worse, Muriel. Being physically alone, or psychically alone. Or are they one-in-the-same?

You were such an enigma to me. Longing for company, but never enjoying anyone in your house, living in bungalows on the park boundaries while your head was filled with images of white colonial houses in pretty movie towns. A lifetime spent in, or on, the edge, of a village full of people you despised or at least disrespected. That walk-in closet full of designer clothes with nowhere to go but the United Church, a shopping day and splurge of lunch up in Moncton once a week, and a yearly visit, if you were up to it, with us. And, later, the agonizing, and increasingly infrequent visits to Donny up at the Georges Dumont Hospital the last four years of his life, your life.

In the Georges Dumont last week, after Agatha spilled her guts, when Jamie and Alexis were busy making arrangements, I asked about you. "Why was Muriel always so stuck-up?"

"You mean her air of superiority," Agatha corrected. "That would be Mother's fault."

In the old days, I would have run to you with that one, Muriel. Only I'd have to change the wording to make it sound that I was on your side. The way you and Agatha kept me up in the air like a ball, playing me back and forth. I was willing, because I wanted you both to like me. I never transcended that first impression Agatha formed of me the day we met, when she caught Jamie and me fooling around on your living room floor. One look from her and I was thoroughly ashamed. I would never make it up. I'm sure you told her all about my mother. So you each played on my insecurities, using me as a sly pathway of information, because almost everything was kept unsaid and unacknowledged — certainly anything emotional, the stuff everyone wants to know about. A whole lifetime together and you two never found a way to face each other. That's one thing I always admired about Alexis, she refused to play your game. But it was easy for her, wasn't it? She wasn't on the outside wanting desperately to get in. She had all the background knowledge I've been left guessing or piecing together with a remark made here and a fragment of information dangled there, with a little bit of research on the side.

You never could have known that I'd end up working with curators in the contemporary art department of a major museum, could you? Do you know what we do? We research, collect, catalogue, describe, and exhibit — with interpretation. That's heavy on the interpretation, Muriel. We institutionalize meaning. We do it for the public good. We do it so the next generation can come along and tear it down and write a new interpretation. This is something you never quite understood. Meaning is something you have to make up on your own. It can't be handed down with the family silver. It's how we learn who we are.

But it's hard to change old patterns. Here I am, still telling you what Agatha said. Only there's been a power shift, hasn't there? I think I'm going to like this. Now I don't have to make it sound like I made an innocent remark and Agatha walked into it. I can be straight now. I'm heading away. There's nothing left to lose.

I've got to get off this road. My hips ache and my legs are stiff. Grand Falls is up ahead. I'm not going to make it to the border tonight.

WELL, HERE I am in this shitty little motel room. It's supposed to be non-smoking but all the artificial fragrances in the world can't disguise the fact that in another life, this was a room in which people smoked. Heartily, I'd say, sniffing out the fetid ghosts of nights gone by embedded in mottled gold carpet and deflocked wallpaper. You can't disguise the past. If you really want a fresh start, you have to lay waste to the stinky layers.

Getting into bed I set the photograph on the Arborite nightstand of you and Agatha that I snitched last night. On the back it says *Wilson Studio, December 1918.* Was it taken to celebrate the Armistice? For Christmas? You were a little over four and Agatha five-and-a-half going on six. What was it doing on the whatnot outside your bedroom, Muriel? Why had I never seen it before? Who on earth put it there?

I gaze at you and Agatha as young girls for quite some time. You are both so recognizable. Dressed-up identically in knee-length, starched-white eyelet pinafores, with cape-like sleeves fitted diagonally over matching blouses with three-quarter sleeves edged in lace. Overly large stiff white bows of the same material fastened to your heads. Agatha's bow sits squarely over her crown while your bow is fastened jauntily to the side, pointing somewhere off in the distance of a hazy, classical-looking background. You are both wearing long, somewhat baggy white stockings, and black patent leather shoes with bows and thick ankle straps. You are each adorned with silver bracelets and gold christening lockets. Agatha is wearing a ring on the middle finger of her left hand. I can't tell if you wear a ring or not because your left hand has been placed between your chubby little knees. You are sitting on some kind of ornate bench with a thick, curling arm, legs crossed at the ankles. Your left shoulder slightly forward, right shoulder back, elbow bent, hand flat on an open book with your fingers splayed, taking the weight of your upper body. Your round plump pouting face is thrust out, making your head appear as if it is sitting directly on your shoulders, with no neck to support it. Agatha is standing erect with her right forearm resting across the top of the bench. Her left arm hangs limply, as if not attached to her body. All fingers are curled in. Ankles together, but ever so slightly, the right foot is turned out. A serious little face, revealing only the slight whisper of a smile, rises sternly from a strong neck. Light glints off your soft blond ringlets. Agatha's tight dark ringlets almost disappear into the background.

Taking the silver-framed photograph into my hands, I begin to look at your bodies and faces. You have been posed so well. How many takes before the photographer got this perfect shot? How did he know to make a provocative display of you Muriel, an *I'm going to marry Daddy* look, innocent and winsome. How did he know to make a retiring yet haughtily independent lone figure of Agatha with those arms that wouldn't reach out to embody life? Was he blessed with prescience? Or was Philomena in the background, stage directing?

I see her getting you girls ready for the big event. She is wearing a black rustling dress that smells old as Methuselah. Her only acquiescence to personal vanity has been to anoint herself with something a little biblical, perhaps Lily-of-the-Valley toilet water. She knows a few behinds will stir and tongues quietly cluck when the villagers get a load of the way she has her daughters gussied up and she makes a strange little humming sound in her throat, knowing she will suffer the slight. She swallows hard. Pulls her chest up. Austerity is fine and well for those of modest means; better standards are for those who can afford them. She will obey the family standards of frugality and pass on to you all of Agatha's everyday clothes, but for photographs she will demonstrate her ideal. After all, her husband Perley is an up-and-coming mercantile man. What does she care what the villagers think? She has come to regard them not as less fortunate, but as less enterprising. And, since she understands there is suspicion of those who do well, she makes regular charitable donations for missionary work in faraway places, though it is worrisome that some will think her proud rather than virtuous. So, she claims her dignity by raising money for the church and hospital, and will not let her reputation rest on her husband's rising position alone.

She had big plans for you girls. She decided that you would attend Mount Allison University and achieve full bachelor degrees. From the cradle, she has provided for you identities with which you can go away and prove your worth in a man's world. She won't have you sent off to Normal School as she was. Philomena still has a bad taste in her mouth for being pressured into coming home from Fredericton. But when her family holds up to her the sacrifices of her younger sister, Clara, who walks the five miles to Point Wolfe to give piano lessons for pennies several times a week, she buckles. Submits and pitches in, sacrificing her teaching wages as well to help the family recover from that bad business deal with the railway, believing, as she was told, that she'd get her reward down the road. Her parents have always been firm believers in progress and predict there will be new ventures and never-ending opportunities in Alma. The family stands together. They get by but they do not prosper. Philomena does her part. She obeys. She contributes. In no time at all she becomes a rigid do-gooder like her mother, and her mother before her.

Seven years after her return from Fredericton, when they have saved enough to give themselves a good start, she marries Perley

Steadman. He is just a farm boy from out Berwick Mountain way, but he has drive and a good head on his shoulders. She supports his plans to take over the company store when the last of the lumber barons departs for good. She believes in Perley's aspirations.

As for Perley himself, he believes in hard work, but he does not wish to rise too much above his station in life. He is fond of his own gentle manner, and goes a good distance to cultivate his belief in the betterment of those less fortunate, as his Methodist upbringing dictates. He believes that with the right training and education, and by the grace of God, a person will have the power to overcome all of life's obstacles. On Sunday mornings, he honours his wife by attending worship in the Baptist church with her, but only after his own Methodist services are over.

When you and Agatha are born, Muriel, he does not resist your being registered in the Baptist Cradle Roll. He simply wants it understood that when you girls are of age, you will be free to make worship preferences for yourselves. Although by the time you are rigged up for the photograph, he has begun to wonder if you have not become too set in your ways. The Baptists, he has sorely noted, hold an unremitting bent of sticking to themselves.

This is on his mind as he escapes into the leather armchair in the back room of his general store after the family noonday dinner. He does not smoke and he does not drink, but concocts a confection of his own sweet mood into which he dips himself day after day, night after night, until his lustre is as hard and deep as his given name, Perley Joseph Steadman. Well regarded for his humorous nature and who, after the Depression, will be honoured far and wide for being a man who never called in a debt. But on the day the photographer comes, he wonders about the future and Philomena's plans for their daughters. In the light of day he fully agrees, convinced that providence will point the way. But at night, he worries how, living in a location where the economy is depressed — a word used before anyone even thought of the capital D depression — he will ever save the money.

Philomena leaves such matters in the hands of her husband. It is her job to teach their daughters how to be ladylike and hold their bladders all day and make sure they do not grow up reckless, getting mixed up with some ignorant backwoods degenerate oaf. There will be no tainted blood in the family. To that end, Muriel, you and Agatha are kept under strict observation. You are not allowed to leave the yard. You were never allowed to ride a bicycle, or learn to swim, like the other village children, over in the millpond. And because she is the oldest, Agatha was trained to observe these severe measures over you.

The morning of the photograph Philomena, a pair of hot tongs in her capable hands, struggles with Agatha's hair. After twenty minutes, Philomena solves her problem by wrenching the little girl's hair back from her scalp and securing the bow to her crown. Agatha's head smarts from the attack. Behind your mother's back, you Muriel, stick your tongue out at her, then cock your head to one side with a little shrug of your shoulders, wagging the bow that has been fixed at a stylish angle. Soft blond natural curls frame your fat little face.

When you girls are paraded before the photographer, Agatha tries to make herself invisible, while you respond by playing up to him when he flicks your chin and wiggles your nose with is index finger.

"Muriel. Sit still like your sister," Philomena admonishes.

Agatha holds the smug feeling of superior behaviour deep in her throat and chest. Her face is blank. She swallows repeatedly, savouring the feeling she has captured for herself. She hides so many feelings here that by the time she is a middle-aged woman her jaw is set.

Flash. You girls are set for life.

To make the most of her daughters being all dressed up, Philomena has arranged a tea party in her parlour with her sister Clara and her daughter Marjorie, who is the same age as you. Clara has also made a purposeful marriage to a bright young man. Both sisters can afford a hired girl. Eventually Clara and her husband will make their way west, but not before you will spend twelve years in the same grade as Marjorie. You and Marjorie will come to hate one another because you each will have to endure your mother's insistence that you hold the place of top student. There can be no second best. The competition between you will be so severe that the young teacher will often go home at night and cry. You, Muriel, will never trust, nor ever learn to form close, or long lasting, relationships with females.

Agatha will be spared this particular drama. As luck would have it, her grade is filled with that tribe of Rossiters from up the back road, so she learns to compete with herself and keep an eye on you, becoming a self-sufficient high-achiever. At university, and later as a professor, she will develop close collegial relationships with her contemporaries that will remain intact all her life. Agatha's drama with her mother revolves around the terror of keeping her clothes — which are to be handed down to you — in immaculate condition. No spots, stains, rips, tears, or undue wear will be tolerated on the clothes that Philomena works her fingers to the bone, and tires her eyes, sewing at night under the dim light of an oil lamp.

While Philomena and Clara take their tea and cakes in the parlour, Agatha, you, and Marjorie are treated to hot buttered biscuits and strawberry preserves in the kitchen. Agatha is mortified when a drop of the slippery red preserves plops onto the front of her new dress. Sickened, she excuses herself to go to the bathroom before anyone notices. Standing on tiptoes to look into the oval mirror over the basin she sees that the largest red dollop has landed in the V of the chain of her gold locket. After many attempts, her little fingers succeed in undoing the clasp. She places it next to the soap dish. Wetting the end of a towel, she dabs at the soap and gently swabs the strawberry stain. Agatha rinses the end of the towel and gives it a good squeeze, hoping it will dry out quickly. Her dress, she sees, is almost spotless.

In the parlour, Agatha takes a seat next to Philomena. Marjorie sits beside Clara. When you join them, Muriel, you manage to seat yourself in a corner where the mothers cannot spy you. Facing Agatha, you sit straight up with your hands folded in your laps, dutifully maintaining silence while your mother and Aunt Clara discuss the arrangements for an upcoming pie social to raise money for the church. Time passes very slowly. You start to fidget but Agatha stares at you coldly before your mother has to reprimand you. You stare back at her and when you are sure no one is looking, you open your mouth and stick out your tongue. Although Agatha remains as composed as a marble statue, a shock wave of revulsion surges through her lifeless little body, for on the tip of your hot pink, biscuity tongue, is Agatha's precious gold locket.

When you girls are excused to play outside, you send Marjorie to the sun porch to fetch the carriage for your dolls. Then you dangle the gold locket under Agatha's nose. Agatha snatches it from you and runs behind the woodshed to vomit a lumpy pink mass onto the snow-spotted grass.

That night she hides the locket under her mattress. When Philomena comes to tuck her in, Agatha confesses, very calmly, that she believes she has lost her gold locket. It must have fallen off when she was playing outside.

All you do is disappoint me, Philomena said to her eldest daughter. "Say your prayers. And tuck those little hands of yours under your chin. Keep them there and don't let them go wandering through the night."

Agatha receives her scolding with great stoicism. She doesn't understand her mother's appraising look, or know why her mother is concerned about her hands. She inches down into the covers, leaving her hands to the mercy of the frigid night air and prays to Jesus to be forgiven for the sin of telling a lie to her mother. She will never do it again. Her little body is cold and not comforted at all until she thinks of the words "duty" and "service" spoken so often by her mother and father.

In the dark, listening, but having already been tucked in, you snuggle down into your covers, afraid to open your mouth. Nobody said anything about your little hands.

Downstairs in the kitchen, stretched out on the daybed near the woodstove by the lone electric light bulb, Perley reads an article in the *Methodist Magazine and Review*, "Pure Thoughts on Avoided Subjects." Coming from an old farm family, and being the seventh child of eleven, he holds a natural belief that a man should not waste his seed. Reading this article, his belief is challenged by the notion that he could be weakening his vital force by spilling his seed too often. He is swayed by the argument that if he conserves his vital force he will be lifted to a higher plane of living. He looks at his reflection in the tall windows hoping for an answer.

Before Philomena enters the kitchen, she stops to pat the tight braids that wrap her head, licking her fingers to tame stray hairs. Entering, she immediately reads the look on Perley's face and knows he will ask her to retire early. She is of two minds. She feels caught between the world of her mother who, on the day before her wedding, advised her that a household runs smoothly if the man of the house is never refused relations and a world she has read about in a series of articles sent to her by her radical cousin in Boston.

Philomena had written to her cousin in dismay that even though she was nursing she became pregnant with Muriel so quickly after Agatha was born. Her cousin, a staunch believer in Family Limitation as a means to establish a strong, prosperous middle class, sends Philomena pamphlets and newspaper clippings about Mrs. Margaret Sanger who writes knowledgeably about the means of birth control. She asks Philomena to distribute the information, but Philomena does not believe it is up to her to save the ignorant from themselves. She is grateful for the pamphlets. She does not plan to spend the rest of her childbearing days wondering if she is pregnant every time she and Perley engage in relations. She does not plan to put their prosperity at peril by bringing a baker's dozen into the world. She has no intention of telling Perley about the Dutch Cap her cousin has sent. She sees no reason why Perley should shirk his responsibilities. She supports the Methodist belief that a man should raise his level of continence to better himself, so insists that Perley pull out from time to time so that he will not grow suspicious when she does not provide him with a male heir. He has had his chance. She takes her place in the rocking chair on the other side of the woodstove and settles into a housekeeping magazine. When the lights blink, she and Perley make their way quietly up the stairs before the mill at Point Wolfe shuts down the power for the night.

I place the photograph face down on the nightstand and hold its image in my head as if viewing it from a great distance. I see myself on the edge of low tide on a moonlit night, holding Jamie's hand. We look across the vast, exposed beach and he points out Philomena and Perley's house. I now know that the house I am looking at isn't the house where Muriel and Agatha lived when they had their photograph taken in the eyelet dresses; it is the house that was rebuilt after the fire eight years later. But the location is the same. What Jamie is pointing out isn't really the house itself. He is pointing out family and family history. How Philomena and Perley treated him like a prince.

"Jamie's grandmother was not the same woman as my mother," you said one time Muriel, in a rare, wry, moment. And then you hissed. Not that you would have had Jamie treated in any other way — after all, he was your little man, and nothing was too good for him. But you could not understand how Philomena showed all the patience in the world for his walloping energy, while for you she had none. You could not understand and you could not forgive. This split caused you the greatest outrage and you did not know what to with it.

That night Jamie pointed out his grandparent's house he told me, so matter-of-factly, "My grandma died about a month ago."

"Oh dear, you must feel really bad," I said.

"I don't know, she was old. It was her time."

He had just turned twenty and his reaction was drained of any feeling as the beach was drained of water. Yet he told the warmest stories of Philomena and her cookies and tearing around her house with Jerry Cooper after school until she'd shoo them out in gales of laughter.

No wonder you were so mad, Muriel.

And what about Perley? He would stand behind the heavy old-fashioned oak counter and reach around to the stacked shelves behind him for any item Jamie pointed to while they engaged in their game of "store." When Jamie was tired of the game, he'd be sent off with a pocketful of penny candy and Perley would patiently clear the counter.

Doesn't their indulgence of your son get to you, Muriel? Doesn't it just get under your old, dead skin? I wonder if the memory of injustice and outrage is sloughed off in the cells, if it still lurks in that skin ash — if the resonance of the past is not only in our minds but also under our fingernails in the here and now?

Do I hear you clawing to get out and smack me across the face just as Philomena smacked you the day you came home from school and asked *What does fuck mean*? Even when you told me this story I could see very well in your waxy wrinkled face the insolence of your young face coming home with that word. You might not have known exactly what it meant, but you knew it meant something, because the word vibrated. You dared. And you got knocked down.

You turned to Daddy, but there was no penny candy for you. There was no supper and no story that night. Only Perley giving you an extra tuck-in after the lights blinked.

Perley always comes off with a bit of a glow. Except for when he denied you your second chance at nursing school — for your own good, mind you — but we'll get to that tomorrow, when I get to Montreal.

For now I'm still stuck with the dead and I think about the supper-time eulogizing and how Perley died on his daybed in 1962 of a heart attack and wasn't it wonderful that he died at home in his favourite resting place, and how Donny rushed in from work with his warden's first-aid credentials and tried to resuscitate Perley, but it was no good. Perley died in Donny's uniformed arms. Donny broke down and cried and cried. But what about last week when Jamie and Alexis and I sat in extreme discomfort in that very same kitchen and Alexis cut the bullshit with a remark I can't get out of my head.

I remember when my father wasn't welcome in this house.

Jamie didn't know what Alexis was talking about and all Agatha could do was tremble and say, "Indeed." She had such complex feelings about the Gallagher family as I had just learned up at the Georges Dumont. But those feelings aside, I was as curious as all get-out. I knew it must have had to do with (Donny's drinking). Then something you said, Muriel, rang in my head. *I lost Alexis to them and I wasn't going to make the same mistake with Jamie.*

I see you Muriel, like a black and white movie, late at night, Alexis bundled in a blanket in your arms as you scurry across the street from the neat little white house with the gleaming hardwood floors you and Donny had just built, hoping the neighbours aren't looking, and deposit Alexis for care-taking with Perley and Philomena, so you can go back and confront *that man* without worrying about what Alexis might see or hear. She spent a lot of time with them didn't she, Muriel? And you couldn't have been married for that long because, as I very well know, you had conceived Alexis on your wedding night.

When Jamie came along it was a different story. You didn't bundle him off. You battened him down. I didn't stop to ask you how you did it but now I think I know. The confrontations stopped and the big silences started. You turned Jamie into *your little man* and forgot about your disappointment with Donny. Jamie was protected and you were placated.

When it all started to crumble, Alexis, and then Jamie, had to be sent away to private schools. But Jamie had seen what was coming. He had climbed up the highest tree in the village one day and looked out at all he knew and understood in the deepest part of him that he could not stay.

That tree is where he went after Perley died too. In all the commotion, you forgot about Jamie. He was brushed aside while the mourners took centre stage. I understand this because it has happened to me too. Why is it that adults forget that children have to grieve too? It's not true that young minds are not affected. It's not true that we grow out of it. In fact, I think we grow more deeply in to our grief.

That's why Jamie didn't show much feeling when Philomena died. It's not that he didn't have feelings. It's that he didn't know how to show them. Not until last week when he collapsed into me did I ever really see Jamie crack open. It was such a connection; I will feel it forever. Like the night out on the beach when he first kissed me and I thought the top of my head was going to blow off.

What does this mean, Muriel? Is it hope?

When I turn the light out, the image of the logging truck light jostling in the rear-view mirror floods my head and a train of fear and heat rushes through my body. All the molecules under my skin are speeding. I am all alone in this stinking little room in the backwoods of New Brunswick with no one to talk to but the dead. Now all those miles ahead of me loom monstrously. All those miles and talking in my head. Maybe I am going crazy. Maybe I'm afraid to make a sound because it might get so loud that it will transform into a big black hole into which I will disappear. Maybe that's what silence is about sometimes. Fear.

But this feeling is not unfamiliar. It has lived with me for so long that I have come to regard it as normal. When Jamie started working away for ten days or two weeks at a time, I would shift over to his side of the bed and hold the covers over my head to sniff the comforting scent of our goodbye lovemaking. I never washed the sheets until the day he came home. But I could only hold that comfort in my head for so long before it would fade and I'd find my head riddled with thoughts of being alone. Eventually I learned to live my life like this by pushing these thoughts away to make the best of our situation, because it was all for the family good. I learned that lesson from you, Muriel. The family good. But I know now that it isn't true. It is never good for the family to spend much time apart. All you can hold up to the mirror of so much separation is the false face.

Jamie so often accused me of not living in the real world because I was sheltered in the house looking after two little girls, or off to school learning how to make art. He didn't understand that learning how to draw, or paint, or to make a video, first required me to look, look hard and long until I could be faithful to what I saw, whether it existed in the external world or the internal world of my head.

What I see now — that girl on the beach, with her longing to come up against the fact of her own existence — is someone being chosen. Someone who mistook the choosing for a gaze of really being seen, really being heard, really being felt. Why was it so easy to dismiss myself? Now I feel ashamed and lonely.

My fists punch the pillow down into a comforting shape into which I ease my tired head. My eyes close. I feel the weight of Jamie collapsing into me. Cracking open. But, I wonder, what the hell cracked open?

There is no answer, though it occurs to me that I don't have to make the best of it like the rest of them. Maybe I can just let this godawful feeling in my body be what it is. *It won't kill you.* My mother's voice. But I want more than just staying alive, or making do. I want real hope. I want to flourish.

Goodnight, Muriel. Sleep tight.

SIX

IN THE EARLY innocent glow of my surprise pregnancy with Andrea, Jamie and I made a list of the things we would never, ever do as parents. My access to the events of those months of pregnancy and childbirth is as open to me as the road here this morning leading to the Quebec border; but, for the life of me, I can't remember one damn thing we wrote with such solemn sincerity on that fresh white sheet of paper.

Oh where, oh where, do our intentions go?

My first thought upon wakening today: Andrea and Caitlin should have been with us for their grandmother's funeral, especially in the flux of what happened that day. I don't think Jamie and I made a plan to exclude them from the mourning process, we simply didn't make a plan to include them. Perhaps we thought about them missing too much school, but to tell you the truth, Muriel, I don't think we thought it out at all. We were so shut down and so far apart that they simply fell through the great big gap we had created between ourselves.

And of course, there was always that other issue swimming not so far below the surface of every decision we ever made: money. It costs an arm and a leg to fly from one end of this country to the other. How does that make you feel, Muriel? Your grandchildren weren't included in your funeral plans because of tight fists and careless neglect. For some things you get second chances, but not funerals. I feel pretty damn shitty about your granddaughters' absence at your funeral. For them and for you, because no matter what else I can say about you — and you might have been wilful in your relationship with your mother — when it came to being a grandmother, you strove to be like Philomena. Or you strove to create for your granddaughters the kinds of memories Jamie had of her. From you, Andrea and Caitlin experienced indulgence and warmth. You loved them in all the ways you could love them and they were imbued with your ideal of grandmotherly behaviour. All you required from them was that they carry your blood.

In the beginning, you were over the moon with the arrival of your first grandchild. A grandchild was a rite of passage and you were sixty years old. Time was pressing. You were afraid that Alexis and Ed would never have children after he announced *If Alexis ever gets pregnant I'll have the goddamn thing ripped out of her before I'd let any offspring of mine come into this godforsaken world.* I was stunned by the enormity of pregnancy and birth and the responsibility. For me, time almost stopped. I felt betrayed and abandoned by everyone. Especially you, because I looked to you for guidance and support. But you, I can see so clearly now, you were overcome with panic. The debris of your own ordeal with Alexis, and such a deep sense of compound failure, washed into the present and swamped the both of us.

Oh god, Muriel, my false sense of security! Now I find it almost funny to think how that sense of security was constructed around such skinny strands of narrative and clues I picked up watching you. Those red hands of yours, happiness always slipping through them and you didn't know why. The scalding water I couldn't get near. A steamy dishrag swiped across the face of the chrome toaster leaving long streaks of oily lemony bubbles that I'd polish up the moment you left the kitchen. You instructing me how to make up a good tight bed with hospital corners in your teacher's voice that made me go limp. The fine art of burping a hot water bottle. Your shock that my mother had never taught me. Your nursing school tricks. Your old puzzle face heaving and contracting as you told me in your own words for the first time, down on your knees, searching through your cedar chest for something you wanted to pass on to me before Jamie and I got married.

I see you so clearly, neat and spry, walking down the corridor of the Royal Victoria Hospital in Montreal. The year is 1937. Young Dr. Moore leans against the nurses' station consulting with the older, moustached doctors. With one eye, he steals up the space between you as you walk his way. You know the rules: probation student nurses are not allowed to fraternize with doctors, but nothing can protect you from his gaze. Not Matron's shrewd patrol. Not the mingled smells of phenol, urine, and vomit. Not the permeating vapours of illness. You are caught in his spell. A mixture of seduction and caution rests in the tilt of your head. Nose down, eyes up. Mouth unsure. The small hole of a smile.

An advanced nursing student teases you in the cafeteria with a word of warning. Dr. Moore's a charmer; he has his eye on you. You do and don't entirely understand. The nurse explains that he intends to get you into his bed. He has a reputation with the country girls. *Your Baptist mother won't want you showing up with a little bun in the oven, will she?*

Being called a country girl makes you steam. You hate being obvious. Yet here in Montreal you are so confused. You are overwhelmed by the ethnic mix. In Alma, everyone looks more or less the same. Prosperity and poverty are the distinguishing features. Back home you know where you stand. In Montreal, you are unsure. The afternoon you are introduced to friends of your colleagues, you are described as *Our little nursing probie from New Brunswick*.

One of the friends eyes you, then steps back to get a full view. *You really can't tell.*

Can't tell. Can't tell what? These thoughts smear your mind. *What can't they tell?*

The advanced student replies that though you have a BA from Mount Allison, you hardly have any accent at all.

Accent. What accent? You worry at night. You know you don't twang like the people in Alma. Your grammar — even if you do pronounce *measure* as *may-zure*, and *butcher* as *bootcher* — is perfect. Yet you can't get the picture of the friend stepping back to take you in. You can't help but think it's something in your clothes, your appearance, as much as your speech. You wonder if you were overdressed with that glossy muskrat stole around your shoulders, the pointy face with its tail in its mouth. You wanted to stand out. But you also wanted to belong. You couldn't make the fine distinctions in this diverse, bustling city. You only felt safe in your uniform, dashing between the dormitory and hospital in the soft wool nurse's cape that you clutched into your heart, wrapping yourself in the crimson lining, protected from the world, if only for those few moments, by the navy blue mantle of the nurse's pride and joy. The cape. The announcement to the world that you belong to a community of women who are bound by your sense of compassion.

To push these thoughts from your mind, you run variations on the scene of Dr. Moore giving you the eye. In these scenes, you have graduated and are renowned for your skills and soothing touch. You and Dr. Moore meet in the corridor, alone. Your hands brush accidentally and just as he is smiling intently upon your gentle, uplifted face, about to tell you that he is falling in love with you, he is flanked, en masse, by the moustached doctors. From nowhere, you hear the older nurses laughing. Over the next few weeks, no matter how many times you practise this scene, you can't stop the sudden appearance of the moustached doctors, or quiet your cheeping colleagues.

The corridor in your mind to Dr. Moore never closes. As you learn how to give subcutaneous injections, master the smelly art of applying hot foments — which you perform with precision but without art: *apt to be mechanical* is written on your student history card — you take yourself to dinner with him. Mustard plasters, dressing procedures, and sponge baths, you approach clinically, finding these duties distasteful. But you must endure if you do not want to end up teaching elementary school back in New Brunswick. Even the endless cleaning and bed-making doesn't grind you down. When Matron snatches the sheets from the bed, having detected a ripple, and shouts, *This is not acceptable*, you blink once, then set your mouth grimly and remake the bed perfectly, knowing it was perfect in the first place. This is not unlike your relationship with Philomena.

What you hate most are the classroom hours. Memorizing anatomy and physiology makes you fidget. There are so many procedures to be copied neatly into the Dominion loose-leaf notebook. You blame your mother for your intolerance of study because of the years spent studying for a degree you did not want.

Near the end of your three-month probation, your pride is stung when Matron accuses you of trying to get out of work when you break down and tell her that you are feeling very ill. Feeling dismissed, you wind up that determination of yours, saying *I'll show her* under your breath, and work as hard as you can. Your fingers steeled to pain as you wring out steaming wool blankets between two sticks. You begin to feel a little dizzy. Your throat is so sore; your head aches badly. You are hot and weak. Almost delirious when the best scene with Dr. Moore starts to play out so well. The altar. The kiss ...

Your ears barely register the clatter when a tray of sterilized scissors and tweezers falls to the polished floor as you collapse. Matron is summoned. She rolls you over to loosen the collar of your uniform. A red thrush is creeping up your neck. Further examination reveals a rash in the armpits, chest, and groin. By the time a doctor steps in to take over, a ring of pallor surrounds your lips, your throat is inflamed, and red spots are appearing on your palate. Your tongue is big and strawberry red.

"Tell me, woman," the doctor bellows at Matron outside your room. "Tell me how one of your students got into such a state."

Matron is not pleased. She has drilled her students in germ theory and the careful application of asepsis and antisepsis. It is the very foundation of modern nursing. In a teaching hospital, the prevention of cross-infection from patients to medical staff is crucial. Off Matron stomps, looking for the charge nurse responsible for supervising the probation nurses.

You spend the next week on the isolation ward. A letter arrives from Perley and Philomena announcing that since you don't seem to be up to the task of nursing, they have put a good word in for you with the school board.

You need to write home and tell your parents how hard you have worked to prove yourself, rising before dawn to start the daily round of ward service and ward housekeeping duties. How every move is watched, noted, and commented upon. You need them to understand about the short lunch breaks, then more study before returning for the evening ward duties. How your beautiful long fingers have been scalded to the bone.

As you lie in the hospital bed — hoping against hope that Dr. Moore will whisk into your room with flowers and a potion to cure your ills, even though you are afraid that he will be repelled by your red scaly flesh — you begin to feel smaller and smaller. You long for him to lay his cool hand on your forehead and whisper, *Oh, my darling, you have suffered so much*. But he never appears. Tracing the ridges of skin caked and cracked with calamine lotion all over your body, you cry yourself to sleep.

A week after the fever breaks and you are released from quarantine, a small group of classmates gather to wish you a safe journey home. In vain you look for Dr. Moore. You tell yourself he's busy, perhaps he'll send a card, a signal to return.

When Matron leans her body over you in the wheelchair and says, *You must return to us after your convalescence, Muriel*, you are barely able to answer. You do not think she means it. You wither at the way she says *Muriel*. You know from your fellow students that

Matron is still on the warpath for being publicly scolded by the doctor who examined you after you fainted.

As she pulls her 5'9" frame up to its full *may-zure*, Matron regards your small wasted body depleted of defiance. The long fever burned out your stores of resistance. It will be a good long time before you rekindle to a fighting mood.

You cry like an infant, rocking, in the noisy arms of the train from Montreal to Moncton. Your jelly muscles throb, your scaly powdery skin hurts, your scalp itches from the residue of dry shampoo, your eyes are sore and through your ears, a deep thucking whoosh drives into the sides of your head as the train trundles on. Because your voice is weak, little is spoken to the private duty nurse who accompanies you. Just the sight of her dashing cape fills you with despair. You can't imagine you will ever feel worse. When Philomena and Perley greet you at the train station in Moncton, you see their horror at your appearance. *Look at you. Just look at you. A rack of skin and bones. Look at what nursing has done to you*, Philomena cries. You understand that she is a breath away from saying: *I told you so*. Agatha will be the one to deliver that one when she comes home from Fredericton at Christmas from her job teaching high school. And you will hear it from her over and over until the day you die. What you don't see is that Philomena had wished to protect you from failure.

I see so clearly now that Philomena missed the moment when she could have saved her daughter's love with a few words of sympathy.

Twenty-three years old, eighty-eight pounds and defeated, Muriel, you maintain a long, slow recovery in your little bedroom that looks onto the street and the big blocky house across the road. If you sit at just the right angle, there is a view of the bay. Feeling strongest the hour before Perley comes in for lunch every day. The hour before the mail is brought, when you still have hope. Each day you are disappointed. Downstairs you pick at your food, push it around on your plate. Take weak tea then retire back to your room until the evening meal. As your rash dries up and the layers of skin peel away, you gradually emerge, thin-skinned, invisibly marked by failure. Rent of imagination.

Then one day, when Perley doesn't walk through the door for dinner at 12:03, something like lightning flashes through what is left of your body. You crash through the side door and look out into the back field, your mind white hot, and are stopped dead on your size five feet. Flames from the oil barrel lick high into air as you witness your sweet round father poke the remnants of the navy blue, red-lined, wool nurse's cape deep into that narrow inferno. The very ground beneath you disappears. One thought emerges to save you from disintegrating right on the spot: *He's doing it for my own good. He's only doing it for my own good.*

Like a phantom, you retreat into the house and the unappetizing plate of warmed over beef stew and hot fluffy biscuits, which you overload with heaps of butter and strawberry preserves. Fortified, you learn to cope by scaling down your expectations. You solidify. You tell yourself that there are hungry people right here in your very own corner of the world. With each bite you put into your mouth, you work hard at swallowing the idea of being stranded at home with your parents and a full-time teaching position.

That night when you fall into bed, you press your two blistering hands together and tuck them up under your chin and keep them there for the better part of a decade.

What else could you be expected to do?

HOT FLUFFY BISCUITS with heaps of butter and strawberry preserves. Now I feel hungry, even though I ate less than two hours ago. Maybe I'll stop at Tim Hortons in Edmundston. Wait. There's an Irving Station up ahead. I might as well fill up now. In the last couple of days, at least half a dozen people have warned me to make sure to gas up in New Brunswick before I cross into Quebec. Most people in Alma hate the French. They blame them for taking away good government jobs in the park. They hate bilingualism. They hate having French crammed down their throats. I have to admit I used to harbour some of these feelings myself before I got out and saw a bit of the world. Now I wish I had applied myself in my French classes, or had taken it at university. Now I see what a privilege it is to speak more than one language, although sometimes I figure I can barely get by in English. I have no fears of getting gas in Quebec. I had no problems seven years ago when I drove down from Mississauga. "Bonjour," I said to the gas jockey. "Fill 'er up, s'il vous plait." Not a big effort on my part, but at least I wasn't defensive, I had a half-assed offering. "That's because you're a woman," Jamie harrumphed when I related this little scene. *A woman*? From the man who doesn't believe in feminism. Maybe he meant sexism, I don't know. But it seems to me that if you admit to one, you have to accept the other. I'll get a cruller and a coffee.

What would you like, Muriel? Is your appetite back? What was it you said to me last winter on the phone? *Ever since I was forced to eat when I got back from Montreal, I wanted to be thin again. All those diets I suffered through. And now I'm as thin as a rake. What was all that worrying for*?

What is worry for anyway, Muriel? I thought you might know, being the champion of worry.

Dear God, does everybody in the Maritimes still smoke? I'm not staying in here. C'mon, Muriel. We're getting back on the road.

As I wolf down this cruller, I think about your fiendish appetite and your recovery that went on and on. Do you know what Agatha said last week? *Dad always thought there was a natural waywardness about Muriel. It worried him to death*. But I think it was more than worry.

I CAN SEE him too. Perley thought he had done the right thing by burning your cape. Freed you from indecision and the natural waywardness he feared in you. When you buckle down to teach elementary school and rise up out of the ashes in the image of your father, throwing yourself into good deeds for the benefit of the needy in the parish, he believes you are finally developing a sense of compassion for those less fortunate. But how could you, Muriel? How could you develop compassion for others when you had not a speck of it left for yourself?

When you married Donny, there was fear about your choice. Donny had a reputation. He had been running the roads in his father's Model T since he was fourteen, with a pint of rum tucked under his belt. He had his father's charm, but none of his drive. He rebelled when sent to business school at Horton Academy and opted for the outdoor life as a linesman. *Wasted his father's good money*, Agatha said. *What a disappointment he was to that man. Donny had his chance. He really had no business to come looking to our family*. But so handsome, wasn't he Muriel? Tall and quick-witted, what a catch. He towered over you. And, after the birth of your children, you gave birth to something else, didn't you? Great disappointment and failure and oppression gave birth to a tower of your own. Almighty rage came forth into your world, but it did not fully manifest until 1961.

Well, Muriel, here we are in Hartland, home of the world's longest covered bridge at 391 metres. Not as pretty as the red covered bridge in Fundy, is it? Do you remember what Jamie said when we came home for that week in 1990 and you took us down to look at the new covered bridge that had been built to replace the old one that the maintenance contractors blew up by mistake when they dismantled the old dam? "What a bunch of fucking assholes," he said under his breath. He didn't mean for you to hear him. But you did. And you pinned me down later that night.

"Why does he say things like that?" you wanted to know.

"Oh Muriel, don't pay any attention. That's the way they all talk in the oil patch," I answered, wondering if I should protect you or him.

"Make him stop!" you huffed.

Who can ever stop anybody from doing anything? You of all people should know that. Who could stop you from the things you did? The chocolate cake is my personal favourite. Though now I wish I had asked you your version of this event. As it is, I have to rely on Jamie's rendering.

As I remember him telling me, it was the first year Alexis went to Netherwood. You had gone back to teaching and were still living at park headquarters. Jamie was ten. He had lunch with Perley and Philomena every day. You both went there after school to wait for Donny to pick you up and drive you back up the hill to your bungalow. One day you all came home to find a doubled-layered chocolate cake made by the hired girl. Donny was mightily impressed. You didn't say anything. Jamie got a queer feeling so made himself scarce up in his room. He heard you clanking and banging around in the kitchen, pulling out drawers and throwing in the metal utensils that were left in the drying rack, muttering *That girl could have at least put away the baking things*. Then the house went silent. The story goes that you spotted a sliver of chocolate batter dried onto the side of your best mixing bowl. Before Donny knew it, you grabbed the chocolate cake with the boiled icing and tromped down the hall, juggling the double layers. Hunks of cake were wiped onto the wall and gobs of icing splattered onto the ceiling. Donny was so stunned that he didn't move for a minute; he reached you about the same time Jamie snuck down the stairs. The hall runner was a smear of crumbs and stickiness. And there you were in a heap on the floor crying your heart out, all over cake. All over your hands, your hair, all over your good school dress. Donny grabbed you by the elbow and hauled you into the kitchen. Then he got the broom and dustpan. *Goddammit, Muriel*, he said. *You clean up this mess right this instant*. You wiped your snotty nose on your sleeve. Then, snivelling and whimpering, you swept the chocolate goop into the pan. Donny stood guard while you got down on your knees with a bucket and rag and mopped up the mess you had made of the hired girl's cake. While this went on, Jamie ran down the hill to Perley and

Philomena's. *Mom's got a bad headache*, he explained. Philomena hissed and Perley sighed. They set a place for him at the table. When they drove him home there was only one light in the living room. *Don't worry about it, boy*, Donny said, when Jamie came in. *Your mother's only going through The Change. Someday you'll understand.*

Someday he'll understand. It's about high time that day came, don't you think, Muriel?

Jamie's only response to me asking if he and Donny ever found out what was bugging you was to shrug and say, "Jeez, how should I know? It's just a funny story, that's all. She was going through the change. Either ranting at me — *do you want to wind up as a ditch-digger or a pulp-cutter* — to pick up my marks or wringing her hands when I did something stupid at school whining *don't make waves, don't make waves*. You couldn't take her seriously. Anyway, we never had a hired girl after that. No one suited her. She was funny like that anyway. A bit of a loner. Know what I mean?"

Maybe a loner, without a confidant, but you found me back in the winter of '72. There we are, Muriel, even though I'm all thumbs we have just made the bed in Alexis's room with perfect hospital corners. I don't tell you I couldn't care less about hospital corners. You go to the window and look out to the view of the bay. "I probably would have married a doctor if it hadn't been for my mother and father."

"What about Donny?" I ask. "I thought he was the one."

"What do you mean?" you say, but you don't answer my question. Instead, you open the drawer at the bottom of the cedar chest, taking out a slim dark green rectangular box.

"Mother gave me these to put in my hope chest after I started teaching school. She was trying to make up for ruining my chances. It's the sorrow of my life."

I'm not sure if you mean the scarlet fever or the ruined romance, but I can tell that you are not expecting any more sorrow. That you bore such sorrows already — *the conniving sister, the mean mother, and the bad husband* — and had no vision of future sorrow, that you could imagine nothing worse to befall you, as if your quota of bad things had been filled up, as if your experience was so bad it had forever inoculated you. You sit on your haunches, as if your five-foot frame holds up the weight of two, a bright twenty-three-year-old, who had nine wonderful weeks following her heart, and the older woman who had submitted. I feel sorry for you. I even notice that you have shifted the blame of your nursing school failure from your father to your mother, though it is so clear in your story that your father made you stay home *for your own good*. And your story is so big that I make the mistake of thinking that it was only weeks or days from your graduation. I thought that for years. I even stake my life on that misconception. But back then, even though I couldn't make hospital bed corners or didn't know how to burp a hot water bottle, I did know that as long as a person is breathing, a person's card of bad things isn't any more filled up than a person's card of good things.

You pass me the slim dark green rectangular box that you had been looking for. "You can have these," you say. "I was going to wait until your wedding, but you might as well have them now."

Inside are six ornamented sterling silver teaspoons from the Hudson's Bay Company. "They need a bit of polish."

That's when I begin to realize that you had been waiting for a long time to tell someone your sad story. You give me these spoons even though I have handed my mother's difficulties over to you, and you have begun to suspect there's something fishy about my stepfather. You give me these spoons because you already have so much invested in me. Then you lean forward to brace yourself and give a mighty grunt as you hoist yourself up from the floor. I lend a hand to steady you.

"My arthritis. I can't depend on this old knee anymore."

That's the knee you had your little hand tucked next to in the photograph.

I take the spoons and give you a hug. You sink into me, all soft and round, and hold on for a few minutes. Then before I know it, something terribly fragile and sorrowful seeps out of you and into my open heart. Lifting, for the next fifteen years or so, the burden of your disappointing life from Jamie's shoulders, and resting it onto mine — until the problem of what-to-do-about-Donny engulfs everybody.

Perhaps you're right, I think. Perhaps your card of bad things is already filled up and you have paid your dues. I feel a little stab of love for you, you who have made your way in the world without dying babies, or crashing sisters, or nervous breakdowns. Who comes from a family where people die from old age. How easy it would be to love someone like this, someone who didn't make it so hard. All I had to do was listen and feel sorry. I thought loving you would be so much easier than the complex emotions demanded by my own mother. Loving you, Muriel, would be a piece of cake. A piece of double-layered chocolate cake with boiled icing.

WHAT I COULD have really used, instead of silver spoons or any of the other fine things you gave me, was some compassion when I filled the toilet bowl with blood in the women's washroom at the Moncton Airport the day we flew home from Halifax with six-day-old Andrea. Isn't that what nurses are supposed to be about? Compassion? At least knowledge, Muriel, grant me that. But you weren't paying attention. You were giddy. The baby was fussing. And your past was about to collide headlong into my present.

SEVEN

AS I HEAD for Rivière-du-Loup, I realize that I have now descended from the Appalachian Mountains into a landscape where, with the exception of the summer I drove from Mississauga down to Alma, I have no personal history, just the history lessons of the wars between the French and English, with the good guys winning and our pathetic high school French classes, the teacher's turgid accent. Most of us were smart enough to know we never wanted to sound like that. Somehow, the province of Quebec always seemed out-of-bounds for me.

Whenever the subject of the James Bay hydro development was brought up, Jamie became bombastic, infuriated that he could not get a job up there because he didn't speak French. He never tried, never found out for himself. Some buddy or other had told him, had planted this belief in his head and off he went half-cocked, tilting at enemy windmills without checking it out.

It's funny about those things that get planted in our heads; they germinate into truths we never question. Like your nursing school story. In my mind, you were so close to the finish line. I accorded you all the virtues of being a nurse. Even the reason you gave me for not going back to Montreal to finish your training. I didn't question it. In fact, your story — *my father wouldn't let me* — was already familiar to me. My mother was denied nursing school by her father for the same reason: nursing is not a fit and proper occupation for a nice girl. But Perley's wasn't the only reason, was it? I've got the goods in those letters to Philomena from Montreal right here in the basket on the front seat. You wrote them but you never sent them. Do you recognize them, Muriel?

I was flabbergasted when they turned up in the hatbox with your white nursing hat and that muskrat stole. Fifty-six years you kept them and they probably hadn't seen the light of day until I read them at breakfast this morning before crossing over the border. I can't believe you merely forgot them. You were too cunning. Even after your devastating prognosis, there was plenty of time to destroy them. You left traces — evidence of your insecurities: the endless tasks. The longing for Dr. Moore was replaced by your story about knowing Donny was *the one* when you were only six. It's all up for grabs now, isn't it Muriel? The truth. When I was young, I took everything you said at face value. I fell for your authority, your age, your education, your possessions, your endowment of respectability. I fell for it all. But it's not that you weren't telling the truth. I realize now that you were telling the truth you could live with.

But is this the truth that I can live with? Did I ever tell you that the first year Jamie and I were married and lived in High-Rise II at Saint Mary's that I was at a dead loss to experience so much loneliness and disappointment? I was simply not prepared for the amount of time he needed to study. The engineering students worked in tight groups every night of the week. I'd get home on Friday, from a week at hairdressing school, with a whopping headache from the chemicals. I'd make supper, and then Jamie and I would snuggle into bed to watch *All in the Family* and *The Sonny and Cher Comedy Hour*, I'd fall asleep and when I woke up on Saturday around eleven or so, Jamie would already be gone. I'd spend Saturday cleaning the apartment and cooking. Late afternoon, Jamie would come home and we'd go shopping for groceries. Saturday night we were back in bed watching *Academy Performance*. We always slept in and made love on Sunday mornings, then had a breakfast of fried eggs and bacon scraps that came cheap in a greasy, plastic-covered lump from Capital Foods. Sunday night, Jamie was back at the books and I poured listlessly over my *Standard Textbook of Cosmetology*, boning up for Monday morning's test.

How I hated Michael's School of Hair Design. You thought I was having fun, Muriel. Guess again. The only part I liked was cutting hair. The chemical stuff, the perms, colours, streaks, toners all made me sick. But that's where the money was. The instructors made it quite clear that a shop wouldn't make any money if there wasn't a lot of chemical stuff going on. Hairdressers have to push product to make a living. Out of thirty-five students enrolled with me that year, only two paid their own tuition. The rest were paid for by he government, most of the women in their late twenties or early thirties, burned up and desperate.

We were so broke. Buying a Coke was a big deal. Jamie's student loan didn't cover our expenses. If Phyllis MacPhail, that flame-haired instructor of mine, hadn't wrangled me into the government program too, we would have been sunk. The help from home came wrapped in the fine brown paper of your agenda. Jamie couldn't imagine working anywhere but the National Parks for the summer. He put in for a position near Halifax because I still had two months left on my hairdressing course. But the only job that became available was foreman of the survey crew back up in Fundy National Park. How astonishing! You got Donny to pull strings, didn't you? Even Jamie thought so. And then you put in word with Agatha who had just moved back from Fredericton into Philomena's house and as a retirement project had opened up a well-heeled craft shop, featuring oatmeal-glazed pottery and thick blown glass. Don't get me wrong, I was grateful not to be waitressing once again. But the whole thing felt contrived. It wasn't easy, sucking up to Phyllis MacPhail to get permission to disrupt my course. When I arrived back in Alma, my heels were kicking.

Then you offered us to stay in your new roomy house. *Think of all the money you'll save*, you said, *We'll all have so much fun!*

"Think of all the money we'll save," Jamie seconded. I felt bamboozled. But I caved with only one condition: that Jamie and I move all the bedroom furniture down into the basement to make a space of our own. Ed and Alexis were going to be around all summer, too, and I couldn't bear the thought of our six big bodies cooped up on the second story emitting nighttime noises in the summer heat. I knew you lay awake at night, with Donny across the hall from you with his snoring and nightmares, listening. You grumbled and gave in to my demand.

My clearest memory is a June Saturday evening, Jamie and I slumped over one another on our bed, reading, when the doorbell rings insistently. We untangle and pound up the stairs from the basement.

"I wonder what's going on?" I ask.

"Geeze, I don't know," Jamie says. "I thought Mom was in the living room watching TV."

We get to the door and there you are, Muriel, standing outside. Alone. Facing your own back door. Arms falling loose from your shoulders, hands turned up as if they might simply float away.

"Is something wrong, Mom?" Jamie asks.

"Nothing sweetheart, I was just playing a trick on you," you say, and laugh in a forced, embarrassed way.

Jamie and I return your underwater laugh. "Okay," he says. Then he starts down the basement stairs. I follow, whispering, "I think she wants us to watch TV with her or something."

"Why? It's all repeats. There's nothing any good on."

"She must be lonely. Your dad's at work."

"He'll be home soon."

I feel sorry for you Muriel, though annoyed at the same time. After all, Jamie is my husband now. We try to resume the easy mood we were in before you rang the doorbell, but it has vanished into anxious air. I remember something you said to me about Alexis and Ed the first Christmas holiday we spent together, a year and a half earlier. *I don't understand why they go out for drives by themselves. They're married now. After all the things I do for them, I don't understand why they don't invite me to come along, especially when Donny's working.* At the time I deferred to you with complete support. Snuggling into Jamie I get a niggling sensation in my solar plexus. This is the early warning bell, but I don't hear it properly. I only hear your loneliness. I don't hear that you don't understand that marriage needs caretaking. I don't get this because I have no idea myself.

Several days later, I find a note tacked to the door: *Turn Off the Lights!* signed *The Management.* A touch provided by Alexis, because I know that you, Muriel, left to your own devices, would never think of such a thing. I sit on our bed in the cold dark basement, hot-faced with shame, imagining the pair of you plotting against me. Nostalgic for my mother's voice: *Who left the goddamn light on?*

I don't know how to respond to a sneaky note pinned to the door.

Why didn't you come to me, instead of complaining to Alexis? And how the hell did you know that the bedside light was on? I always closed the door nice and tight. Was it a dim sliver of light that caught your eye on the way to the cold room for a tin of ham? Or was it because you were rooting around in our stuff again? Like the day you found the green garbage bag of porno magazines and books under our bed.

Jamie and I were so quick to disclaim ownership of the green bag of porno that we forget to ask what you were doing, looking under our bed.

Vacuuming, you explained later, when it occurs to you. *I was only helping out.*

"The Old Lady's always been a little weird," Jamie said, when I complained to him about your snooping. "It's no big deal. One day when I was a kid and pissing her off about something, she screeched 'Do something with this child,' at poor old Dad the minute he got home from work. He took one look at her, then turned around and looked at me, and with a shrug upped with his boot and gave me a good swift kick in the ass. So what do you want me to do? Go up and give the old lady a good swift kick in the ass?"

Probably wouldn't hurt, I figured. But I didn't dare to say anything. You were a loyal bunch, Muriel. You nattered behind each other's backs all the time — your bitter, relentless diatribe about Agatha getting Perley and Philomena's house, how you had to hand over the keys, how you couldn't even go up to your old bedroom without asking permission;, how Agatha was sitting on a pile of gold. My personal favourite was your dismissal of her education when I asked where Agatha got her PhD. *Oh that, it's only honorary*. But Agatha was as critical of you as you were of her. She dismissed your claim that you had to have Caesarean sections because Philomena had dropped you on the floor when you were an infant, which caused you to have a tipped pelvis. She pointed the finger at you for the appalling lack of social life you and Donny had, even going so far as to say, *Poor Donny, he was such an outgoing man.* She was enraged with you for not doing your bit with Philomena in the last addled years of her life, *I took early retirement to look after mother, I could have co-written a math textbook. Do you know how much money textbooks make?* She would not say this to your face. She took back your key to the old house instead. No, you never said anything to each other but you did get defensive if an outsider said anything. It was made clear to me that I wasn't one of you yet, married into the family or not.

I'm finally out of the woods and onto the four-lane highway. Passing back there, with only two lanes, was making me a nervous wreck. This is much better. I wonder if the cruise control works. I learned to drive in Sussex, which didn't need a red light. Driving on highways used to make me nervous. I didn't even attempt to drive in Halifax or ask Jamie to teach me. Traffic jams made him anxious and volatile. That didn't leave much territory left over did it? I used to be just like you, Muriel, driving only in the most familiar places. I didn't question that the car really belonged to Jamie. I never got the knack of driving that shit-brindle brown Maverick with the shifter on the column that you and Donny gave us for a wedding present.

All those frightful long holiday weekend trips back and forth from Halifax to Alma. The carnage we witnessed on the road. Even our first trip down to Halifax the night we moved all our stuff the first time, the girl my age who died when hit from behind by a couple of drunks in a truck. We were there within seconds. I covered her with a blanket. Her boyfriend was screaming from somewhere in the ditch, "Where's Debbie. Where's Debbie." She looked perfect, lying on the side of the road, except for a gouge in her ankle, but her neck was broken. I still see her so clearly. Not a frightening image, just real and sad.

I keep thinking about the night Jamie and Alexis and I arrived in Moncton the day you died. How we were whisked straight into the funeral home in Hillsborough on the way down to Alma. How exhausted we were from the anxious preceding days and then the long haul flying across the continent. It must have been close to 11 pm. The funeral home director and his daughter were kind as they led us through the arrangements. When he asked what flowers we would like, Jamie and Alexis looked at one another and said, "No flowers, nothing fancy." I put my foot down and insisted on a spray of roses for the casket lid. Then we were led to the basement to choose the casket. This was really weird, Muriel. When Jamie and Alexis chose the cheapest coffin, the funeral director asked if we'd like to see the body. Jamie and Alexis visibly stiffened and replied simultaneously a resounding, "No." The man was clearly disappointed. He must have worked hard to get you presentable for our arrival. I was shocked, too. It's not that I was exactly looking forward to seeing your body, but I was prepared. I thought it necessary. But I lost my chance. I should have spoken for myself right then, but I didn't want to embarrass them.

This haunts me, Muriel. Not seeing you before you died. Not taking a moment to witness you in your death. What was your children's fear? Have you any idea?

To me it was nothing like the fear that possessed me on those dark slippery nights we drove back and forth from Halifax to Alma.

Or the unearthly shrieks that rove my body the night my mother got the call that her sisters had been killed.

THE SECOND YEAR we're down in Halifax we rent the upstairs apartment in an bright red Edwardian house with white trim on Henry Street, near Dalhousie. I don't feel the isolation of the year before. After I graduate from Michael's School of Hair Design there's a flutter of excitement when I land a job in that small, exclusive unisex shop on Spring Garden Road, owned by a wealthy widow. She draws most of the clients from her upscale circle of friends. I like them and they like me. They're working women who have the kind of professional jobs I have never heard of, and are married to men of substance and power. They ask me why I became a hairdresser. They think I could do better. I believe them. Especially the one who owns a public relations firm.

"Someone like you would be a real asset to my company," she says.

When I ask her how I would go about doing that, she replies, "Go to university for a couple of years. Learn a little about the world and a lot about yourself. Then come and talk to me." I want to be just like her. Wear a suit with a pretty blouse and black high heels and swish along Spring Garden Road in a long trench coat with a silk scarf tied at my throat. I want a briefcase. That woman hooks me. So I enrol in high school correspondence courses and knuckle down to the homework I couldn't face just two years before. Elated, I walk back and forth to work cutting through the Public Gardens and the Camp Hill Cemetery, fuelled by possibility.

Jamie is all for this new direction. He thinks hairdressing is bullshit. He hates me coming home hairy, overtired, overworked, and underpaid. He escorts me to see the Assistant Dean of Admissions at Saint Mary's University, who just happens to be the son of Jamie's former headmaster at King's. The Dean admires my ambition, promising that if I can manage to complete three courses in good standing that he will consider admitting me into first year in September. I can't believe it! In April, when it's time to head back to Alma and the park for the summer, we don't even blink twice when I quit my job. We are so sure the future will all work out. I am just about to turn twenty.

This year Jamie applies directly to the park superintendent to rent the chalet out on the northern boundary of the park. I'll never know if you had a hand in our success or not but it's my guess that you didn't want us living in your basement any more than we did. To hell with that *saving money* and *we'll all have so much fun together* ploy. But we do have to stay with you for a couple of weeks until the ground thaws and the plumbing in the chalet is operational.

You are in a foul mood when we arrive, only talking to Donny in two- or three-word sentences, hardly giving us the time of day. For an entire weekend, you hole up in your room refusing to talk to anyone. Donny is baffled, has absolutely no idea what's up.

Then you announce your early retirement.

"Good for you, sweetheart," Donny says.

"Hey Mom, whatever turns you on," Jamie says.

"She must be going out of her mind," Agatha says.

And this, you confide to me, is exactly why. *I am going out of my mind.* You proceed to lay the blame squarely on Donny.

"He's been out to the legion in Sussex off and on all winter. I can't be trying to teach and have to worry about him all day, too. My pension won't be as good, but there's nothing else I can do. Anyway, I have done my bit for the world."

When I question Jamie about your weird behaviour, he just says we're lucky it isn't like the old days.

"One day Dad came home and she was mad at him and started leaping around in a ball of fury and ripped the curtains off their rods faster than Dad could react."

"What had he done to make her so mad?"

"How would I know? I wasn't there. It was when I was away at school. Dad told me about it later. Apparently she practically ransacked the entire house. Then she just stood in the middle of the living room and yowled like a cat in heat."

"So what did Donny do?"

"He threw himself into the car and drove into Sussex and picked up his cousin Harvey Elliot. They spent the rest of the night in the Legion, knocking back rum shooters in honour of the mysteries of the fairer sex. The next day, when Dad got home for his Sunday dinner, the house was tidied up and Mom was preparing her school lessons. They didn't speak until the following Saturday when Dad took her out for lunch in the Eaton's cafeteria, where they went to buy new curtain rods. End of story."

I'd prefer ransacking to this punishing silence. My guess is Donny must have nipped into the Legion before this latest incident as well as after, but I know it's useless to say so. Jamie protects his father, like the one and only time Donny ever protected him from you. Do you remember the first night Jamie came home pissed to the gills? He does. He remembers you storming out at him and Donny turning you back with a firm hand. Then he stood in the open doorway to the bathroom laughing while Jamie puked his guts out.

You both did a good job sheltering him didn't you, Muriel? Good enough to pretty much silence him about his father's behaviour for most of his life. If I dare bring anything up, I end up sounding like a shit-disturber.

He protected you because of the deep sorrow of your failure to become a nurse. He protected his father. I protected him. But Jesus, wasn't there something in the wedding vows about protecting me?

All that sheltering setting him up.

We think things are settled, but you withdraw again the next weekend. Silence hovers in a pool of cool air around your door. When Jamie's old school buddy is expected, your door opens and a trail of frigid air follows you into the kitchen. You throw a Swiss steak into the oven, then disappear again.

"Mom's got the flu," Jamie tells his buddy. "Real bad."

A few days later, you start talking again.

"Would you like baked or mashed potatoes tonight?" I ask.

"Mashed."

"Would you like pie with your tea?"

"Yes."

And, finally, later in the week, "Would you like to go for a drive with me and Jamie in the park tonight?"

"That would be nice."

I'm learning the house rules: least said, soonest mended, be cheerful and act like nothing is going on, and grovel.

You don't really come out of your funk until we plan a family retirement party. We get all gussied up and take you over to the clubhouse in the park. When the waiter asks if we'd like to order an aperitif, the four of us stumble, but Agatha clasps her hands with her index fingers pointing steeple-style, touches them to her lips, and orders Dubonnet with a twist of lime, then winks at the waiter and smiles.

She's so sophisticated, isn't she, Muriel?

And gallant. A few weeks later when she comes down with shingles, Jamie and I visit her in the hospital. She is clearly wracked with pain but puts on a good show. One I'll never forget. There she is, decked out in full slip, pantyhose, and an eighteen-hour bra under her matching nightie and duster, sitting up in bed, hosed legs crossed at the ankle and a pair of bone-coloured pumps hiding her feet from the world. Under her bed were tucked a pair of brocade slippers.

"You've still got great legs, Aunt Agatha," Jamie says.

"Thank you, dear." She winces as she tries to smile, an archipelago of pocks swaddling her left eye. "Your mother had quite a good figure until she had you children. It's a shame she let herself go."

Perhaps it was the painkillers. What do you think, Muriel?

Back in the car, Jamie and I take up our ongoing discussion as to the likelihood of Agatha's virginity. "No way," he says. "Look at her. Someone must have bagged her along the way. She was engaged to that insurance salesman for twelve years. I mean twelve years, who would wait twelve years? And then when I was a kid she used to show up in Alma on weekends in a convertible with a guy she taught with at teacher's college, he was way younger than her, you know, the famous politician, what's-his-name."

But I had done up Agatha's long spindly grey hair many times in pin curls and she had told me the story about becoming engaged to a handsome Frenchman, from France, no less, when she was at summer school upgrading her BA to a B.Ed., before going off to Columbia to get her MA. The way her outrage still made her body shake when she revealed that he had explained it would be his right to take a mistress when she was pregnant or having her period, made me sense that she was still a virgin, and that somehow I sense that her virginity should be defended.

An enduring question though, Muriel, n'est-ce pas?

Though why should I be on her side? It seems Agatha does everything in her power to scatter my energy that summer. She schedules me to work split shifts and weekends. I know she resents the moments I steal to work on my correspondence courses when no one is in the shop because you told me. As a professor of education at a teacher's college for so many years, you'd think she'd be more encouraging.

What was it she said? *Robyn had her chance*. You can hardly wait to tell me that one. *She'll never make it through those courses*. Then she complains to you that my idea of dusting in the shop is to blow into a cup, and you get such a kick out of demonstrating to me how she mimics me blowing into a cup and saucer. You two were so funny.

I dust her damn shop and dip into my courses whenever I get the chance, deciding that if Agatha wants me to do a better job she'll just have to tell me herself. My sales are way better than hers. Even that she complains to you about. *Robyn is too forward with the customers for my liking.*

YOU DID COME to my rescue in the end, Muriel; you and Jamie both, pitching in to help out with the endless assignments as the end of August drew near. I think you did it to prove Agatha wrong just as much as to help me. Agatha turned a blind eye to the cheating. She didn't think I had a hope in hell of getting into university with three grade eleven courses anyway.

But I do. I'm on my way up in this family.

Everything seems to be going our way. We'd even dumped the Maverick and found a nice big heavy car, going cheap because of the oil crisis. Cleveland engine. Automatic. Not as hard on gas as you'd think. I love whizzing back and forth to Agatha's shop, hands on the wheel, foot on the gas.

Driving that car, even though it's only in the park, gives me a real sense of being a grown-up. One morning I get up the nerve to hurdle across Kyle flat at ninety miles an hour. Scared shitless, but the only thing I'm worried about is a deer jumping out. Imagine, Muriel: ninety miles an hour — a little reckless, maybe, but such a spurt of confidence for me.

Let's say we gun up your little Buick here. What do you think?

Most of my new-found confidence came from the women I met at the shop and the faith of the Assistant Dean. This promise held me through your family tactics all spring and summer. It was one of the rainiest seasons anyone could remember, fog almost every day, damp and cold. The tourists never stopped complaining. I never stopped working and studying. And Jamie and I made love every night, snug in the glow of our bright future.

Before we know it, the summer is over and we're back in Halifax. I sit before the Assistant Dean of Admissions at Saint Mary's in September. I had busted my gut to get there. Three top marks. The Dean is looking at my transcript and pulling on his moustache. "Oh dear," he says at great length. "It seems you have taken a course which we don't recognize. You managed to do jolly well in it, but I'm afraid it doesn't count. This leaves me in a rather difficult position." He looks into my face and shakes his head back and forth.

The phone on his desk rings. "Please excuse me a moment. I've been waiting for this."

As he turns in his swivel chair to face the tall leaded windows behind him I stare at the herringbone pattern on his tweed jacket. I feel very small and scared and hopeless with Agatha's remarks *She had her chance, she'll never finish* whipping in my head, a tattered flag in a strong wind. The course that Saint Mary's doesn't recognize is current events, the one that you and Jamie pitched in on. How smug Agatha will be.

Funny how I don't even think about my own parents as I sit calculating how disappointed everyone will be in me if I didn't manage to wedge myself into university. Somehow, whenever I think of my education, I think only of you and Agatha. I don't have one single thought about how my parents would have reacted if I hadn't mustered up. I don't even have one of my mother's ready remarks to recall. She and my stepfather were so preoccupied with themselves and the final, torpid days of their dismal marriage.

Desolation seeps into me, like water into clam holes on the rising tide. A flood of tears wells up behind my eyes, my throat constricts. I know the Dean is going to say no. I saw it in his face just before he swivelled around. I see it in his back. I am desperate to disappear without a trace from that office, but am rooted to this chair. When he hangs up the phone and swivels back to face me, he raises his eyebrows and forms a tent of his splayed fingers, touching the tips of his index fingers to his lips.

"This is your lucky day, young lady. I was going to say no, but something the person said in that phone call has made me change my mind. I think since you have given up a full time job and worked this hard, you won't let us down. I'm going to give you a chance. But if you're not doing well at Christmas, out the door you go."

The Dean's voice is as clear as a bell to this day. I often wish I had pressed the question about his change of heart and asked who the other person on the line was and why he or she called at that moment and shifted the whole course of my life. But there is something about the mystery of that incident I don't want to ruin.

I wisp out of his office, euphoria flowing through me, propelled down the corridor and out the tall heavy double arched wood doors of the dark granite administration building. This euphoria propels me every weekday on my walk from our apartment on Henry Street across Coburg Road and down along South Street turning onto Robie Street to Saint Mary's and back again. I experience a deep sense of freedom breathing in the air of an old, rooted city: the trees hardening off for the winter in the damp fusty air with their leaves day-by-day burning into the magnificent colours of an eastern fall, the smell of grit and oil sifting up from the lower city on the fetch of the North Atlantic with its fresh salty overtones, often tinged with a sense of Europe, a sense of ancient ancestral ties, and, once in a while, a whiff of the exotic, Africa perhaps, something deep and mysterious that comes from away and stirs me in the deepest regions of my being. I have not been so present in my own existence since I was a child, roaming the beaches and boggy lakesides and heavily scented mossy woodlands around the places where my family had lived.

These walks become a sacred act as I begin a great conversation with myself. Whereas my high school days were bondage, university is a revelation. I take in the lectures on English literature, British history, the economics of the North Atlantic community, and introduction to political science as if they are my birthright. Only in sociology do I flounder, but there is a general malaise in that class, where nobody pays attention to the indifferent professor and, by the end of the year, only thirteen of us are left from a class of fifty. As I purposefully stride back and forth to school, I imagine conversations with my profs or the authors of the texts. Never once do I think about *the curtains, the cake, the kick in the ass*, or *the dead mother, the missed funeral, and The War*. Let alone Agatha's machinations or my parents' debacle. For the first time in my life, my mind is liberated from the confines of family drama.

I see myself so clearly one bright morning waltzing into English class, wearing a short, cherry-red shirtwaist dress with long sleeves and a black belt, shaggy dark brown hair bouncing on my proud shoulders, fresh air wafting in around me. A handful of students are gathered near the instructor by the blackboard and they all turn at once to mark my presence. Until that moment I have more or less felt invisible at Saint Mary's, holding my breath, not sure I belong. What I see reflected back to me is part of my old self, the musical performer and cheerleader with the great legs, before the final tragedy struck my family its death blow; and part my new self, a confident young woman making her way in the world.

Do you see me, Muriel? Remember how you felt in your cape?

Jamie is entrenched on another campus over at Nova Scotia Tech, where he has finally made it to the last two years of his engineering degree. He, too, is feeling a sense of purpose and belonging that he had never experienced at Saint Mary's, slogging through his engineering diploma. I am happy that I pursue this direction by myself.

These are the halcyon days, Muriel. That's what our ceaseless trek after Jamie graduated was supposed to be for, so we could come back with enough money to buy a big Victorian house and recapture those days. Halifax, the city we loved.

Back then, we had spaghetti dinners with Alexis and Ed, candles stuck in lopsided Chianti bottles. Ed was interning at the Victoria General. Alexis had given up her elementary school job to enter a master's program in biology at Dal. *Why does she want to do that?* you ask, with your face all scrunched up. *Why couldn't she just take home economics if she doesn't want to teach? She's going to be a doctor's wife. What does she want with a master's degree?* But I know what you don't: Alexis wants to apply to med school herself. She doesn't just want to be a doctor's wife.

All this potential. We are energized. Fearless.

LOOK AT THAT, the St. Lawrence is so wide here it almost looks like an ocean. Except I can see that the water is flowing, and guess what, we're not going with the flow, we're driving against it. I never thought yesterday as we drove up along the Saint John River that we were going against the flow then, too. It does cause me to wonder about the fact that we're going against the flow. Although I guess where you are, you can go in any direction you please. Or can you? Do we have to finish this story before you will be released?

The things that bind us, Muriel; so many little things.

One morning, getting ready for class I gag while I'm brushing my teeth, nearly vomiting. Befuddled, I can't remember when I had my last period. They've never been that regular anyway. Something's fishy, Ed says, and sets me up with the best ob/gyn to check out these symptoms. Something's fishy all right. The gynecologist confirms that I'm pregnant. How could that be? Ed had always lectured us on the hopelessness of me ever conceiving — *you'll never get pregnant without intervention, you'll have to get artificial insemination* — based on the fact that Jamie had had a bad case of the mumps when he was fifteen. I went off the pill, but we still took some precautions. But that summer in the chalet on the northern boundary of Fundy National Park, when all the world seemed open to us, we could not be bothered with spermicides and rubbers during the endless nights of making love.

I leave the doctor's office and float down Henry Street, encased in a funny bubble of my own where I can see out and people can see me, but they can't see the life that is growing inside me. I feel quite happy, but somehow I don't feel quite real. Stunned, I make my way to Alexis and Ed's to share the news. We have a celebratory dinner with their neighbour and light a series of firecrackers in the backyard. I participate as if from a distance, waiting for Jamie to come home, so I can tell him the good news, too.

What do you say about times like this, Muriel? When you look back on your life? I love my children with an intensity that sometimes scares me, that sometimes makes me want to control their every move, and sometimes makes me want to run away from them as fast as I can. To question their existence is to question my own.

But this pregnancy is not good news. Ed had planted a falsehood in our heads as surely as Jamie has planted a baby in me. We laughingly blamed him. Big mistake.

And a bigger one is about to take place. Jamie and I close in on my pregnancy like vultures waiting for the kill and decide that we cannot risk the possibility that I might fall on the ice during the long walks I have to make to school. We have to move. We even ask your advice, Muriel, and you concur. Walking is too risky when pregnant. So we leave our beloved, somewhat shambling apartment on Henry Street and move back into the married student's residence in High-Rise II at Saint Mary's, where I don't have to go outside to get to my classes.

What the hell were we thinking? Why didn't we stay put? Why couldn't I have taken the car to school? Why didn't we consider that possibility? It wasn't any farther to walk to Nova Scotia Tech from Henry Street than when I used to walk to the hairdressing shop. They were right across the street from one another. Here it was 1974, and the thought didn't even cross our minds that Jamie could surrender the car to me.

I'm not a women's libber.

I want to work in the National Parks just like my father.

When you and Donny get back from your retirement trip out to the Rockies, you come down and help us with the move. While the men contend with the heavy stuff, you take me on a shopping trip and buy me two pairs of maternity pants, two blouses, and, after you saw the sorry state of my shoes, a new pair of penny loafers. I have such mixed emotions about this extravagance. Grateful, but embarrassed. I know my mother should have been the one to go shopping with me, but I've never been shopping with her in my life. At the time, she was too preoccupied with her divorce. But you, you are beside yourself with pleasure that you are finally going to become a grandmother, just like Philomena. You are pleased that although I have experienced some queasiness while brushing my teeth, I have not had one moment of morning sickness. "The only women who get morning sickness are the ones who deep down inside don't want their babies," you assure me. "I never got sick, either." You give me an impromptu hug to celebrate our no-morning-sickness bond. I'm back in your good books.

That night, you and Donny take us all out for Chinese food to celebrate. When the toast is about to be made I somehow think it's going to be about me, but when Jamie raises his glass and says *If it's a boy, Dad, we're going to name him after you*, I feel like some long arm of the past has snuck up behind me to take my breath away. My hand flies down to my slightly mounded belly as if to protect my baby from something that sounds like a curse. I don't like Donny all that much. How could I, Muriel? I only see him through your eyes and all you do is denigrate him. Jamie and Alexis and even Ed revere him, but all I see is his self-conscious Irishness, his superficial, happy-go-lucky top-of-the-morning charm.

Name my baby after him?

Buy me all the clothes you want, but I don't think so.

Nor do I want to ponder the other predicament of the naming the son custom. Our son will take my maiden name for his middle name. Just like Jamie is James Steadman Gallagher, our son will be Donald Southerland Gallagher. Not that that isn't a fine sounding name, but I am so ambivalent about my stepfather's name. And about my mother's maiden name, well, I feel mostly shame.

At the time, there is so much to think about that I put the whole idea of naming my baby after Donny out of my mind. There is the apartment to sort out and essays to write and exams to study for. I made my commitment to the Dean and I don't plan to let either of us down. Then, before we know it, Christmas arrives and we're back in Alma for a couple of weeks. When we open our presents on Christmas Eve — because you could never wait until Christmas morning — I have to hide my great disappointment when all my presents turn out to be things for the baby-to-be. This might sound childish to you, Muriel, but these baby gifts make me feel invisible. I sit with a glass smile, while at my very core I am shaken. I hear my voice exclaiming delight over the stupid ugly baby booties and mint-green crocheted blankets and I know I have been in this place before, been made to keep my silence or simply be good and nice when the real me wants to howl and protest.

Back in High-Rise II at Saint Mary's, in our apartment with the brick-red tiles and off-white walls that back onto the garbage chute for the entire building, I try to out-study, out-clean, out-smart this terrible feeling. I try to out-eat it. The harder I try, the worse I get. Sleep is fitful with the garbage clanking and crashing down the chute day and night. I am suffocating. Outside is winter and danger. I puff along the concrete corridors and tunnels from the high-rise to the classrooms with no one to talk to. All the light is florescent. Everything looks slightly green. Smells used-up. Sounds hollow. My body is unrecognizable to me. I think nobody can even see me. Fat and fluids accumulate under my skin and Jamie won't touch me except to give me a back rub from time-to-time. He claims to be under too much stress from the seven courses he takes each semester at Tech, so I excuse him. Deep down, I know that he is repulsed by me. He has not wanted sex since we found out that I am pregnant. If not for the baby kicking inside, I would think this terrible existence of mine is somebody else's nightmare. The only thing that keeps me going is a fierce attachment I am forming for this baby, the classes I attend, and my promise to the Dean. I know that back in Alma bets are being made about whether I'll make it through the term or not.

By the middle of March, my behaviour has become so downright obsessive that I take to making donuts and ironing my nightgowns and underwear. I wax and polish the ugly red floor. The doctor keeps asking me if I'm taking it easy and I reassure him that I am, but I do not know what either of us means. I simply tell him what he wants to hear. How can I take it easy with all these classes to attend and an apartment to keep in order, meals to fix, and the baby's layette to get ready? My blood pressure is going up. My ankles swell and my face balloons. I can't wear my wedding ring.

People start looking at me curiously and I realize that rather than being invisible, I stand out, an anomaly puffing along the corridors of a Catholic university, looking like someone who got knocked-up and abandoned. For the first time in my life, I feel like I have sinned, but I don't know against what.

Coming out of the library one day, I start to cry as I head down the tunnel to the administration building that connects to High-Rise II. Big heaving sobs I can't control. Everything blurs. I bump into someone and try to stumble away. A hand catches mine. "Come with me," a firm voice says. The voice belongs to my economics professor. "My office is just down this way." He settles me into a chair and passes a box of tissues. "My wife and I have five children," he says. "And there were tears with every one of them. Tell me when you're due."

"April 24th," I blubber.

"You won't be able to write your finals," he says gently.

As soon as he says this, I know without a doubt that he is right. This thought has been pressing down on me and I haven't been able to face it. If I don't pass, I won't be able to get a student loan next year and we will need both loans to get Jamie through his final year.

"I'll tell you what," he goes on. "I'm willing to pardon your final and give you the mark you have going into the exam. It's been my experience that if a student has an A going into an exam, they will write an A exam. I'm willing to give you the benefit of the doubt. And I'm willing to bet your other professors will feel the same way. Go to each one and tell them what I'm going to do. If they have any problems, get them to call me."

You know what, Muriel? That man reaching out to me was one of the greatest acts of kindness I have ever experienced. All my profs agreed with his plan. I know you and Agatha rolled your eyes, thinking I am getting off scot-free. But tell me; what else could I do?

That night I think all my problems are solved. I sit in front of the TV with the sound of garbage rattling through the chute and with a tender love that has been welling up within me; I smooth my hands up and down the enormous kicking, Braxton Hicks clutching mass that has become my belly. All of a sudden the thought dawns on me that there is only one way this baby is going to get out. This is one final I won't be able to squeeze out of. In fact, this mass is going to have to squeeze out of my vagina and I don't know how in the world this can ever be accomplished. I don't know how such a thing as big as a baby can come out of such a small hole, a penis-sized, tampon-sized hole. I know that millions and millions of women have done it before me, but at the same time, the idea seems preposterous. To put this absurdity out of my mind I turn on a rerun of *The Partridge Family* and pray really hard for a Caesarean section to get me out of this mess.

My prayers are almost answered. In the final days before my due date, after packing our summer things up for our annual trek up to Fundy for Jamie's summer job, I begin to experience dizziness. A monumental fatigue overtakes me, body and soul. There is so much to do. We are in the process of shifting all our furniture to a quieter apartment next door that we're going to sublet for the summer. Jamie and a friend move all the furniture while I lie in bed feeling guilty about not being able to help. The next morning, at my biweekly check-up, the doctor is alarmed to see I have gained seven pounds in less than five days, there is protein in my urine, and my blood pressure is heading sky-high.

"I want you in the hospital in twenty minutes," the doctor says in a voice that frightens me. "I don't mean half an hour. I mean twenty minutes."

Less than hour later, I am strapped down to a hospital bed in the labour room. Attached to my lumpen body is an electronic fetal heart monitor. Into the top of my hand is an intravenous drip. Contractions start almost immediately with a violence I never imagined. There have been days when I've tucked up in bed with a hot water bottle and 222s for bad period cramps, but the intensity of induced labour literally takes my breath away. In fact, breathing is hardly an option. I suck in air between contractions that come like

Niagara Falls. Student nurses check my blood pressure every fifteen minutes. One nervous wreck of a girl can't seem to get the hang of the procedure. She pumps up the cuff over and over, but can't hear the blip. Finally, she flees the room, leaving me with the cuff still inflated. I think my eyeballs are going to pop out. Various edgy interns traipse through to check my belly and poke their heads under the sheet to feel around and see if I'm dilating yet. They never knock. They never know what's going on and I never know what to say. One tall fellow with an enormous Adam's apple slips in and stands by the bed looking as if he's about to be executed. Several minutes tick by before I rescue us both.

"I'm on the pan," I finally manage to confess.

"Oh," he pips, like your eardrums popping in an airplane, and out the door he escapes. Lucky fellow. I never see him again. I squeeze my eyes shut and wish the world would just stop marching through the door.

Then sometime mid-afternoon, Muriel, the fetal heart monitor goes berserk with beeping. Two nurses crash into the room. One rolls me over so I can't see the machine and the other whips the intravenous out of my hand.

"I told that idiot the dose was too high," the charge nurse says with a heavy eastern shore accent. "We coulda lost them both."

Do they think I'm deaf?

Rolled over like that, while those women save my baby's life, I enter a hyper state of lucid consciousness. The whole world shrinks down to my body: those hands, that monitor, the wrenching pain, and, most of all, my baby who has been kicking my guts out for several months. I am beyond prayer. When the nurses roll me back over, I search their faces. They look relieved, so I follow their cue. I don't feel their relief; I simply monitor them as they monitor me. When the doctor finally breezes in with new instructions, I regard him with distrust.

"A little fright, no worries," he says.

I don't believe him.

The contractions start again. There is some breathing space this time. Not much, but enough to get through the minutes and the hours. At 6 pm I am detached from the machines and sent to a room up on the ward to rest for the night.

Jamie pops in for a few minutes. He's been in and out all day. Our new apartment is almost set up. You and Donny are arriving any time now, but there's the old apartment to be scoured, and this and that yet to be done. I can't keep up with him. He's always such a busy man.

In the morning, stabilized, and shifted to a new labour room, the doctor sits on the bedside and informs Jamie and me that the baby has to come out today. He runs through various methods of pain control and recommends an epidural when the going gets rough. If my water doesn't break soon, he'll have to do it manually. And if the labour doesn't progress in a timely manner, he'll have to do a C-section. Expertly informed about what I can expect for the day, and flat on my back all strapped-up, the drip is started again.

"By the way," he says with a smile, leaving the room, "no more students today. We need to keep everything under control. So don't worry."

Moments later, the rollercoaster of induced labour pounds through me once more. The breathing exercises I practised are useless. An hour later, the doctor comes back to break my water.

"Out you go," he says to Jamie. "There will be tears."

Those words scare me more than you'll ever know, Muriel. I brace against the contractions. I brace against that man reaching up inside me to pull the plug that's stuck in the drain. After rooting around for a bit there's a scream from me and with a loud pop and whoosh, warm water floods between my legs as hot tears spill down my cheeks. A mantra starts in my head: *Nobody ever told me it could be like this. Nobody ever told me it could be like this.* My mother told me that she walked the halls throughout her labour with me and that she nearly had me by herself in the toilet. And you, Muriel, you had your C-sections.

Jamie comes in to comfort me but his face is so contorted I can hardly bear his presence.

"Better sign these," the doctor says, waving papers for the epidural under our noses. "There's always the slight risk of paralysis but nothing to really worry about. Just make sure you keep still."

Jamie and two nurses hold me down on my side as the contractions rage and the anesthesiologist murmurs, "Don't move. Keep still now. That's it. Don't move. Keep still now," as he threads a needle through my spine and pumps me with a fluid that is sickeningly cold and branches up through my backbone and under my shoulder blades and out into my hips like liquid lightening. When this sensation settles down I realize that I am somewhat frozen — but only partially.

"Oh dear," the anesthesiologist grumbles. "You only took on one side."

He makes this sound like my fault. I start to cry. Jamie is so shaken after this procedure that I can't bear his suffering as well as mine, so I send him out to have a smoke.

At 3 pm I have dilated only two centimetres. The lopsided epidural has done little to quell the storm in my body. "Time for a C-section," the doctor says and gives us more papers to sign.

I am given a light hit of Demerol, then left on my own while the doctor makes off to get ready for surgery. The Demerol makes me heave and vomit thick green bile. When a nurse comes in to attend to my mess, I am suddenly gripped with the sensation that a cannonball is about to emerge from my lower regions.

"I have to bear down!"

"Nonsense, my girl. This is your first. What would you know? Anyway, you were only two centimetres not twenty minutes ago.

Oh god, the cannonball is breaching. "I have to bear down," I wail.

"Calm yourself. Calm yourself. They'll be taking you out to the OR in a few minutes."

"I have to bear down now!" I groan and the nurse finally takes a peak.

"Oh my god. I can see the head! Don't push! Don't push!"

Once again, I am left stranded in a cheerless room as the nurse slams through the door shouting instructions. Then in a kind of frenzy, I seem to be attended by the whole hospital as they grab the gear attached to me and wheel me down the hall into a delivery room. Jamie appears by my side in a green gown and mask. The doctor whisks in, ordering people about then stops long enough to grin at me, "Aren't you full of surprises today."

You know Muriel, at that moment I was scared silent, but today I wish I'd had the presence of mind to say *Fuck you*.

He ducks behind the sheet draped over my feet. My legs are in the stirrups. "You'll just feel a little sting now," he says. Then he makes the cut and tells me to push.

"Do you want to watch in the mirror?"

"Christ no! Just get the baby out of there."

Push. Push. They don't think I can do it with the epidural, but I do. I push like hell. I only need a little help with forceps near the end and one more big push and out comes the baby.

A girl!

She is wiped off, bundled and handed to me to hold and I can't believe this little squirming cannonball is all mine and Jamie's. I think this might be a good time for Jamie to say something wonderful to me. But, if he does, I don't hear it. The agony is over and I am so relieved I don't have to call her Donny.

Then I hear the doctor's voice as he makes way to leave. "This is our resident, Dr. So-and-So. He'll be sewing you up." I look into the face of this strange man who is about to sew my vagina and perineum back together. Oh god Muriel, he looked more like a *bootcher* than a sewer-upper.

Once he has established that everything is tickety-boo, and Andrea is wheeled off to the nursery, Jamie says, "I have to go now. I called Mom and Dad and they'll be here soon."

So, with a peck on the cheek, off he hot-foots-it out the door. I am left with two nurses. One kneading my belly. One cleaning up. When it is time to get me off the delivery table I find the epidural has not quite worn off and I can't move the frozen side much at all. As the two nurses struggle to heave me onto a bed, the sheet falls away exposing my legs. "Oh my god," the assistant nurse exclaims, "look at the size of the thighs on that girl."

All the way up the elevator and into my room *Look at the size of the thighs on that girl* pounds in my head. I am given a sponge bath, put into a fresh nightie like a plastic doll, and am advised that Andrea will be brought in to me shortly. My mind is numb. I hardly understand the curt instructions for the sitz bath. I nod weakly when warned not to get out of bed unless someone is there to help me. But as soon as I get some feeling back in my leg, I struggle into the washroom to get a good look at myself.

I check out my breasts, which are erupting in a post-partum Rocky Mountain balloon-a-thon horror show. Hard. Hot. Pale green. They hurt like hell. I touch them with my hands and they ooze colostrum. Then I do something I wish I had never done: I lift my nightie to get a load of *the size of the thighs on that girl* but what I encounter first is a great slab of flesh, like an apron of liver, which used to be my cute little belly, hanging down to my knees. I am twenty-one years and ten days old and my thighs are nowhere in sight. I can't look up to my face. So I shuffle back to bed and gingerly heft something that used to be mine, but now feels like something that sat in a wasps' nest, onto the bed.

EIGHT

THE RIVER SUDDENLY seems narrow. Quebec City, already. I see the Chateau Frontenac across the river, its four towers and steep copper roof. Funny, I haven't thought of this for a dog's age: how militant Jamie was when René Lévesque's Parti Québécois took power in '76. It was as if Lévesque had waved the separatist flag right under his nose. He got so worked up, declaring he was ready to go to war to make Quebec stay in Canada.

"You mean you'd leave me and Andrea and put your life on the line for stupid old Quebec?"

"You bet I would."

"But what business is it of yours if Quebec wants to get out?"

"They can't go around breaking up the country just because they want out. They have no right."

"What if you got killed?"

"My father was willing to die for this country and so am I!"

"But what about me and Andrea?"

"A man's gotta do what a man's gotta do."

IT CAME AS a shock that he could even think about abandoning Andrea and me, that we weren't the first in his books. He was so charged up, I found it hard to credit his behaviour when set against the background of daily life. This rage brought on by René Lévesque should have served me as a warning, but when the referendum failed and the issue of Quebec separating from Canada was put on the back burner, I tucked away my fears about Jamie abandoning us.

Odd, isn't it, Muriel, what we're willing to risk our lives for when we're in our twenties. Jamie would have gone off to fight his own countrymen, you worked yourself into a potentially fatal fever when Matron accused you of malingering, and I couldn't open my mouth for fear of being sent back to the hospital the afternoon I hemorrhaged in the women's washroom at the Moncton Airport.

You'd never been on a plane. You had the heebie-jeebies about flying and I'd only flown a couple of times. I was nervous, too, and really wobbly. We ended up flying from Halifax to Moncton because I wasn't recovering quickly and Andrea had lost a little weight, so the doctor did not recommend the long drive. But Jamie had to start work on the survey crew and we already owed you more than a hundred dollars. Since we were running out of time, you offered to pay for the three of us to fly home. You and me and the baby, while Jamie drove the car up. Donny had already gone back. There I was again, in the position of having to be grateful. Only I didn't feel grateful. I wanted to fly with Jamie. Not you. I wanted you to drive, but I knew that was out of the question.

But why, Muriel? How hard could it have been to drive to Alma from the Halifax International Airport? Turn right out of the parking lot. Right onto the Bicentennial Highway. Keep to the left at Truro to head into the Wentworth Valley. Go straight across the border from Nova Scotia into New Brunswick. Stay on the same road until you near Moncton, then take the left turn with the big sign that says MONCTON AIRPORT/DIEPPE and head for the centre of the city past your beloved Champlain Mall, turn left and follow the sign to cross the bridge for Riverview, turn left after the bridge, and follow the road all the way home — all the way to where you have lived for sixty years. Why couldn't you do that? Why didn't I ask?

Even my mother got in her car one night and drove all the way to Dartmouth to my grandmother's — never to return. She didn't have your education or five cents in the bank, but when push came to shove, she had the guts to drive off. So there I am, cooped up on a DC9 with you and your nerves. By the time we touch down in Moncton, I'm struck with killer cramps and feeling faint. I hand Jamie the baby and make a mad dash for the bathroom. You scurry right behind me.

As I squat over the toilet a great whoosh of blood streams into the bowl as I double over in pain. The bright red is so violent against institutional white. I am scared to death and recall a snippet of conversation from two nurses who had come into my hospital room in the morning. "If her doctor had any sense he wouldn't be letting her out of here today," one said. "I guess not," the other said, "look at her. Pale as a ghost." "My mother-in-law will look after me," I say lamely, even though they had more or less been talking through me, not to me.

I can't bear the thought of being in the hospital again. The embarrassment of it all.

"Not a flower in that room," one said to another as they were leaving my room a few days after Andrea was born. "Is she allergic?"

"Nothing on her chart."

It's not your life you think about when you're in your twenties and faced with danger. It's your pride.

The second day you came to visit, you brought a fruit basket that looks like it's been on sale. "I thought of bringing flowers," you apologized, "but Alexis said flowers are a waste of money. She picked up something more practical. And, by the way, I cleaned your oven. You must have been baking pies all winter."

Jumping Jesus Muriel! A flimsy basket stuffed with green plastic straw and great big four-pointed mushy red and golden delicious apples and spongy oranges draped with limp green grapes all smelling of over-ripe bananas when I peel back the plastic wrapper. I don't like red delicious apples. I like a nice crisp Spartan.

This is what's going through my mind as I stare at the toilet bowl full of blood. I even think *I'm going to die* but I don't know what to do about my situation. Who would look after the baby? As I change my pad and jam a wad of toilet paper into my panties, I reason that if you, practically being a nurse and all, do not notice anything strange about me when I come out of the stall, then I will just ignore what happened and carry on with the fifty-some mile ride down to Alma.

So you and I, Muriel, you and I stand in front of the mirror washing our hands and I'm holding on to the side of the counter to keep from folding over sideways. *I'm going to die* I keep thinking as you jabber away, high as a kite. "Just imagine, I'm sixty and Andrea is six days old and we've had our first airplane ride together. When she grows up and has children of her own we'll tell them all about it ..."

That's when I kind of check out. A poor body accompanies you back out to the luggage carousel and takes the baby back from Jamie, but it isn't me. I'm out of there. The next thing I remember is arriving in Alma with a sticky warm mush of blood-soaked pads and strings of toilet paper between my legs. I'm stuck to the toilet seat when I remember that I need a container to do the sitz rinse. I don't want to call out so I poke in the cupboard and come up with the pink plastic cup that Donny keeps his false teeth in at night. This is one secret I'll take to the grave.

The next morning, Jamie is out the door by 7:30, raring to get back to work. I am barely able to rise long enough to feed Andrea, change her, rock her, and crawl back into bed. I can't eat. It's all I can do to dig through our suitcases stacked in messy piles all over the room to find clean panties. I'd been shoving all the bloody ones into the garbage pail under the bathroom sink. Andrea is fussy. We don't have this breastfeeding business down pat yet. My hot rocky breasts ooze pale yellowish-blue milk all day long. The poor babe gags, she seems to be drowning in the stuff. The bleeding is still heavy. My hind end throbs like it's been opened by a can opener. I feel like a swamp. I am going down.

Late in the afternoon, you tiptoe into the room while I'm dozing. "I managed to get all the blood out of your panties and slacks by soaking them in cold water and salt. Then I scrubbed them good and hard on the old wash board."

"Oh, thank you. Thank you so much. I'm sorry to be so much trouble."

I could have just died. I never felt so pathetic in my life. When you close the door, I look over at the stack of fresh laundry on the dresser, then turn my aching unfamiliar body to the wall and cry my heart out.

My god Muriel, there was blood down to the knees on my slacks! I was going through Kotex like a women's dormitory on the full moon. Didn't you suspect anything? As much as I was humiliated by my body and its fluids, at heart I was waiting to be rescued by your superior knowledge and skills. The least I expected was an expertly burped hot water bottle. Not the indignity of you rescuing my worn-out maternity pants.

The next day you and Donny traipse up to Moncton for your ballroom dancing lessons. You had missed them the week before. How could I begrudge a woman who has scrubbed my bloody panties on the old washboard? Jamie plops himself down in front of the TV after work to watch the early news. I make hamburger in a can of tomato soup, mashed potatoes, carrots and frozen peas, between feeding, changing, and burping Andrea.

Andrea wakens me all night long. *I want to die. I wish the baby would die.* When these unspeakable thoughts enter my consciousness, I take Andrea downstairs and hide in a corner with her in case anyone can hear what I'm thinking. Thereafter, whenever she is quiet for a few minutes, I am compelled to check up on her, always alert.

In the morning, I'm disoriented. I wonder if I should call a doctor because I've lost so much blood and am having such bad thoughts. But again, I defer to your experience, Muriel. I'm waiting for you to say something about my appearance but all you have to say is,

"Alexis was a terribly fussy baby, too. You're just lucky you didn't have to have a caesarean like I did."

On cue, I ask, "How come you had to have a caesarean?"

"Mother dropped me when I was a baby. The fall tipped my uterus. We didn't know until I had been in labour for almost a day. I've always felt such a failure not having been able to have my children the proper way."

"But you went through the labour?"

"For Alexis, yes."

"Well that's the hard part, Muriel. You did all the real work."

Is this the passive woman that Alexis had as a mother? Someone who could manipulate me into making her feel better when I'm hoping to die? Do you recognize that passive woman, Muriel? Was it me, or you? Is that what Jamie saw when he watched me standing in the bay, waiting for the tide to turn?

Just to get your point across you went on to complain, "When Alexis was born I was in the hospital for over two weeks, and when I got home I had no help at all. Donny worked six days a week and needed his rest."

You forgot that I already know this story complete with the information that Perley came and took Alexis every Sunday for the whole day. And not for one minute do I think that Philomena didn't help out somehow. She lived down the road.

"Poor Donny. He never got home until just after six and by then Alexis was put down for the night. He hardly saw her at all the first year."

"Why didn't you keep her up for an hour or so?"

"Oh, I couldn't. The doctor said she had to sleep from six to six. Feedings were every four hours. Those were the rules. We just had to make the best of it."

"But why not seven to seven?"

"I think I hear Andrea crying. If you kept to a schedule, she wouldn't be so fussy. Jamie was a perfect baby. He never fussed at all. Even from the beginning I only had to attend to him every four hours just like the doctor said. All he ever needed was a bottle and changing and then be put back in his crib."

AS JAMIE AND I wait out the late spring for the pipes to thaw in the summer chalet, this sort of conversation becomes the routine, you telling me how lucky I am while you lord it over me about your miserable rotten life. If you can call that a routine. Andrea still wails all night long. I don't know what I'm doing wrong. I can't seem to get the hang of breastfeeding. You and Jamie urge me to put Andrea on the bottle. I resist.

"Sometimes it just doesn't work out," you say, during the commercials one afternoon when we're watching *Another World*, eating yogourt. "I couldn't breastfeed Alexis because I took a beal breast."

"A what?"

"A beal breast. An infection."

"Oh." How can I question such medical language? Funny though, Muriel, I've asked and checked since then and I can't find the reference to *a beal breast* anywhere.

When Andrea is almost three weeks old and I actually feel like I am going to live, Jamie and I ask you to babysit one Saturday afternoon so we can pop over to the tennis courts at headquarters. You pout, but agree. Jamie seems content enough to bat a few balls around that I more or less hit back to him, but every once in a while he can't resist slamming a killer serve at me and I just about jump out of my skin. I could cry. After forty-five minutes of this, I've had enough and off we go for a little toot down to Point Wolfe and back again.

The downstairs is eerily quiet when we come in. I hear Andrea whimpering and charge up the stairs. There you are with Agatha, Agatha's old friend the nursing instructor from UNB who is visiting, and my baby, my Andrea, plunged into a sink of tepid water.

"What the hell are you doing?" I yell.

"The baby fussed and fussed from the time you left. She nearly turned blue and I didn't know what to do, so I called Agatha and she called Marg and Marg said that putting her into cool water would calm her down."

Really, Muriel, the mother of a girl and a boy and you called two old maids for help with your grandchild?

"Get out of the way," I say and scatter the three of you like a bunch of hens.

I bundle Andrea up, nurse her for a few minutes, then walk her back and forth along the corridor until she drops off to sleep.

When I confront you again in the living room you defend yourself by saying, "If the baby was bottle-fed you'd be able to get out a bit more."

I look at Jamie and he shrugs. You'd obviously talked this out while I was upstairs.

In a heap of exhaustion, I gave way. Quit breastfeeding. But it was no use. Andrea still cried night and day. I'd no sooner put her down and hop into the shower, than you'd be banging on the bathroom door shouting. "The baby's crying. The baby's crying."

So I'd turn off the water, wrap a housecoat around my soapy body, and go to Andrea. You were afraid to pick her up after the tepid bath episode, you had gotten arthritis in your elbow, your knee was a problem, and you feared you might drop her. I was afraid I'd never get a full night's sleep again.

I could have used Jamie's comfort in the evenings, but he's always out in the back forty helping Donny put up a new tin shed, changing the oil on the tractor mower. I don't know why he mows the whole goddamn two acres anyway. Then they haul that stupid Spitfire down from Donny's sister's place where it had been up on blocks. It's been there for three years, I don't know why they have to get it out now. I don't know why Donny can't move ten feet without calling Jamie to give him a hand.

Couldn't you see, Muriel, that I needed my husband?

When did his father begin giving Jamie the time of day? When you guys were getting the driveway paved and Donny asked Jamie about the slope, Donny just clapped him on the shoulder and said, "Well boy, an expensive education is all fine and dandy, but what really counts in this world is experience." Experience? Even I could see that Jamie pointed out the right slope for the driveway. Away from the house, not toward it. I wish I could remember the convoluted reason Donny gave for sloping the driveway toward the house. It was a real winner. That man, always on automatic, if someone said white, was bound to say black. And here he was, taking up all of Jamie's time when I needed him.

When I think about it, Muriel, you and Donny showed so little interest in us unless it had something to do with you. Did you ever ask us about our courses or what we wanted for the future? I remember the day I got the letter in the mail from Saint Mary's congratulating me for making the Dean's List. I had to ask what it meant.

"Oh that," you said. "It means you got high marks."

Don't you think we could have had a little celebration? We had a dinner all right and Agatha was invited over, but what did we end up talking about? Something that had happened in 1927. The big fire that burned down half the village started by a spark from a portable sawmill. "Eleven houses, four stores, the school, the Orange Hall, the United Church, and all the mature maple trees along the main street were destroyed. Including our store and house."

"Was anything saved?" I ask.

"The hardwood mantle which is in the house now. Mother's good dishes," Agatha says.

"A basket of Mother's magazines from the attic," you add. "Our Easter hats."

"Yes," says Agatha. "And you bawled like a baby when they were stolen."

"I did not!"

"Oh yes you did. I remember clear as a bell Mother scolding you. 'Control yourself young lady,' she said. And you cried even harder later in the day when Nellie and Betsy Green from up the back road paraded through the village sporting the stolen hats."

"That's not true!"

"How can you forget? You wanted to confront them, but Mother told you to learn to put your feelings aside and show a little family pride. 'Everyone knows who the rightful owners are,' she said. 'What else can you expect from a backwoods tribe of degenerates?'"

Donny's attention drifts off. He's looking out the big picture window where the most fascinating event in the world is taking place.

"Well, well," he coos. "Looks like Gertie has given poor old Rud the heave-ho for the night again."

Sure enough, across the road, Rud Spencer is making his way to the shed he keeps for himself in the backyard down by the brook. His wife Gertie is standing on the porch with her hands on her hips.

"Regardless," Agatha continues, her voice hard and clipped, "the looting wasn't the worst of it. Later that afternoon Dad remembered what he had been about to do the day before when he heard shouts of FIRE! He had been about to call the insurance company to transfer liability from the transport company to his store. But he never made the call. The six months of provisions he had unloaded into the store were not covered by insurance. Though he and mother made the best of it, it was a loss from which they almost never recovered." Then she spoke directly to you, Muriel: "I have often wondered how they found the means to send us to university during the Depression."

"Don't look at me," you shrug. "I never asked to go."

"It was a privilege," Agatha pushes.

We sit uncomfortably for a few moments until I ask if anyone would like more spaghetti. Jamie and Agatha take a second helping.

"My diet," you say, and shove your plate to the side.

Donny pushes around the last mouthful on his plate, "I have to watch my girlish figure," he grins, patting his washboard abdomen, wolfs it down, wipes his mouth, shoves his chair back and announces, "I am sufficiently sufficed. Anything more would be super abundant. Thank you!"

DONNY SITS GRINNING like he wants to say something else but can't think what it would be. When you serve bowls of chocolate ice cream with marshmallow topping, he looks disappointed for a moment then claps his hands and says to no one in particular, "Muriel makes the best chocolate cake."

A terrible hush descends like winter fog. After you serve the tea, you quietly disappear.

"Where's your mother?" Donny asks Jamie when they're clearing up the dishes.

"Upstairs, I guess," Jamie says, and briefly, unconsciously it seems, touches his father's back.

Donny gazes longingly at the puffs of smoke that have begun to belch out of the oil drum stove down in Rud Spencer's shack.

That's the last we see of you for the night. Everyone's on pins and needles. During the night, Andrea is fussier than usual so I take her downstairs and pace the hallway trying to lull her into sleep to keep the house quiet because, as I've been told, *The men have to get up in the morning and go to work.*

At some point, I realize Andrea is sound asleep. Moonlight streams through the picture windows. There isn't a sound in the world. Only Andrea's even breathing, bundled against me in a flannel receiving blanket. I slip into the living room and pull an afghan off the back of the couch, slide down into Donny's big padded rocking chair and ease it into the reclining position, covering myself and the baby as best I can with one hand. Soon I am asleep too.

I'm wakened to a kiss on the forehead and a glass of juice. Andrea is just starting to stir. Jamie already has a bottle warming in a pot of water on the stove. My feet are freezing and I really have to pee.

"Take Andrea, will you?"

"Okay. But I've got to get going in a couple of minutes."

"Where's your mother?"

"I don't know. She isn't up yet."

I have a bad feeling about this. She always gets up to make the men's breakfast.

Later I pack Andrea into her Snuggly and take a long walk. On the way back, I stop at the store to get a bottle of gripe water. Feeling a little woozy, I lean against the counter and try to make small talk with the clerk. Andrea starts to whimper so I jiggle her up and down. Then she starts to wah-wah-wah. My breasts haven't dried out yet so they let down milk. Sticky and weepy, I turn to leave when the door opens and in walks Agatha. I take one look at her and start to bawl.

"Good Lord," Agatha says. "What in the world is the matter with you?"

"Nothing," I snivel. "Just hormones." And brush past her.

Instead of going back to your place I lumber up the hill behind the schoolhouse, rubbing Andrea's round little rump and tiny tender back through the corduroy of the Snuggly. Finding a big flat rock, I gingerly set down my bottom, which is beginning to feel normal again. The cold feels good. All of a sudden, I miss my mother. I cry harder. Stupidly. Rocking side-to-side as I sing "Mockingbird" to Andrea and look out over the water.

The tide is almost all the way out; a vast expanse of beach exposed, stretching almost a mile to the water's edge. Long slicks of red-brick mud glimmer against the edges of the gravel flats. Springs trickle around the sandbars; the channel has dwindled down to a slate blue stream. In the far distance loom the hazy wooded headlands of Nova Scotia. A strip of pale blue hugs the shore. Whitecaps arc and peak in the silted turquoise bay, bleeding into streaks of saturated mauve and teal along the shore's edge where mud and sand churn against the tide. Low clouds are mounting one on the other, tinged with pearly grey and baby blue. The afternoon sun punches through here and there, lighting the swirling mass with a pale golden hue.

I FISH DR. SPOCK's baby book out of the diaper bag and write a letter to my mother on the end pages and back cover.

Dear Mum,

I'm sorry you had to get back to Moose Jaw so soon. But I guess you were right, it would have been awfully crowded in the yellow house if you had come up to stay. I don't really think Muriel even wants the baby and me here.

I'm glad you've got your own apartment now and I hope your Nurses' Aid course goes well.

Jamie and I are going into Sussex next weekend to see Dad and David. He's leaving for boot camp next week.

You might as well know that I'm not doing so hot. I quit breastfeeding. I feel so guilty because I know in my heart that breastfeeding is the best thing for a baby. They told us to make sure we hardened up our nipples in the pre-natal class and I guess the few swipes I made at it didn't do the trick. Really, Mum, there's no way a towel would have done the trick.

And the truth is, I'm so tired and so scared. I can't really talk to Muriel. She and Donny hog all Jamie's time and I don't think he understands that I really don't know what to do with this baby. I mean, he'll change her diaper and give her a bottle and everything, but Muriel told me not to make too much noise when I get up with Andrea because he works and he needs his sleep. And I don't know how to tell him that I don't know much more about babies than he does. I'm afraid I might do something wrong. I've read the Dr. Spock book and I took the pre-natal classes but nothing has prepared me for all this dampness and stitches and soreness and fatigue and wailing and all this helplessness. If we don't get out of Muriel's house and into our chalet soon, I think I'll go stark raving mad.

XOXO
Robyn

LOOKING OUT OVER the bay, I remember so clearly when my baby sister died of crib death. How my mother lay on the couch with an ice pack over her face, hands clenching and unclenching. My stepfather's back and shoulders caved-in over his heart. We couldn't turn the lights on at night. Or the TV or the radio. Any noise, any light, fell like razors on my mother's skin.

Count your blessings, I say to myself. Count your blessings.

When I get back to your house, you're in the living room watching *Another World* so after I tuck Andrea up for a nap I slip in and join you, hoping that your mood has changed. But your face is waxy and you hold your body stiffly away from me. You don't even look at my bloated face.

"I think Andrea's getting diaper rash," I say, trying to bring you around.

"Happens," is all you reply.

I take *Dr. Spock* out of the diaper bag and look up *diaper rash* and then Andrea squawks so I put the book down by the side of the chair and sprint up the stairs before she bothers you. While I'm checking her diaper, I hear the soft click of your bedroom door.

You hole up for days. A pall descends over the house, so low we'd rather be stuck out in the bay in a small fishing boat. We are perplexed about what set you off this time. Maybe it's the baby fussing all the time. When Alexis comes to visit, she braces herself with a tray of tea and squares and enters your forbidden chamber while Jamie and Donny and I cringe in the kitchen, waiting for the verdict. Out she comes to announce, "It's you, Robyn. She read the letter you wrote to your mother in the back of *Dr. Spock*."

"She read my letter!"

"Indeed she did," Alexis affirms, raising her eyebrows above her specs. "She feels so betrayed. She doesn't know how she will ever be able to face your mother again."

All eyes fall on me.

Donny springs up from the table and rubs his hands together uttering, "Ha-ha, he-he, ho-ho," just like he gestures unconsciously every time he's dealt a great bridge hand, and bolts for the door.

Jamie just shrugs his *what-the-fuck* shrug.

"Oh great, it's all my fault that Muriel won't talk to anybody," I moan. And then looking for something to grasp onto in this disintegrating atmosphere, I add helplessly, and somewhat obtusely, "And Agatha hates me!"

Alexis regards my statement for a moment then answers, "I don't know if I'd put it that strongly."

Her clear, cold message leaves me with no allies, no ground, just pure anger.

What the hell did you think gave you the right to read my letter? I feel naked and belittled. I have no rights in your house.

Brace yourself, Muriel, because I feel one hellacious mood sweeping through me. Even after all these years. Did you really think I would actually send such a letter to my mother? You knew about the baby that died. How could you have such little feeling for other people? But really, that wasn't the issue, was it? You just tried to use what I wrote against me to turn the tables away from your own sin of snooping again. You, who wrote letters to your mother that you never sent, either. Wherever you are, I hope your cheeks burn with shame.

WELL THERE, TROIS-RIVIÈRES is behind me now and the river has widened again into Lac Saint-Pierre. If I get to the other side of Montreal by tonight, I'll be pleased with my day. Last night, I laid out a map of Montreal on the round blond table wedged between two orange chairs and the air conditioner. I don't want any screw-ups with bridges and off-ramps. I've only done this once before and it scared the wits out of me. But that was before I lived in Calgary, before I became one of those manic city drivers. Merging at high speeds doesn't scare me anymore. I'm just as ruthless as the next guy. Still, I wanted to get the lay of the land in my head before I got there.

There's something nice and peaceful about this lake. I don't feel the current pull against me. It must flow somewhere way deep below the surface. Like these feelings I still harbour, Muriel. It's so humiliating to discover someone has read a letter or a diary. I was so enraged. I am still enraged. And now, I have read your letters, and gone through your personal belongings with a fine-tooth comb. How does that make you feel? Does it make a difference that you are dead?

Should we treat the dead with the same respect we treat the living? Should I have burned your letters unopened? Even though I have a better understanding of you now, was it the right thing to do?

What would make you feel better about the way I tell this story? That you bought us a big pram carriage and knit a couple of adorable cap-and-sweater sets. That you fed us when we were broke. Just tell me what I'm missing here.

But the truth of the matter is that Jamie and I couldn't get your first grandchild out of your house fast enough.

Donny puts pressure on the maintenance crew to get the summer chalet ready. Jamie figures they must have opened the water and sewer lines with a blowtorch because in no time we're snuggled down into peaceful digs on the northern boundary of the park. Alexis keeps us posted about your mood. Sends word that we're disinherited.

"Disinherited?" Jamie scoffs, more miffed than angry. "Give me a break."

Inheritance is the last thing on our minds. Anyway, we simply don't believe you, Muriel. You're losing credibility. All that fuss for a letter I never even sent.

So we thought. Was it really the letter? Or were your own inadequacies as a mother stirred up? Your childhood wounds?

In the space and quiet of the little chalet, Jamie and I breathe and relax. Left to ourselves we take delight in our baby, the ever-miraculous fact of her. Her baby smell. The soft spot on her head covered with a pelt of fine reddish hair where we see her heart beat. Fingers and toes and folds of delicate, papery skin. One eye slightly larger than the other. The tiny speck of a mole under the larger eye. Her mouth sucking. Eyes on my face with unwavering attention. We are falling in love. In the evenings, the three of us cuddle on the couch, at last open to each other as a budding family.

Agatha turns an enraged blind eye as I draw on unemployment insurance to help keep us afloat. We are gathering strength for the last big push for Jamie's final year of university.

My body returns to its normal weight, as I count calories and do sit-ups and side bends. The slab of belly cinches up into place. I will not let myself go like Agatha accused you of doing. My thighs scissor-kick back to shape. By July, I'm comfortable in a bathing suit but I'll never wear a bikini again. My nipples are larger and darker and Jamie can't get enough of them now that they're no longer leaking and once more his sole territory. "You look more like a woman now," he says, and his comment gives me both pleasure and pain. My youthful body has disappeared from my mind and I don't think I'll ever walk into a room in a short red shirtwaist dress and turn heads again. Moments of sadness overcome me from time to time but they are fleeting. Getting to know my baby encompasses most of my thoughts — that, and looking forward to school in the fall. I don't think about working in public relations anymore, I have my eye on a PhD in English or History. When Andrea is napping, I spend hours poring over Saint Mary's '75/'76 academic calendar. Years and years of study loom before me. There will be no more babies to complicate my plans.

I felt just like you did when you announced your retirement, Muriel. I've done my bit.

Jamie and Donny see each other every day at work and eventually Donny informs Jamie that you're out of your room but your mood hasn't improved. Jamie and I are still disinherited. Then before we know it, Donny jumps into that Spitfire and off he goes, on a bender. His ulcers kick up, of course, and he ends up in the DVA in Lancaster again. But, still, no contact from you, Muriel.

A few weeks go by and we're into serious black fly season with swarms of no-see-ums. They come right through the screens and make a beeline for Andrea, leaving bloody trails on her forehead and neck.

"This is bullshit," Jamie announces one night near midnight. "We're going to Mom's."

So we pack up Andrea in the middle of the night, drive the twelve miles to Alma, and knock on your door. When the porch light goes on Jamie and I notice the FOR SALE sign on the Triumph. We exchange a look.

"The baby's grown," you mumble when you let us in.

"Would you like to hold her while I put on the kettle?"

"Okay."

"So what's new, what have you been doing?"

"Shopping."

"Did you get a new dress?"

"No."

"What then?"

"Look for yourself." You point toward the living room.

I dutifully trot in expecting a new lamp or something, but you have bought a new chesterfield and matching chair. They are large, overstuffed, and festooned in a huge floral print in gold, acid green, avocado, and shit-brindle-brown on a beige background. You got the set on sale.

"Oh this is beautiful," I exclaim.

"Do you really like it?" you ask, torn between looking at your new furniture and the baby in your arms.

"It's perfect."

"It really goes, doesn't it?"

I stand back to admire the effect of the monstrosity on your minty-green mottled carpet, set against your drab olive-green custom made drapes and sepia and rust patterned rockers.

"Oh, it just — goes." I exclaim and I wonder who the hell would want to inherit this godawful furniture.

NINE

I HAVE OLD ideas about Montreal. That it's a city of charm, fine stone buildings, and cobblestone streets. There's nightlife and glamour, intrigue, and political plots. The exoticism of the Roman Catholic Church is like nowhere else in this country. A place in Canada where the words *bourgeois* and *bohemian* apply. A place the world dropped in for Expo '67 and the Olympics in '76. Montreal is a place of food and wine I have never tasted. A place where clothes and shoes and handbags and high-heeled boots and accessories can be bought that would keep me in disguise for a lifetime, except I'd be unsure of entering these mysterious boutiques, where I assume the sophisticated saleswomen only speak French with perfect accents.

Growing up in Nova Scotia in the fifties and sixties it was hard not to be aware that the very fact of being from Atlantic Canada was a disadvantage. By the time I was ten, nothing made my blood boil faster than to come up against some brat in my class or neighbourhood who came from Montreal or Toronto and tried to get off with rubbing my nose in the idea that I was inferior. I never failed to stand up for my home and native land, which in my tender youth was Nova Scotia. What did I know of the rest of Canada? Less than a hundred miles and I'll be in Montreal.

Out of the blue, a Triumph Spitfire passes me and disappears around the bend up ahead. I never see one of those cars without feeling a sense of loss. Jamie had always counted on the Spitfire coming to him one day. Young as we were, the Spitfire would have meant something as an inheritance. But, to keep the peace that summer, Donny sold it to one of the naturalists who was being transferred to Cape Breton Highlands National Park. I could never figure out why you wouldn't go for a ride in it. But now I remember something you talked about one afternoon when I was setting your hair, about Donny taking the wife of one of the other wardens for a ride in it when he first won it in the poker game. When you asked him why you didn't get the first ride, he cut you to the quick. *Because you're no spring chicken.*

At the time I thought you were making a mountain out of a molehill mostly because you ached and moaned about Donny not being able to get it up. So what harm could a ride out in the country do? But last week I walked in on a conversation between Jamie and Alexis about Donny and *that car* and *Moncton* and *Ladies of the Night*. They clammed up as soon as they took in my presence. I know they're never going to tell me, and I don't really need to know the details. But now it seems clear. After the Spitfire was sold, you came out of your room and started talking again as if nothing had happened. We were so relieved that we never again brought up the matter of the letter I wrote to my mother in the back of the baby book. You and I never faced each other over that episode. It was all fixed up with whispers and winks on the side, the least said soonest mended.

This is how Jamie and I dealt with the first real fight we had the following February. We were cramped in our one bedroom apartment in High-Rise II at Saint Mary's. Andrea had the bedroom and we set up our bed in the living room. I had dropped from five courses down to three and even that was tough going with the demands of looking after the baby, but I needed to take at least three courses to keep my student loan. Jamie was going flat out in his last year at NS Tech. Most of our emotional effort was directed at this achievement.

I arrange for a sitter and take a rare night out at the Valentine's Dance at Tech. Jamie plunks me down at the end of a table full of people I barely know and disappears to get drinks. Strolling back, he hands me a beer, and takes an empty chair next to an older student he admires at the other end of the long table. As the evening wears on, it becomes apparent to me that perhaps he admires this fellow's wife even more. I'm sipping at my by-now warm beer, while Jamie knocks them back. I want to dance but Jamie doesn't like to dance. I retreat into pretending I'm really digging the band. Then I notice Jamie's empty chair. I track him downstairs, to the washroom. When he comes out, I accuse him of coming on to the older student's wife. He nearly pops his cork. "How dare you?" he bristles, body stiffening, face tightening. He pushes me against the wall then ducks back into the washroom. Having said my piece, I scurry back to the table upstairs and wait.

The band takes a break. I wait until this funny feeling starts to seep into me and I become aware that Jamie has snuck off. I feel disconnected, as if my heart and mind have become untethered. Feelings of shame wash through me. I grab my coat and slip out of the building to check the parking lot.

Our car is gone. I feel invisible, as if, somehow, only my eyes are left floating about in the cold, overcast night. Not knowing where to turn, I start walking down Spring Garden Road. Crusts of black speckled snow are sunk into the curb along the street. My footsteps sound like drumbeats. Terrified of attracting attention, I dart down South Park, building catastrophic scenes of murder and rape in my head. In the half hour it takes to get home I imagine Andrea growing up sad and motherless, Jamie old and alone, remorseful and heartbroken. These scenarios I alternated with possible explanations for Judy, the woman I exchange babysitting favours with, as to why I arrive home abandoned, shivering, and tear-streaked. Though I needn't have bothered, our apartment was dark. Judy is not there. Andrea is fast asleep in her crib and Jamie is snoring, unaware, smack dab in the middle of our bed. In the morning, as if nothing had happened at all, Jamie asks me why I'm sleeping on the couch. When I try to tell him about my midnight odyssey, he stops me. "Why didn't you just ask for a ride home?" he asks. In the bright light of day, it seems ridiculous to me that I had skulked off on my own instead of asking for help. I chalk up the whole episode to stress, and am just as anxious to forget about it. We're both slaving on end-of-term papers. Exams are coming up. Jamie still has some problems to work out on the model earth dam he's building for his graduating thesis. We are both anxious about Jamie finding a real job in the bleak job market. But, more immediately, Andrea needs breakfast and a bath. We put the spat out of our heads.

But somewhere on the tip of my tongue is a question.

How is it possible for a person who feels invisible and disconnected to have the courage to ask for help?

Getting closer. All these French town names coming up: L'Assomption, LeGardeur. I wish I'd looked at the map last night. I know you won't be any help, Muriel. And what did Jamie say when I expressed my anxiety about getting to the other side of Montreal? *Just watch the signs. Watch for the signs.* Don't you think that's funny, Muriel?

Watch for the signs.

After all our worry about the future, Jamie's best job offer comes from Newfoundland Light and Power to build substations in small, remote towns. My plans go up in smoke. The side of me that tries to make everything right convinces me that this move into the boonies will make a good break. I'll be able to read without worrying about term papers. Snuggle up with Jamie on snowbound evenings with no exams on our minds. I grab onto some false pioneering spirit, which I think is my rightful heritage, to hide the profound disappointment that I won't be going back to school in the fall. We pack up all our belongings at Saint Mary's High-Rise II for the last time. Whip out the credit card and take Andrea out to a Chinese restaurant to celebrate. She does not take to the strange surroundings, and after about twenty minutes straightens out stiff as a board in the high chair and yowls until we release her, leaving a heap of chow mein and ginger beef with mushrooms and green peppers on our plates. We drive past our old apartment on Henry Street then head for Robie and the highway to New Brunswick, arriving in Alma in time for Andrea's first birthday celebration, and three weeks holiday before shoving off for Stephenville on the west coast of Newfoundland.

Everyone is lovey-dovey for the birthday party. Then the shit hits the fan. The next day, you corner me in the upstairs hallway. "Why couldn't Jamie find a job up in Moncton?"

"Moncton?" I gasp. "He never even looked. Why would we want to live in Moncton?"

"You could drive down on the weekends. We could all have Sunday dinner together."

I am speechless.

"You know Donny and I could have gone to Whitehorse and then Banff with the Parks. But we wouldn't have dreamed of taking Alexis and Jamie away from their grandparents. I think you're being so selfish."

Selfish? Here I am thinking we're making the best of it, given the circumstances. It's what we believe is required of us. I know it's not the Depression or The War, but at some level, we do feel like we're making a sacrifice.

And, here, Muriel, there's something I know about your son that you don't. He's become ambitious. Two years of professional engineering school has seen to that. He doesn't want a government job and to play golf on Friday afternoons anymore. He's looking for something to do with his life. You don't know your son. You only know the boy in your heart.

"Moncton!" Jamie says wide-eyed when we tumble into bed that night. "She sent me away when I was thirteen. I never, ever, thought of coming back here."

I lie awake, aware of all the space in this house that you wanted us to fill up in your golden years. Oh Muriel, why do we so often set ourselves up only to be disappointed?

The next morning, when the men go to the post office to get the paper, you start in on me again. "I've thought about and thought about it. And the only thing I can come up with is that you and Jamie are moving so far away to punish me. For the life of me, I can't think what for."

"Muriel, you haven't got anything to do with it. More than a third of Jamie's classmates still don't have jobs. His best friend is going back to do a master's degree, hoping the picture will be a bit brighter in a year or two. Jamie doesn't have that luxury. We've got Andrea to support and student loans to pay off. How do you think I feel about it? I've got to give up school. God knows when I'll finish my degree."

"You're young. You have all the time in the world."

"YOU'D BETTER HAVE a talk with your mother," I tell Jamie.

"I haven't got anything to say that you haven't already said."

In the back of our minds is the possibility of *the curtains, the cake, the kick in the ass*. We're too consumed with your distracting behaviour to consider the possibility that you are right. You were your own worst enemy, Muriel. Because now, years later, I have the sneaking suspicion that maybe you were right. Maybe at some level Jamie was punishing you. But with all that family perfection taking up conscious space, it would have been a deep, dark secret even to him. At the time, we still haven't figured out that we are to be the stars in Act III of your life.

WE FIGURE WE need a diversion. Donny had been saying that when Jamie graduates he wants to buy him a dog, a golden retriever like you had when Alexis and Jamie were little. Do you remember how we all trotted off to Moncton to see a litter that was predictably adorable? And how our little jaunt, predictably enough, blew off some of your steam. Jamie chooses a male pup. Donny's wallet doesn't crack open.

"Guess he forgot," Jamie says to hide his shame.

EVERYTHING MIGHT HAVE actually been okay if it hadn't been for Agatha's renovations. Carpenters are busy at work in her kitchen and she has set herself the task of stripping the wallpaper in the upstairs bathroom.

"Oh I'll give you a hand," Jamie says, good-naturedly.

"I'll help," I add, always looking for an excuse to get upstairs in the old house where Agatha guards so much stuff. "You don't mind watching Andrea while she naps, do you Muriel?"

"Suit yourself," you snip. "Stripping wallpaper's not my idea of having fun."

"I'll tell you what," Agatha chimes. Coy as a cat. Cinching the deal. "I'll give you the furniture out of the front bedroom in exchange for your labour."

"Hey, Mom, isn't that the furniture Grandpa gave you when you got back from Montreal?" Jamie asks.

YOU ARE RIGHT. Stripping wallpaper is not much fun. There is more than one layer. There are decades of layers. Jamie steams, soaks, and scrapes morning, noon, and night. His only consolations are the elaborate lunches Agatha fixes for him every day: fresh hot biscuits, lobster, clam chowder, apple pie, ice cream. Then it's back to scraping. And all the while, you are seething as you and Donny and Andrea and I dip our grilled cheese sandwiches into Campbell's tomato soup jazzed up with a dollop of cream. I slip down to help when Andrea's sleeping. Agatha keeps patrol, ruining whatever fun we might have by making sure we don't sneak into any of the rooms to get a load of what she's got stashed away.

Jamie and I are up to our eyeballs in thin strips of slimy wallpaper and your sentences are getting gummy. The afternoon you declare you couldn't watch Andrea because you need a nap yourself, I have the feeling that you're going to come apart at the joints in your brain, the corners where you calculate the sorrows of your life.

We slink off to the beach with Andrea in her Snuggly. The tide is about halfway. A wall of fog hugs the water's retreat. Sea and sky smudged together, the boundary opaque. The whole world appears grey, every surface soaked in fat particles of moisture, vapour puffs and swirls. We crunch out across the gravel in thick cool air. My hair frizzes. Nose is cold. I touch my fingers to Andrea's cheek to feel if she is chilled but Andrea is warm as toast clamped onto Jamie's back.

"Shit's about to hit the fan," I say, giving the boot to a dark green rock.

Andrea squirms. We let her down to play in a tidal stream until her hands start to turn red. Out of the blue, weaving our way back to shore, Jamie says, "Dad only has two memories of his mother. One is from down here on the beach when the whole village turned out for a huge bonfire to burn the Kaiser in effigy at the end of the First World War. He was four years old and terrified out of his wits. His mother carried him all the way home on piggyback. I never thought about it until just now, but it must have been an awful struggle for her because she went to the sanatorium not long after, and was dead in a few months."

"What was the other time he remembered?"

"He'd be about the same age. Playing cowboys and Indians by himself in the house roaring around and he shot a vase off a table with his bow and arrow. Crash down it went and he was scared shitless and started to cry. His mother came into the room and told him it was okay, shushed him up and got the hired girl to clean up the mess. Took him into the kitchen and gave him a molasses gem."

"How did he play cowboys and Indians by himself?"

"Played both parts. First he was the good guy and then he was the bad guy."

"What was her name?"

"Who?"

"His mother. Your grandmother."

"Jeez, I don't know. Isn't that awful?"

"Yes, it's terrible," I say. But my mind is pulling elsewhere. I take a last look at the beach. It's been five years since the summer I had tried to determine the exact moment when the tide turns. For a split second, my old obsession comes zinging back. As we trudge up through the tidal trash, I experience a strong urge to run to the tide's edge and throw myself in. But back to shore I amble with a deep nagging feeling of something left undone.

The house was dead silent. Your bedroom door closed. A hamburger, macaroni, and cheese casserole sits thawing on the counter.

When Donny gets home from work, he takes you up a cup of tea and a sticky bun. Without touching a bite, you send him away to tell Jamie and me that we're disinherited. Donny shrugs. We shrug together. That old saw again. There is no power in that stance.

Couldn't you see, Muriel, we were too young and full of life to be threatened by disinheritance? That was your fear and it came true! We didn't want your house and your furniture. We wanted your blessing.

But there was power in your silent exiles. I felt bamboozled again. What was I supposed to think? Didn't you feel like a fool up there? I certainly felt like a fool, scuttling around, keeping Andrea quiet. How were we supposed to act when you came out? What were we supposed to say? Were we supposed to talk about it? Was someone supposed to say okay, okay, I get the picture? But what was the picture? You made us feel guilty about living our lives.

Like a fog-bound apparition, you make the odd silent appearance over the next couple of days to get something to drink. You're not eating. Your face and throat distort as if clogged with tears, as if you've been choking to hold back the debris of disappointment and foiled desire. You play your part until the eleventh hour.

The night before we leave for Newfoundland, while I'm packing, you quietly open your door and pad down the carpeted stairs. It's about ten o'clock. I slip down behind you, perching near the bottom, out of sight but not out of earshot. That staircase, located in the heart of the house, with the kitchen and dining room falling to one side, and the large, long living room to the other. Solid walls flanking both sides.

The rocking chair in the large hallway by the back door creaks. Then I hear Donny's voice.

"Yes, sweetheart. Of course, sweetheart," he croons. "You have every right in the world to be angry with Agatha."

"She's always trying to steal my children from me."

"I don't blame you one little bit for being upset."

"And who knows if I'll ever see my grandchild again."

"Come on, Mom. You and Dad can come to Newfoundland."

Jamie is in on this sweet talk, too. After all the hours I sat with you, listening to your sob stories, dispensing sympathy, and offering whatever heartfelt advice I could muster — I am thoroughly poisoned by the idea that I have not been consulted. Five years I spent with that bunch of you and here I was hunched on the staircase, like a hired girl, trying to figure out what the hell is going on. I listened to them jolly you along.

Didn't they have any respect for you, Muriel? Didn't you have any respect for yourself? What was the point of respectability, if you couldn't get respect from your own family?

The next morning, when we come downstairs, there you are squeezing oranges. We make cotton ball conversation, teeth gritting on the residue. We're supposed to pretend nothing happened. There's a lot of fuss and mess before we get the suitcases, Andrea, and the puppy packed into the car. Our goodbyes offered in a whorl of diapers and dog shit.

As we headed up the back road I kiss Jamie's hand and play with Andrea's feet in their tiny-tot red sneakers. Your image, waving us goodbye, stuck in my mind. Jamie had you and Donny pose for a farewell photograph. You in your long checked housecoat and Donny in his uniform. He has a big no-care-in-the-world smile on his chops and is sending us off with a wide stretched-out wave with his right arm, his left arm wound tightly around your waist, as if he's holding you up. Your arms are tucked around your middle. You're smiling weakly, bravely.

I am overwhelmed with a sadness I don't understand. Our leaving should have been different. I don't understand why it had to be so chaotic. I vow the future will be different.

When I think now about that first attempt to get away I think it should have been a time of celebration. There should have been generosity and good will. Not pettiness and squabbling. Maybe if it had been a cleaner getaway we wouldn't have repeated the scene so many times. The pull was so strong. Like the tide, we went out and we came back. As though we could never get it right. And the funny thing is, until just now, I have always thought it was about us. How we were leaving you behind. But it was more than that. It was about you. How you had only tried once. And all we ever did — Jamie and Alexis and I — was remind you.

And now here I am driving across the Repentigny Bridge onto the island of Montreal, heading west on the #40. There's the Petro-Canada refinery on the left. You don't want to know what Albertans think about Petro-Canada, Muriel. Now the Shell refinery. I just have to keep my cool as I travel through the heart of the city; it's so easy to get lost. Okay, what's coming up? Autoroute Décarie. Don't want that. Don't need to be distracted by all these funny-looking signs. A red Honda Civic is coming up on the ramp alongside me and is supposed to yield but oh my god I don't think it's going to yield. We are so close I can see the driver, a woman in a power suit with unmerciful make-up. I panic and stand on the brakes. The car behind me blares his horn. The woman throws her hands up in the air then gestures move on, move on. I spurt over to the left without thinking. Where am I going? Somehow I get squeezed onto an off-ramp — who the hell builds an off ramp that exits to the left? Now I'm on Autoroute Décarie.

THERE'S A SIGN for the #20 to Toronto, but god knows what territory that will lead me through. Now another for highway #10 via the Champlain Bridge. Christ, I don't want to land on the other side again. What's this? Bonaventure Expressway. I'm going to take it. As I make a little turn I'm staring at downtown Montreal. There's Place Ville Marie with its four wings. That I know. Jamie and I stayed in the hotel near there with Andrea one weekend not long after we moved to Labrador, but I don't want to go there tonight. Let's see. A big stone turn-of-the-century building, the Sun Life building. St. Mary's Cathedral. Queen Elizabeth Hotel. I remember these too. We took a horse and buggy ride through the old town. Okay. Here's something. Hotel Bonaventure. I like that name. Reminds me of the aircraft carrier HMCS *Bonaventure* docked under the Angus L. MacDonald Bridge that spans the water between Halifax and Dartmouth when I was a kid. All lit up at Christmas. Okay this is it. I'm pulling in. I'm going to regroup.

It's room service for us tonight, Muriel. What would you like to watch on TV?

There's something bugging me about your return to Alma in humiliation from Montreal. You know I've never put it all together before but I think you must have stayed with Perley and Philomena for almost a decade. You were twenty-three years old! I never thought to calculate how long that stretch of time — your great period of dormancy — was. I only thought about the order of events: your illness, your recovery, your father's refusal to let you go back to nursing school, your teaching, the war, your marriage. A little over nine years. Somehow I had always contracted this period, shrunk time down to the sequence.

Perhaps a person can't think in decades until they can start to look at their own life in terms of decades.

How did time pass for you as an elementary school teacher living under the roof of your pious, teetotalling parents? Perley, stretched out, digesting on his daybed; Philomena pinched-mouthed in the chair beside him, embroidering the King's Message on a sampler; you, young and anxious, defeated, knitting sock after sock for the boys overseas; all three in the big kitchen listening to war news on the high, arched mahogany radio after your five-on-the-dot supper. Sundays must have been like a tomb. No card playing, no radio, no diversions aside from church and chicken dinner. According to Agatha, even Sunday picnics were unheard of in the parish until after the park opened and people of a lesser Sunday devotion came spreading their bad habits. Sundays aside, how many diversions could there have been in Alma at that time? Even the nearest movie theatres were either fifty miles away in Moncton or forty in Sussex. What could have been diverting in Alma for a young woman who had spent five years at university, where she bobbed her hair, painted her fingernails, lived from Saturday night party to Saturday night party, played tennis with great panache and, behind everybody's back, had had enough gumption to enrol in nursing school all the way up in Montreal?

"Wasn't it boring?" I asked you once.

"No," you snapped. "We had pie socials. They were loads of fun. Donny always bought my pies."

Really Muriel, how can I be expected to believe that now? How many pie socials could there have been in nine years? Especially when for a great deal of that time, almost six years, Donny was away at The War. How come there aren't any letters to and from Donny during the war sitting here in my baskets? Surely you would have saved love letters. You saved everything else. So what were you doing, Muriel? How did you mark time? I know you didn't cook because there's that story about you not even knowing how to make biscuits when you and Donny got married.

"Mother was just about out of her mind having Muriel home like a child," Agatha told me. So, after nine years, Agatha took it upon herself to find you a teaching position in Sackville and goaded you into applying. At least that's Agatha's version and I've never heard a peep from you to discount it. But the joke was on Agatha and Philomena. Donny Gallagher, who after the war worked as a clerk in War Surplice up in Moncton, started courting you and then you became engaged.

"If Muriel had still been living at home," Agatha said. "Donny Gallagher wouldn't have got his foot over the threshold. Mother would have seen to that and I would have backed her up. But the damage was done before anyone knew. After he and Muriel became engaged, he quit his job and hired on at Dad's store when they moved back to Alma. It's just as well the National Park came along in '48 to save the day, because it was hard enough to make one good living at the store, let alone two."

I love Agatha's tirades, don't you Muriel? They are never full of self-pity, only energetic moralizing. If you edit out her vitriol, she generally has her facts straight. But most often, the moralizing is the story. It's the part you remember faithfully. Right, Muriel? Sometimes I wish I could be more like her. But I don't have the knack for it. I don't share her sense of entitlement.

And I don't have your knack for still points. I push time. It spreads before me like an enemy. There are so many things I want to do and places I want to go.

Sometimes I wish I could make time stop for me the way you could.

I don't know what I'm doing with all your stuff in the trunk of the car. Was I smart enough to pick out the benign pieces? The pieces I can put in a cabinet, look back on fondly, and say without my heart jamming up, "Oh look, this is a lovely piece; it used to belong to Muriel." Will I keep any of it if Jamie and I remain apart?

I FOUND A map in your cedar chest that made me cry. It was one I made with Andrea about five years ago for show-and-tell. We took a map of Canada and traced, in pink highlighter, the roads to all the places she had travelled. The pink spread from the very east to the very west, with trails, like leaf skeletons, running north and south off the Trans-Canada Highway. Then we wrote a little blurb about all the places we had pinpointed with a big lime-green highlighter dot — the places we had lived. I had forgotten that Andrea had sent the map to you as part of her Christmas present that year, thinking you'd get a kick out of it because you had come to visit us in all those places, too. But now I remember when we visited Alma in the summer how Andrea had been disappointed that you hadn't put the map up somewhere in the house, if even on the wall of the upstairs hallway. I tried to explain to her that maybe it made you sad. That maybe it was too much of a reminder of how far away we had gone.

I have brought that map into this hotel room. I spread it out on top of the map of the city of Montreal. As I trace the pink line from Newfoundland to British Columbia with my index finger, I become aware that the blood in my veins is racing, heating up. My heart bumps and pounds. All the space around me begins to fill in. There is nothing but this map and me. What will happen to all the pink lines and green dots if Jamie and I decide to split up for good? Will they peel away like old wallpaper? Or become smudged like sea, land, and sky on a foggy day. Looking at the map, it dawns on me that I have left footprints on the land and heart prints on those around me; that my travels and travails have not been like walking out into the water, when trenches fill in as soon as I lift my heel. I stare at the map and wonder how to plot, and trace, and dot, the geography of something I find hard to contemplate, but may well have put in motion; the geography of a new life; the geography of divorce.

TEN

STARTING THE CAR this morning, I stepped on the gas when I turned the key in the ignition; the engine caught with a mighty roar. I forgot about the fuel injection. I forgot to keep my foot off the gas. In my mind, I heard you hiss. It does feel, from time-to-time, as though you are sitting in the passenger seat, on edge, watching my every move. I try to ignore you because I'm stupid and groggy, having overslept. The weather is overcast and heavy, which suits me fine, I have no attachment to this landscape.

I called Andrea last night. It seems incongruous now, the drama and tears and bawling of Andrea's first year and to think of that baby as the able young woman she's grown into — eighteen already, soon to graduate. She's going to take a year off before starting her BFA in music at UVic. Jamie and I have encouraged her to take some time to think about who she is and what she wants from life. We don't believe in the ramrod approach to education. You would not approve. *Give them an inch and they'll take a mile*, you'd say. *Once a child has had a taste of freedom, they'll never settle into school again.* You'd say this, despite evidence to the contrary. You'd still repeat what you were taught when you were young.

I'm beginning to see, now, how hard it is to unlearn what we've learned from the cradle. Yesterday here I was ready to drive from Montreal straight on to Toronto and then north on the 400 without even considering that I can cut that jaunt out and head straight through Ottawa. I was going to drive to Toronto because that's the way I drove before. If I hadn't got lost yesterday, I wouldn't have figured that out until it was too late.

Andrea's been holding down the fort while I've been gone. I told her I wasn't going to push this drive; that I'd arrive when I arrived.

"No problem," she said. "I've got everything under control."

"Don't forget to water the plants." I said this because I felt inadequate. She's more than capable of looking after the household. In fact, she is far more capable than she thinks I give her credit for. She's ready to move out, but hasn't realized it yet. At least a hundred times, I've told her that one of my jobs as a parent is to send her out into the world as a person who will be responsible. I don't mean just financially, but responsible enough to make good decisions, manage her time, not lay blame on others for her own shortcomings, to be thoughtful of other people, and to be kind when possible. That's one of my responsibilities, I tell her, to make sure she becomes an adult, that believe it or not, it's something you have to work on.

I am not raising her to keep me company in my old age. Are you listening, Muriel?

So truth be told, I want her out — oh hell, let's face it — I've been like a great big bird pushing her out of the nest. She's become so hard to live with. We're at each other's throats all the time. What she doesn't understand is that she is challenging me and testing herself. She's bristling to break out, but she's afraid. I know she'll do fine. But she won't know until she makes the leap. In the meantime, she strews the house with her litter of tragedies and heartaches, not to mention her shoes and boots and sheet music and apple cores, orange peels, and candy wrappers.

And the constant bickering with Caitlin. They drive me up the wall. I don't feel safe from them in my own home. In the evenings,

I fly out the front door on any pretext: gallery openings, book readings, volunteer work. I'm gone two or three nights a week up McLeod Trail, or the Crowchild, or merging into killer traffic on the Deerfoot. You can count on me, I show up everywhere. I'm what you'd call involved with my community.

The closest I came to just letting time be was the eighteen months or so Jamie and I spent in Newfoundland — first in Stephenville, that small town on the north shore of St. George's Bay, where Jamie built his first substation. We rented a three-bedroom apartment in a building that had been converted from the Air Force barracks the Americans built when they had a base there from 1941–66. Stephenville was no great shakes. It was run-down and poverty-stricken. A linerboard factory, one of Joey Smallwood's great schemes, was on its last legs. Unemployment was high, spirits were low. But all the same, we were happy to be there. Our big apartment felt like luxury. As did the time — in the beginning. With no classes to rush off to and no essays to write, no jiggling Andrea up and down to keep her quiet when I snuck her into the reading room in the library, I took pleasure in letting the day unfold. I took pride in preparing from scratch every bite we ate from bread to yogourt. Even Jamie whipped up homemade pizza dough and sauces every Friday night. He also bought me a dishwasher so he wouldn't have to wait for me to do up the dishes before we took long drives on the weekends all summer long, and played on the beaches with Andrea and the puppy. We thought everything about Andrea was perfect, even the yellowish turds she deposited in the surf the minute her little bottom touched the cold water. Through the week, I sat out on the apartment steps with several other young mothers and we chatted about much of nothing while our toddlers and preschoolers played in the dirt on the patchy, ragged weeds that passed for a lawn. In the afternoons, while Andrea napped, I read Penguin paperback classics, or tended the dozens of houseplants I had started from cuttings. Time was restful and lovely. I was content and overcome with a love so intense for Andrea that sometimes when I looked at her I felt something tumble through me, pure and weightless. In those moments of joy, it was as though time stood still. There was nothing else but our connection. There was no difference between us. I didn't want anything to change. I thought the three of us, Andrea and Jamie and I, could go on like this forever.

It was only in the evenings when Jamie took our pup, Cubby, out to a pond to teach him how to retrieve that I felt uneasy. He pushed the poor little thing too hard. Held the pup's head under the water to make him latch onto the dummy. I preferred to stay home.

When you and Donny came on the ferry from Port aux Basques to check us out, I turned myself inside out cooking and cleaning. Everything was perfect — except Andrea's behaviour. At nearly eighteen months, she would not tolerate the time it took to sit in a restaurant, order a meal, and finish it leisurely. Donny was particularly annoyed and accused me of not being able to keep my child under control. I was exasperated, but informed him that it seemed unnatural to me to try and make a toddler's behaviour conform to that of an adult. He was outraged on both counts: my child-rearing philosophy and my talking back. I caught him in a big scowl as the phrase *That girl has a mind of her own* slipped through his skinny lips later that day when he and you had your two old heads bowed together. Things didn't get any better when we attempted the long drive to Gros Morne National Park up the west coast. Andrea had too much hustle and bustle to sit strapped in a car seat contentedly the whole day. She fussed and stormed non-stop. Our nerves were shattered. I was blamed. What was I supposed to do? Smack her? I tried everything to entertain her — rattles, keys, peek-a-boo, sing-along, even bribing her with a banana, which she swallowed whole, then promptly threw up.

It was after you and Donny left for New Brunswick and the days grew shorter and the houseplants started to go dormant, that I did too. That old restlessness I experienced the summer I tried to measure the exact moment when the tide turns seeped back into me. I missed going to school. When moments of frustration began to steal up on me, I immediately felt ashamed. Didn't I have everything I could ever wish for? Something will turn up, I told myself. Just stay still.

I bought an exercise bicycle, a new mattress, a new dress, a cheap set of dishes. Nothing worked. Until one morning when I arranged for a friend to sit with Andrea while I browsed through Woolworth's and came across the remnants bin in the sewing section. There were dozens and dozens of tidy bundles of brightly coloured cottons and corduroys and denims. I drifted over to the pattern books and flipped through the pages of toddlers' fashions. How hard could it be to make children's clothes? I pranced out the door with thread and buttons and 99-cent bundles of cheerful material and three Easy-Sew outfits. Back in our barracks, I set my mother's old Kenmore sewing machine up on the dining room table and cut out my first pattern. Before I knew it, I was whipping up tiny pinafores with ruffled bibs and puffy sleeved blouses with perfect French seams. The most ambitious project was a pale blue duffel snowsuit with a fox tail I ordered from Goose Bay to adorn the hood. My little blond girl looked — if not acted — like an angel in these clothes. I even took to embroidering daisy chains on her cuffs and collars.

When the light changed, and he couldn't take the pup out for retriever training, Jamie started showing his first signs of restlessness. He was almost finished the substation, but we weren't sure where he was going to be posted next. "Can't we transfer to St. John's?" I asked. "I could go to Memorial University."

"The company's talking about Marystown. And even if there was something in St. John's, we're not ready yet. You know I get paid more for being out in the field."

Then one night he confessed that he hated building substations and never wanted to be an engineer anyway. This was news to me.

"What did you want to be?"

"A vet."

"I thought you wanted to be a golf pro."

"Secretly, I always wanted to be a vet."

Imagine, Muriel. He always wanted to be a vet. Did you and Donny ever ask? We actually talked about throwing in the towel and moving to Guelph so he could go to veterinary college, but the thought of amassing more debt threw him off.

I was thrown off by the out-of-the-blue wanting to be a vet business. I encouraged him to buy a good camera, an Olympus SLR.

We waited on tenterhooks wondering where we were going next for Jamie to build another substation. I re-upholstered the old daybed Perley died on with a tough stain-proof acrylic material, then went whole hog and bought a contrasting pinstripe corduroy to cover a bookcase Jamie had cobbled together, and made matching pillows for the daybed, all the while telling myself that I could be good and wait to find out where we were going to move. This was not anxiety. I was not going crazy. It didn't bother me at all that the damp winter air sinks into everything and that I resorted to using the blow dryer to warm our beds at night.

As the white sand beaches of the Ottawa River flash past in a break through the trees, the image of a photograph I had come across while sorting out your things blazes into my head. You and Andrea on the trip to Gros Morne National Park. We had stopped at a rest area. The afternoon was surprisingly warm and sunny. Andrea's Savage shoes snapped like duck feet across the pebbles of the little beach. When it was time to go, you scooped Andrea up into your arms and gave her a hug and squeeze and she wriggled to get down. Jamie captured the moment perfectly. The wind was whipping your tie-dyed kerchief and Andrea's fine blond bangs like angel wings. The look on your face was pure, unadulterated love.

Funny how that photo didn't come across my mind when I was thinking about that trip this morning. Funny how we always want to capture the good times in a photograph, but always capture the bad times in our heads, where they go round and round.

I see your face, Muriel, with so much love. No matter what else happened, I mustn't forget there was always that love.

I pull the Buick back into the slow lane. My eyes are stinging and my throat is tight. I haven't had a good wail about you since last summer. There were few tears in the church last week during your funeral service and I've been a little weepy off and on, but that's it. I think if I pulled off to the side of the road I could have a good hard cry, but I'm not going to. I'm going to keep going. I'm on my way home.

I think it was when we moved to Marystown, all the way across Newfoundland on the Burin Peninsula, that cheery little place, situated on one of the best harbours in Newfoundland, that I started wearing my big disguise. There was a lovely beach, Wild Beach, nestled between two gently sloping headlands with sand flats and stone outwash that reminded us of home. We let Andrea run free there and throw sticks for the dog. We lived in a little bungalow in the local housing authority development along with a contingent of shipyard workers from Glasgow, Scotland. From time-to-time, I was invited to the women's coffee mornings and sat uncomfortably while they complained about their living conditions. They all wanted to go home, they all missed living in a city — St. John's was a hard, bleak 200-mile drive away — but there was no work for their husbands back in Scotland. I tried to put on a happy face and said in the local dialect, "Sure, it's not so bad here, the people are *noice*." I was determined to play my role of mother and homemaker well. But I should have been paying attention to my own body; it was giving me enough clues: tight bands around my head, a leaden feeling behind my eyes, listlessness in the mornings, staggering fatigue in the afternoons. I got hooked on your TV soap *Another World*; it became the pinnacle of my days. The only thing I could be bothered making was a red velvet dress for Andrea for Christmas. Instead of sewing, I fabricated happiness. It took all my energy. Jamie was pestering me to have another baby. He was hot to trot to have that boy to carry on the family name. The way my body felt, pregnancy was the last thing on my mind. How could I think about getting pregnant when we knew we were going to be on the hoof again?

The substation was near completion but we still didn't know where we were going for the next one. Again, I nagged him to lobby the company for a transfer to St. John's, but he didn't think we could afford to live in the city and have me at school while paying off our student loans.

Paying off debt was all we seemed to be living for. At one point, Jamie had banked enough money to buy a very nice little boat, which seemed like a good idea if we were going to live in Newfoundland. Instead, he went grimly to the bank and completely paid off my student loan.

"Don't ever expect more than this little bungalow," he warned not long later. "It's all we'll ever be able to afford."

"But what about after I get my degree?"

"At the rate we're going, I don't see how we'll ever be able to afford that either."

I didn't know how to argue with him. His hysteria about debt was so deep-rooted. I think this came from Perley, who had often advised Jamie when they played store that he could never grow up to be his own man if he owed money. *Buy land* was the other advice Perley gave Jamie as a tyke. *Buy land.*

Buying boats was more of a Donny kind of dream. A big dream. And although Jamie was clearly torn at the time, buying the big dream was put on hold.

Something's bugging me Muriel, the wanting to be a vet, the hysteria about never having a good house, me never going back to university. What was Jamie really telling me?

In the meantime, there was the business of a son to be addressed.

I was still resisting another pregnancy when one day I spied an ad in the paper and thought all our problems would be solved: a junior civil engineer was needed in Churchill Falls, Labrador, the giant hydroelectric project with eighty-eight earth dams. The ad boasted the recreational facilities were second-to-none. The money was good. Good enough to save to buy land and boat. All food and supplies were shipped in from Montreal and sold at Montreal prices. Something about the ad, the promise of it all, got a flame going under me. A couple of years up there and we'd bank enough money to get back to Halifax. Jamie got excited and applied for the job. Maybe being an engineer wasn't so bad after all. We smelled adventure. The company flew us up for a couple of days to check it out. A standard procedure, to make sure they were hiring the kind of people who could hack the place. With no serviceable roads in or out it was an expensive prospect to move a family all the way up into vast wilderness if all they did was turn around and want to run out screaming as soon as they arrived.

ELEVEN

LITTLE DO WE know the ways of the world when Jamie and I fly into Churchill Falls on a grey windswept day in November of 1977. Located on a vast plateau high above sea level in central Labrador, the company town is a model of modernism in one of the world's last wild places. As we descend through the clouds, I watch in awe as the strange dark land, with its endless stands of black spruce, gaunt in the pale light, spread out beneath me. A tapestry of rocks, glacial debris, and patches of tweedy muskeg protrude through the snow cover. Lakes, littered with islets and string bogs, sheathed in thin streaks of dry powdery snow, twist off into the horizon with long cracks from shore to shore. A network of dirt roads disappears into the hills. Off in the distance looms a massive, solitary structure rising from the top of an earth dam; its tall concrete columns, dark rectangular recesses, and double steel tower seem incongruous in the scoured and abraded landscape.

"What on earth is that?" I ask.

"That will be one of the control structures," Jamie answers.

As we make our approach, the mighty Churchill River stretches before us, gouging its way through the great Canadian Shield. I crane my neck looking for the waterfalls when the Boeing 737 banks sharply and the compact, orderly town of Churchill Falls comes into full view. The rooftops and roads are covered in snow and the place looks like a model town. There is not another house for hundreds of kilometres in sight. I shiver. The 737 levels out, then suddenly drops and lands with a screeching stop, thrust reversers full throttle, bringing us up smartly on the short runway. I grab Jamie's hand, leaving fingernail marks in his palms.

"This could take some getting used to."

"It's probably not like this all the time," he says, but his voice is too thin. I have no faith in what he says.

We step out into the blustery landscape. A guide escorts us into town in a four-door, pale-yellow Plymouth, the company logo plastered on the door panels. Bumping along the pitted surface, the guide remarks that the roads are smoother in the winter because the potholes fill in with snow. Oh shit, if this isn't winter, I wonder, what is.

There was no way to imagine, Muriel. Labrador has to be witnessed in the middle of real winter, not the middle of November, to understand.

Except for a few clumps of stunted black spruce hanging on for dear life here and there, the town shows no sign of shrubs or other trees under its thin blanket of snow. It has the look of a military base, but with curves and style. I am struck by how new everything looks. The guide talks about the town with rehearsed pride. "The architects did their best to make all the buildings blend in with the landscape with the varied board and baton feature. The big joke around here is, "When are they going to uncrate the houses!"

"What's the population?"

"A thousand. Give or take the comings and goings."

At the hub is the Town Centre complex that divides the residential streets into three main sections with houses arranged in concentric arcs around it. "The houses were built on only one side of the street to allow a bit of privacy and, it helps with the snow removal," the guide says, then laughs. "A big deal since the average snowfall is 150 inches. But don't worry, it gets cleaned up lickety-split. You never have to worry." There are five basic designs for the houses. Big and blocky, with flat inclined roofs, each fronts an attached garage sporting an orange door. A lot of big shiny snowmobiles are parked where you'd expect cars. At the fringe of town, off to the east side, are mobile homes, arranged in angled rows. In a corner of their own overlooking Blueberry Lake are three huge managers' houses. A clump of four apartment buildings is situated just west of the Town Centre.

"The lake is frozen over eight months of the year, but the cross country skiing is great," the guide enthuses.

I figure I could give cross-country skiing a whirl.

UP AT THE Control and Administration Building the guide shows us a wall-size map of the entire project. "What distinguishes this area from the rest of the Canadian Shield," she says. "Is the fact that practically the entire plateau drains into the Churchill River. The headwaters converge at the edge of the plateau, plunging into a gorge, dropping 1000 feet in less than twenty miles. The *pièce de résistance* of this natural watercourse is the magnificent Churchill Falls, higher than Niagara, at 245 feet."

"Do we get to see them?" I ask.

"They're not on this time of year."

"Not on?"

"No. The only time the falls are turned on now is during spring run-off."

"You mean you can turn significant waterfalls off and on?"

"We have the technology," the guide laughs. "In the late 1960s and early seventies the terrain was manipulated and flooded into reservoirs and fore bays with a system of eighty-eight earth dams covering forty miles, with control structures and spillways that form a water catchment area about the size of New Brunswick."

"So the dark blue area on the map was the original watercourse," Jamie says. "And the light blue area shows how big it is now."

"That's right. And if you'll look at this," she says, pointing to another framed diagram. "The millions of cubic metres of diverted water pounds through an intake structure that is located directly above the penstocks. There are eleven of them — like inclined mine-shafts — and they're concrete-lined. The water spills down the penstocks, whirls through the donut-shaped scroll case and wicket gates, then hits eleven giant turbines. The turbines are like great big hunks of metal made up of rotors and magnets, located in what's called the machine hall, or the underground powerhouse. Come with me and we'll take the elevator down into the largest underground powerhouse in the world."

"This," she continues, "is where electricity is created."

We walk out into a place so extraordinary it could have been the perfect set for a James Bond movie. We are standing deep in the Canadian Shield in a cavern excavated out of solid granite, 972 feet long, 81 feet wide, and 154 feet high. There is a strong smell of rock and concrete. The sound is deafening, I can't think, and it is bright enough to be daylight.

"The electricity goes through a mass of coils and cables up to the transformer gallery in another underground cavern located above and behind the machine hall. From the transformer gallery the electricity goes to the switchyard via electrical cables, and out to Hydro-Quebec on 735 kV lines that cross from giant towers, to span the Churchill River — 6000 feet from side to side. The spent water that has whirled through the turbines goes into the surge chamber. The surge chamber dampens out the effect of fluctuations in water due to demand for power."

Through a special glass window, we peer into the surge chamber, which is almost as big as the powerhouse. The spent water roils and rages. The guide points up. "From the surge chamber, the water is directed via draft tubes through two tailrace tunnels over a mile long, back into the Churchill River. All of these structures — and all that power, 5,225 thousand kilowatts, or more than 7 million horsepower — are managed in the control and administration building, located at the surface via an access shaft directly above the powerhouse, where we came in."

All those numbers I remember. I can almost feel you rolling your eyes, Muriel.

Right now I'm too busy admiring the greenery along the highway. The sun is coming out. Spring up here in the Ottawa Valley must be weeks ahead of New Brunswick. It's lovely. I feel much better than I did this morning. Now, where I was I?

Oh yes, Churchill Falls; an engineer's dream come true. After touring the powerhouse facilities, the guide drives us down toward the river to show off McPharland House, a swank and elegant place overlooking the river where the company holds special functions and houses important guests. At the ski hill, we stop to peer in the windows of the ski shack, built from a half dozen trailers, located at the top of the gorge. Two ski runs plunge down toward the river. "It's not much," the guide says. "But it gets a lot of use. Volunteers operate the club. The company pays for heat and lights."

Sounds perfect to me. Little do I know that volunteering will cause me so much heartache in less than a year.

That evening, we are invited to a party the guide and her husband are throwing. "Nothing special. Just a Christmas warm-up. Come any time after eight."

We are welcomed by about thirty bright and friendly people who have come from all over Canada and Europe, sipping wine, munching canapés, chattering away about the town and its social events. Jamie and I fall a little in love with the scene; we fall in love with the apartment, a split-level with living room, dining room, kitchen on the main floor, two bedrooms and bath on the second. This is style. Back in our well-appointed hotel room we take forever to fall asleep, our heads abuzz with grand ideas.

The next morning, Jamie is interviewed by Frank Dudek, a well-known structural engineer, former pilot from of the Polish Free Army who flew with the Brits and spent a year in a concentration camp, and the man who will become so important to our life in Churchill Falls. Jamie comes away in awe of Frank.

I wander through the corridors of the Town Centre. The brightly lit department store on the second floor draws me. Inside, I finger through an array of men's, women's, and children's fashions of exceptional quality and decent price. Walking down the corridor past the post office, I'm struck by the strange quality of sound and light in the massive building, completely sheltered from the outside elements, its gleaming warm wood ceilings and walls, recessed pot lights, the sienna ceramic tiled floors. When I enter the main foyer area, the light changes completely. I look up to the skylights letting in the blue light of a bright, cloudless, sunny day. All around is bold ultra modern design that signifies wealth and power and austerity. Everywhere I look — the library, the movie theatre, the swimming pool, curling rink, and bowling alley — everything is first-class. On the main floor, I peek into the well-stocked grocery store; there is a wide selection of fresh, frozen, and non-perishable food at reasonable prices, all company subsidized.

A town administrator fills us in on the details of living in Churchill Falls. Since there are no serviceable roads in or out, the company pays for two trips a year to either St. John's or Montreal, plus any trips for medical or special dental care. The hospital is staffed with a surgeon, a GP, a midwife and a complement of nurses. All housing comes with the major appliances and is company subsidized.

"You don't have to worry about your heating bill," the Administrator chuckles.

"What's available for housing right now?" Jamie asks.

"An apartment, downstairs from the one you were in last night."

"What about a house?"

"Well, as you can probably imagine, houses are harder to get. The housing committee keeps a list and meets whenever one, or a couple, become vacant. Several factors are considered; position, length of service, number of children. But since you're an engineer, it shouldn't take too long — especially if you have more than one child."

We smile, completely seduced by this middle class utopia. This is what university has prepared us for, not Moncton. If Jamie is offered the job, he'll take it in a flash. I had my IUD removed the week after we saw the job ad in the paper; we are sure we'll get one of the houses before long. Churchill Falls has knocked our socks off.

And you, Muriel, you would have been knocked off-kilter by our move to Churchill Falls if you hadn't been so preoccupied with Alexis and Ed splitting up.

"They're going to get a divorce," you hiss into the phone when we called to announce that Jamie got the job. Without skipping a beat to absorb what we're telling you, you just prattle on, fully consumed. *Oh where oh where did I go wrong*. If only Alexis had decided to take a home economics degree, as you had suggested, instead of a B.Sc. Then she wouldn't have to spend all her time in the lab working on her master's, she'd be freed up, at Ed's beck and call now that he's a full-fledged doctor and wants to take vacations to Hawaii

"I don't understand Alexis. Ed's a doctor now. She could have a charge account at Mill's Brothers. Why did she have to do this?"

"It was a power struggle, Muriel," I offer.

"A power struggle?"

"You know. He didn't want to have to arrange his life around her schedule. She didn't want to give up her work."

"But he was her husband."

"And she his wife. Not a member of his staff."

"It's just too much for me. There's sure to be talk."

WHO KNOWS WHAT goes on in the head of anyone else? Jamie and I spared you the not-so-glad tidings of our separation last winter. Not that I think you would have understood, given the extraordinary stasis of your last nine months. It wasn't just the morphine was it? It was the perfection of your still points. Against the doctor's prognosis, you held us in your orbit like you had never been able to hold us before. It was one good trick.

At the time, we only thought to put on a good show. You would have been proud, because in your books that's what counted. When it comes right down to it, if I admit it, we'd been putting on a good show for quite some time.

It comes as quite a shock, Muriel, looking out the windshield of your little Buick as I cross the border into Ontario to realize that somewhere along the way I had started to put on a good show. Not just the disguise of happy homemaker I tried out in Marystown, where at least I had a half-assed idea that things weren't quite right, but something deeper than that. In Churchill Falls, I put on such a good disguise that I fooled myself. I wonder where my disguise started. How did it all begin?

ON OUR FLIGHT from St. John's to Goose Bay on January 10th, 1978, we land in the most godawful blizzard. *Bleak* is too good a word for the place in these conditions. It's hard to believe that during the 1950s this was the second busiest airport in the world. We are shuffled off with a couple of dozen other people to an empty, hastily made-up barracks at the air force base for the night because there is no way our plane is going to get off the ground again. Churchill Falls is snowed in.

There is an eerie silence amongst the passengers, all of whom live in Churchill Falls and are on their way back from Christmas Holidays. In early December, on a Friday night, CFLCO's Lear jet had crashed in Churchill Falls, killing all crew and passengers. Two people, a company executive, and the wife of the airport manager who had been Christmas shopping for her three kids, had survived the impact, but blizzard conditions struck shortly after the crash and they couldn't be found. In daylight, the jet was found two kilometres short of the runway. The crash site was strewn with toys. Jamie and I only know about this from newspaper reports. Our fellow passengers know this in a deep and intimate way. You can see it on their faces.

We are invited along to dinner, but we're kind of wiped out from the move and fall into the lumpy cots like they're a luxury. All through the night I keep waking to a desperate parch in my mouth and throat. The building has been so long abandoned that we have been advised not to drink the water. All I can reach for is a half-empty bottle of Fanta Orange Andrea dragged along on the trip.

The next day we make it into town, landing with that abruptness I will never quite get used to. The approach is flown at minimum speed, the leading edge flaps and slats come out in stages slowing the jet down. The amount of energy the brakes have to absorb is huge. The runway is just legally long enough to handle a 737, so the landing has to be planted on the numbers. The instant the weight is on the wheels the thrust reversers are deployed. Spoilers dump the lift. It's a nose-down-put-on-the-brakes-hard-landing every time. Waiting for our luggage, I hold Andrea, who is almost three, while we are being chatted up by a number of people. All of a sudden a fire alarm stirs the crowd, but nobody makes a move to evacuate the building. All eyes are on me and Andrea. I turn to look behind me and sure enough, the fire alarm is inches away. Our arrival has not gone unnoticed. Someone has to follow up with the obvious gag-line.

"My, what an alarming child you have there."

My face freezes into a smile. This is my introduction to one of the undeniable truths about Churchill Falls: everything you do here will be noticed. There is no place to hide.

We dump our suitcases into one of the old trailers left over from the construction days. This will be our home until our furniture arrives. This may take as long as six weeks, as it has to be trucked across Newfoundland, ferried across the Cabot Straight to Cape Breton, then trucked through the Maritimes and Quebec to Sept-Isle, where it will put in a container on the QNSL railway that runs as far as Esker, about 150 miles west of Churchill Falls.

Jamie rushes off to the office. I bundle up Andrea and myself in the ski-suits we have just bought at the department store, and step out to play to wear off our after-travel, pent-up energy. It is mid-afternoon. The sun is low in the sky and the air is clear and cold, the real deal of -40C, but I am afraid that if I don't brave the weather this very afternoon, I won't be able to face it tomorrow. Our nylon ski-suits make a harsh shushing sound in the frigid air. Our boots squeak and crunch with every step. The pure white snow is dry and granular; we cannot make it form into any shape. In the dead of winter, the relative humidity in Churchill Falls is less than the Sahara Desert. My teeth ache when I try to smile. Andrea's face turns bright red as I watch for telltale white patches. Time seems suspended. I keep checking my watch. Five minutes. Ten minutes. Fifteen. Twenty. Twenty-five. At half-an-hour, I scoop Andrea up and flee inside. We have braved the cold of Labrador. As I pause on the fold-out aluminum steps, a deep, animal kind of fear penetrates my freezing body.

When Andrea is snug in bed that night, Jamie and I sit at the kitchen table talking over the events of the day. The electric heatalators groan and crackle. To me, the thin walls of the trailer seem insubstantial, like tinfoil, hardly capable of protecting us from the arctic air sweeps down over the plateau. We were advised to leave the tap in the kitchen running all night so the pipes, which are protected by heat-tracing, don't freeze.

"It's not like this all the time," Jamie says to comfort me. "This is just a cold snap."

I sip tea and blow my nose. "I can't stand this dryness."

"We'll buy a humidifier when we move into the apartment."

I don't know what I am going to do with myself for six weeks. The town administrator loans us an old black-and-white TV but all we get up here is CBC North. *Another World* is on CTV. I am ashamed of how panicky this withdrawal makes me feel. As if reading my mind Jamie looks around the 10 x 48 trailer and says, "You'll be able to rest up after the move." If *patronizing* had been a word I understood then, I could have thrown it at him but he never could have caught it. He is only trying to relieve me of anxiety the way Donny taught him to relieve you. Regardless, rest is not the cure for what ails me my first night in Churchill Falls.

You know, Muriel, I could never have named it then, but now I think I was suffering from a feeling of acute abandonment. Not abandonment by Jamie. I abandoned myself.

There is a false cure for anxiety caused by feelings of abandonment, and that is to place your faith in something that exists outside of yourself. Whether Jamie intended to fix me, or was suffering from exile himself, he starts to talk about buying a snowmobile, then seamlessly eases into his childhood stories about the outings he and Donny took on park snowmobiles during the Christmas holidays when he came home from King's. And the times you, or you and Alexis joined them, building a shelter and a bonfire, drinking thermoses of hot chocolate, and roasting wieners and marshmallows. I hover on the edge of these perfect childhood stories, a voyeur. Little by little, he weaves a spell that cocoons us against the frigid night. I begin to glow inside and feel cozy. A long time has passed since Jamie and I have been so bound together without intrusions of family or duty, or worry about security and the future. Feeling safe, we stay up most of the night talking.

At one point we veer into the territory of my past and that old heartache of mine from the hockey-playing boyfriend. This reminds Jamie of his hockey playing days and he tells me how he quit the team at King's when he realized he wasn't that good, he was only being used as an enforcer. Only for a moment does our euphoric mood darken when he reaches up to the shoulder that he broke playing rugby and, in a rare moment of candid reflection, he confesses, "They used us you know, got us all hepped up with school spirit and sent us out onto the ice or the fields to get slaughtered. They taught us not to feel anything but pride."

"I thought you loved playing hockey and rugby."

"Yeah. I liked the team spirit and the guys and hanging out, but I didn't like being used and I didn't like being pushed. They didn't care about us as boys, only the strong men we were supposed to become. They didn't give a shit about broken shoulders or broken ankles."

This is when my female mind rushes right past his male revelation, and I think to ask, for the first time since I've met him, this question, "Did anyone ever break your heart?"

"Nope," he says. "You're the only one I was ever in love with."

A flash of cold, like the epidural, branches through me as I think *Everyone gets their heart broken sometime*, and for a split-second I worry I will be the one to break his heart. But the moment Jamie reaches over to kiss me warmly, I simply bask in the part of his statement that declares *You're the only one I was ever in love with*. We tumble into bed, keen to make a baby, and I even begin to hope it will be a boy and make all of Jamie's dreams come true.

From time-to-time, over the years, Jamie will be able somehow to weave this spell that holds us in hope. He will never be happier than when recounting his mythological past. Only in the last couple of years has he failed to draw me into his spell. But back then, fifteen years ago, I could still be lulled.

TWELVE

EARLIER, I WAS thinking that I might stop in Ottawa to tour the new National Gallery. I haven't been here since Jamie took me on a conference almost fifteen years ago. We explored the Parliament Buildings, walked passed 24 Sussex Drive and up to the Governor General's Residence, went to the symphony, wandered around the Sparks Street Mall and whipped through the old National Gallery, then spent hours at the Aviation Museum.

This was the part Jamie liked the best, checking out vintage warplanes, especially the Lancaster bombers. He talked about Donny nonstop. Being in contact with these aircraft brought Jamie closer to his father than anything I had witnessed between them. Jamie felt his father's sadness that he couldn't be a pilot, because of his eye stigmatism; and when he signed up with the RCAF in 1939 he trained as a radar operator, but wasn't good at pattern recognition. Then, with a great deal of pride, he explained how Donny's steady hand and unusual ability to remain calm in the face of extreme danger were the qualities that fit the job of an armourer.

Or gun plumber, as one of the old vets who volunteers tells us. "Those guys had to be on the money. There was zero room for error.

The gun plumbers were always out in the cold and wet. They didn't load in hangers. It was always in the middle of the night, always in the dark. They waited around for the Lancasters to come back from a raid. The bombs were hung mechanically and if one of the shackles jammed up then what they had on their hands was a hung bomb. If the Lancasters had hung ordinance it had to be declared before landing, and they had to land last. It was a big deal. The armament trucks would follow the Lancaster down the runway. The flight crew would be running away from the aircraft and the gun plumbers would be running for it. And they'd be wondering, in what shape was the hung bomb. Was the fuse armed or not. If it's live, it's ready to go *boom*."

The volunteer clapped his hands hard and we jumped.

Which dislodged from Jamie the story of Donny and Rumboldt, Donny's best RCAF buddy who used to run out with him to the aircraft that hadn't dispatched its payload. They were on leave for a couple of days and stopped at a park bench on a sunny afternoon just to let the sunshine touch their faces. A prim little sign PLEASE DO NOT TREAD ON THE GRASS amused Donny and unleashed his youthful attitude: *You can't tell me what to do*. He realized he hadn't set his bare feet on green grass for a dog's age. So off came his boots and socks and he waltzed out to the centre of the green in his bare feet. Out of nowhere a German plane flew across the skies above the park, strafing it. When Donny turned around, Rumboldt and a nanny with a baby in a pram beside him were shot. Donny walked away in his bare feet.

I never missed the fact that Jamie admired his father; he often mentioned the commendation Donny was awarded for single-handedly stopping a riot in one of the campgrounds on the May long weekend in 1970. I just never understood this worship. But now, in remembering Jamie's excited face that day in the Aviation Museum, I think I see how Jamie was looking for some way to measure up to what he considered to be his father's heroism. It only occurs to me right now that one of the things Jamie probably wanted most in life was to be able to walk off in those boots his father had abandoned on the desecrated green.

It's hard to understand these men of ours isn't it, Muriel? They tell us so little. Hells bells, they tell each other so little.

I am thinking now of the time Jamie went duck hunting with Wolfie, his Chesapeake Bay retriever. They went out on the marshes, down past Waterside the first fall we went out together. Jamie would have loved to go hunting with Donny, but he respected the fact that Donny had no interest in hunting since the war, so Jamie went out alone. Do you remember the look on his face when he got back? He was ashen and trembling and full of rage. There was blood all over his sweater. Wolfie wasn't with him.

Jamie threw his shotgun down on the porch steps and told us in a deadly quiet voice, "I had to shoot my dog." The story came out in clotted bursts.

"Wolfie was heeling real good on the trail out to the marsh. His nose on the ground, astride with my left leg. I must have stepped over the trap. But I heard it. I heard it snap and I heard Wolfie yelp and I knew before I even looked back what had happened. The bear trap had him right around the neck and he was down on his side. I couldn't budge it. I looked at Wolfie and Wolfie looked at me and I shot him right through that eye. I couldn't let him suffer.

"That old bastard who lives in the shack down by the marsh laid his trap right on the goddamn path. He's the one I should have shot."

Two thoughts immediately filled my head. The trap could have snapped on Jamie's leg and how did he know for sure Wolfie couldn't be saved?

The next time Jamie had to take such decisive action, I was present. The summer we lived in Marystown we got a kitten for Andrea. Jamie and Andrea and our golden retriever Cubby and the kitten were out in the backyard playing on a Sunday morning while I was making pancakes. I just happened to look out the kitchen window to witness Jamie smash down on the kitten's head with a two-by-four. I screamed while he whipped the kitten away before Andrea could see what happened. He came in the back door with this limp little fur ball in his hands while I looked at him in horror.

"Cubby and the kitten were playing. Cubby got a little rough and broke its neck. It was still alive but jerking in spasms and I couldn't let it suffer, I couldn't let Andrea see what had happened. So I just grabbed what was at hand and put the kitten out of its misery."

Oh god, Muriel. I still get sick to my stomach when I remember that two-by-four coming down on the kitten's head. I had to take Jamie's word for what happened. But there was always this lingering doubt. What if the kitten could have been saved? Shouldn't that be the first thing to do? Bundle it in a blanket and rush off to the vet?

AT THE TIME, I wondered what in life prepares a young man for such swift and decisive action? I was so sure I could never do such a thing. I was so suspicious of men's ability to act with such thorough decisiveness.

I'm not much in the mood for the National Gallery. If I stop now I'll never get to Sudbury before dark.

Sudbury. Now there's a place we managed to avoid in Jamie's rising career. I read in a newspaper recently that Sudbury began life as a company town for the CPR and the big copper and nickel mining boom didn't explode until after the Second World War. When I was growing up, that's where everyone down on their luck in Atlantic Canada seemed to go — there or the military. Now Sudbury boasts the world's largest urban re-greening and rehabilitation scheme.

It's hard to imagine rehabilitating the landscape around Churchill Falls. All the rubble from the building of the earth dams and control structures, but since it was covered with snow most of the year it didn't matter much. Who was there to notice? Even in the summer, the rubble blended into the landscape. Remember the joke we told you: God created the world in six days and on the seventh he threw rocks at Labrador.

I figure he must have abandoned Labrador after he roughed it up. What a godforsaken place. But after we settled into our apartment and made fast friends with the neighbours, we felt as if we had arrived. We had made it. We ordered cross-country and downhill skis and the latest sewing machine. Jamie practiced photography with his new SLR Olympus. We were set.

In this atmosphere we get down to the business of making an heir by following instructions I read in *Chatelaine*: tracking body temperature at ovulation, waiting for it to go up slightly, then we make love with my legs pointing straight up to heaven so that the squiggly little buggers that grow boys get a really good shot at rooting deep down into the well of my baby-making apparatus. We practice this for several months before hitting pay dirt. Now everything seems tickety-boo. What more could we want?

One day, Jamie, comes arrives home with a big second-hand IBM electric typewriter he bought from work for $150, thinking I'd like to learn how to use it in my spare time.

"You might want to be a secretary someday," he suggests.

"What?" I say.

The novelty wears off after the first weekend. What is the good of typing when I can't think of anything to type?

I prefer my new sewing machine and fill the closet with maternity clothes for me and spring outfits for Andrea. Hold off making anything for the new baby, thinking *What if it's a girl*? I keep this thought to myself.

For me everything would be perfect if not for my persistent nausea and fatigue from insomnia. The woman who lives upstairs plays Fleetwood Mac's *Rumors* over and over, all day long. She washes her dishes at midnight, banging her pots and pans around in the kitchen, which, because of the unusual layout of the two-floor apartment, butts right next to our bedroom. I try to have sympathy for this woman and her moods, because she was supposed to be on the Lear jet that crashed before Christmas. At the last minute, she got bumped by a vice-president and lost her seat. So she made her way to the main terminal at Dorval for the EPA flight leaving two hours later, arriving in Churchill Falls like a ghost — her name still on the Lear jet's passenger list. Her best friend was the one who unstrapped herself from the seat at the crash site but froze to death soon after. Now my neighbour walks the floors at night and moans and cries. She threatens my fragile sense of safety. I don't want to live in the presence of such grief while I am pregnant.

When I think of her I can still remember the deepness of her grief, how it seemed to permeate the floors and walls. It reminded me too much of my mother and her dead sisters and the pall we lived under for so long. I am preoccupied with life and procreation, not death. I don't want tragedy breathing down my neck. I grew up with that.

So unlike your grief, Muriel, which was all for yourself and your unlived life. This woman grieved for her friend and the unfairness of a mother taken from her children while she, childless, had been, at the last moment, spared. Perhaps I'm too hard on you. Do you think that's an unfair thing to say? It's so strange, driving alone in this car. Seeing things in a way I've never thought of before.

When spring trickles in — we're talking late May here — I am eager to see the waterfalls in spring run-off. It's about a twenty-minute hike from the road to the falls through a path in the woods. All I am aware of, as I tramp toward them, is being swarmed by blackflies and mosquitoes and stouts, waving my arms madly about my head. Distracted, I begin to care less about the natural wonder of what I am about to see. When we arrive at the viewing spot, I take one desperate glance at the falls in all their glory and flee back to the car. I have almost no visual memory of the falls — only the roar in my ears as I retreat.

I wish I'd prepared myself with more protective clothing. I certainly wish I'd tried again another spring. The Labrador winters were a lot easier to master than the three months of spring and summer when the big snow banks finally melt and it becomes so painfully apparent that there is nothing to do and nowhere to go. Unless you're crazy about blueberry and partridgeberry picking or fishing — apparently some of the best fishing in the world. These can only be considered recreational activities if you don't mind being eaten alive and keeping a sharp lookout for black bears. A lot of people have camps along these roads by the water. Oh yes, lots of rugged recreation free for the taking out and about if you don't mind dousing yourself in fly-dope head-to-toe — not a good idea if you're pregnant.

Every once in a while we get a weekend with a good stiff breeze so we can get out and have a "boil-up," as the Newfoundlanders say, while exploring the dirt roads leading to and from the fore bays and control structures.

I remember one afternoon in particular when we take Andrea out into the bush with friends. The temperature only reaches about 4 or 5 degrees Celsius, which is good, because that means no bugs. The sky is leaden and heavy, the air dense with the smells of forest and wildflowers. On the ground covered in mosses and lichens, we set out a picnic. I lay back on the moss, hands resting on my belly waiting for the baby to kick. Andrea builds a village for the squirrels with her plunder of sticks and stones from the area, which she laboriously decorates with wildflowers. While Jamie cleans up from our feast, I close my eyes and run my palm over the spongy, yet brittle, heads of the caribou moss, and a warm electrical glow spreads through me. I'm content, camped out in the bush with family and friends, and realize that though I don't think about it very often, I am happy to be alive. It's one of those moments when all the ingredients are just right. Jamie and I don't know the names of the shrubs or the flowers, the tapestry of moss and lichens, let alone the names of birds twittering in the background. We are young and smug, contained in our family unit, in many ways the outside world doesn't exist for us at all.

We have surrendered to the idea of living here and are waiting to hear about our application for a house. We get a good laugh from the housing committee. *You have to wait your turn.* Housing squabbles — who gets what and why — is the major feature of town politics. Everyone wants one of the big new houses, but they're at a premium. When a house becomes vacant — usually because someone is leaving town — the housing committee meets to determine who's in line for it. Several factors are officially considered, but how much pressure is exerted by senior managers seems to weigh in the most. There is also the unofficial housing committee, which pretty much comprises the whole town, though divided into various groups with their own agendas. They all make their own lists that hardly ever turn out to be the same as the official one.

Jamie takes this put-down personally. A slap in the face. After all, he's an engineer. Not a technician or a labourer. What about his status? *You have to wait your turn.* (We do not fail to notice there are four women pregnant in our apartment building alone.) To ease demand, the company is bringing in a dozen spanking new 12′ x 65′ trailers.

"Couldn't we move into one of them?" I ask.

Jamie puts his foot down. He doesn't want to live on the edge of town. Engineers don't live in trailers. He doesn't understand that my days and nights are disturbed by our neighbour's anguish. I can't stand it. I can't sleep. But Jamie sleeps like his old man — a log. I badger him to put our name down for one of the trailers. He balks. He likes the apartment. It's driving me crazy.

Six years of marriage and push has come to shove. We move into one of the new house trailers, but Jamie does so reluctantly, silently, thinking I bullied him. He takes refuge in his work.

This is our first real power struggle, Muriel, where I demand and get my way. I often wonder if the trouble was worth it. The trailers aren't ready until the first of October. I am six-and-a-half months pregnant and the move just about does me in. My blood pressure is on the creep again. I am ordered to take it easy, but Jamie is wrapped up in a special project, working twelve or more hours at a time on the night shift. He can't lend much of a hand. I feel all this duty to make our home homey. The doctor's words fall on deaf ears.

Sinkholes have been detected in one of the major dykes. A team of specialists have been called in from San Francisco for this challenge. Nothing like this — grouting sinkholes in an operating damn — has been attempted under such hostile conditions. Jamie's manager, Frank Dudek, knows this will be a big break for Jamie and loans him from the Water Resources Department to work with the big guns. The work proceeds twenty-four hours a day, seven days a week, for over three months. Working on this project is the most exciting thing Jamie has ever done.

I feel left out.

"How come there are sinkholes?" I ask.

"They're caused by the migration of fines within the core."

"Oh. Do you think you'll be getting a day off soon?"

"Not that I can see."

An early cold snap hits in November. My world becomes opaque. With the electric heat turned on full blast and the humidifier running day and night, the aluminum windows and doorframes have iced up not only outside, but inside as well. The closet doors need to be kept open so the clothes don't freeze to the walls. I don't dare complain; after all, I am the one who couldn't stand the noise in the apartment. I don't want to admit it's strange, living over here, isolated from the fast friends we had in the apartment building. Still, I keep telling myself, it's better than trying to sleep while Fleetwood Mac and deep grief filter through the walls.

But restlessness and the duty to take Andrea out to play kick in; I face the cold and venture out, shoving my body, which feels as vast as the Smallwood reservoir, into an old brown mouton coat. As I waddle up the empty, crunchy street I feel sorry for myself and my mind turns to absurdities, like being mistaken for a bear in my brown coat, scarf, and boots and getting shot.

The evenings are so long, I let Andrea stay up late playing hairdresser to keep me company. Such a comfort, her little legs straddling my shoulders as she perches on the back of the couch, brushing and combing my hair, learning how to make braids. I remember doing the same thing with my mother when my stepfather worked away from home.

I stand at the living room window sometime around midnight. The temperature is -42. The wind chill is below imagination. I hear my mother's voice *Don't touch your tongue to metal.* I am tempted to put my tongue on the iced-up window frame. I wonder how Jamie would react if he came through the door in the morning and found me there, stuck. Cheek against the frosted pane. Pregnant belly pressed hard against fake wood paneling.

You only get what you deserve.

That's your voice, Muriel.

I trace the frosted pattern that covers the window with my long fingernails, the crystalline shavings melting like tears on the smock pulled tight across my massive belly. There doesn't seem to be another soul in the world. Christmas is coming. The cards are written and mailed. What about all the presents and the cooking? I haven't been able to manage these duties yet and they press down on me. I breathe two holes onto the windowpane, side by side, scratching in eyelids and eyebrows around them. The cold black night stares back at me. There is nothing to see and nothing to reach out for. The temptation to press my moist lips to the blank eyes is overwhelming.

I leave a note for Jamie to please fill up the humidifier. I can't manage it tonight.

EARLY IN THE morning, I waken to the sound of Jamie trudging back and forth in the hall sloshing pails of water. He comes quietly into our bedroom, sheds his clothes and dives into bed with a shiver. Though I ache for him to do so, he will not roll into my warmth.

I'M OUT OF the trees and farmland now heading north, just past Petawawa. Deep River ahead. Then Mattawa. More blackfly country. What's that song? "The blackfly, the little blackfly ... always the blackflies picking my bones?"

When the engineering wonder of plugging the sinkholes is finally accomplished, Jamie signs up to take a photography class on his first day off in months. I am outraged and can't hold back the tears. I want his attention. I need help with Christmas. I need a lot.

"Jeez, are you going nuts, or something?"

This is an accusation. Not a compassionate query.

I nod my head to all four points of the compass. No. Yes. Maybe. I don't know. You tell me. Do I look nuts? But of course I can't get my mouth open. Jamie is flabbergasted, but he cancels the class and we spend a marvellous day together.

I brood about the sinkholes. Perhaps something like that is starting to happen with me, with us.

My spirits plunge, my blood pressure skyrockets. Next thing I know, I'm in the hospital on the drip again. This time there are no student nurses or interns or residents, I am the one and only patient, with a certified midwife to guide me though induced labour. We take it nice and slow and Caitlin comes wailing into the world three days later.

Another girl. Jamie and I fall for her the moment we clap eyes on her. Love hurdles back into our lives.

When I get home from the hospital with Caitlin, Jamie begrudgingly helps with the Christmas shopping. I fall into a pattern of obsessing about getting it all right and all done on time. Not wanting anyone to think I can't cope. We have to send our parcels out by Express Post and they arrive for Christmas.

Christmas Day, Jamie flops on the couch and snoozes away while I provide the feast and nurse the baby and deal with Andrea, who is wildly out-of-sorts about the presence of a little somebody who needs a lot of attention. She sits under the tree with Caitlin spilling out over her lap and when she thinks nobody is looking, she bops her over the head with a hand puppet of Tigger.

This is the beginning of Andrea acting out. She insists that I lay down in bed with her every evening, refuses to wear the clothes put out for her, demands to have her hair brushed.

"You don't have to feed that baby with your breasts, Mommy," she says, creeping out of bed in her ruffled flannel nightgown, her little round face earnest. "I will get up and feed her with a bottle for you."

"Thank you sweetheart, but this is Mommy's job."

I grit my teeth and let my nipples bleed and run my fingers through Andrea's hair while she sits at my feet watching a movie on television. We now have two stations.

I turn a deaf ear to Jamie's grumbles about wearing the nursing bra to bed, or how my milk lets down every time he lays a hand on me. This is motherhood and if it conflicts with our love life so be it.

THIRTEEN

I WISH I'D gotten off the highway at Petawawa and sat at the park by Allumette Lake for a while, instead of just grabbing a sandwich at the gas station. What did I say to Andrea just last night? I wasn't going to push this drive. I'd arrive when I arrived. So what am I doing today? Pressing on, keeping up the momentum.

What is all this pushing about, anyway?

Jamie pushed our puppy, Cubby; he forced him into the cold water to retrieve the dummy. Poor little thing was just too young to get it; all he wanted to do was play. But Jamie was only interested in pushing him into the water, holding his head under until he took the dummy with a soft mouth. After a while, Cubby became wary. He'd obey, but he didn't warm up to Jamie. He was always running away. Every time he got the chance, he'd be out the door between your legs like a shot and not come back for days.

"I pushed him too hard," Jamie admitted not long ago. "He wasn't ready."

Jamie surprised me with that remark. I didn't think he ruminated. I always thought he spat out his cud along the way. "You think too much," he accused me, more than once. Perhaps I do. Maybe that's my downfall. I get stuck on the highway of the past like it's the Trans-Canada. But how will I know if it's time to get off, or if I should keep on going, if I don't examine the landmarks along the way?

So this pushing. It's about power and control — or the illusion of control. For the first time in my life, I feel like I have some kind of power out here on the open road. Power to think out the past without interruption. To have a long conversation with you, Muriel. How often does this come along in a lifetime?

I keep thinking back to the waterfalls. We've had a stunning aerial photograph of the falls in glorious run-off hanging in all our living rooms since leaving. But it is so silent.

I go over this silence in my mind: the stupendous feat of imagination, engineering, and construction that makes it possible to turn the wonder of the falls off and on, like Christmas lights. This is what is meant by diverted. Dry as a bone. The natural watercourse held back. The flow is controlled, backed up to the intake in order to create a higher head to generate electrical power. It's the biggest withholding project in the world.

Diverted. That's the word. That's what the place was all about: diversion and power.

I think I would have cracked up after the winter in the ice-cave, if that summer we hadn't got the reward Jamie figured we deserved. The anxiety we suffer waiting for the next housing committee meeting is almost unbearable. Jamie has great conviction that our turn is now. He pushes Frank and Frank pushes the housing committee. It doesn't matter who gets in his way, he's bound to get what he wants. On some level, I know that we are definitely not the most deserving. All of our friends who live in the same apartment building we did when we first arrived have all had second children. One of the couples has had a third. They all arrived in Churchill Falls a couple of years before us — and these are just the people we know about. Yet Jamie's conviction is contagious and marries my desire.

Getting a house is all we can talk about. Getting a house is the thing that binds us back together. We mistake this obsession for something real. We mistake it for togetherness.

When I fly down to Alma with the kids, the committee hasn't met yet. I try to get you, Muriel, to understand our anxiety over the matter, but you don't seem interested. All your attention is focused on Alexis and the new man in her life — a younger man who works at the lab. You don't like the sound of it.

"If she and Ed hadn't broken up, none of this would be happening," you say.

I look at you wide-eyed. You never had a good word to say about Ed.

"You should be happy for Alexis. After all those months alone, she has someone to keep her warm at night."

Now you go wide-eyed.

"You don't possibly think they're sleeping together? Do you? There could be talk."

What ever happened to *Boys have needs*? Now we're all grown up, presumably men have needs. Not to mention women of a certain age. Say, women just over thirty. Divorced. Eligible. Exceptionally attractive.

"Are you serious, Muriel? Alexis was married for nine years. I'd be surprised if they weren't sleeping together."

Oh, but you are, aren't you, Muriel? It was one thing to take care of your young son's needs, another to think of your daughter's.

JAMIE GRABS A house for us. The unofficial housing committee clucks. Jamie is shameless. I am so proud of my husband who is working his way up in the world and has worked our way into this house. When one of our friends expresses her opinion that we have butted to the head of the line, I hide behind Jamie's well-developed sense of entitlement, and act as if it had nothing to do with me. I am overjoyed with 2 Jackson Street, one of the crated houses situated on the first street in town. It's a four bedroom with a finished basement I have painted a soft vanilla yellow from top to bottom inside. Everything seems perfect when we move in.

OUT OF THE blue, there is a wedding announcement. The new man in Alexis's life turns out to be working on a post-doc at Dalhousie. Brian's a Rhodes Scholar. Published poet. Plays the guitar. Best of all, his father is a professor at Guelph, in Ontario. Brian's not a medical doctor, but he ain't bad. You treat yourself to a mink stole for the event. Jamie flies to Halifax and a good time is had by the tribe. I've seen the pictures. I am not included. I am the one outraged now. The excuse was that a second ticket was too expensive but nobody said that they wished I could have been there. I hate you, Muriel, for leaving me out.

I resent Jamie for his indifference to my feelings, but I can't say anything because he holds our upcoming trip to Bermuda over my head. The day he leaves for Halifax, I come down with a hellish sore throat.

Two months later, our trip to Bermuda assuages me to an extent. It's the only week in all of our marriage that we ever spend alone on a real holiday. "Our honeymoon," we call it, more than seven years after the fact. I can still feel the jasmine-scented warm, moist air on my skin. The hot pink sand under my feet. The easy sex. We fall in love with the place and vow to come back as often as we can.

I have you to thank for being such a good sport, Muriel, to take on an eleven month old and a five year old for a week, though in the end it was too much for you and Donny. You were frantic when we got back to pick them up.

When we're packing up for Labrador, you rush into our room and thrust a brown velvet skirt and suit-jacket into my hands.

"Here," you say. "You might as well have this. I bought it for Alexis as a going-away outfit, but she said it was snug around the tummy."

Did you know, Muriel? Had you guessed? Alexis had told us the day before, but she hasn't found the courage to tell you.

There could be talk.

I take the suit and skedaddle.

When you and Donny and Agatha troop up for Christmas, I relish this family visit on my own turf and welcome you all into my resplendent domesticity. Knowing how you honour hard work, I am looking to make good in the family books.

Every week, I fit a cloth dampened with lemon-oil over the long nail of my index finger and lovingly trace the curlicues on the antique sideboard; sterilize the kitchen counters with Javex; polish the toaster and canisters; scrub the bathrooms; wash and fold and iron hampers of laundry; vacuum the lamp shades; and, though Jamie often whips out the machine after supper to get rid of the day's rubble, I am responsible for nooks and crannies and suck dust and animal hair and cookie crumbs from every conceivable gathering place. I keep the corners clean, the baseboards gleaming. No blowing in tea cups around here. I take pains with decoration. Make macramé plant hangers, woven lampshades, and, under a light garden, raise rare African violets propagated from single leaves that continuously bloomed little pink and purple flowers.

You arrive to fruit pies and chocolate chip cookies, biscuits and homemade whole-wheat bread. Banana bread. Freshly made yogourt and granola, vegetable beef soup, lasagna, clam chowder. Dozens of muffins. The turkey dinner with summer savory stuffing and deep brown gravy made with my own stock and thickened with flour. No Bisto for this baby. I whip up fluffy omelettes, scramble perfect eggs, and lightly butter toast from edge to edge while it's still hot.

"Can't that Robyn just fry an egg?" says Donny.

"Mmnh, hhmmn," you respond.

We not only have Christmas to celebrate, but Caitlin's baptism. I have been taking confirmation classes from the Anglican priest. I love to get dressed up and go out to sing hymns on Sunday mornings while Andrea attends Sunday school. My private confirmation class is the only intellectual game in town and I am truly thirsty for it.

But what surprises you the most is that the priest's wife has consented to be Caitlin's godmother. Even Agatha is impressed.

Jamie isn't. He thinks church is bullshit. He humours me all the same. Pats himself on the back for cleaning up after bacon and eggs and watching over Caitlin on Sunday mornings.

I'm proudest of my efforts at mothering. You have drummed it into me that the first three years of a child's life are the most important. I need you to know that I have given my daughters the best start possible. Andrea hasn't even begun school, but can read; we practice five days a week with flash cards. She has earned her first swimming and figure skating badges. Caitlin speaks in complete sentences, knows her primary colours, easily rattles off the alphabet, and counts to twenty in both French and English. In her pair of water wings she is fearless. Their bedrooms are treasure houses of Fisher Price toys, books, puzzles, dolls, crayons and coloured pencils, all shiny clean and displayed artfully on bookshelves and dressers. They are lively, but well mannered. I encourage a certain amount of piss and vinegar. I want them to have minds of their own. They keep you and Donny and Agatha on your toes. Every night, after Jamie bathes them and tucks them into bed with a story, I tidy up. They are fast asleep by 7:30 and sleep soundly for a good twelve hours, which leaves plenty of time for us to play bridge without interruption.

This is my work. I work hard. I want credit for my achievement. Acknowledgement. I want you to lavish me with praise. Especially my pies; they could have been in commercials. You compliment me to the hilt on my cooking, and what hearty eaters you old gals are. I take it in. Still, something nags at me. All those dutiful compliments. What did they mean?

I figure I have finally achieved some kind of status in the family. But I am not totally satisfied.

I also want something like my own page in *A Woman's Home Companion to Complaints and Suffering*. But you won't let me in. You keep the upper hand.

You've got nothing to complain about.

Last year when Andrea flew out to visit you before you fell ill and you were baking pies together, she was practicing rolling out the crust, and you stopped her and said, "Not like your mother, sweetheart. Thinner." There's a complaint for you.

IT'S NOT JUST real compliments I want. I want you to see me as I am. What I get for my efforts is an afternoon of complaining about Donny and Agatha when they're out of earshot.

WHILE I'M PUTTING away the pots and pans that Donny left sitting on the draining board the last night of your visit, Agatha creeps into the kitchen for a glass of water to knock back the aspirin for her bad hips. Everyone else is asleep. "I couldn't help overhearing Muriel complaining as I was coming down from my rest this afternoon," she says. "Don't let her make you feel guilty about the life you live. She and Donny had their chances to make some good money and see a bit of the world, but she kept them behind for reasons other than she is willing to talk to you about."

"You mean the move to Whitehorse?"

"Of course. There was a bonus to be made for living in the north, but they were too scared to take the chance."

"What do you mean? I thought they stayed in Alma to keep Jamie and Alexis close to their grandparents."

"Don't believe it for a minute. Muriel didn't have the nerve to re-write her teacher's certification. She was afraid she'd fail and wouldn't be able to teach."

"What about Donny? Did he want to go?"

"It's hard to say. He holds his cards close to his chest. My guess is that he would have enjoyed it. And after all, staying in Fundy prevented him from advancement in the Parks system. No moves, no promotions. That's the way it is. Muriel held him back with her own fears." Agatha swallows her aspirins. A sour look flits across her face. "I don't know why she saw marriage as the salvation of her life. What a shame a woman like her, with a university degree, should bow to the sexual demands of a man when she was quite capable of making a good living on her own."

How long has she been saving that one up? I finish tidying up. And what does she mean *bow to the sexual demands of a man*?

Oh, she was good, wasn't she? Two birds with one stone.

She got me thinking.

I'm going to take a little detour into North Bay, Muriel. Do you feel like a stretch after that insult? I do.

Agatha has always had a way of getting under my skin. I dare-say the feeling is mutual.

With time and distance, I've begun to see how you might have been seeing me. Why you wouldn't give me the acknowledgement I craved. There I stood beside you, six inches taller, slim, beautifully dressed, artfully made-up, everything under control; my big house, my robust daughters, the fancy food, the decoration, the social life, my involvement in the community, the minister's wife being Caitlin's godmother, your son a very able provider. My skilled hands. Even the haircuts on the blessed heads of my husband and daughters. The whole presentation. I was only twenty-five and I had everything you had ever dreamed of. And the confidence. I didn't doubt myself — domestically — for a minute.

As a family, we had such a narrow range of permissible emotions. Emotions and behaviour were all mixed up. The goal was happiness and goodness, as if one equated the other. If one of us felt sad, that was bad and we were expected to snap out of it. There certainly was no tolerance for anger. The ideal was normal. The standard was Perley. *Salt of the earth. Never raised his voice in his life.* Donny. Happy as a clam. So what were we supposed to do about all the inevitable emotions that arose?

We weren't supposed to have them, were we, Muriel? And if we weren't supposed to have them, then we sure as hell weren't permitted to see them in each other, let alone name them and deal with them.

THAT REMARK — NOT *like your mother. Thinner* — still rankles me. Why, Muriel, does this bother me so much? It seems so petty and I hate that about myself.

Not like your Mother. Thinner.

I REMEMBER LISTENING to Agatha climb the stairs one at a time with her glass of water. When I sense the house has settled down completely, I turn off all the lights except the light garden and sit next to my beautiful African Violets. One by one I take them out and gently remove debris from their dense hairy leaves with Caitlin's baby brush. It's the perfect instrument, catching dust and dog and cat hair without scratching the dark green surface. The action is soothing. I snip off the dead flowers and pinch back new growth that suckers from translucent stems. With toothpicks, I gently nudge the leaves to train them into a crown of perfect symmetry. Thinking about Muriel's fears makes me realize how I have become such a careful person since Andrea and Caitlin were born. Everything I do I evaluate in terms of how it will affect them. When I downhill ski I make the turns as slowly as possible, hardly ever falling down, always thinking *What if I broke my arm*? *What if I broke my leg*? *Who would look after everybody*? I can hardly get through a glass of wine. Smoke only a few cigarettes after supper to be sociable with Jamie. Even my choice of clothes has become conservative. I shop at Muriel and Agatha's designer store now. Gone are the days of short skirts. I wonder if this is what I will be like for the rest of my life. I begin to think that something has been lost. As I brush the quilted leaves of my African violets, I begin to see that I have padded myself in safety. My heart plunges.

"I'm so afraid that I will turn out to be just like you, Muriel," I whisper to the brightly coloured blooms.

I switch off the light garden and sit in the dark, listening. There is not a sound to be heard, except a faint hum from the streetlights dotting the concentric streets. When the refrigerator's motor kicks in I scoot up to bed and wedge my chilly feet between Jamie's legs. In a wilderness of hopes and dreams, I lay stiffly beside him trying to hold onto the peaceful brushing sensation of removing dust and debris from the leaves of African violets in the quiet of the night. But deep inside, I detect low voltage thoughts vying for attention. A terrible power and I don't know what it means or when it will surge. When I shift my weight, Jamie senses my presence and slides his hand between my legs. I turn toward him, passive as an African violet, while he strokes my currents into desire, but my response is mechanical. I come with my mouth shut.

THAT SUMMER, JAMIE is seconded to another sinkhole project. He bundles me and the girls onto the plane and sends us off to you with a promise that he'll join us at your place. "Two weeks. Tops."

So here I am stuck with you and Donny with nothing to do but lie around in the backyard or help the girls make a fort and listen to your litany of complaints. This summer the big deal is Alexis's "premature" son. I try to keep a straight face whenever the subject is brought up at the store or over at the restaurant.

"Congratulations, Muriel. I hear you have a new grandson."

"Yes. He was born two months premature."

"Oh my, and how is the little tyke doing?"

"What?"

Honestly, Muriel. Why all the fibs in this day and age?

We spend the days waiting for the tide to be right to go to the beach. I don't have a car. You never offer yours. You never pass the keys to me and say *You drive sweetheart.* I call Jamie every couple of days and he informs me there has been another delay with the project. I read half the nights away. Don't bother making the beds in the morning.

One hot afternoon, when Donny is over at his sister's helping his one-armed brother-in-law get in the winter's wood, you suck in your breath and let out a mean hiss when you hear a car in the driveway.

"Ye gods, I'll bet that's Eileen Black," you yelp, and jump out of your chaise lounge. "Agatha told me she might show up today. Get her into the living room while I run up and change."

I dally a few minutes saying hello, then usher Eileen and her daughter — the certain second cousin you didn't want Jamie fooling around with the summer we met — into the hot stuffy house. When we open the doors to enter the living room, we are hit with an airless wall of heat collected from the sun blasting on the two picture windows. The jungle room. Your cacophony of colours and colonial furniture.

"Hello, Eileen," you say. "What a surprise, you caught me doing the crossword."

What a surprise indeed. How you managed to get out of your bathing suit and into your foundation garments, pantyhose, dress, and bone-white pumps to deposit yourself in the living room with the newspaper folded over your lap is a marvel to me.

We spend the next fifteen minutes trying to find something interesting to say. Finally I excuse myself to put Caitlin down for a nap and release Andrea back to her fort in the yard. You, you old sourpuss, give me a dirty look, but I don't intend to make the child sit next to you all afternoon.

I make a pot of tea and put out a few cookies. I'm puzzled that you don't take the opportunity to escape to the kitchen and give me a hand, but you don't look like you're going to budge. Then it occurs to me that you may not want to prolong the visit. I begin to feel uneasy.

After the tea, we sputter into a social sinkhole. I plunge in with the news that you had your very first swim out in the bay the day before. In fact that's where we'd be now if Eileen and the certain second cousin had not come a-knocking. We were waiting for the tide to warm itself coming back in over the hot mud flats.

"Swim!" Eileen gasps. "Wellwellwell." She looks at your thighs like she can see right through your layers of clothing. You shift your weight. Give me a look.

"When on earth did you learn to swim?"

"Last winter Agatha and I took our very first swimming lessons up in Moncton."

"What in the world possessed you to take swimming lessons at your age? I never heard tell of such a thing."

"I think it's wonderful," I say, and really mean it. "It's something you've wanted to do all your life, isn't it, Muriel?"

"Well, yes," you say. "Mother never let me learn to swim."

"Your mother never let you learn how to swim," Eileen mocks and slides a look over at her daughter. "Imagine."

Something is going on that I don't understand. I gather up the tea things and take them to the kitchen. And then it hits me. All of a sudden I see how ridiculous it is to be over sixty years old and still blame your mother for never letting you do something. Just when does a woman take responsibility for herself? I wonder. When she leaves home, turns 21, gets a job, gets married, has a baby? Becomes a grandmother. And then I wonder if you ever really left home, or if you just shifted yourself down the street with your husband and children.

"It seems a shame Jamie has to fend for himself while you're here enjoying the beach," Eileen says when I go back into the living room.

"I filled the freezer before I left. Almost all of the wives and kids in Churchill Falls go away for the summer. It's not healthy up there. The kids develop swollen glands from all the black fly bites. If we want any summer at all, we have to go away. We miss him, too, you know."

"Just thank your lucky stars it isn't the war," you say. "Some children didn't see their fathers for years."

Uh-oh. The War. I guess the Depression can't be far behind.

"Oh my yes," Eileen says. "And during the Depression, many men had to go away to work."

You and Eileen bond in your shared memories of the great sacrifices, but it doesn't last. We cross and uncross our legs until a length of silence reaches some cosmic moment that cues Eileen and the certain-second-cousin that the visit is over. We all stand up except you.

"You see them out Robyn, dear."

I know there are two stories you're going to tell me as soon as we're alone. The sad first cousin and the mean mother.

Poor Eileen, you will begin. *You know her husband committed suicide when the children were still small. Not long after, their daughter climbed through a window after school to get the homework assignment she forgot, and as she was getting back out through the window it slammed down breaking her neck.* Then she'll lower her voice to say, *The father drank*, and she'll tell me the son died of an overdose in the bathtub, when he was only seventeen. So I will know that Eileen is a failure. She somehow deserved all these sorrows. She lacked control as a wife and was not a dutiful mother.

As I brace for these stories, I'm surprised to find you still pinned to your chair when I enter the living room. You have a peculiar look on your face and don't say a word until I slump onto the couch beside your chair. Then you start to giggle and pull up your skirt. Your queen size hose are slung like a half-cooked donut around your knees. You lean forward so the top of your dress falls open to reveal your bathing suit.

Honestly Muriel, you slay me in that moment. We laugh so hard. Things have been so good between us since your visit at Christmas.

"Don't Robyn, don't," you sputter. "I have to go to the bathroom. Give me a hand, I've kept myself in this position so long I can't move."

You hold out your hand and I clasp it firmly to pull you up. Your body quakes into an upright position, almost throwing me off balance. You duck-foot it to the bathroom then return, pantyhose in hand. Again, we fall into a ball of laughter on the couch. Bouncing off each other, wiping tears away with scratchy paper napkins.

"Poor Eileen," you start, right on cue.

I look at you, but all I can see is the deep crevice and little bump on Eileen Black's lower lip.

"Let's go to the beach now," I say to get you off track.

"We can't go swimming now," you retort. "I'll have to get Donny's dinner ready. Why did they have to come here today of all days. Why did those women have to spoil our fun?"

I always wondered why Eileen bothered to come back. Now I sense that Eileen's summer visits were a stoic insistence on showing her presence in a family that had come to disregard her. Year after year, she stopped by with one or both of her daughters to claim familial territory. I imagine these shows were no treat for her, either. Why brave such smouldering contempt except to say *I'm still here*.

It's ironic, though, isn't it Muriel? The way Eileen came back into those last few months of your life. What did it feel like? Bedridden, knowing that the cousin you shunned and mocked all those years had swooped down and fetched away the man who had come along with the promise of a happy ending. It must have felt like having your head held under water. That smile of yours put well and truly in its place.

That afternoon was the end of our easy-going summer. Later that evening, Agatha dropped in for supper and just happened to mention, right at the table, that Ed had called to give her his new telephone number.

"Don't forget to remind Jamie to give him a call when he gets here," she says, examining the tea leaves in the bottom of her cup. "He'd like to get together."

Up your back comes and you are onto me the minute Agatha leaves the house with a mouthful of *How could you* and *How dare he* and *I worked so hard all of my life I sacrificed the best years of my life* and *Oh why oh why do you and Jamie want to have anything to do with that man?* You don't dare say anything about the fact that it's obvious Agatha still has contact with him too.

I try to tell you I am not in the business of letting Jamie do anything. But if there's one thing I've learned in this house, it's that all moral responsibility rests with the wife. It seems that men cannot be expected to do what's right.

You hole up in your bedroom and I get on the phone.

"Jamie, I want to come home. Now."

"Hold on. Hold on. Hold on," he says. "I'll be there in a few days. Don't worry about Mom, she'll get over it. Anyway, Ed's a great guy."

My mouth is speechless but my mind is furious. I know, I know. Jamie spent the best summer of his life with that guy. It doesn't matter that Ed fucked around on his sister or made unreasonable demands on her time.

"What's wrong with Grandma?" Andrea asks when you won't come out of your room the next day.

"She's sick. You have to be quiet."

Andrea and Caitlin are quiet as church mice. We have several hot sunny days when the tide is just right, coming back in the afternoon over the baking mud flats and scorching sand and gravel. I walk miles back and forth with the kids, turning over big rocks to see what scampers beneath, collecting broken bits of shells, writing our names in the sand, building sand castles. When the idea to find the exact moment when the tide turns strays into my head, it seems like something I remember from a movie or a book. I try to enjoy the here and now, slipping and sliding over gooey red mud. Mud larking, there's nothing like it. We experience the three best days in a row in years when all the conditions are just right on the Alma Beach. You missed them, Muriel.

YOU ONLY COME out of your room long enough to arrange for a hitch to get put on the car because Jamie had mentioned on the phone that we could go camping on PEI. When he does arrive, ten days after the initial blow-up, the travel trailer and car are at our disposal. You come out to give a muffled hello and pass over the keys. We take off to PEI for three days. When we come back, you're almost back to normal. But the weather has cooled and the tide is all wrong for swimming.

"See?" Jamie says. "I told you she'd be back to her old self in no time. These things always pass."

"Waiting for you to get here was awful. I could hardly stand it."

"Yeah, but if I'd told you how long I was going to be working on the sinkholes, you wouldn't have stayed and we wouldn't have had such a good time on PEI."

"You mean you knew from the beginning how long you were going to be?"

"Well, yeah. But it all worked out. Right?"

"How long did you know?"

"Oh I knew the schedule before you even left."

Honest to god, Muriel, I could have killed him. And what about you? He didn't even question that you might not want, or be up to me and the girls hanging around for five weeks. He just played it out the way he saw fit.

These things always pass.

I don't think that's true. I think *these things* simply fester. Nothing passes unless we bring it out into the day of light. In our minds, somebody has to be right and somebody has to be wrong.

So what was wrong with me? How come I could figure out how silly it is for you to still be blaming your mother for your miserable life, but I could not ask myself if I took responsibility for my own life? Why didn't I just get the hell out when I knew things were going downhill? Was it just my fear of putting out the bucks and renting a car and a cabin somewhere else? No. I didn't think about that. I was too busy pondering you. I thought everything was okay with me. I thought my life and my choices were fine. And why wouldn't I?

WE ARRIVE BACK in Churchill Falls with seventeen pieces of baggage because we all went on a little spending spree to help clear the air after the camping on PEI. We've bought new duds for everyone, a tea table and kitchen cabinet from IKEA, and a set of Royal Doulton earthenware dishes.

I've got nothing to complain about.

But since getting back, I've been slouching around, feeling enervated and crampy. My periods, never easy, have been getting heavier and heavier. They go on forever and all I want to do is crawl into bed and stay there with the heaves and waves of intense pain wrenching through me.

I lose interest in the house. And lose interest in sex.

I like it. Just not as often as before. My body is in demand. I'm constantly being handled: four little sticky ones all day long, and two big sweaty ones at night. I ask Andrea to mind Caitlin in the mornings so I can take a shower after Jamie leaves for work instead of in the evening when the girls go to bed. I do this, because Jamie always interprets my bathing ritual as a signal for sex. Now, more often than not, I simply want to get into bed and go to sleep. I want the light out by ten but Jamie wants to read so we make a compromise: he can read as long as he rubs or scratches my back. All that fall and winter, he reads and rubs through all three volumes of *The Gulag Archipelago* as I lay in a half-sleep, devoid of dreams.

We argue about birth control. I don't like being on the pill. I'm convinced that it makes all my symptoms worse. So I go off it and insist that Jamie take some responsibility. He digs in his heels about using rubbers.

"It doesn't feel right," he complains.

"Feels all right to me." I don't know what all the fuss is about. Anyway, they're a lot less messy if you ask me, and no one gets stuck in the wet spot.

"I shouldn't have to go through this shit. I'm a married man."

I hold out. It's up to him. He lets the supply run out. Then one night in complete frustration whips out of bed around 11 pm and roars down to the Staff Club, arriving home with a stash.

But he has one more move in mind.

"Let's have another baby."

The minute he makes the suggestion it's as if an army of archers has been lying dormant in my head and they all flash up at once, fully armed. No way. No more thermometers and jack-knife legs for me. I'm out of the baby-making business.

"Over my dead body," I snap, surprising us both.

When I relate this to the doctor, what I say is, "I feel like if I have another baby I will just die."

"You're not far off the mark I'm afraid, my dear," he responds. "Two pregnancies with toxemia is not a good sign. I think you should consider a tubal ligation. It's an easy procedure; I could do it right here sometime within the next month. You go home and talk it over with Jamie. Then make an appointment for a check-up before we go ahead."

Jamie takes the news stone-faced. "If that's what Dr. Price says, that's what he says. Who am I to argue?"

I figure he has a she-cock, anyway. I figure we'd have a string of girls and Jamie would always want to go for the boy, again and again. I see no end in sight. All of a sudden I have a whole new understanding of what *the sexual demands of a man* could mean. It isn't just giving in to the pleasure that can hold you back; it's the frequency, the progeny.

"Listen," Jamie says, trying again. "We'll hire a housekeeper and a nurse if we have to. You can stay in bed the whole time. I'm sure everything would be okay. Ask Dr. Price. You know I've always dreamt that I'd have a son to name after my father."

"No Jamie. I don't want to go through another pregnancy. I don't want another baby. I want to get on with *my* life."

As soon as I say the words I know they are true. My feelings are as true as Jamie's desire to carry on the family name. There's a number that does a little turn in my head: *If it's so important to carry on the family name, then it only makes sense for your sister to go ahead and do it. Alexis can carry on the family name. You're all so goddamn clannish anyway. Ask that new husband of hers if he wouldn't mind giving up his name. After all, you don't mind asking me to give up my life.* I am stunned by the ferocity of my emotions. But I keep my mouth shut.

When I proceed with the check-up, I yelp when Dr. Price probes my ovaries. "Oh dear. How have your periods been since you had Caitlin?"

"Let's just say I bloat like the fore bay and flood like the falls during run-off. I lose a couple of days to cramps and swampiness."

"Do you experience ovarian pain at mid-month?"

"Yeah. I get a lot of twinges. Enough to know what's going on."

"Well, I'm afraid that tubal ligations often turn out to be more trouble than they're worth in situations like yours. For some reason, there is often severe ovarian pain. We usually end up doing a hysterectomy. I suggest you consider that option and save yourself a lot of fuss and bother. I'll make an appointment for you in St. John's. In the meantime, I suggest you discuss this further with Jamie. If he has any questions tell him to give me a call."

WHEN I FLY out to St. John's, the surgeon asks a question that knocks me off my feet. "Will your husband still think of you as a woman if you don't bleed every month?"

"What?"

What kind of a fool question is this? How the hell else could Jamie think of me? So help me god I am beginning to think that all men are cracked. I am a woman. What else could I be? I fly back to Churchill Falls with my mind set like a bear-trap in the wrong place.

The phone calls start from Muriel. Don't do it! From Agatha. Don't do it! All the way from Edmonton, where Alexis has moved with her new husband. Don't do it! Jamie has squealed on me. What business of theirs is this? I haven't even informed my own mother. I don't know what all the fuss is about. I'm not getting a lobotomy. I'm going to keep my ovaries. I'm still going to experience the whole wide range of emotions that go with the full menstrual cycle; I'll still get bitchy and break out in the odd pimple,

I'm just not going to flood the place anymore, I'm not going to have the full baby-making apparatus deal anymore. So what? It's my body, not theirs.

When you whisper, "You'll get fat, you'll change," to me over the phone, I don't trust you.

"On the contrary," I snip. "I plan to lose weight. Major surgery has to be more efficient than counting 1000 calories a day and starving to keep myself trim. I'll be on drugs. It'll make a nice change."

"Don't do it."

What did you know, Muriel? You knew something. I didn't pay attention. I didn't trust you. But it wasn't me anyway, was it? You saw the threat to the marriage.

When Jamie drapes himself on the edge of the couch one night and says, "You don't have to do this, I'll get a vasectomy," I know you have called him at work behind my back. In my head, I hear the wedding march playing backwards. The words plodded out of his mouth. Good god, Muriel, he wouldn't even consider getting the dog fixed. His body is perched on the couch beside me in a way that makes me think of a hung bomb. And what, I wonder, if in his old age, he turns out to be a blamer, like you?

"That's okay, Honey. You don't have to worry. I haven't changed my mind. I'm still going to go through with it."

My arse doesn't fall off.

That's what the surgeon in St. John's says, shaking my big toe a few days after I surface from a Demerol stupor and the great waves of pain are subsiding. "Well your arse didn't fall off did it, my dear?"

"Yes, my son, and *tink* of all the money I'll save on pads and tampons," I retort back to the surgeon, who pretends to be shocked.

The procedure isn't as easy or painless as I thought, flying down to St. John's by myself, going under the knife. I do lose five pounds.

I also lose something else. My innocence about how I think Jamie regards me. When he calls just hours after I come out of the OR he assures me that everything is fine at home, that the housekeeper, a young woman in her late teens, is working out. "In fact," he says, "she gets everything done in no time. Even the vacuuming. I haven't had to touch the thing since you left." I am cut to the quick. That remark keeps surfacing throughout my recovery.

WHEN JAMIE PICKS me up at the airport, the first thing he says is that he's sorry he has to get back to work right away. At first I think he's being caring about me, then with a nudge and a wink, I understand that what he's saying is that he's horny, and expects, after a ten-day absence, for me to be horny too. *What do you think I've been through*? I want to scream. Instead, I very calmly announce, "Jamie, it's like having a baby. You have to wait six weeks."

"Get serious. We never waited six weeks."

You just wait, Mister.

When I walk into the house and Jamie proudly shows me how well they have done in my absence, I want to sit down and cry. Oh sure, things are neat and tidy. But the dirt! The cookie crumbs and the dog hair hugging the dusty moulding, the dust rings around the ornaments. Couldn't the girl lift anything? The stains on the kitchen counters. The smelly dishrag. It didn't look as if it had had a good rinsing or squeeze since the minute I left. And Andrea and Caitlin, they look adorable, but how can I put it? They looked rumpled. Where are all the loving touches? That's when I realize Jamie doesn't have one shred of an idea what I do with my time. He does not appreciate the details of keeping a good home. He does not appreciate me. What does he think I do all day, I wonder? But not for long. I get it. He doesn't think I do much of anything.

During my recovery, I nag him about small things, like always putting the scrambled egg spatula in the dishwasher when I have told him a thousand times that the dishwasher bakes egg to a hardness that is permanent.

"Why the hell can't you remember anything I say?" I shout at him, hounding him up the stairs. He turns on me.

"Because," he spits through his teeth, "you never have anything important to say."

FOURTEEN

IT'S DARK. I'M tired. Sturgeon Falls is behind me and Sudbury is not far ahead. Good old Sudbury, known affectionately as the arse-hole of Canada, home of the world's tallest smokestack.

The Biggest. The Tallest. The State of the Art.

Boys Have Needs. Men Have Needs.

There's a picture in my head that my stepfather once took on top of the intake structure the last November we lived in Churchill Falls. He captured the starkness of the place with his unerring eye. On the right of the photograph your eye zooms down the concrete platform, covered in patches of snow, and, on the left, your eye is slowed down along the same view by concrete huts that jut up at even intervals, like checkpoints. About a third of the way up the picture there's a solid mound of rocky hill, with dustings of snow in the gouges and on the outcroppings. A few scraggy black spruce stick up like a week of stubble. The sky above the mound is blanched to a kind of nothingness. The whole set-up looks like the still from a war movie. All that's missing is the firing squad.

This is the place where Jamie and I learned the ways of the world. He summed it up for Andrea and Caitlin at the supper table this winter, just a week or two before I asked him to leave. "This is how you get a big job done," he said. "You tell people what they want to hear and then you do what you have to do."

This line lives in my head like an airplane advertising banner.

Here's another one: "Do you need to see a shrink?"

That's Jamie's response to me for whatever.

Do you need a shrink? It isn't a remark made out of concern. It's an accusation. My problem is that I don't live in the *real world*. The real world to Jamie being his work world. The world of quantifiable and measurable facts: over forty miles of earth dams and dykes that required twenty-six million cubic yards of sand, gravel, rock spalls, riprap, and processed sand and gravel. The real world is where you get a monthly salary. Company towns like Churchill Falls are not designed with jobs for women in mind. Women are expected to volunteer. We make the social organizations run smoothly. We're expected to keep the men happy — not the other way around — so they don't crack up at some critical moment when billions of cubic metres of water are rushing down the penstocks into the giant turbines.

By our fourth autumn in Churchill Falls, I've had my turn as social convenor of the ski club; I am the recording secretary on the church board; treasurer of the figure skating club; vice-president of the home and school association. And the only woman who worked on a committee that managed to convince the chairman of the board not to deliver our company-funded school into the hands of the provincial government.

But this is not the *real world*, the world of women and children. We come as strangers to this land of caribou moss, black spruce and bogs, partridgeberries and lichen-covered rocks. We become a congregation who work for each other's salvation. We confess our sins and listen to the sins of others. We like each other. We are like each other. We are the wives of technicians and managers, engineers and accountants, teachers and millwrights. We are mothers and craftswomen. We sew and knit and bake. We bundle the kids up and take them to the pool early in the mornings. We congregate for coffee and tea, supervising the socialization of our children. We gossip. Argue. Plan future events and complain about the grocery store and who got what house. We are an underground powerhouse.

"You've got it made," Jamie says, belittling my life. "I'd like to have the Life of Riley, too. Go for a swim in the mornings and sit around having coffee, gossiping all day."

This is bearable because we women have each other. So we can complain about our complaining husbands. So we say, "Do you want to have the Life of Riley with or without children?" And then we titter about the poor things giving birth.

Beyond the jokes, however, I begin to wonder. If I don't live in the real world, where do I live? Buried beneath the real world? The unquantifiable world of babies sucking cracked and bleeding nipples? The immeasurable world of a good hard cock working its magic deep inside me? My world is my body and it does not measure up. Being constantly reminded that I do not live in the real world, I found my unquantifiable and immeasurable world lacking.

You thought I had nothing to complain about, Muriel, but it's not so smart to design a company town with all the amenities and not figure out that the women will need more to do than volunteer and arts and crafts and fit into one of the morning coffee clacks. The only jobs for women are a few positions for teachers, nurses, secretaries, waitresses, and store clerks. All this power generated here — more than thirty-four-and-a-half-million kilowatt-hours per year — and there is only one important job for a woman, the bank manager. She just happens to be the wife of one of the electrical superintendents.

So, when one of the two part-time tour guides leaves town with her husband, I take the job for a few months. But it's not a real job though. I'm not in charge of anything critical or dangerous. I don't float down the penstocks in a raft looking for cracks or check out all the control structures below water.

I've got nothing interesting to say, or interesting to do.

But even Jamie wants out. He claims he's getting bored. In part, looking back, I think this has to do with Frank Dudek dying of a stroke the year before. Jamie has nobody to look up to anymore. Nobody to believe in or emulate. So after three and a half years working in the land god threw rocks at, Jamie wants to get out, too. I push for Halifax, but Jamie says there's no work for someone like him there and we don't have enough money saved up yet.

I say all this, Muriel, as if for ninety percent of the time we don't live our lives each day as a normal happy family in our Enchanted Kingdom in the north. When there are no special projects on the go, Jamie leaves for work at 7:45 am, comes home for lunch at noon, and is home again by 5:10 pm. As a family, we spend a lot of time together. It's all very cozy and satisfying in that way. Ideal for our two young children. Yet there's this hunger we both experience.

But there's something harder to talk about. We started hanging out with a different crowd for the odd party. It used to take me all night to down the better part of a beer; but, at one of the dos at McPharland House, I discover an affinity for Grand Marnier — such an elegant name, such sweet nectar. You wouldn't call it booze. Still, I do manage to swill it back from time-to-time. How to talk about the night, down at the ski lodge, when Jamie pulls back the collar of my turtleneck and tosses a glass of scotch down my back because he wants to go home and I say, "Fuck off Jamie, I'm having a dance with Bob." Or how to explain Jamie pissed to the gills at a fondue party crawling around on his hands and knees asking where the wife of his best friend is. The same woman who is having tea with me late one afternoon when Jamie walks in and when he sees her he gets the same look on his face that he had when I met him at the altar. This look strikes me with fear. We don't talk about this. No one does. The place is too small.

In silence, we build up a liquor cabinet just like most of the other folks in town and congratulate ourselves on our new-found sophistication.

What happened to the girl who sat in your kitchen and declared she would dump all the alcohol in the world into the ocean, if she could?

She gave in to the ways of the world. Every once in a while, I'd jump into the ocean for a bottle and swim to the bottom of the sea. All I had to do was follow Jamie's bubbles.

Then, out of the blue, one of the consultants tells us he'll be leaving soon for a big coal-mining job in British Columbia. Perhaps Jamie would be interested. It's a billion-dollar megaproject. Jamie has an in. The construction manager is someone we already know, an operations manager who left here a couple of years ago. I often had tea with his wife, a woman fifteen years older. I looked up to her. We have connections: we went to the same high school back in New Brunswick. I know her nieces. Agatha taught her at teacher's college and remembers her vividly. All these connections I think mean something.

"Ground hasn't even been broken yet," the consultant says, as if Jamie needs further lures.

This is when he really lights up.

A man has needs. He needs to strut his stuff with the big boys on a big construction job with the world's biggest equipment and work long hard hours to make a lot of money to buy a house for his wife and kids. He needs to go places and do things and above all, be mortgage-free.

And a wife needs...

Trouble is, I don't know what I need. I've been dammed-up so long and too isolated to know. My ideas about going back to school have become vague. I don't remember what I liked about it. Suddenly, it seems more important to have an adventure. I think about British Columbia in a dreamy, wishful way. Beautiful British Columbia. Who wouldn't want to live there?

So this thing, this obsession that Jamie and I shared about getting a house becomes activated again. He flies out to Vancouver in September for an interview. It's all good; they're going to make him an offer. Then there's a hiring freeze; the financials aren't in place. We get put on hold. We obsess. We think that if we don't get out of Churchill Falls soon, we will just die. We can't tell anybody, because if it falls through Jamie needs to stay here. He needs the job. We need the job. So we share this dream and we go round and round with it. It brings us closer together. We have a common goal. To get out and far away. The adventure of a lifetime.

One chilly morning in November, almost four years to the day that Jamie and I flew up to Churchill Falls for his interview, we buzz into Moncton for a couple of hours on the company's King Air. Our mission: to break the news to you and Donny that in all likelihood, we will be moving all the way across the continent sometime early in the New Year. When Jamie broaches the subject, you are deftly angling the heel of your fork to pick up the last few crumbs of strawberry rhubarb piecrust floating in melted ice cream. The light goes out of your eyes. You had been so excited to whip up to Moncton just to have lunch with us. Everyone in Alma would know by the next day. You even have to tell the waitress, a stout woman in her mid-fifties. "This is my son and his wife. They flew all the way from Labrador in a private jet just to have lunch with us."

"Well isn't that grand. Just imagine. He must be very important." The waitress plays up to your ego with obvious finesse. Her mouth says one thing, but her body says another; she walks away to get the bill, her backside swaying with indifference. She's heard it all before.

"The King Air isn't a jet, Mom," Jamie says earnestly. "It's a jet assisted prop."

"Well I'm sure she wouldn't know the difference," you reply, a little miffed.

Donny is sitting back, his mind more on getting the waitress's attention to make sure she gives the bill to him, as per usual. He only snaps to when the word *moving* is brought up. "Where are you going, boy?"

"British Columbia. A couple of the guys who used to work in Churchill Falls have gone out there on a megaproject. They put my name in. Dad, it's going to be the biggest open pit coalmine in the world and I'll be able to get in on this one from scratch. It's my big chance."

"Well, good show," Donny says.

"But you're all set where you are," you say. "I don't see why you have to go so far away."

"They're going to build two mines, a whole new town, a rail spur, and a port facility. It's going to come in at over a billion dollars. A billion dollars, imagine that Dad. You can come out and see it too."

"You know Daddy doesn't like to travel so far."

Somehow I don't think Donny is taking it all in, he seems distracted. As he and Jamie get into a tug-of-war over the bill, you lean over to me and say, "Come to the washroom with me, dear."

"Talk to Jamie," you demand as we apply fresh lipstick. "I'm sure he's making a big mistake with this job thing."

"To tell you the truth Muriel, we're both pretty fired up about it."

"But I thought you wanted to move back to Halifax."

"There aren't any jobs right now."

"But why move at all. Perhaps I'm just a stupid old woman, but I don't understand. Jamie has a secure job. You have everything here. I don't see what you have to complain about."

Remember *Boys have needs*? I'm thinking. Remember how you disinherited us when we first moved away. Remember?

"Men have needs," I say, trying it on, but all I get is a blank stare. "Jamie needs a bigger challenge. He's bored. All the interesting projects have been all wrapped up here."

"Talk some sense into him."

"How can I? I'm bored too. There's a whole world out there."

"But you don't even have to work."

"We're young; it's too soon to throw in the towel for security."

"You wouldn't say that if you'd lived through the Great Depression or the war."

"Where's Agatha today?" I ask to distract you.

"I didn't tell her you were coming. Sometimes Donny and I need to do a few things on our own."

"Of course. I understand." I am always ready to support you when I can.

"I hardly saw her all summer when that old roommate of hers was visiting."

And now I really understand. This is payback time. *Girls will be girls.*

While we're getting our coats on, you throw yourself at Jamie and cry, "Oh, you're off so soon. By the time we get home, I'll hardly be able to believe you were even here. Can't you stay the night?"

"Oh Mom, I told you on the phone, the King Air's only going to be here for a couple of hours while they pick up a part for one of the helicopters. We were just lucky there were empty seats. But this was fun, wasn't it?"

"Yes." Your eyes start to mist up. "We have to make the best of what little time we get together. Especially now."

Jamie shifts his weight to the leg that toes in. He never liked to play the bad guy. "Well why don't you and Dad come up for Christmas again?" he suggests.

"Really? Again? We were there just last year. You're sure it wouldn't be too much?"

"We'd love you to come. Wouldn't we, honey?"

"Of course," I say, smearing a little lipstick across my front teeth as I smile. "What could be more perfect?"

And you came. Do you remember how Donny's eyes appear spring-loaded when he lays them on our fully stocked liquor cabinet, taking up the whole top shelf of the pantry cupboard, in particular, the forty-ouncer of Crown Royal. I wondered about the wisdom of this display, but Jamie figures it won't be a problem. His father's too old to get into trouble now.

So with no fuss at all, Donny and Jamie have their rye and ginger every evening before supper. You are so obviously relieved, you take a short one with them on Christmas Day. I sip a glass of white wine as I tend the gravy. This is just like a movie, you say to me, enjoying what you consider the height of refinement. Your face always changed when you thought you were getting what you deserved out of life.

When a storm blows in on the 27th, we're housebound; you suggest we play bridge. I love bridge, but I hate being Donny's partner; he's such a loose cannon in the bidding department, he always takes us down. You're an over-cautious bidder, but Jamie plays by the seat of his pants and takes you into bidding heights you have never dreamed. "Oh Jamie, we're going to go down," you squeal; but, more often than not, you make your bid and then some. Then you gloat. The mother and son powerhouse. I can't stand it. I'd rather be playing with Agatha. At least she plays by rules I understand. The Blackwood Convention is a cinch compared to whatever you and Jamie have going on.

But Agatha's not here. You've left her out of the family visit.

"She must have known when she stayed an old maid that she'd be spending holidays by herself," you'd said over the phone when we were making arrangements. "And don't you remember? You said Donny and I don't have to do everything with her."

I meant things like going to the mall. I never imagined you'd be so spiteful as to leave her out of the biggest holiday of the year. I feel shitty.

I pack the girls off next door. Jamie gets out the Crown Royal around four.

"Just one now, Daddy," you warn.

"Oh, sweetheart," Donny croons, giving you a wink.

When the girls trundle back at five o'clock, I make a salad and get the potatoes going, while they pin you down in the living room showing off the paintings they've made. Jamie clears away the card table and Donny comes nosing around in the kitchen. He seems restless.

"Hungry, Donny?"

"A little peckish," he says. I don't think food is on his mind. He darts back to the living room, leaving behind an air of aimlessness. I don't like it. When Jamie opens a second bottle of wine at supper, Donny actually smacks his lips. Half his tourtière is still on his plate and he has barely touched his potatoes. I notice that his w's are getting thick and his s's stretched out. He reaches for the bottle and slops some into his glass. "Well, boy," he starts, then stops, his mouth moving up and down silently as he struggles for words. Then he scrapes his chair back and puts his hand on his thigh with his elbow sticking out. His face darkens. "Well, boy," he starts again. "I hope you're up to this big project you're talking up. It's all very well to have a grand education and such, but what something really comes down to is experience. Experience counts in the end. I hope you're up to it."

All cutting and chewing comes to a stunned halt.

"Bath time," I announce, and whip the girls away.

"Daddy, don't start in," you warn again.

Donny laughs. "Just kidding, boy, just kidding. You know your old man." He doesn't look at you.

"Yeah, Dad. I know," Jamie doesn't look like he knows anything; the wind has gone out of his sails. "I'll do the girls, Robyn. You can get the tea on."

You follow Jamie upstairs. "I'll give you a hand, sweetheart."

"Just a second," I say, running down to the basement. "I've got to get some pyjamas out of the dryer." When I get back up, Donny has his gob stuck in my pantry.

"What do you think you're doing?" I bark.

Donny backs out, topping up his glass. "Just getting a taste more of that delicious wine."

I look at the bottle. "That's port!"

"I don't mind."

"It cost thirty-five bucks." I snatch it away from him. "Go and sit down while I get dessert."

"Someone's in a mood," he says under his breath as he slinks back to the table.

You come into the kitchen wringing your hands. "Jamie's just tucking Andrea and Caitlin in. Where's Donny?"

I nod toward the dining room. "Hand cream?" Helplessly I squeezed a dollop into your outstretched hands. We peek into the dining room to find Donny in a chair, his back to us, elbow on the table, hand holding his head up. There doesn't seem to be a breath coming from his body.

"Donny," you hiss. "Are you awake?"

Just then, Jamie enters by the hall door and gives his father a tap on the shoulder. "Tired, Dad?" Donny shakes himself to and looks around, clears his throat a couple of times. "Just resting my eyes," he says. He straightens out and smiles at everyone.

"Give me a hand will you, Jamie." He carries the tray while I bring the hot mincemeat pie cradled in a pair of grubby oven mitts. He can't look at me. He can't look at anyone.

"Doesn't this smell good," Donny says, his mouth full of marbles. I stare at Donny's profile. His eyes are at half-mast, the skin around them sagged. When he finally feels my gaze on him, he turns to me in slow motion and blinks. His oily irises drift in and out. He starts to list forward, brings his hand up to steady himself, but miscalculates, elbow landing on his plate instead of the table, fork crashing to the floor.

"Why don't you go to bed," you say, eyes filling with tears.

"S'alright. S'been a big day, that's all."

You start to sob.

"It's alright, Mom. Nobody cares."

"He should go up to bed." You take a tissue from inside your bra and hold it to your eyes.

Donny refuses to be banished. While the three of us half-heartedly watch TV, he flakes out and for two hours gives us the pleasure of witnessing his head lurch and roll. Every once in a while he grumbles in semi-consciousness, peering through his amphibious eyes, "Yes, that's the ticket," he mumbles, then recedes into his stupor.

"You help Daddy up the stairs," you say to Jamie when the movie's over. "I'll be along in a few minutes."

I know what's coming. One of our talks. You settle beside me on the couch, where Jamie had been.

"I'm sorry about tonight."

"It's not your fault."

"We were having such a good time. I don't know why he had to go and ruin it."

I don't know what to say. You have shrunk into old age in a matter of hours.

"You see why we can never go out anywhere. I can't trust him."

"Yes. I see that."

"Why do you suppose he does it? I know he had a hard time growing up without a mother. I know it must have been awful during the war. But I've made a good home for him. Why do you think he does it?"

"Perhaps it's simpler than you think. Perhaps he just starts and then he can't stop."

"But what makes him start? You would think if he loved me he would never start."

"I don't know, Muriel. You would think if he loved any of us, he would never start. Perhaps he always thinks 'it'll be okay this time.'"

"You must have to tell yourself an awful lot of lies if you're a person like Donny."

The streak of red I have witnessed so many times before shoots up between your eyebrows and peaks at your forehead. Your eyelids and rims glow a sort of neon pink, tears well up. Oh Christ, I think, my heart twisting, it's an awful thing to see tears on an old face. I give you a hug. Partly to comfort you, and partly so I won't have to look at you. You push away and blow your nose.

"I've always done my best to protect Jamie from his father. I never wanted him to see Donny like this. I never wanted anyone to see Donny like this. When Alexis was little, I always sent her down to Mother and Dad's — that's how I lost her to Agatha. But I wasn't going to make the same mistake twice. I didn't want to lose Jamie. So I made Donny leave the house. I made him sleep it off in the car. That's when he started going down to the Legion. Sometimes he'd be gone for days."

"But there haven't been any problems lately, have there?"

"No, not since the summer Andrea was born. And one night when we took the bus tour to Florida. That's why I'd never go again. He always wants to go back to Europe but I've put a stop to that folly. Can you imagine what he'd be like re-visiting all his war haunts?"

Up in bed, I ask Jamie if he remembered his father sleeping out in the car. "No." Did he remember his father taking off for days? "Let's get some sleep, Robyn."

I don't get to sleep for a long time. There was one last thing you asked before we turned in. "What did Jamie mean when he said, *Don't worry Mom, nobody cares*. Doesn't he think I am somebody? Doesn't it matter enough that I care?"

I don't know the answer. I know Jamie feels sorry for you. Until now, I have always thought this is enough. Isn't that what you wanted? But that night I'm not so sure. Feeling sorry for someone is, after all, easy. Understanding is the hard part. While my mind searches for a word to describe this relationship, it occurs to me I'm just the same. I try to please you, because I feel sorry. It's my easy way out, offering no resistance.

Just as I begin to fall asleep, my body jolts, and I unhook from that releasing state of oblivion.

Doesn't he think that I'm somebody? Doesn't he think that I'm somebody?

This thought haunts me all through January, as we wait in desperation to get the final word about the mining job. We're told the financials are all in place. The hiring freeze will come off. We wait in agony. We still can't share this news.

Jamie works off some of this tension by towing the big mean-machine company snowmobiles on his truck out to the control structures where he and Alex, one of the guys from his department, roar through the bush to inspect some of the off-the-beaten path installations, and take a few detours to check out Alex's traplines. He has a nifty little business on the side, supplying Montreal furriers. Jamie starts to get it in his head that he'd like a souvenir of Labrador. He'd like to shoot me a fur coat. So one day he arrives home with the carcass of a big silver male wolf. It's over eight feet from nose to tail. The guard hairs along its back were black and grey, the undercoat silver and white. A male in its prime. The soft black outline where its eyes had been, and the smooth velvety hair around its muzzle, fills me with the deepest sadness because it had been killed in my name.

Jamie wants to try his hand at tanning the pelt himself so it hangs in our garage for three weeks. Almost every night I keep vigil, slipping out in my bare feet to stand beside it. I wonder about his mate. Did she feel lonesome when he didn't return the night Jamie shot him?

I don't want to be implicated in the deed. My desire to ever own a fur coat goes down the tubes every time I lay my eyes on the carcass. Jamie, my he-man, expects his due. He did it for me. I lavish him with praise out of the side of my mouth, hoping to hide the look of disgust that I'm sure flickers across my face.

One day, I tell my best friend Cathy about our impending move, swearing her to secrecy.

But the secret gets out in the oddest way. The manager over at the general warehouse drops by Jamie's office to show him a telex he'd just received from a major moving company with a query about crating up our furniture to ship it out to B.C. Jamie makes a fast what-the-fuck call to the new company and they telex him the offer while he stands guard over the machine. The news is out!

You try your best to act happy for us. I can only wonder how Donny and Agatha will have to pay for your real disappointment.

Jamie and I are well and truly relieved that we are far enough away not to have to live through your histrionics.

I should have known we'd never get away without some kind of mishap.

We're supposed to have our goodbye dinner at Cathy's, next door. Jamie's being taken out to the hotel first for a drink by the guys in his department. He never shows up for the dinner. He gets so pissed-to-the-gills that he has to be carried home to the trailer we stayed in the last week we were in town. I can hear the water resources guys in my head, "Aw yer old lady will do the packing. She'll make sure everything is cleaned up. You don't need her bossing you around all night."

By three o'clock in the morning, everything is finally packed in seven suitcases and a small trunk. The cat and dog cages are assembled and ready by the front door. Andrea and Caitlin are finally sleeping after being hyper and cranky all evening. The bathroom is wiped clean. Clothes are laid out for the morning's departure. An assortment of colouring books and dolls are crammed into carry-on baggage. There is just one thing left to do — cut the wolf skin down from the back porch and cram it into the trunk. The tanning process had not been far enough along to pack it with the movers so now I'm the one left to take care of it.

I drag the trunk down the hall and lay it on its end so I can climb up and cut the pelt down. I'm angry enough with Jamie to leave it, but there would be hell to pay and I don't want to start out on this move across the continent on the wrong foot. He's inordinately proud of his kill and has big plans to hunt a couple more B.C. to get that coat made for me. A horrible thought steals into my head as I cut the wolf skin down: young men do what they want and take what they want from life and they do it with little remorse.

FIFTEEN

I COULD BE anywhere. This motel could be anywhere. This lone little dandelion springing up from the crack between the cinder-block walls and crumbling asphalt could be anywhere. This curtain of fog could be anywhere. But let's face it, I am here on Route 17 on the outskirts of Sudbury, 350 kilometres north of Toronto and, as the crow flies, 1500 kilometres west and south of Churchill Falls. Thunder Bay, which is roughly in the middle of this great big country, is 800 kilometres from here. Nothing but rocks and lakes and forest as far as the eye can see. I'm feeling a long way from anywhere.

I'VE BEEN HERE before. Seven years ago, in my blue five-speed Jeep Cherokee, following Jamie in the yellow Ryder moving truck, which had a fifty-mile an hour governor. The girls took turns riding with us. We had left Mississauga the afternoon before in pelting rain and headed out on the 429, then the 401 and finally the 400 going north, me stuck to Jamie's bumper. The combination of the rain and the streaming traffic frightened the wits out of me. If he changed lanes, I prayed and changed lanes too, even if I couldn't see a thing. We arrived here in the dark, the same motel, the same diner — the same weather the next morning, starting out.

It came as a shock last night with the map spread before me that I didn't have to drive down the 401 to Toronto and up through the 400 to North Bay, that the best route is to stay on the Trans-Canada and head past Ottawa and Petawawa to North Bay and, if everything goes well, make it to Sudbury for the night. When I left New Brunswick, three days ago, I thought that leaving Quebec I'd recreate the drive I did from Mississauga to the prairies in 1986. But I'm getting ahead of myself. I see now that I can re-plot the whole thing. My stops will be out of synch. It comes as a relief to figure out that I'm not just re-tracing the past. I'm re-mapping it.

I can feel that hour now. The time shift. Last night, in Montreal, I couldn't feel it. But now I do. It's odd how going through time zones makes you feel a little outside of yourself.

Where the hell did I think I was going that morning we headed out of Churchill Falls? True enough, I was primed to skedaddle off to the construction of world's largest open pit coalmine, but I was still just the tag-along. I couldn't see that then. God help me, I still trusted that something good was waiting for me besides the possibility that Jamie would shoot more wolves to make a fur coat.

You know, it's funny, I just thought of something right this minute. Jamie came home with that wolf skin and presented it to me like a cat dropping a mouse at my doorstep. "I shot this for you," he said. I believed, too. But if the wolf jumped out in front of him, he wouldn't have had time to think. He shot, then made up the motivation to fit the story on the way home.

Is this how we do it? Is this how we tell the story of our lives? Inserting the motivations and the epiphanies as we go?

How can I explain my behaviour that morning and for the next couple of years? It's enough to make my head spin.

There I am, in a rush and a huff. No time to look back at Churchill Falls the February morning we drive to the airport. I catch a glimpse of Whitefish control structure as we disappear into the clouds. Block out heartache of leaving good friends with the hope of new adventure.

Not understanding my own misplaced anger in Montreal later in the day when we change planes. Outraged with the flight attendant because it's a 737, and not a 747 like I booked. Making such a fuss that a CP representative is called aboard. The sting of the flight attendant's words *Get this woman a wide-bodied jet, now, get her off my plane.* My capitulation and later embarrassment when we are settled comfortably in the near empty business class section. Jamie feigning sleep when we're at cruising altitude and I'm relaxing with a large Grand Marnier and the flight attendant can't resist disturbing me to ask *Has Madame calmed down?*

WHEN I SEE Dawson Creek from the jet window, it's like I'm having a déjà vu nightmare. Below are flat fields of snow as far as the eye can see as the plane banks for landing. To the west are waves of forested hills, crusted snow, and leaden sky. I can tell it's deadly cold because smoke and steam rise from buildings in straight fat columns and vehicle exhaust huffs out plumes. As the 737 lets down its landing gear, I begin to roar with disappointment.

"Is this it? Are we landing in the right place?"

"This is it," Jamie says.

For all the world, under snow, this looks just like Labrador. We have travelled over four thousand miles from fridge to freezer. I see no opportunity down these frozen roads. What the hell is happening? I thought we were moving to Beautiful British Columbia, home of giant forests, green rivers, misty coastline, and majestic mountains.

The mining project will be built in an undeveloped area of the Peace River coalfield, on the edge of the northern Rocky Mountains. Jamie left Churchill Falls with the understanding that the construction team would work from Dawson Creek until the mine is well underway and the new service town, with all the amenities, is ready to go. Then the families will move out together, with the opportunity to stay on for the operation of the mine after construction is complete. The pay is good, so our plan is to stay for five years, save money, then go home to Halifax.

So there I am, a month later, my face into the blanket on the king-size bed in our three-room suite at the George Dawson Hotel. I mutter, "Hello," when Jamie comes back from work. "Any news yet?" I turn to look at him.

"Nope. They're still working on it."

I want to know if the new company has figured out our housing policy yet. I don't know how much longer I can stand being holed up in the hotel.

"Why is it taking so long?"

"I don't know. Do you think I like it any better than you? They're working on everything. It's a big, big job."

"I know. I know," I mumble. But it doesn't matter how much I know. The idea that we will stay for five years in a town that hasn't even been built yet seems like a mirage. I'm looking for a horizon, but I can't see it.

"Did you stop at Nancy's today?"

Every weekday morning I take Andrea and Caitlin in a taxi over to the Rivers' so Andrea can walk to school with their kids, then I hang around with Nancy for tea and gossip and sometimes lunch. At first Nancy and I have a lot to talk about. She lived in Churchill Falls for seven years and sucks up everything I can think to tell her, but now I sense that she doesn't approve of my restlessness. Restlessness is a mark of disloyalty. There's not much left to say, so our friendship floats like fresh water over salt water.

"Yeah. Nancy had an appointment at the dentist, so I babysat Debra. I did the most awful thing. I knew I shouldn't be doing it but I couldn't help myself."

"What?"

"I scoured her kitchen."

"So? I'll bet she was glad to have a hand."

"I'm not talking about unloading the dishwasher or anything. I scrubbed her draining board. I sterilized the countertops and scraped globs of mouldy drippings off the trim. I took an SOS pad to the kettle and the teapot. Don't you see? I shined everything up. I knew it was no business of mine, but I just couldn't stop."

"What did she say?"

"What could she say?"

"You're making a mountain out of a molehill."

I doubt this. Nancy will take my interference for the indictment it is.

"I hate this fucking hotel."

"Someday you'll look back and think, there was this time in my life when I was treated like the Queen of Sheba," Jamie says and slaps me on the behind. "C'mon. Tell the kids to turn off the boob tube and let's go down for dinner. I'm starved."

I stare at a menu I know by heart and see absolutely nothing. "You've got to do something about this, Jamie. I mean it. We're going to get sick on this food."

A couple of weeks later, we move into a two-bedroom apartment. Six weeks after that, a yellow split-level — exactly like the one my parents owned in Sussex — on a corner lot in a new subdivision without a tree or a shrub. Not a week passes by before Jamie arrives home with the news that the whole construction office is going to move out to site by the end of the summer.

"Where are we going to live?"

"They've ordered a bunch of trailers. Isn't that great?"

"But I thought it would be a least a year before you had to be working out there. I don't want to live in a trailer way out there. It's bad enough here."

Out there in the mountains. When I try to imagine what this might look like I have something Swiss in mind, something all cute and cozy and established, although lately it's beginning to dawn on me that it's going to be a lot like Labrador, only mountainous and with bigger trees. At least there's a road in, I tell myself for consolation.

To top off the ever-shifting company announcements, a few days later, Jamie rushes home at noon. "Sorry, there's been another change of plan, the construction team's moving out to site now."

"Jesus, Jamie."

"Come on, honey. This is just temporary. Think of all the loot I'll be making." He packs a bag. "See you in a week."

This act, that Jamie can just up his tent pegs and hightail it off to the woods without any warning or consultation, outrages me. I have been put in my place and I feel it. It really hits home that all of my movements are pinned to his. My rational mind tells me that Jamie has no choice; after all, he is the breadwinner and has to march to the company beat. But what really gets my goat is his pleasure. He leaves, with great glee, a kid going off to camp. He is free and I am stuck. I can't get over it. I am stuck in our split-level in a bald-ass subdivision on the edge of a homely town with a double-wide main street, Mile 0 of the Alaska Highway, and a mall with a Safeway pinning down one end and a Woolworth's pinning down the other. There is a Merle Norman Studio; all the women who work in Safeway look exactly the same, with thick pancake and layers of burgundy eye shadow. Not like the women I am used to. The weeks inch by. Jamie leaves our house at 5 am, on Monday mornings and doesn't return until just before supper Saturday afternoons. Six and a half lonesome days I'm at loose ends.

Winter lasts until the end of May, then one fine morning summer arrives with day after day of menacing sunshine. I miss the fickle sun-fog-rain of the Maritimes. How the hell is a person supposed to get on with all that stabbing sunlight eighteen hours a day? Or the monumental four-in-the-afternoon thundershowers. The dry, ceaseless wind and the dust and the dirt of the prairies. Not a drop of water in sight. No rivers, no lakes, no swimming pond, just a couple of mountain ranges to crawl over to get to a beach.

I find no enthusiasm for the split-level. In Churchill Falls, I had not realized how much Jamie's schedule organized my life, especially the fact that he came home for lunch every day for forty minutes, and divided my day into four easy pieces. Now, he isn't even home for supper. Between the hours of 4:30 and 7:30, I flounder. Andrea and Caitlin miss Jamie, too, and so make more demands of me. It's all I can do to keep upright and put a decent meal on the table for them. I flop over the tub when I bathe them; shuffle through the pages when I read their nighttime stories, my lips and tongue like last night's liver. Do they notice, I wonder? I hope not. I try hard to carry on the bathing prattle, the dabbing of little noses with soap. Scrubbing a little blond head and an even smaller brown one with baby shampoo, while they each squeal "my eyes, my eyes!" Helping them get their warm damp bodies dry and into clean fresh pyjamas. I could have held on to them for hours, but I don't want to suck them into my complicated adult world. I tuck them in and kiss them safely into childhood dreams. Only when they're safely asleep do I give in and grieve through the night, stultified, watching anything on television until I'm so zonked that I won't worry about that horny husband of mine as I lumber up the half-flight of stairs to bed.

It is 1982. Most women work now. They have jobs and careers. I feel like I have nothing to show for myself. I think about finding some kind of job, but we are going to move at any time. Sensing that I am coming apart at the seams, Jamie encourages me to enrol in a correspondence course through the University of Waterloo. I sign up for Psych 100 to get back into the swing of things. Although I find it stimulating enough, at some level it only reminds me how alone I am because I have no one to share it with.

The summer is devastatingly barren; I almost jump for joy when you and Donny dare to make the trip out to visit.

THE WEEK BEFORE you arrive, Jamie and I celebrate our tenth wedding anniversary. It's twilight in the living room of our temporary home and still no word when the families will be moved from Dawson Creek to join the men out at site. There are building delays in the new town. I'm still hanging on to my first date illusions. *When I graduate, I want a job in the National Parks like my Dad. Play golf on Friday afternoons and not work too hard. Take my kids out on picnics*. I'm hoping for an outward sign, a diamond ring perhaps. Our student loans are finally paid off. I want something tangible from Jamie to hold me in place. I buy him a new lens for his camera, but he has nothing for me. Not a rose, not a card, nothing but his needy body.

Jamie is slouched in an armchair; I'm on the carpet, my head in his lap, watching the prairie sunset, trying not to think about diamonds in the sky, trying to concentrate on the scarlet dust buzz of colour. I'm trying to keep a question off my lips but it won't dissipate with the draining sky. It just tumbles past my good sense and over my cracking heart.

"I have to ask you Jamie. Which is more important, your job, or me and the girls?"

Silence percolates through my bloodstream.

"I don't know," he sighs. His long, blunt fingers stroke the short dark bangs from my forehead.

LOOK, THERE'S A road sign for Elliot Lake. The same company Jamie worked for at Quintette had a big stake there. Uranium, I think. Totally bust now. Like Tumbler Ridge. Another perfectly conceived town would have been down the tubes if someone hadn't got the bright idea to promote it as some kind of retirement community. I hear it's a real going concern. Oh boy, the life of the retired, Muriel. How you and Donny looked forward to your retirement.

When you and Donny arrive it's only been nine months since we all spent Christmas together, but I can't get over the change in you both. All of a sudden, at sixty-eight, you look like an old woman. Exhausted. Sagged. Deserted. Perhaps you have a sneaking suspicion there are no happy endings. I am alarmed.

"Donny got all mixed up and got us lost in the Toronto airport," you announce before we even get in the house. "I kept telling him we were going the wrong way, but he insisted he knew where he was going. We would have missed our connection if I hadn't finally got my courage up and asked someone."

I think you're just off on a new jag of Donny complaints so don't pay too much attention. It's weird for me to get stuck with the two of you without Jamie around. Do you remember your disappointment when you realized that he wasn't going to get the entire time of your visit off? He's home for two days, then back he goes. After he's gone, I start to believe you, there's something amiss with Donny. He's as full of good-natured shit as ever, but fudges when asked anything. He's fidgety, and lets fly quite improbable answers. Can't remember he's in northeastern B.C., gets it all mixed up with Labrador. A few days later, when it's time to take the bus down to Edmonton to visit Alexis, he thinks you're going to Halifax, and Alexis is still married to Ed. Wait till he sees the grandson, I think to myself. But he never fusses, never complains, and is quite happy reading the same *Maclean's* magazine article over and over.

"There's something wrong with your father," I inform Jamie on the phone the minute you leave. "I think he's got Korsakov's Disease."

"What the hell is that?" he snaps.

He wishes I could have found something else to take but psychology. He wishes I wouldn't inform him of things.

"A kind of amnesia usually brought on by alcoholism," I prattle, breaking the rules. Knowing *alcoholic* and *alcoholism* are forbidden words. Even you never used them. "I read about it in my psychology course."

"There's nothing wrong with Dad."

After you and Donny come back to Dawson Creek from Edmonton, you tell me that Alexis's verdict on Donny's confusion is that he probably has *a little hardening of the arteries* and *he needs to remember his hearing aid*. Alexis doesn't like to talk about alcoholism, either, and believes that in the past Donny only went on the occasional binge because you wouldn't let him drink in the house. She had remarked a few years earlier that she felt her very best when slightly cold, slightly hungry, sipping single malt scotch, straight up. I believe Alexis thinks she's just like her father, but I don't have the nerve to tell Alexis that her father isn't a sipper. I don't think *a little hardening of the arteries is* responsible for making Donny look like loneliest man in the world. He's unable to join conversation, unless the topic is fond old stories.

"He wakes up at night barking," you confide. "It's not like his war nightmares. I can't say 'Wake up Donny, it's only a dream, the war is over' because he is awake. That's the scariest part. He's wide-awake in the middle of the night, sitting up in bed, barking. I can't make him stop."

"Have you talked to Alexis and Jamie about it?"

"Oh, no. They're so busy. I don't want to be a burden."

No. You want me to be the burden.

I don't know why Jamie can't see it for himself when the four of us pound over washboard logging roads on a tour of the mine-site. Donny shows even less interest in this billion-dollar undertaking than he had in Churchill Falls. Jamie's been so anxious to show his Dad that, after all these years, he has finally built a big road. He stops on the way to the truck shop and gets us all to hop out. We stand on a wide, substantial gravel road, built to last a lifetime and to take the wear and tear of heavy equipment. It's a thing of beauty. Jamie waits for praise, hands in his pockets, right leg turned slightly in, chest high and hard, face soft.

"What do you think, Dad?"

"Good show, good show," Donny offers.

We wind our way up the mountain past the tree-line, through a series of switchbacks, dust whirling up behind us in a brown cloud, all the way to the truck shop, where we witness the monstrous green shovels fill 170-ton trucks, two and a half stories high, with over-burden.

You scrunch up your face. "With what?" you shout.

"Over-burden. The useless material on top of the coal seams."

"What do they do with it?"

"Throw it over the waste-dump located on the side of the mountain. After the over-burden is removed, they blast in benches to get the mining drills and excavators in."

Donny is nodding, but his eyes aren't focused. When he senses us looking to him for a response, he finally shouts, "Forgot my hearing aid."

"Daddy's always forgetting his hearing aid," you chime.

Undaunted, Jamie continues, "This is called the grizzly." He laces his fingers and slides them back and forth to show how two huge grated metal plates work to screen the coal from the over-burden. "After the grizzly, the coal goes to the surge bin feed conveyor, then the surge bin, and from there to the 13.6 kilometre-long overland conveyor — what we call the beltline — to the raw coal silos. That's the next part of the project I work on."

"Well," Donny shouts over the roar and the wind and the dirt. "Can you beat that?"

You're not even feigning interest now. You go straight for matters of the heart. "Do you think you can get a few more days before we leave, sweetheart?"

"Jeez, Mom, I can't. I've already taken an extra day. We're on a tight schedule."

Down in the plant-site, Jamie points out where the fifteen-storey preparation plant will be built. He explains the kind of equipment they'll use for the process of screening, washing, crushing, and floating the coal. He goes on to describe the dryer, clean coal silos, and the train load-out, and how the final product will be shipped by rail to Prince Rupert, and then across the ocean to Japan's steel mill industry.

"Are you sure you can't take another day or two?" you ask again while we're having coffee in the construction office trailer.

"Sorry, Mom."

You button down a hard smile.

"Can a fellow get a bite to eat around here?" Donny asks.

Fast-tracking and megaprojects are not in your scope. We trot off to the 600-man camp for lunch. Donny helps himself to two desserts.

So do I and so do you.

After lunch, Jamie tours us around the roughed-in roads, survey stakes, and fire hydrants that mark the birth of Tumbler Ridge, the town that's being carved out of the mountains. Located thirteen kilometres from the plant-site, on a steppe, surrounded by three rivers with a view westward of the Rocky Mountains, it's expected to shelter 6000 people in 500 new homes and a dozen apartment buildings. They're going to build a recreation centre, strip-mall, schools, everything within a year.

"I can't imagine how this will be liveable," you turn to Jamie. "When did you say you were supposed to move out here?"

"We were supposed to be here by now, weren't we Jamie?" I wade in.

"Well, you've got to expect a few delays on a project of this size," Jamie answers. "The trailers will be here any day now. So it shouldn't be long."

We're learning a hard lesson, aren't we, Muriel? There is not much family time on fast-tracking construction projects. Even though I'm here to witness the whole shebang, I hate the way heavy industry makes the family unit feel like a pipsqueak, even though we are the pipsqueaks that oil this industry.

SIXTEEN

OH SHIT. I left my goose down pillow in Sudbury. I've had that pillow since Dawson Creek. Bought on one of my shopping sprees not long after winter snuck into town, a week or so before Halloween. Over a decade ago, but the sudden shift from dry warm days into the icebox is still fresh in my mind. That town, wind-swept with snow, bent grasses and weedy stubble poking out of the thinly crusted cover of grimy white. At the time, I almost can't bear the flatness. I feel it in my soul, its dryness in my body. All that space, filled with desire. My worst shopping spree is a fast trip to the Merle Norman Studio one afternoon when I spend $157.36 on make-up — gobs of pancake and burgundy eye shadow. Jamie is not impressed. We're supposed to be saving money. I feel silly and sick about my purchases, but looking back, I see it was harmless. Though a marker of things to come. After all, I could have got a sitter and skulked over to the lounge at the George Dawson Inn and bellied up to the bar to watch the famous stripper who could do that thing with the ping-pong balls everyone was talking about.

Can't you just see it, Muriel? Buying make-up is the best thing I can think of for a dose of escapism, while I wait for news about the move into Tumbler Ridge. There's a labour strike out at the town-site. The provincial government is footing the bill for most of its development and has a policy of open shop for the building trades. But the unions want total control; they're lobbying for a closed shop policy. The talk is they want to get on at the mine-site, because that's where the money is. At one point, it looks as if I could be stuck in Dawson Creek until late May. Sound familiar? You can't hook up trailers to water and sewage service if the ground's frozen. That's the problem now. If the strike isn't over soon, the ground will be frozen solid as the hubs of hell, which is where I think I am anyway.

One afternoon the phone rings and it's someone important from the job-site. He relates a conversation he heard on the plane going down to Vancouver. Two union leaders were discussing their strategy of holding off work indefinitely in Tumbler Ridge until the wives of the mine construction team, who plan to move their families out there, become such basket cases, that they drive their husbands crazy, who in turn drive the bosses crazy until the company relents in the union's favour, just to keep domestic peace.

"Want to turn the tables on them?" I'm asked. "You bet your sweet bippy," I jump right in. It's one thing to wonder about your own sanity, it's another to let some strangers describe you as a potential basket case. "But what can I possibly do?"

"You organize against the unions. Make a public stink. Play for sympathy before they do."

"Get out. Me? Organize against trade unions? Cause a public stink?"

"Anything can be done, if it can be imagined."

I'm thinking, if waterfalls can be turned off and on ...

"Here's what you can do. Get a list of all the wives in Dawson Creek from the main office on the pretext of holding some sort of gathering. Then tell the wives this story you overheard somewhere — use your imagination. Ask them to fall in with you. Call the newspaper, radio, TV. Don't tell anyone you got this from me. Especially my wife."

I keep my lips sealed and get the list. Make the calls. Find one enthusiastic supporter and hatch plans to march down main street right to Mile 0. We paint posters — and call the media. I get my two-cents in on the morning talk show. I'm all set up with something important to do and something important to say. Before we know it, the unions relent. We get a move-in date. The trailers are on their way. I am pumped and Jamie is proud. Almost as proud as he is for the very idea that someone important would take notice of me and have confidence that I have enough aggression in me to take on the unions. This puffs him; it's a good reflection on him.

I am convinced that everything will be okay as soon as we are all under one roof again, safe and sound. I wait for news of the moving date. I wait with an almost debilitating restlessness. It's not like the obsessions I shared with Jamie about our house in Churchill Falls, or our move out here. Jamie is perfectly content in his new enchanted kingdom out in the mountains. Now we are disconnected. I feel alone in this.

I feel guilty that motherhood doesn't fill me up. That soft little arms and legs wrapped around me don't make up for the loss of Jamie's company. Days and weeks go by and the move-in date gets pushed further and further back by one stupid delay after another until finally the date to end all dates is supposed to be settled. I pack the 12,000 pounds of stuff I unpacked seven month ago. I scour everything with a thoroughness that would make your old matron smile. I even take the dog to the vet and get his nuts lopped off with the hope that his behaviour will improve. We're ready to go.

Jamie calls from work. "Hi. It. Ah. Looks like you can't move out for another week or so."

"A week or so. Everything is packed and ready to go. I am moving somewhere today. Did you get that, sweetheart? Today."

"What do you expect me to do? It's not my fault."

"Figure something out. I'll wait for your call."

I sit on a box in the middle of the dismantled house and wait for the phone to ring. On the third, I answer.

"Okay. Everything's okay. You can calm down. The boss says you can stay at the hotel and the company will pay."

"I want two rooms and an adjoining suite."

"You got it."

"Animals to the kennel."

"I said, you got it. Whatever you want. Just calm down. Don't go berserk on me."

I figure he's thinking *the curtains, the cake, the kick in the ass.*

It's funny how this didn't turn out to be one of your favourite suppertime stories, Muriel. You must have heard some version of this before, and yet, I don't hear a squeak from you. You don't approve, do you? Hits a little too close to the heart, eh? Don't worry. Settle down. We're just getting to the best part. It's about me. Not you. And you won't want to miss it, though it's a shame you won't be able to hightail it down to Agatha with this one.

WHERE WE ARE? Coming up to Sault Ste. Marie. First settled in 1622. Adjacent to the rapids between Lake Superior and Lake Huron. We're in iron ore country. Algoma Steel is Canada's first employee-owned steel mill. No union problems there, I guess. And here's another fact for you I read on a placemat at lunch, this is the home of the world's largest fleet of planes for fighting forest fires. Now what would Donny say? *Good show.* After all, he fought in the world's biggest war. What could all this world's biggest stuff possibly mean to him?

That was a little snippy, wasn't it? More about me than poor old Donny perhaps. I always get irritated when I'm going to talk about moving.

When moving day finally arrives, I load our Bronco with Andrea and Caitlin, pick up a load of groceries, rescue the animals from the kennel, and beat our way out to Tumbler Ridge on the winding, rutted, slippery snow-covered logging road. By the time the movers shove all our stuff into the 72″ x 14″ trailer I am wiped-out and too tired to cook. Jamie's coming down with the flu, so takes us up to the mine-site for supper in the camp. The variety of food is astounding and plentiful. Six hundred men chow down with gusto.

I am a bag of bones. Everything aches. Everything sags. I can't remember if I washed my face this morning. Doesn't feel like it. I can barely lift the fork to my mouth.

If the town of Churchill Falls was bleak because it looked so barren, Tumbler Ridge is equally unappealing to me because we're hemmed in by waves of mountains and dense forests. Everything is in trailers: grocery store, post office, school. The grocery store is barely adequate. Trips still have to be made to Dawson Creek for anything but the basics. Caitlin always throws-up and I never know when it's coming. All of a sudden there will be a whiny groan accompanied by a projectile of vomit. I keep my trips to town to a minimum.

Still, winter in the house trailers, snuggled together in a cul-de-sac on thirty-foot lots, does take on an aura of refuge after a year of eroded expectations. There's a certain something, a spirit of adventure in the air that holds me for a few months. I get busy making the trailer into a home. As a peace offering to Jamie, I drape the wolf skin across the back of the couch. He resumes his ritual of getting Andrea and Caitlin ready for bed and reading their bedtime stories. He often looks tired though. His days are long and hard. Fifty-four hours a week with ten more months to go at this pace. Every once in a while I glance at his face and it looks strange to me. As if I have never seen him before. For a fleeting moment, I wonder what the hell I am doing with this strange man in this strange place. Although we cuddle in the evenings watching TV, there is something missing. As if we are playing at our old roles. At Easter, when the construction site shuts down for four days, we fall into our old family rhythm again. Jamie scrounges some lumber to build a deck and a tree house for the girls off the back of our trailer. I'm not that handy with a hammer and nails, but I'm good at giving instructions and providing tasty snacks and meals that we eat outside picnic-style. There is such pleasure and comfort in this family. I am content. The girls are thrilled with their tree house. Jamie seems relaxed and happy to be doing something physical. But the days fly by and, before we know it, Jamie is back at work. The spell is over. By the time all the snow has melted and I reenergize with spring, I am plagued by the treadmill in my head again.

Still, I try to keep my spirits up — as advised by the older wives, the wives who don't question and don't complain and never withhold sex as a power play — and become obsessed with *Jane Fonda's Workout*, going for the burn four or five days a week. As my idea of myself ravels away, I continue the process I began in Churchill Falls when I altered the inside of my body. Now I alter it on the outside. With sweat and determination, I nip and tuck little rolls of flesh, which all of a sudden offend me, into smooth sleek lines. My body becomes quantifiable and measurable: bust: 36″; waist: 25 and 1/2; hips: 35 and 1/2; thighs: L 20 and 1/2, R 20 and 3/4; calves: 13; weight: 123. I am twenty-nine years old, living in the mountains under the shadow of a ridge, and I want someone to notice.

To break the monotony of a June afternoon, my friend Gen and I drive up to the plant-site and brazen through the security gate to pay a surprise visit to our husbands. The spring rains have stopped. Dust hangs in the air. As we come close to the construction offices, the noise is all-encompassing. I know enough about heavy equipment to pinpoint individual sounds and train my eyes on brutes like the picker cranes lifting pipe and structural steel, or fork-lifts and crawler cranes setting equipment. The night before, Jamie had mentioned that the big task of the day would be setting the enormous vessels for washing coal.

Inside the office trailers, the secretary points to the far end where Jamie and Gen's husband, Bryan, are bent over a large drafting table with a group of men. As we walk toward them a guy named Pozzi looks up. There is quite a buzz about him in the gossip department. He's the rock star of construction stiffs: tall, single, charming, strangely good-looking and, in his mid-thirties, one of the youngest construction managers around. Word has it that he's being groomed for the top job in his company. Both men and women are drawn to him. There's a mysteriousness about him, and an air of tragedy, due in part to his hair which is a sandy colour streaked with silver and white, reported to be the effect of a car accident he had when he was nineteen. Part of Pozzi's charm is that when he talks to you he has the ability to look completely absorbed by what you're saying. In his quiet voice he asks questions, nods his head, touches your arm so you know he's paying attention. Yet he somehow remains aloof.

As I walk toward him, it's like I had not really seen him until this moment. His hair reminds me of the wolf skin. His eyes, the same shape as the wolf's empty cavities, are locked on me in flashing silver blue. He draws me toward him. I'm stunned to feel a flutter of excitement. I'm locked into the moment. A voice like my mother's — *You have no business looking at me this way, mister* — is trying to take control of the situation. *Shut-up Mum*, part of me insists. Walking toward Pozzi is like swimming underwater — slow, cool, suspended. Eventually I have to break the surface for a breath.

I tap Jamie on the shoulder.

"Hi, honey," he exclaims. "What are you doing here?"

The spell is broken. Pozzi excuses himself. Jamie and Bryan get us a coffee, take a few minutes to chat, then turn back to their drawings. As Gen and I drive away from the plant-site, the construction noise becomes less distinct. Concrete mixers and diesel welders meld into a general rumble. Gradually the only sounds are car wheels on a gravel road and the whoosh of the air conditioner.

And a tiny little tick tick tick from the bottom of my heart.

The heart ticks a little louder a few days later at an informal get-together at Gen and Bryan's, when one of the town employees, who when drunk likes to brag about being an ex-con, makes a lunge for me asking 'Who's your husband, sweetie-pie?' A big hand clasps his shoulder and a slightly familiar voice announces *I am*. Saved by Pozzi. As the drunk lurches off, Pozzi puts a territorial arm around my waist. His long frame dangles over me like a question mark.

"I broke up with my girlfriend," he grins.

"How come?"

"She was hounding me about a commitment."

"What's the problem?"

"It's not my bag."

"Too bad."

I amble off to find Jamie, brushing Pozzi dust from my head and shoulders where he had dangled over me, sprinkling a little disturbance.

JAMIE IS HAVING second thoughts about staying on for the operation of the mine. The position he has been promised has been snapped up by the son of the vice-president and Jamie feels snubbed. Other positions are available, but he's not interested. Now he's not so keen on operations. The construction guys work together tightly, like a well-practised professional sports team, with one goal in mind: get this mine built ahead of schedule and under budget — and then get out. With the operations guys, they are always preening and manoeuvering for their positions in the years to come. Each group thinks the other is a bunch of assholes. In operations, Jamie claims the politics are dirty. Then there's the whole business of putting up our own money to build a house. We don't want one of the small bungalows that are going up; we want a two-storey, four bedroom, like Churchill Falls, and that will cost us a whopping $130,000. This is 1983, interest rates are sky-rocketing. The economy is shaky. There is a general smell of disappointment in the air about the whole deal.

CBC sent *The Fifth Estate* in the fall and they gave the project a bum rap. The newspapers are full of angry articles that so much money is being shunted up here at a time when the rest of the province seems to be sinking. Within six months of moving into town, Jamie and I are thinking about moving out. But where to go? What to do?

I get the heebie-jeebies with an excess of something I can't define and I can't shake off. Like I'm tumbling full-speed-ahead into I-don't-know-what. Even though the town is shaping up with foundations poured for the town centre and town hall, the roads get paved and a few playgrounds are installed, and a giant above-ground swimming pool is set up for the kids, I develop the worst hankering to get away.

All I think about is home and a familiar landscape, the beach and the swimming. Jamie says no, forget it, it's too expensive to fly five thousand miles and anyway, he can't get the time off. But I'm not thinking about him. I'll go without him. And, when it comes right down to it, I don't really want to let you know how much I want to go home. I don't want to give you the chance to say, "I'll bet you miss your two company-paid trips a year."

I consider going to Moose Jaw to check up on my mother, but I know it would be a nightmare. She lives in an apartment in a small town with a man I have never met. I can't imagine taking refuge there. Invoking her image gives me a succession of weird dreams about old boyfriends where she always barges in, pissed-to-the-gills, and lectures us on the refinements of birth control while I keep insisting, I haven't got a uterus anymore. But did I really think Mum would listen? Not even in my dreams.

After a lot of nagging, Jamie arranges to take ten days off at the end of July. We drive down to Vancouver and take the ferry to Vancouver Island. I pray this will save me.

In the meantime, there's a party to look forward to. On the Saturday of the July long weekend, I'm juggling a load of groceries in a rickety cart when out of the corner of my eye I spy Pozzi across the dirt parking lot.

"Hey!" I shout before I think. "Want to give a lady a hand?"

He's never seen me barge through an airport with toddler and diaper bag on my right hip, while my left hand clutches the hand of a five-year-old to a cart loaded with seven suitcases, so he bounds over and helps stow groceries into the Bronco.

"Going to the party tonight?" he asks.

"Yeah," I say as off-handed as I can manage, giving him the once-over. He's got a great haircut and is always close-shaved. Trim and extra clean — the mud and dust of construction doesn't seem to stick to him. What does stick to him is speculation. He's become a topic of conversation among the women. We all think we should set him up with someone we know. I, too, play this game.

A lot of the parties are official functions for the staff of various contractors or foreign investors, like the Japanese. I usually feel stranded, so stand back, watching, never really knowing what the hell to say. Jamie is familiar with all the people and moves about freely. The party we're going to tonight is different. It's over at one of the apartments; most of the people there will be the crowd from the plant-site. A lot of singles looking for action, the real deal of parties. It starts off like most. Most of the crowd is strange to me, so I try to horn in on a conversation Jamie's having with one of the contractors from the belt-line.

"Buzz off, Robyn," he says, flicking me away. "I'm trying to talk to the guys."

Dismissed, I drift off, my neck flushing, when through the door, in walks Pozzi. Looking positively Pozzier than he looked even a few hours ago, except he's wearing a nondescript beige sweater. It doesn't do a thing for him. He pops a beer and sits on the floor near the stereo. I make my move and sit cross-legged beside him.

"My sister gave it to me for Christmas."

"What?"

"The sweater. You were giving my sweater the hairy eyeball."

"It's not your colour."

"What is my colour?"

I take a long moment to look him over. All six feet and four inches. "Probably the winter colours, but you'd have to get draped to know for sure." Not that I don't know for sure. I trained to do colour draping in the spring. I know exactly what colours will look good on him. But I don't want to look at him; I want to dance with him.

We try to pick out a few tunes. Much to my embarrassment I have to confess that I had somehow missed out on the Sex Pistols and the Police when we lived in Churchill Falls — they were more a Stars on Long Play, Barry Manilow sort of crowd. Pozzi convinces me I'll like Prince so we give it a whirl. "Why not?" I say. "I'll try anything once." But for the damnedest reason something about the aggressive beat makes me think about my mother.

"Don't you just hate it," I say, "when someone walks in and out of your life through dreams, and you can't make them go away so you're left with this hangover feeling of that person all the next day?"

"You mean you get like that, too?"

Our eyes lock.

Then I would swear that that man's sweater turns a deep saturated red before my very eyes. It smoulders. I catch a piece of the fabric between my fingers and stroke it. For a second, the music stops. Flooded and flushed, I wonder where the hell Prince has been all these years. Like a wolf spider, Pozzi's hands pose on my hips. Arched and hesitant, I reach up and skither my fingers through his dangerous wolf hair. His opalescent blue eyes reflect mine. Coming to his senses, Pozzi pushes me away.

"You'd better go find your husband," he says gently.

I find Jamie over in a corner with the belt-line boys. Announce that I'm tired. And I am. All of a sudden I am exhausted. Pozzi follows us out to the truck to say goodnight and I trail home a little starry-assed, none the worse for wear.

A FEW MORNINGS later, I'm folding the day's wash, wondering when I'll get to see Pozzi again, when a scruffy black bear, about two years old, saunters into the backyard. For a split second my mind goes blank with pure fear. Where were Andrea and Caitlin? I tear out of the trailer door just as the bear settles down to examine the contents of a garbage bag he's toting and helps himself to leftover Chinese food. There's only one restaurant in this town, one of those places with a sign outside that announces *Chinese Buffet and Western Food Available*, in red and gold lettering.

The sound of 500 houses being built fills the air. I don't see the girls anywhere in the bright sun as I sweep my eyes across the cul-de-sac. All I see are three shiny ravens. Magpies screeching from a lodge pole pine. Heart in throat, I race to the playground — scattering the ravens, frantically searching for a splash of turquoise and pink from their matching outfits. I spot Andrea's bike first, slung across the gate, then hear their voices coming from under the monkey bars where an assortment of blankets is draped.

"Andrea. Caitlin!"

A blonde head pokes through the blankets.

"Mum. You're stepping on our fort!" Andrea yaps.

I bend down and peek in. Seven kids, aged about nine to three, are huddled together. Caitlin is hanging upside down by her knees.

"She's in jail," Andrea explains.

"You're going to have to spring her," I order, trying to keep the panic from my voice. "I want everyone to come with me. There's a bear in our backyard."

"A bear! A bear! A bear!" eight little voices chirrup.

I herd the kids to a safe trailer, alert a couple of mothers, then pound back to my place to see if the bear is still there. Bear is sitting under a fir tree. The contents of the garbage bags are heaped around it. I shout, "shoo, shoo!" but bear ignores me. Frantically, I look around. There isn't another soul in sight. Then like a dream come true, I hear a vehicle coming and turn to spot Town of Tumbler Ridge lettered in a half moon on the side door of a half-ton pickup.

"Stop! There's a bear having lunch in my backyard and it won't go away."

Until that very second, I have been a bear-hugger, a strong advocate of trapping nuisance bears and letting them loose in unpopulated areas. Now I'm shouting, "Shoot it!" to the driver, recognizing him as the ex-con who had asked me where my husband was at Bryan and Gen's party. I figure it stands to reason that anyone who's been in jail must know how to use a firearm.

"It's against town policy." He jumps down from his truck. "We've been instructed to call the forestry people when there's a bear in town."

"There isn't time. Shoot it!" I drag him by the sleeve to my back porch.

"I'm not allowed. I'll get into trouble. You're sure it's a bear?"

A man from down the street appears. One of those operations guys who works shifts. He sneaks a peek in the backyard.

"There's a bear all right."

I'm pissed-off that a man is required to confirm the presence of a bear.

"Shoot it!"

The operations guy is so startled he puts his hands up, victim style.

"I'm going to call someone." He disappears.

"Listen, if that bear gets away, it'll come back. Once they've had food in someone's backyard, they always associate that place with food. Everybody knows that. If it gets away, I'll never know when it's coming back. I've got two little girls. If that bear gets one of them, I'll come looking for you."

By the time I finish my spiel, I have the ex-con rounded up in the back porch where Jamie keeps his guns in a rack on the wall.

"Okay. Okay."

"Pick your weapon. I'll get the ammo."

Ex-con chooses a shotgun, which he loads with some difficulty. He charges into the backyard and takes aim at the bear that has stood up to see what all the fuss is about. Ex-con fires and hits it in the shoulder. Bear lunges forward. Ex-con reloads and shoots again, getting bear in the leg. Bear growls. Stands stock-still. Ex-con fires another round and bear thrusts forward.

"Get more ammo!"

I'm crying my heart out as I grab another box of shells. Ex-con reloads as bear staggers toward us. Bang. Reload. Bang. He finally gets bear in the eye and bear drops to its knees. One more shot and bear rolls forward and topples onto its belly. By this time operations guy is back on the scene. He looks at me and he looks at ex-con. He looks at bear. He looks back at ex-con dangling the shotgun in his shaking hand.

"God almighty. A shotgun to kill a bear? Are you crazy? You two are damned lucky that bear didn't get you."

I'm almost on another planet. Nothing seems real.

"I never shot a gun in m-my life," ex-con confesses.

I hadn't even considered him through the whole ordeal. I've only thought about my children. Who would figure? An ex-con who couldn't use a gun. It dawns on me that I might as well have shot the bear myself. At least I would have known enough to choose the 7mm Donny brought back from the war.

When the shooting stops, everyone comes running from the trailers. Caitlin jumps up into my arms, crying. I pull down the turquoise and pink terry top that has scrunched up and slide my hand under to the smooth soft skin of my child and in the moment feel vindicated. Andrea races around like a hornet, looking at the bear in awe.

"Did you do that, Mum?"

"Sort of." The shock of the deed starts to sink in.

"Wow. What's Dad going to say?"

Jamie is proud of me. Over the next few days, I think about the wolf Jamie shot and how bad I felt; but now I have to question those feelings. Obviously, I'm capable of being a predator. But is it the same? Jamie killed for sport and I had killed in self-defence. Is there a difference? I don't know. All I understand is that the act has made me feel alive, from the first moment when I spotted the bear and my gut clenched until the final moment when the bear rolled over. Perhaps I crossed some kind of line, Muriel. The episode puzzles me to this day. I often wonder if I did the right thing. What would you have done? There's a constant bear threat in the early days at Tumbler Ridge. So much land has been blasted and bulldozed for the mine and the town, their natural habitat is shrinking.

A few days after the bear incident, Jamie calls to inform me that after work he and Pozzi are going to paddle a rubber raft down the Murray River from a spot near the plant-site to the bridge a couple of miles from town. Do I want to meet up with them and go for a drink at Pozzi's apartment afterwards? *No*, I want to tell him. *I don't want to join you after. I want to float down the river too.* But where would I get a sitter at the last moment, so I simply go and wait by the bridge to pick them up with one of the guys from work. Twenty minutes after their estimated time of arrival and no sign from them, I start to get antsy.

"Don't worry," the guy I'm waiting with says, reading my mind. "They only took a six-pack."

When the pair finally comes into view I can tell by the set of Jamie's back, even from a hundred yards off, that he's absolutely sloshed.

"The fucker tried to drown me," he shouts, pointing at Pozzi, when they get within earshot. "Rocked the boat while I was taking a piss." He waves an empty bottle of Grand Marnier. A six-pack of empties rolls around in the raft. The boys get into the Jimmy droop-eyed and soaking wet. We drive over to Pozzi's apartment and call some of the belt-line gang to join us for an impromptu Monday night party. Pozzi and Jamie get into fisticuffs in the bathroom, trying to beat each other to the shower. Jamie pulls the toilet paper hanger off the wall. "Pretty piss-poor construction," he snorts and lunges into the shower to warm up. Pozzi wanders around with nothing but a towel wrapped around his middle. What a hairy guy, I think, a great big tomcat. When Jamie staggers out of the shower, he makes it to the bedroom and passes out in Pozzi's bed. Sooner or later — even I get too pickled to tell — everyone leaves but Marilyn, the secretary on the belt-line. She and I hatch a plan to drape Pozzi, and decide for once and for all what season he is. We empty all his drawers, gathering a miss-mash of garments and colours to drape the pleasantly passive and pissed-to-the-gills Pozzi. After Marilyn and I declare him a winter, Marilyn makes to leave. "I've got to work in the morning. Don't get into trouble, boss."

So there we are. Me and Pozzi all alone — if you didn't count my passed out husband — sitting squeezed up tight on the sofa gazing goofily upon one another. He stands up and fiddles with the stereo.

"Let's dance," I say, and before I know it, we're smooching in a serious way. If I'd been Pozzi-dusted the night he draped his arm across me, now I'm absolutely Pozzi-salted and red-hot peppered. It's working both ways. I'm about to bust my yoke when an image of Jamie snoozing away on Pozzi's bed floats before my squeezed-shut eyes. I break free.

"Time to wake up Jamie. Time to go home."

Pozzi doesn't resist. We trip across clothes strewn all over the apartment and drag Jamie into Pozzi's truck. He drives us home. Kisses me on the cheek and says, "You're going to get me into trouble."

I crawl naked into bed and lay awake the rest of the night, aware of Jamie snoring contentedly beside me. While my mind cleaves open, I begin to talk to myself in parenthesis. (It was only a kiss.) (Only a kiss, how could you?) (You're a Commissioner of the Girl Guides of Canada.) (Only an acting commissioner.) (He didn't try to feel me up, no harm done.) (No harm done? Anyway, what's wrong? Am I ugly or something?) (This has to stop at once.) (I haven't felt so good for years.) (This is torture.) (I haven't felt so bad for years.) (Jamie will kill me if he finds out.) (Jamie doesn't care what I do anymore. He's in love with the job. I'm just the over-burden now.) (He's a good father who reads to the girls every night and gives them a bath.) (Pozzi's a ladies' man, everyone knows that.) (Maybe he's misunderstood.) (Give your head a shake.) (I am the mother of two little girls.)

All the while my mind is busy, a river of pleasure wends its way through my body, irrigating every tender aching inch: my fingertips, my lips, my nipples, and my labia are drenched in pure liquid gold. At times this river flows deep inside and at others surfaces and floods over me so I can't tell the difference between my body and the sheets. I can almost hear the rush of current. My hands slowly circle my breasts and belly. The shape of my hipbone pleases me. The creaminess of my cunt pitches me into ecstasy. I lift the bedcovers to inhale my sweet dense odour and moan around the hard, intangible, ball of desire that I can feel but cannot reach out and touch. I am alive. I am viscous. And not for one second do I consider rolling over and pouring myself into Jamie.

By the morning, the pleasure wears off and I'm shit-baked, wondering if Jamie will corner and accuse me when he gets home for supper. When he leaves for work, I lay in bed staring at the open door, goose down pillow scrunched under my pounding head. It was just one kiss, I tell myself again, and hold my hand out in front of me, my index finger pumping up and down like a miniature Jane Fonda. Amazed at how one little finger can block out a whole doorway.

Finger. Doorway. Finger. Doorway.

SEVENTEEN

DID YOU GET a glimpse of Lake Superior back there, Muriel? I know it's miserable and foggy, but every once in awhile I get a good look at the cold grey water under this canopy of fog and drizzle. In a way, it doesn't matter what I see. I feel its vastness out there to my left. Did you know that the Great Lakes compose the largest body of fresh water on the face of the earth? I suppose you did, being a schoolteacher and all. Still, it's never a bad idea to reacquaint yourself with information like this. When we get stuck in our own far-off corners of this great big country, we tend to forget the majesty of the endless, varied geography. Do you remember those television spots that would start out with the cry of a loon on a lake and a deep, warm authorial voice would begin a narration about the "hinterland"? And then we'd see some guy paddling a canoe along a rocky granite shore, alone, at one with nature. The romance of it all. The picture we hold of ourselves. I looked up the word *hinterland* in the dictionary one day and it means something like the land directly adjacent to and inland from a coast, remote from urban areas, backcountry, that sort of thing. With a broad definition like that, it could mean places like Fundy, or the west coast. But in the Canadian heart, *hinterland* means this area. The Canadian Shield. Home of the Group of Seven. It doesn't matter if I don't have a clear view of the area today, because in my mind I see it as it was painted. The mixed forest of maple, birch, poplar, and spruce. That magnificent fall display of colour. The bite in the air. Brute headlands that push out into the water. Outcroppings of pink rock. Brooding clouds built up like blocks on the far horizon. Blueberry blue water rumpled with turquoise and more. Somewhere along here, there must be bleached-out silver trunks of dead hardwood trees like monuments. Oh where, oh where is that wind-wracked jack pine?

It's over on Georgian Bay. Doesn't matter. The spirit of the thing is here.

All that splendour, and today on view the raw green of spring growth struggling against the leaden sky. What do you think, old girl?

The roads we take. The risks we take that don't seem like risks at the time. They seem inevitable. In hindsight you think, I don't know. I might have wanted to think that one through a bit. Well, there's never any shortage of hindsight is there? What I've lacked in my life is a well-developed sense of foresight. I'm hoping this trip will help me out.

When I get up the morning after draping Pozzi, I can't think at all. Whenever my eyes close, I experience all the rush of the night before and the imprint of Pozzi's body holding me as we danced. At suppertime, when Jamie's truck crunches into the yard, my tummy clenches and my heart lurches. I don't know how to explain what happened. My only defence is that nothing really happened, but I know my face will not lie — something had happened. I just can't name it. So I brace, ready for a lambasting, but Jamie is his usual good-natured self, laughing about his trip down the river with Pozzi. I am puzzled, but relieved.

All that week I pitch from household activity to household activity, an explosive mixture of birthday sparklers in my belly; by the time Saturday night rolls around, and we plan a little get-together with Pozzi and the crew, I know I'm not going to be challenged by Jamie. The closest he comes to broaching the subject is, "You'd better watch out for that guy. He's a ladies' man." What kind of warning is that? I began to feel the most powerful feeling of all: I am untouchable. I can play this game and get away with it.

I still have a desperate hankering to get out of town and, although I was the one who pushed for this vacation, when we leave for the coast my heart isn't in the trip. We leave in a rush after work on a Wednesday afternoon and drive through to Chetwynd and down the Hart Highway until dark, stopping at a roadside motel at Hixon, about an hour and a half after Prince George. What we don't see in the dark is a small construction project next to the motel and we're wakened abruptly by the growl of a backhoe early the next morning. Just what we wanted to hear on vacation: more machinery moving earth. As we travel farther south, the day heats up. The girls are crabby — why couldn't we fly like we did in Churchill Falls? By the time we stop at a red light in Cache Creek at four in the afternoon, with the full blast of the sun on my side of the Bronco, which I take unreasonably personally since Jamie bought a vehicle with no air conditioning, and I look out to see dry sandy hills and pearly green sage brush, I'm in a bitch of a mood.

"Will the wonders of this province never cease," I say. "We're in the goddamn desert."

The red light stays red for what seems like eternity. I breathe in sizzling dry air; the sand hills suck the life right out of me.

"God almighty, it's hotter than the hubs of hell," I say as we move along and I fling my arms toward the dashboard trying to cool off my armpits while Jamie shoots his Has-Madame-Calmed-Down glance my way. As we pick up speed, I feel a bit of relief as the hot dry air blows over my skin. The girls are so far past restless they're almost catatonic. As we drive out of the intense heat and climb another set of mountains along the Fraser Canyon heading for Hell's Gate, I zone into parenthesis again. (It was only a kiss.) (Only a kiss?

How could you.) And on and on. Nothing has changed in a couple of weeks — except a vague awareness that I am living a life of my own in my head.

I say *vague*, Muriel. It's hard to figure out what I knew then and what I know now. For the first time since being a teenager, standing ankle deep in slack water trying to figure out exactly when the tide turns, I had become the central character in my own drama. I don't think I could have named that then, but deep down, at some level, that had to be part of the attraction of Pozzi. All the agony he caused me provided some relief from that other treadmill: where are we going to go, where are we going to live, what am I going to do with the rest of my life? An image haunts me from the day before we left. A woman shuffles in the parking lot of the grocery store. She comes from the direction of the construction camp, where the workers who are building the town live. She's in her early fifties. Looks she's done this so many times before in so many different places that she doesn't give a damn anymore. She scares me witless. I do not want to end up like this woman. I will not spend the rest of my life tagging around after any man from construction site to construction site.

I can't image staying in Tumbler Ridge for five years. We are so far away from home. Jamie is making all kinds of noises about some other big construction job somewhere. He can't imagine himself working in an office in some high-rise. Not after the thrill of a fast-tracking megaproject.

I get nowhere with this line of thought, so I hop off one treadmill and get on the other and between the fits and starts in my head I relive every moment of every occasion I have been in the company of Pozzi since we first moved to Tumbler Ridge.

The restaurant at Hell's Gate is closed, but it doesn't matter. We're too tired and miserable. We take one long look at the raging water in the rocky gorge, a passing glance at a billboard that explains something about the construction of the CPR wiping out the sockeye salmon stocks, and decide against taking the aerial tram ride into tourist heaven. Back on the road, after the fatigue and heat and guerrilla warfare I am silently waging against myself, and coupled with the state of constant daydreaming arousal and continuous vibration from thrumming over rugged asphalt I feel like a day-glow skipping rope run over on a hot street.

We find a motel room in Hope and I settle the girls into the bathtub. Andrea moves her hand through the water like little fishes and says the most amazing thing. "Hey Mom, the water here is so soft."

She splashes Caitlin and Caitlin splashes back. Laughter and splashing in the soft water. I watch my daughters and am revived by their simple beauty in the bath. Andrea is right, the water is soft. I hadn't let myself realize how hard it is in Tumbler Ridge. Not just the water. Between the cool sheets in the motel room, with Jamie's hand slung across my belly, I wonder if I have anything important to say or if he has anything important to ask me. The next day, when we drive down the mountains from Hope into the lush, farm-studded Fraser Valley, I sink into the peace of the thick, wet, cool air. I sniff the sea in the distance.

Vancouver is busy and beautiful. The beach at Stanley Park is a welcome relief, if crowded. The citiness is foreign. Even the magnificent ferry ride from Tsawwassen to Sidney, through Active Pass and the Gulf Islands, doesn't appease me. I see the beauty, but it stands back from me. The drive through Cadboro Bay and Oak Bay into the summer throng at Victoria's inner harbour is astounding in its display of wealth and refinement. Memories of Halifax seem dingy in comparison, but I'd trade the harbourfront in Victoria for a walk through Point Pleasant Park in a heartbeat. As we head up and over the Malahat Highway along the eastern coast of Vancouver Island, all I long for is something familiar. The forest meets the water in a way that leaves me out. We fight traffic through Nanaimo as I check the map for likely places to spend the night. My heart aches for the mystery of Long Beach, out on the far western edge of this country, but the girls are giving signs that if we don't stop soon they are going to heave. In Qualicum Beach, where we stop for the night, the tide is low and the smell of sand flats and seaweed with scatterings of shells quells my aching heart, but the beach is a pebbly sight for eyes that crave an eastern sandy beach. The next day I relax into the drive. In the picturesque town of Campbell River, and for the first time since I can remember, a comforting thought enters my head: I could live here. But as we continue north to Port Hardy the weather closes in and so does my soul. We depart on a ferry for a ride through the Inside Passage up to Prince Rupert, one of the most magnificent passages in the world, and I might as well have missed it. My heart has shut down.

I am aware that I'm as bad as you, Muriel, that summer you locked yourself up in your room. I'm too goddamn miserable to find pleasure, because things aren't going my way. I let my thoughts drift into the possibilities of Pozzi: the graze of his hand, his tongue on my ear, the fibrous touch of that wolf hair of his in my hands. By the time we arrive back in Tumbler Ridge, the only way I can explain my preoccupations to myself is that I must be in love with Pozzi.

AN OLD ENEMY or two seems to have slid into the car with me this morning. No, not you, Muriel, stop being so insecure. The old enemy is the urge to name things. As if naming will solve the problem and point the way. Not a way, but the way. And naming love must be the very worst. It is so full of promise and hope. What could I possibly have known about that man? My back is sore, my neck stiff. My shoulders ache. Hands are clenched onto the steering wheel at ten and two in a death grip. I should get out and stretch, but I'll wait for the next gas station. I'll check out the steel statue of a Canada goose coming up at Wawa. I'll bet you dollars to donuts it's the world's largest. We're just a few miles away.

I wonder: is it really the car that's so confining, or is it the memory of being confined? It took me years to work out in my head what my body knew then, when it started to act out. Not long after our 3000-kilometre B.C. marathon, Jamie comes home from work with word that the development of a second potash mine in Sussex with the promise of a third on the horizon, in good old New Brunswick, is a go-ahead. I think our problems are solved. Everything will sort itself. I'm not that fussy about going back to Sussex, but from B.C. it seems like a stone's throw to Halifax. Jamie's reluctant. He wants to try his luck in Calgary or Edmonton, to see if he can get on with the oil patch where the big money is. I can't see it, but I don't want to end up being a blamer like you, so I decide to take another page out of your book, and become a schemer.

"Listen honey," I say, "your parents aren't getting any younger. They could use our help. And just think how good it would be for the girls to spend more time with their grandparents."

Jamie remains impassive. Life goes on in Tumbler Ridge.

While we were away, Pozzi acquired a new girlfriend. A good-looking thirty-something divorced chartered accountant who had come to set up a practice in boomtown. Obviously gaga over Pozzi, she's eager to glean what info she can.

"Watch out for that guy," I tell her. Repeating Jamie's advice. "He's a bit of a ladies' man."

Ladies' man or not, nothing had changed. Pozzi and I continue our love affair of the eyes and casual touches. We dance the long slow dance of arousal in tune to the mystery of mutual attraction. I am ready, willing, and able every time Pozzi comes near me.

"This is like high school," he whispers in my ear during an agonizingly short, slow dance while Jamie and the attractive accountant pair off.

Yes, it's just like high school, where everyone is on view and everyone is trying to figure out the rules. Wondering who will get the girl and who will blow the whistle. And, just like high school, there is a long enough line standing behind Pozzi to keep me dancing all night. I don't care. I am in love.

OH GOD, MURIEL. Was I present enough to be the good mother I thought I was? They are always first in my heart. An unfathomable love I sometimes take for granted.

"I wish you weren't married," Pozzi whispers one Friday at the end of the dinner party as he's about to go through the door.

"It could be eradicated."

"There would be too much grief."

His answer silences me. Is this the tender gel that keeps the two parts of myself from falling completely away from one another? Do I know somewhere, at some level, deep within the rifts and seams of my mind, that this is what makes Pozzi and I so safe for one another: the dish will never run away with the spoon.

A marriage can be destroyed. But it can never be eradicated.

Whose grief was Pozzi thinking of? I should have asked him. But here's the thing. We never talked. We operated in the realm of covert glances and spurious meetings, always in the company of Jamie. Our desire made us so compellingly attracted to one another, but rendering us totally impenetrable to each other's thoughts.

There is grief all right.

By mid-fall, Jamie makes up his mind for sure that he isn't going to stay on for operations, and since no other projects are jumping for his expertise, he gets revved up about the idea of building a state-of-the-art potash mine, even if it's in New Brunswick. He's merged with the beltline gang now and feels part of their family. A lot of them are jumping on the potash bandwagon. There's all this loyalty in the construction crew. He goes for that.

Then one day, after the dog has run away for the umpteenth time, Jamie hands him over to one of the guys from the plant-site. "That dog's got no sense of loyalty," he says. "Good riddance." He turns his back on our dog and that's that.

With this act, I experience the strangest sensation. *Walking on your grave*, I think it's called; a presentiment. He'll do the same thing to me some day.

So when the idea comes up to buy a house in Sussex, I'm all for it. I fly out ahead and buy a house so we don't have to go through the moving agonies of the recent past. At least that's our excuse.

We put so much stock in having a house. As if four walls we label as our own will keep us safe from the big, bad world.

You must remember, Muriel, all the excitement attendant with this purchase of our first house. I stay with my stepfather during the house hunting days in Sussex and before returning to B.C., you come into town and pick me up for the weekend. You are just about beside yourself with the news that your family is coming back. You go out of your way to make me comfortable. Even presenting me with four blown glass wine goblets that you knew I always admired and wanted.

For all my craftiness, preying on Jamie's sympathies about you and Donny so we could move back east, I see that I wasn't far off the mark. You and Donny share a life with little in it. Saturday nights playing cards at the Seniors', you've taken up church again on Sunday mornings, Agatha up for supper once or twice a week and perhaps a shopping trip to Moncton or a doctor's appointment. There are no more dancing lessons. Only evenings while you watch television distractedly, knitting socks or doing the crossword at the same time while Donny snoozes in his recliner. Then, after the news, shaking Donny awake and prodding him up the stairs to bed. Every damn night.

You and Donny look frightened.

I begin to realize that, for better or worse, after all these years, I really am attached to you and Donny. Somewhere in all the family disturbances and petty annoyances, you have become part of my ground substance. I truly hold you in a quiet spot in my heart. Somehow, we are more than a package deal. I remember the summer night, ten years earlier, when Jamie and I had been so wrapped up in ourselves, and you had rung your own doorbell to ferret us out of the basement. You stood on your own back step, looking sheepish, wanting nothing more than our company for an hour or two. I understand this loneliness now.

I understand for the first time what a big risk it could be to ring your own doorbell. How disappointing it would be if nobody answers.

Can I add some measure of comfort to your life and take care of my own needs at the same time?

WHEN YOU AND Donny drop me off at the Moncton airport, Donny's perpetually cheerful look suddenly slides from his face. "Do you think Jamie will ever be out this way again?"

You stupid old fart, I'm thinking. What the hell do you think all this fuss is about buying a house? Then a closer look at his not-understanding face makes me understand that his question is serious, pleading even. So when I said, *Your parents need help*, I had been more right than I imagined.

Oh god, Muriel. We're not going to make it to Thunder Bay tonight, that's for sure. I think we'll have to stop in Marathon, not far ahead. There's talk of a trio of gold mines opening up not far from there. Hemlo or something. Apparently there's a lot of recreation in the area. A couple of big provincial parks and some kind of archaeological sites nearby. Marathon has the same kind of history as a lot of other towns scattered across the country: company towns at the mercy of boom and bust cycles. Jamie was telling me about it last week because he's been putting his feelers out about possible work, but that's only if something doesn't open up for him with a sour gas plant in, guess where, Chetwynd — an hour and a half from Tumbler Ridge.

No matter how hard we try, sometimes it seems like we don't get anywhere.

It doesn't matter how much recreation there might be in an area near a big construction site, if the guys work sixty hours a week, there isn't a lot of energy for recreation. We spent a year in Tumbler Ridge and never saw Kinuseo Falls, the centrepiece of the newly created Monkman Provincial Park.

I wish I hadn't left that stupid pillow back in Sudbury. I'm going to miss it tonight. It'll be the first time in a decade I haven't had it with me.

Back in B.C., I take up your cause with Jamie. "There's something terribly wrong with your father," I inform him. "Your mother is tuckered right out."

He gave me the standard answer, "A little hardening of the arteries. Leave him alone."

Is Jamie suffering from a little hardening of the heart? What will happen by going back to New Brunswick? Could our love be renewed? Could we go back, in our minds, in our bodies, to the starting point? Is this what I really want?

For the first time in many years, I wonder about the slim girl who stood in the water trying to figure out the exact moment when the tide turned. Where is she now?

Our last six weeks in northeastern B.C. seems like a lifetime. The plant is being commissioned and Jamie works full-out non-stop. The contracts that were supposed to appear for the potash mine in New Brunswick still haven't materialized. A lot of people on this job are depending on that job. What if it doesn't go ahead? Everyone is edgier than usual.

Then the day the Wabco truck dumps its first payload from the coal seam into the grizzly, most of the rubble stays on top. Where's the coal? Seems like there's a lot more over-burden than anyone predicted. There is a bad feeling in the air. What if someone important with camera and a microphone figures out the boys blew the top off the wrong mountain?

The big stress-buster is a round of going-away parties up at the plant-site. A few days before we're supposed to leave, Pozzi cups my ear and grazes my earlobe with his tongue as a bunch of us sits around in one of the trailers listening to music, shooting the shit.

"I think I'm falling in love with you."

"Every Breath You Take" by the Police conceals our chatter. I am awash in pleasure. Transported to the state of arousal. Is this what it's all about? I feel like my heart is being put through the crusher.

From across the room Jamie shouts, "Hey Robyn."

I hold my breath. Has Jamie finally chosen his moment to take me to task about my coziness with Pozzi? I've been waiting. Is there no green-eyed monster lurking in his heart?

"Come here and tell Elsa about the house you bought us."

I breathe out and tear myself from Pozzi. Elsa, ten years older than me, is married to one of the superintendents and works as a secretary in the office.

"You remind me too much of myself at your age," she says to me.

When moving day arrives, and there is still no contract for the potash mine, I begin to doubt everything. The movers refuse to leave town without a company P.O. Twelve thousand pounds of furniture plus our Bronco is loaded into an Atlas moving van with the engine idling. "Who's gonna pay for all this?" The moving guys are outright grumpy. It's been a year to the day that I moved all this stuff out here. What have I accomplished?

Heroically, Pozzi saves the day, coming through with telexed purchase orders. Jamie and I are on our way again.

Pozzi is coming too.

In hindsight, Muriel, I see now what I never saw then. I worried for nothing. I'm going to let you in on a little secret. It wasn't just me who had a crush on Pozzi. Oh, no. It wasn't just me.

EIGHTEEN

I CAN'T STOP yawning this morning. I seem to be in the throes of a revolt. The clock says 10:15 am. I should be bright-eyed and bushy-tailed, but honestly, 10:15 on the clock doesn't make any sense as to how I feel. How I feel is more like *What day is it, how long have I been here, how much longer will this drive be, when will I get there? Where am I*? I'm in no-man's land and no-man's time. I left Calgary for New Brunswick by air two weeks ago yesterday. Jamie and I had to plunge into the three-hour time shift from day one because there were so many details to be taken care of that demanded we be on local time. When I left with your car five days ago I was habituated to Atlantic Standard Time. Now I'm in the middle of this continent on Eastern Standard Time and sometime today hope to drive into Central Standard Time. My destination, Calgary and Mountain Standard Time, does not seem real. All that seems real is the road and the story. I have stopped looking out the window. This landscape is meaningless to me.

Last night when I talked to Andrea and Caitlin, they told me that Jamie is thinking about selling your house. Every insurance company he has contacted has given him the same unwelcome news: insurance for a second home is twice the price as a principal residence. When he first heard this last week, it made his blood boil and he took it personally, as if in his great hour of grief the world was out to get him. The second disappointment was when Eileen Black, that cousin of yours, and the paramour she stole as you lay dying, refused Jamie's generous offer of letting them live in the house so it wouldn't sit empty, on the condition that they wouldn't mind us moving in for a few weeks every year when we came home. Thank god they had some sense. *Shit out of luck*, Jamie said. My stepfather wasn't interested in moving out from Sussex, either. Jamie was so disheartened. He couldn't imagine renting the place.

To tell you the truth, Muriel, I couldn't imagine the cousin and the paramour living there. Or sharing the space with them in the summers. They are more or less strangers. Wouldn't that make your blood boil? How would you like her polishing your good furniture? Everything was happening so fast anyway with the two funerals. The whole idea was pretty weird. Desperate.

The day after your funeral I sat in the little vestibule on one of your rockers, by the patio doors, and tried to imagine coming back to live someday. I couldn't do it without visualizing all the walls being torn down and opening up the space, a complete renovation. Expressing my thoughts openly made Jamie panic. He offered his standard response: *It would cost too much*. But I wasn't thinking money. I was thinking of the effort we had to make to be the ones you needed us to be in order for you to love us.

I have no more effort like that in me. Coming back didn't work the first time. Why did we think it would work a second time?

The night we arrive back in Alma from B.C., there is a full moon in a clear sky beginning to cloud over. I fall into bed with the sensation of jet travel coursing through me. Next morning, I awake, dying to go to the beach, needing to reorient.

Though things seem familiar — particularly the woody, musty smell of firewood stacked all along the back wall of the basement that permeates to the upstairs — there is something different. I'm a little detached, a little removed, from wanting to belong. I sniff the air, thick with the past. Outside, a wall of fog clings to the slate siding, its presence bores into the house impregnating the cold, lemony air with a fat dampness.

You are bustling away down in the kitchen. Laughter from Andrea and Caitlin darts up the stairs. As I roll to the edge of the bed, Jamie reaches out and pulls me back to his side.

"Don't get up yet," he says, fumbling for my breasts.

"The kids are down there with your mother."

"That's okay. She won't mind."

"No. They'll have her in flap in no time and then she'll fill them up with pudding or something and they'll be on the tear all day."

"So what?" He dives under the covers trying to shift my panties in the tangle of sheets.

"Nope." I dislodge.

"The story of my life," Jamie mutters, sinking back into the pillows as I hit the floor.

In the hallway, I'm surprised to see the door to Donny's room still closed. How strange. Donny is always up at the crack of dawn doing sit-ups. I am annoyed he is still sleeping. The bugger kept me awake most of the night.

"He sleeps in," you explain, as I crack eggs. Sleeping in has always been a no-no in this family of hard workers.

"Well, well, well," Donny exclaims when he finally comes down, his surprise to find us all the in the kitchen more than apparent. "Look who's here. Isn't this the ticket?"

He claps his hands.

"Grandpa!" Andrea and Caitlin laugh. "You're so funny."

We all laugh with him.

"Who's coming to the beach?" I ask when breakfast is over and the kitchen sufficiently tidied.

"The beach?" you whine. "Look outside. The weather's so dirty. Stay in with me and have another cup of tea. There's no hurry to get to the beach. You're back now. There's all the time in the world."

"I'm saturated with tea. Wait until I get back."

"Tide's in!" I announce to the girls as I park on the verge across from the entrance to Fundy National Park.

"Dirt's out!" Caitlin chimes back and I realize that at the age of five she only knows about tides from detergent commercials on TV.

The girls scramble over the riprap on the park beach while I head for the water's edge. Though the dense morning fog is beginning to break up and scatter, feathering up over Owl's Head, Nova Scotia's headlands across the bay are still cloaked. Lazy muddy breakers roll onto shore, tumbling stones and tidal debris. As the wave pulls back, I am mesmerized by the crackle of foam and the lacy pattern left in its wake. The next breaker hits shore a few feet away then floods in over my runners.

"Whoops!" I screech, the cold December water so shocking.

"Mummy got her feet wet!"

"What's Grandma going to say?"

Andrea and Caitlin surge toward me, grabbing me by the arms, pulling me away from the waves.

"Grandma won't say anything if you keep your lips zipped."

I swing them around.

"Let's all get our feet wet!"

We hold up our arms, hands attached, wailing as we rush the swell.

We line our runners up on the electric heaters. No reaction from you, you're busy making bacon and eggs for Jamie, who's looking kind of glum.

"Where were you guys?" he asks.

"You were sleeping," defence primed. "We went to the beach."

"I wasn't sleeping."

I glance at you first. Your back stiffens, but your fat little arm works away at beating a lump of cold butter into submission on a slice of toast.

I don't like where this is going so I call on you for distraction.

"Muriel, you'll never guess what Caitlin said yesterday in Dawson Creek as we waited for the plane."

You turn to face us, your underwater smile showing.

"It was all a big rush. We stopped for Egg McMuffins, but took them to the airport so we could check in the cat and the luggage in good time. When we finally sat down to eat, the McMuffins were cold, and there was some kind of announcement. I thought I heard the word *cancelled*, and got a little tense —"

"Yeah, a little," Jamie throws in.

"Caitlin leaned forward, looking at all three of us, and said, 'We've got to get the hell out of here.'"

"Out of the mouths of babes ..." you start, then stop. We know there is something dark and truthful about what Caitlin said.

"Where is Dad?" Jamie asks.

"I think he's in the living room watching *Sesame Street* with the girls," you say. As soon as Jamie's back disappears down the hall you turn to me and add, "Or I should say, they're in the living room watching *Sesame Street* with him." I look at you uncomprehendingly. You elaborate. "He watches almost every morning. In a way, it's a relief to keep him occupied for an hour. I don't know what to do with him anymore. Everything I say goes in one ear and out the other. I send him to the store and he can't remember what to get, so I write him a list and he doesn't know where he put the list. One day, he comes back to ask, 'Where am I going?'"

"Oh dear," I utter.

"I get so exasperated because he keeps me in a perpetual game of hide-and-seek for his glasses, his keys, his wallet, which I suspect he is actually hiding, because he won't part with one red cent. I have to pay all the bills with my own money."

"Oh-oh-oh."

"And on top of all that, he nearly drives me crazy taking his clothes out of the washer and shoving them into a wet ball at the back of his closet. He never went near a washer in his life."

"Don't I know it!"

"Some days I think I'll go out of my mind."

Oh dear. *The mean mother, conniving sister, and the illness; the bad husband, the wrong husband* usurped by *the unaccountable husband.* I look at you and I believe you. Your face is the colour of an abandoned beehive.

I pat you on the back, knowing that sooner or later something more concrete will be required of me. For now, I am happy to put off future obligations by throwing myself into the mania of putting my new home in order.

The energy I threw into that house.

What were we thinking? The potash mine is scheduled to be finished in less than two years. There is a lot of talk about a third mine being built. But that is all speculation. We allowed ourselves to be seduced into thinking it will happen because we want it to. Need it to. We all feed each other this promise and speculation that we'll probably end up living here at least four, if not five, years — what feels like a lifetime to us. For a month, I believe that everything will be fine, just fine.

Then Pozzi arrives. I am catapulted back into the snake pit. I not only begin to think in parentheses again, I begin to live in parentheses. Pozzi is introduced around. Remember the day Agatha parts with the piano in the old house and gives it to Andrea? Pozzi comes out to Alma with us to help pick it up in a company truck. After a hearty lunch, you and Agatha corner me asking all kinds of questions about him.

"Why isn't a man like that married?"

"He likes to be footloose and fancy-free, I guess," I answer nonchalantly, sneaking a peek to see if you suspect me.

Who knows what's going on? Thursday nights, Jamie and Pozzi take a computer class while I try my hand at drawing again at adult education classes at the new high school. Afterwards, we go for a drink at the Maples Hotel. When I get home there is no other thought in my head than wrapping my legs around that long, hairy body of Pozzi's, convinced I'm in love with him. Some weekends, Jamie and I get together with our old Tumbler Ridge friends. Pozzi is always there. Some weekends, we spend with you and Donny. Pozzi's always breaking into my thoughts. For a moment I stop breathing, then I go back to whatever I'm doing, playing cards, helping with supper, getting the girls ready for bed. Lightheaded for a moment, but it doesn't last. If something doesn't happen soon, I think, like you, I'll go out of my mind. Only I can't talk to you about this. I'm relieved you're distracted by Donny; you can't see my restlessness.

By the way, the other thing the girls mentioned when I talked to them last night is that Jamie has decided not to pursue the Hemlo gold mine projects. He's got his heart set on the Chetwynd job. He claims it will be better for all of us because it's easy to fly home to Calgary from Fort St. John.

Us is a very small word for what it implies. *Us* is that indent in my body where Jamie collapsed into me just ten days ago. The connection we felt again.

Us is part of the *we* Jamie always used that I finally balked at a couple of years ago. I'd listen to him going on and on about when we were on the Tumbler Ridge job, or we were on the potash job. My mind finally anted up after one of these episodes and I said, "What? What *we*? I was never on those jobs."

"Yes you were, honey," he protested. "We were there together in the excitement and spirit of the project."

"No, we weren't. I never worked on those jobs. My experience was not the same as yours."

JAMIE WAS CRUSHED, Muriel. He always thought of us as merged in some way. I have to admit that in the early years of our marriage I viewed us in a somewhat similar way. But after being left in Dawson Creek on my own for seven months, I never saw us that way anymore. As time went on, I saw myself more and more as a person separate from him. But I wanted to be my own person. Isn't that what we're supposed to be when we grow up?

Adjust your watch, Muriel. We just passed a sign announcing that we are now entering the Central Time Zone. Although I suppose that's nothing compared to the Eternal Time Zone you have just entered. How's it going up there anyway? What do you do with yourself when you arrive in a new place and don't have the distractions of unpacking to help establish a new point of reference?

I have hardly gotten ground under my feet in Sussex when out of the blue, my mother bursts into town. "I moved back to Nova Scotia," she informs me on the phone the night before she arrives. "So thought I'd come up. The bus gets in around two."

While Mum sits at my kitchen table, I scrub the counters with a weak solution of Javex and dish liquid.

"I'm fed up with the prairie winters. Fed up working at that nursing home, and fed up with that goddamn Bill — the thing likes the sound of his own voice a little too much. I'm going to move in with Mumma and Dad and look after them. God knows they could use the help."

"God knows."

I have not seen my grandparents for almost ten years. I suppose that now I will have to make the effort. They live in a haze of cigarette smoke, blue TV light, cheap rum, and regret. They both came from good families and are perplexed by their decay.

"Can't you sit down for five minutes and talk to me?" Mum demands as I dump Comet on a tea ring and scrub viciously. "Do you have to be on the move all the time?"

"Hold your horses. I'm almost finished," I say as I look out the window. My stepfather pulls into the driveway in his nifty Nissan 300 ZX. Before I can open my mouth, he trots up the stairs and steps into the kitchen and tap-dances right through to the living room. "Oh hello," issues somewhere from the top of his throat and out the side of his mouth.

I inhale sharply and follow right on his heels.

"Hel-lo Rob-bert," Mum says through a cloud of smoke.

"She just arrived," I whisper. "I didn't have time to warn ..."

"I can hear youuuuuu," Mum yodels from the kitchen.

"I came to drop off these tapes." He exits safely through the front door.

"What tapes?" Mum asks when I come back to the kitchen.

"Some of the old stuff. You know. Jelly Roll Morton. Bix Beiderbecke."

"Oh that old stuff. I thought this new girlfriend would have him on to something new by now."

"She does. Mel Tormé."

"Mel Tormé. Now isn't that the cat's ass. So what's she like, this new one?"

"Her name is Jane and she's really nice. I really like her."

"Nice? Is that all you've got to say? Nice."

"That about covers it."

Mum stays for a week watching my every move. She isn't falling for my resplendent domesticity the way you always did. By Saturday night, I'm on pins-and-needles when Jamie and I take off to Pozzi's housewarming party out in the countryside, packing sleeping bags to spend the night. No sense driving after a party when there is a grandmother so handy.

It's a drinking, dancing, flirting party. For a few hours I moult the burden of responsibility and experience a rush of possibility. I have made up my mind. Tonight's the night.

Somehow I think having sex with Pozzi will liberate me from my suffering. All night while gyrating to *Thriller* and Huey Lewis I wonder whether I actually have the nerve to do it. I change my mind a hundred times. When people start to leave, I make myself busy, emptying ashtrays, loading the dishwasher.

When I enter the front room, I catch Jamie pawing one of the secretaries sitting on the floor next to the stereo.

"Ah c'mon now Sandy, your boyfriend's gone. Let's have a little fun."

I backtrack into the kitchen, figuring I've just been handed permission. "I'm beat," I yawn, dragging Jamie off to bed in the spare room. When I'm sure he's conked out for the night, I slip out of bed and slink up the stairs to find Pozzi. He's getting a towel from the linen closet. When he faces me, I almost lose my nerve. I don't know how to get from standing in the hallway into Pozzi's bed.

"I can't find my toothbrush," I say in a little voice.

"Use mine." Pozzi leads me by the hand into the bathroom.

The simplicity of standing in the bathroom next to a man while washing my face and brushing my teeth with his toothbrush is so familiar that my fear slips off. I follow him into his bedroom as if it's the most natural thing in the world.

I sit on the edge of Pozzi's bed. He kisses and undresses me in slow, even turns. He folds me into his arms, and my ordinary life falls away. A column of pleasure bleeds through me when he enters my body. I rock into him. I am fearless.

"I love you," I whisper.

Pozzi digs his fingers into my back and arches toward me, his head shifting back and forth as if in agony. His eyes scrunched shut. My heart stands still as he comes into me. When he is spent, I clamp down into him and lay very, very still until he falls into a deep sleep. Disillusionment is so swift to enter. *What have I done?*

How are you doing up there in your Eternal Time Zone? I hope there's a rocking chair or something now that you've heard this one. Did you ever suspect? I don't think so. Too bad. It might have served you in some way down the road. I've thought about this over the years and have come to understand that my desperate act was not the ends I hoped it would be. Somehow I always thought that the very act of having sex with Pozzi would take care of everything. It would be a revelation of monstrous proportions. The next step would be self-evident. Nothing was revealed, except my own naked desire. My act was a means for getting unstuck. It took me so long to see that.

I remove myself from Pozzi's bed, feeling oddly cheated, and creep back into bed with Jamie. Just after dawn, when he begins to rub the small of my back I realize he wants sex. I can't think how to refuse him. In terror, my mind clamps shut and my legs open wide. I let Jamie in before he can smell Pozzi on me, and find that my hips keep time with him, as if erasing the act of a few hours before. I am void of feeling in this act of erasure.

Later, when we're leaving for home, Pozzi drapes himself across the couch in his brown velour robe. As he turns to his side, the robe parts and his scrotum peeks through.

"Put those away," Jamie says in mock disgust.

Pozzi just snorts and, taking his time, covers himself up.

In the car on the drive home, I am not compelled to make a confession, but I am compelled to ask a question.

"Is Pozzi real?"

"What do you mean?"

"You know. The way everybody looks up to him. Admires him. His knowledge. Generosity. Is it real? Genuine?"

Jamie is quiet for a few minutes, then he declares, "Pozzi is all of that and more. He's just the greatest."

We're pretty much silent the rest of the way home. As soon as we walk through the door, Andrea and Caitlin rush us with hugs and kisses.

"Nanny taught us how to sew."

"We made you potholders!"

I am immediately disoriented. I've got the smell of two men on me. Here are my babies, bearing gifts. Can my mother sniff me out? Do I look sly? The girls stick their potholders in my face.

"Whose do you think is best?" Andrea asks, elbowing Caitlin out of the way.

"They're both beautiful!" I examine the lumpy squares of yellow and blue check with big loopy stitches.

"So how was your party?" Mum asks.

"Oh. It was great." I shrug. "Everyone had a good time."

"Well, I'm knackered," Jamie adds. "I'm going to have a smoke and a beer and hit the hay early."

"Jesus, Jamie. Is that all you think about? A smoke and a beer. I wanted you to fix the shower rod in our bathroom."

Four sets of female eyes fall on Jamie. He goes over to the fridge, plucks out a beer, and heads down to the poolroom.

Mum gives me a sharp look. "What flew up your ass?"

"Mum. Watch your language."

"You don't fool me Robyn. You always did wear your heart on your sleeve."

"C'mon girls," I prompt, turning from my mother. "Let's find a place to hang these pretty potholders."

Sometime over the last half-hour it seems like my mother has infiltrated the car. *Why-in-the-name-of-god did you have to tell him you loved him?*

Good question, Mother.

I wish I could talk to you, but you always find a way to silence me. Do you remember what you said to me the night I had my first real kiss? I had just turned thirteen. I had told you everything up until that moment.

You didn't let that thing put his tongue in your mouth did you?

After that, I kept you guessing. So why should I confide in you now? Let's see. I'm all alone somewhere on the North American continent between a place called Terrace Bay and another called Nipigon. Lake Superior is out there to my left with thin light shining through the high clouds, making the water look like the underside of tin foil. I haven't seen another car go by for at least a half an hour. I'm really tired. Everything hurts. I'm sick of talking to Muriel. So let me think about it for a minute.

Maybe it has to do with a feeling of spilling over, of needing to spill over. I felt I'd been a reservoir of love contained for so long that action was not enough. That action was almost meaningless if I couldn't get my mouth open and say something really big. And that was about as big as I could get at the time. I couldn't think of anything else.

I love you.

I never thought three little words could hurt so much. The silence that came back to me was so much bigger than the words that went out.

One day I put on my runners and, like my mother, simply walk out the front door. I don't get in my car and drive to Moose Jaw, I start to run. In no time I am pounding down the sidewalks wearing a cute little pink and white striped outfit with Nike Airs. First I run around the block and quickly build up to a mile, then two, now three. My calves and thighs are sleek and hard in full stride, arms loose at the shoulder shunting back and forth in easy rhythm to John Cougar Mellencamp and Tina Turner as I burn up the sidewalks in the town where I dropped out of high school. When I bump into people I knew from the past they always have the same question for me: *What do you do?*

I suppose I do colour draping. Though that mad eighties fad hasn't hit here in Sussex, I give it a shot. My picture is in the local weekly paper, demonstrating my skills on our next-door neighbour who is caped in a sort of barber's rig and capped in a white kerchief while I smile knowingly and fake draping one of the colour swatches across her chest. The photo is of course in black and white and very grainy so unless you're familiar with the routine, it looks somewhat like the cheerful execution of a female member of the Ku Klux Klan. A few brave souls book appointments, but I can't muster any enthusiasm for the home parties. I know I have reached the end of my colour draping career when one night a group that booked for six appointments expanded the shin-dig to eight without bothering to tell me, and as 1 am approaches and I am trying very hard to apply make-up to a very homely, and very unsatisfied customer, I inform her that for thirty-five bucks, I don't do plastic surgery.

I toy with ideas about my future career. Muriel and Jamie and my mother think I should go into nursing. We still have high hopes about the third potash mine, and staying in Sussex. I could go down to Saint John, only a forty-five minute drive, and get into nursing school there. "Just think how perfect nursing would be," you all say. "You could get a job anywhere."

For a while, I take on all this big feeling about nursing, sacrificing myself for others. Though in the pit of my stomach I know these reasons have nothing to do with me. In the end, it is Agatha who disabuses everyone of this idea.

"A nurse!" she says. "You couldn't be a nurse, Robyn."

"Why not, Agatha?"

"Because, Robyn, dear. You would want to be the doctor."

This is an accusation, not a compliment. I take it and run.

"What about being a psychologist?" I say to Jamie. "I'm a good listener."

"Takes too long. And remember, you'd have to take statistics courses. You're no good at math."

"Oh yeah, I forgot."

That's the story.

Is it true? I'm not smart enough to take statistics?

Just get a job.

Get a job.

I don't know how to say something as sophisticated as *Why is it men need careers and a woman only needs a job?* But I feel it, and resent it in my bones.

Agatha tells me she heard on *Morningside* that no intelligent Canadian should miss reading *The Aquarian Conspiracy*. I take up her challenge, order a copy. Covering up the little dents Jamie and Pozzi have left in my heart. I order more books. Maslow. Jung. Rogers. Huxley. Hatch new ideas. If I haven't got anything important to say, I'm sure as hell getting something important to think about. Agatha can make neither head nor tale of the *Aquarian Conspiracy*. I enjoy a taste of smugness over that one.

Jamie tries to listen to me talk about self-actualization and synchronicity while he soaks in the tub after his after-work run of 10k. He's into marathons and endorphins. I accept the fact that he can run circles around me, that I will never have a career like he does, that he comes from a more respectable family than I do. But I keep trying to talk to him.

What to do about his diamond cock, forever hard and bright and shiny oozing pre-cum just for me; predictable as the tides, twice a day. I'm giving the offering the snub more often than not. I think his forever hard-ons have more to do with his genes than me. I'm running hot and cold, becoming a bit of a touch-me-not. It's not that I'm any less horny, it's just that I want, well, I want to be the seducer. I want something that's not so available, under my nose all the time. I'd like Jamie to take me away on holiday, but there's not a holiday in sight.

I keep reading. Register for a ten-day watercolour landscape painting course down at Mount Allison, even though I've never held a paintbrush, even though I'm not that interested in landscapes.

I'VE BEEN FOLLOWING this eighteen-wheeler for an eternity. The diesel exhaust is getting to me. There has to be a place to pass somewhere soon.

Back in the fall of '86, when I made this drive in tandem with Jamie in the yellow Ryder truck, most of the time I was content to shift up and down and follow along. Every once in a while I'd come out of my stupor and whiz past him and keep going a good clip for a half hour or so. Then I'd duck into a pull-off and wait. Sometimes he'd stop and the girls would stretch and change vehicles. Though more often than not I'd simply fall in behind again and adjust myself to his rhythm.

God, there must be a passing lane coming up. Nothing. This is so frustrating. I take a peek around him. Coast is clear. Hold on to your hat, Muriel. Off we go. This is not a bad little car you know.

Which reminds me of the time Jamie and I take Andrea and Caitlin over to the park playground. You and Donny come over in your car a little later. The day is mild and sunny; tennis courts dry as a bone.

"We should have brought our old racquets," Jamie says.

"Oh that would be fun," you smile. "I haven't played in a dog's age. Daddy and I will run back and get them. And since it's so nice, I'll make us up a picnic."

"I'll come and give you a hand," I offer.

From the backseat, as we drive down Church Hill, across the bridge into the village, I get the distinct impression that Donny doesn't seem to realize he is actually driving. His arms go slack when he gazes over the bay. He's not looking at anything so much; his look is just hovering, disconnected.

"Do you think Donny should be driving?" I ask you as we make up ham and cheese sandwiches.

"Why?"

"Have you told Jamie the things you told me, about the washer and the money and the forgetfulness?"

"I don't want to worry him."

Somebody should be worried.

"Your father shouldn't be driving the car," I tell Jamie in bed that night.

"Oh he's all right," Jamie answers.

"Well, I'm telling you right now, you can do what you like but I'm not driving with him and the girls aren't, either."

"Okay, okay. You're probably right," he huffs.

You know I never paid that much attention to Donny. He just seemed to occupy this space between Jamie's adoration and your belittlement. He never really had anything to say. But after months of being in his presence on a regular basis, I start to get the feeling that nobody's home. It seems odd that I'm the only one to notice this absence. Something else I start to notice: the way you respond to his handsomeness. Maybe I could never see your behaviour before, because I never thought he was handsome. But now I catch you looking at him. There is no penetration in your gaze. Before then I would have said that's because Donny has no depth, no soul. But now I'm beginning to wonder if he only seems that way because nobody really sees him.

Maybe I'm noticing that because I don't think anyone sees me either.

What I'm thinking about here is the first time Jamie and I made love. The weekend after he kissed me out on the beach and nearly blew the top of my head off.

Jamie and I arrange the furniture in his apartment and unpack some of the boxes. We make up the bed. When we're finished playing house, I hop in the shower. Then Jamie. I sit on the bed, towel still tucked up under my arms. Anxious. He comes into the bedroom with a towel wrapped around his waist. Kisses me. Removes the towel and lays me down, looking at me reverently, and says, his voice trembling, "You're beautiful," softly kissing my slim young body, head to toe, and back again. He makes me feel beautiful and I kiss him back every inch of the way. When he enters me, his eyes do not waver from my face for even a moment. He locks on and holds on until we liquefy into our journey home. I think I will never leave that place.

I try to remember when Jamie and I stopped looking at each other. I can't think of a particular time or incident. I think about the tide, and how you can only tell it has changed after the fact. Such longing, but I can't imagine how we'll ever get back to that place.

CAITLIN, WITH HER sea-green eyes and shiny brown hair, looks up at me and says, "Mummy, you look so pretty when you get dressed up to go downtown. I'm afraid some man will take you and run away."

That comment from that earnest little face stops me dead. I kneel down and hug my little girl. "I'm not going anywhere, sweetheart. Don't you worry. Not for a minute."

This one, tiny incident, makes me think long and hard about what is at stake.

I resolve to keep Pozzi-thoughts at bay.

But, hard as I try, I can't stay away from him. The construction gang continues to party.

Late one night, Pozzi and I are slow dancing, swaying to "Michelle." Pozzi holds me a lot closer than he should. Everyone's around. I feel we will shatter when the song is over. When the music stops, Pozzi holds on and whispers, "What are we going to do when this mine is built?" "I don't know," I whisper back.

What I mean is nothing, unless he makes his feelings clear, we are going to do nothing. I cannot say this. I cannot speak. There is just this on-going grind of silence.

Later, Pozzi and Jamie get into fisticuffs out on the deck and have to be pulled apart. We'd been shooting ice-cold vodka. We were pissed. Then fisticuffs. Nobody knows what to say about the skirmish. It's tough. All these guys work together and play together. Pozzi is Jamie's boss. Everyone keeps their eyes down except Jimmy, the drawings clerk. He touches my arm as I head for the car and says, "If you ever need anything, give me a call."

All the way back home, Jamie drives like a rock. I'm terrified he is going to ream me out. I feel like puking. He shouldn't be driving.

Back home in the hallway, on our way to bed, Jamie grabs my arm. "I don't know, Robyn," he says. "You and Pozzi always seem to be hanging around together. It makes me wonder. Do you still love me?"

The wall hard behind me is unforgiving as I slump down to the floor. I've been so sure that he does not love me anymore. Of all the questions I've been dreading for over a year, this is not the one.

"I have great regard for you," I muster.

"I know you have regard for me. Do you love me?"

I surprise us both with my answer.

"How can I know if I love you, when I don't even know who I am?"

We sleep back to back. Through the night, I doze fitfully. Like it's not real time in the real world.

Who asked that question? Who said *How can I love you when I don't even know who I am*?

NINETEEN

THE SIGN UP ahead reads THUNDER BAY 103 KM. I often wonder why the highways people don't just round off these distances, or at least put the signs at distances where it's all neat and tidy. *Thunder Bay 100 km*. How do they figure out where to put the signs, anyway? Are they in the places where the signs used to be in miles?

I've been to Thunder Bay once, for a week, with Andrea to visit a high school friend when we lived in Churchill Falls. While touring me around, my friend explained how this part of the city used to be Port Arthur and that part Fort William. To this day, people who hail from here still hold on to old loyalties and more often than not say I'm from Thunder Bay but *really* Port Arthur or *really* Fort William.

Too bad my friend still doesn't live here, because I could use a break for a few days; but I don't feel like holing up in a motel or hotel, so my aim is to push on. If I remember correctly, once I'm past Kenora it's a pretty easy drive. One more day of Great Canadian Shield, Muriel, then we'll be into that transition landscape around Kenora and out onto the tabletop of the world. It will feel like coasting. Then we'll be home safe and sound and I will drag your stuff into the house and divvy it up between the girls. They've already told me that Andrea wants the silver jewellery and Caitlin the gold.

You know it would have been a lot easier on us if you had taken the time to sort out some of this before you shuffled off to the great hereafter. How were we supposed to know what to do with everything? Your will was so simple. The house to Jamie; the money to be split between him and Alexis; the car for me. Nothing else.

But why the hell did you give Alexis the mink coat? She still dresses like a grad student, albeit one who has a certain amount of cash to spend at high-end places like Mountain Equipment Co-op. "She dresses just as carefully as anyone else," I tried to explain to you. "It's a look." But you would have none of it. You couldn't believe that a daughter of yours would choose to dress like that. Now I think it has more to do with contempt for the way you dressed. I can't imagine Alexis wearing that mink coat — unless she makes it practical by turning it inside out to keep out the northern Alberta cold. She'd probably wear her old orange anorak over it. Me? I could wear it inside out, too — to an opening at The New Gallery. I could at least turn the mink into something ironic. Or maybe it would be more ironic to wear it straight. But then that would make the act of wearing it straight ironic. Or would it? These days I can't even keep my theories in perspective. Isn't this supposed to be the age of irony? Although after what happened at your funeral, I think I'm done with irony. I haven't read one line of contemporary cultural theory in the last few years that holds a candle to being upstaged at your own funeral. Alexis might not even still have that old orange anorak. She bought it back in the halcyon days. I remember those frantic Christmas shopping treks before we all rushed back home for the holidays. That's when Alexis bought that ugly anorak. She couldn't resist it. I couldn't believe she wanted it. Even then the only thing we had in common was the fact that I was married to her brother.

Time does nothing to close this gap of awkwardness between us, it only makes things worse. When she and that second husband of hers fly out with their two little kids for a family visit and we all crowd into your big yellow house and struggle to get along for your sake it doesn't quite work. The real shocker comes with the showdown between Jamie and Alexis. I don't think you are aware of what was said, but you must have known, despite everybody's best efforts to hide their feelings.

The showdown starts because Jamie finally acknowledges, after I refuse to let the issue drop, that something has to be done about Donny. For this discussion, he and Alexis head into the yard. I watch them pace up the back forty trying to make things right. When Jamie comes back, his face is set like concrete. He recounts the conversation and I make the mistake of thinking his rage is directed at Alexis, that it arises from the moment.

He starts off telling me that Alexis still can't believe there is anything wrong with Donny other than a little hardening of the arteries. She has some theory of farks or maybe it's something she heard on *Quirks and Quarks*, he can't remember because she talks biological rings around him. She throws in depression as a possible reason for Donny's unaccountable behaviour. Of course Jamie agrees Donny is depressed, but where they differ is the reason for Donny's depression. Jamie thinks his father is depressed because he retired too soon and hasn't got enough to do. Alexis believes that he's depressed because you never let him bring booze into the house. And then, to Jamie's everlasting surprise, she launches into an attack on you that he can hardly believe. In fact, never accept.

"I couldn't believe it," he tells me later. "There she is colder than a witch's tit wondering why I don't see that not only did Mom thwart every move Dad tried to make, but that she tried to thwart every move that any of us ever tried to make. That she was always trying to get us to do things her way."

This is not the way Jamie remembers his childhood.

"It isn't true," he insists, his face contorted. "It just isn't true."

How could he believe these things? He didn't think you had any power. He only saw you as wounded, the nursing school failure.

Jamie is full of anguish and for the time being I let drop the conundrum. But it works away in my thoughts. What does the truth of the past have to do with the way things are now?

And if someone denies your truth, your experience of things, does this mean that you don't have any right to your feelings?

Alexis doesn't have the right to feel thwarted?

Jamie doesn't have the right to feel he had a perfect childhood?

Donny doesn't have the right to feel hamstrung by you?

You don't have the right to feel Donny ruined your life with his drinking?

Even then I could figure out *truth* isn't the real point. Emotions aren't about right or wrong. They just are. They are what we say they are. There is nothing else to go on. But I can't get this across to Jamie. Like Alexis, he is balled up in right and wrong. I am the one left holding the paradox. If they had asked me, I could have at least pointed to all the evidence of suffering. Your face was a tired maze of lines deepened to a map of despair, a map to nowhere. I could have pointed out how the twenty-five pounds you had struggled so hard to lose had packed back on, and that you have given me your favourite fine grey wool designer suit because you know you'll never squeeze back into it again. I could have pointed to the evidence of a furtive, bewildered man suspended between the story he used to tell about himself and the story of what you want him to be. He suffers short outbursts of anger. He comes at you yelling and shaking his fist: *Don't you come here and ... Don't you come here and ... Don't you ...* He never finishes. You don't know what he wants to say, but it preys on your mind.

But Jamie and Alexis don't want to know what I have to say. I don't have the right to my observations.

Jamie needs an ally if anything's going to be done but it won't be me because he doesn't trust my feelings about his father. And it won't be Alexis because she can't bear the pain of seeing there's anything wrong with him.

They don't ask Donny how he feels.

After all is said and done, Alexis manages to stall the question by convincing Jamie that there is really nothing wrong. Jamie lets it drop, but he is left with a bad feeling, haunted by something Donny had said years before after a game of golf just before Donny retired. He looked Jamie straight in the eye with the dark blue eyes that had guided the hands that released hung bombs for five years during World War II, and said, "I get scared when I can't remember things."

There is enough fear to go around. When Alexis flies back to Edmonton hard feelings are left between Jamie and Alexis.

"You'd think we grew up in different houses," Jamie says.

"Were you treated differently?" I ask.

"No."

"Nothing?"

"Well, Mom kind of nagged Alexis about keeping her room clean and tidy. You know how Alexis is. Sometimes Mom really lit into her, but no worse than we do with Andrea and Caitlin."

"Didn't she nag you, too?"

"I was a neat and tidy kid — place for everything and everything in its place."

I think the gentleman doth protest too much.

There is no ripple of irony across his face. He is completely earnest. I explode with laughter and outrage.

"You were the boy. I bet your mother picked up after you all the time and did your room up when you were outside playing."

"That's not true," he argues. "I've always been neat and tidy."

"Well, Jesus," I launch into him. "That's pretty funny, because you were a slob when we got married. I was always picking up after you."

"I had to study."

"So did I. When we were going together, your mother always made your bed."

"She did not."

"Oh, yes, she did. Don't you remember the morning she ruffled your hair and said 'Don't mess your bed up in the morning, sweetheart, I only have to come in and re-make it.' Smile-smile, nudge-wink."

Boys have needs.

I have him cornered.

"And, while we're on the topic," I gallop on. "What about the Sunday morning your folks drove down to Mount Allison because they were suspicious of what was going on between Alexis and Ed and parked out in front of his apartment building and watched their one and only daughter, Daddy's Princess, back out of Ed's place to leave footprints in the snow so it would look like she had just walked in. Paid the piper then, didn't she. But that was all Ed's fault, wasn't it? Alexis would no more want to have sex than cook with spices if she hadn't met Ed."

Boys have needs.

"The only time I ever heard your mother say anything about your messy behaviour was when she asked you not to put your great big hands on the goddamn copper pole in the kitchen."

"Sweetheart," I mock. "Don't leave your handprints on the pole. I have a devilish time getting them off after you go."

Then I bat my eyes.

Silence.

"Well?" I ask. "Is there anything you can think of? Anything at all that would show you were treated differently?"

"Yeah," he answers, as he leaves the room. "They bought me a car when I was sixteen."

"And," he adds, echoing down the hall. "I was a neat and tidy kid."

It must be nice to have a neat and tidy mind, with all that room for denial.

Talking about denial. How about all that money Jamie and I put into the house after I got the job selling advertising at the weekly newspaper? We do everything we can do to hold on to the illusion that we are going to stay in this house: install a new picture window in the dining room, stained-glass light fixtures. Rip out the wrought-iron railings Jamie detests and hire a pair of cabinet makers to build in more up-to-date wooden ones.

Or pretending I like the job. I do like the part about buying new clothes and a briefcase and getting out of the house. I do like chatting up my customers and drawing up ads. I certainly like getting a paycheque, meagre as it is. It's not engaging enough to take my mind off my addiction to the exquisite Pozzi suffering that wafts through me. Even though I have a dim idea that saying to Jamie *How can I love you when I don't even know who I am* applies to Pozzi, too, this emerging knowledge doesn't stop me from wanting him.

Or the fact that Wanda, the office manager, a woman three years younger than me who still lives with her parents and grandmother, met Pozzi when he first came here apartment hunting. Now she wants to know all about him, hinting that she wants me to set them up. After six weeks of lunches and coffee breaks, I decide to hand her over to Pozzi and be done with it, inviting her to the company Halloween party. She sews a tight shiny red dress with a tail and heart-shaped bodice set off by long slinky gloves and a considerable amount of rhinestone jewellery, thick make-up, and hair teased high and wild. I simply don a black and hot pink spandex aerobics outfit and add a pair of wings — I'm going as a disheartened butterfly — and Jamie gets himself up as one of the Blues Brothers. When we walk into the party, Pozzi bounds to my side. He and his roommate Randy are decked out as the Jolly Green Giant and the Little Green Sprout complete with dyed long underwear, Robin Hood tunics, and green grease paint.

"This is Wanda," I say shoving her between us. "She's single."

Then I flounce off to try and enjoy myself. Ha! Given the nature of the night, everyone just goes for flat-out drunk from the very beginning. I don't lay eyes on Wanda for about an hour, until she comes to tattle that while she was sharing a joint outside, Jamie made a pass at her. Fuck a duck, I mutter, I can't leave the bugger alone for five minutes. I tromp off to find him before he gets into trouble.

"Why do you care?" he asks.

"We're still married in case you haven't noticed," I answer.

"You'd never know it. How do you think I feel?"

"How the hell do you think I've felt since you told me in Dawson Creek that work is more important than me and the girls?"

"That's not true. I only said I didn't know. And I thought about it, and I do think you and the girls are more important."

"So how was I supposed to know?"

"Don't I show it? I work my ass off for you guys every goddamn day of my life. What more do you want?"

"I want you to see me."

I haul him into a bedroom when I notice our voices getting a lot of attention. We end up making out on a stranger's floor. The next thing I know it's the middle of the night and people are starting to go home. I reattach my wings and Jamie straightens his fedora. We meet up with Wanda and Pozzi in the hall. She's saying something to him, but I can't catch it. He says they should check with me first.

"We're trying to sort out our rides." Wanda gives me the eye.

"Well," I say. "I'm afraid that I deliver but I don't pick up."

With that, I leave Wanda to her own devices.

On Monday morning, we don't even pretend to work; we simply lock ourselves in Wanda's office while she spills her guts. "After you left," she says, "he just picked me up by the tail and took me home, and there I was the next morning smeared with green paint and my rhinestones all mucked-up when Randy comes bounding into the room and bounces up and down on the bottom of the bed and says, 'You're artsy aren't you?' And as soon as we got rid of him, the Jolly Green Giant and I were doing it again. It was amazing, he just kind of slid me on top of him, front to back, and talk about the jolly green giant ...

This is just so sleazy. I know I shouldn't be listening, but I'm riveted to the side of Wanda's desk. Confused and jealous. I manage to try and ask Wanda, nonchalantly as I can manage, "So, does this mean, like, you're dating?"

Oh yeah, that's what it seems to mean all righty-roo.

We waste a couple of months talking about him, Wanda wanting to know more, and me being held by the spell of all the delicious, torturous details that Wanda is only too pleased to share. We can't stay out of each other's offices. Until some point — I can't name it — I have to face the fact I can no longer indulge myself in this tacky behaviour.

"There's something I have to tell you." I face Wanda while we're loading the dishwasher after a quiet gathering sans Pozzi, who has taken a quick trip back to Ontario to visit his ancient mother.

Wanda freezes over the dirty dishes and eyes me for a moment. "Oh god." Her face caves in. "Don't tell me. I think I know. It's something about you and Pozzi isn't it?"

I nod.

"I knew it. You two were falling in or out of something. I didn't really want to admit."

Leaning against the counter, while we drain a half bottle of wine, I confess the sorry story.

"Didn't you ever talk about it? Try to figure out what to do?"

I shrug. "It's too hard. Everyone's afraid. I think we all always knew how it was going to turn out. But this silence has been killing me. I mean it's really, really awful. And the worst thing is, I have no answer for any of it. I just began to feel like a real shit. A totally useless, unlovable, little shit."

"Oh, fuck," Wanda moans. "How come I'm feeling sorry for you when I'm the one who's been made a fool?"

"We're all a bunch of fools. But if we can't risk being foolish, how will we ever get out of our stagnant lives?"

IF YOU LOOK out there, toward the lake, Muriel, you'll see lumps of what looks like a massive figure sprawled in repose across the lower part of Sibley Peninsula in Sleeping Giant Park poking through the low dirty clouds. It seems to me that there are many sleeping giants lying to be wakened in all of us — giants of potential, of suffering, of desire. Unless we go into the world at least halfway, these giants will remain as inert and ungiving as that granite, tree-covered giant sleeping in the cold, clear waters of Lake Superior.

BY THE END of January, that old longing to get away bubbled up again. An ad I have just taken from the local travel agency grabs my attention: LONDON SHOW TOURS. Flight, accommodation, three show passes, and bus or tube fare to and from the airport all for the price of the airfare.

"Let's go," I suggest to Jamie. "We haven't been away together for five years."

"Can't afford to take the time off."

"But ..."

"I mean it, Robyn. We can't go."

Next day I slump into work and complain to Wanda. She looks at the ad.

"I'll go with you."

"Really?"

"Sure. Why not? It's a deal."

So we book. You hand me a hundred bucks spending money. Even Agatha doles out a travel diary. The girls are in awe. Jamie is silent. He's been out manoeuvred and he doesn't like it. I see his mind working: *first that ten day painting workshop in the summer, now this trip. What next?*

Who knows? That's part of the excitement of getting on an airplane bound for London. Who knows what ideas this trip will put in my mind? Who knows what I'll get up to with Wanda? The meeting of my feet on the sidewalks in an ancient city on a different continent dislocates me from my usual attachments and fills me with a sense of the wonder of myself as a person — a person with likes and dislikes of her own. In London, trudging the grimy gum-polka-dotted streets, amidst massive historical buildings that feel like they've been lumped together by a cyclops, I come up against my old self in the red dress, who swung her arms in the excitement of walking to class. I visit Buckingham Palace and take in a show of the Royal Faberge Egg Collection. We listen to the ethereal voices of the boys' choir practice at St. Paul's Cathedral, stopping outside to feed pigeons on our way to the Tower of London. The crown jewels and regalia aren't as shiny as I expected, but there is something about being in their presence that fills me with majesty. And then the unforgettable experience of entering the White Room, where the great historical figures were kept prisoner; I make contact with the history I studied. Ghosts peel off the wall. Something palpable seeps into my pores and fires a deep and mysterious recognition of my connection with the suffering of those who have gone before. Time collapses. I am there with the imprisoned, body and soul. When I walk out, I am not quite the same person as when I walked in.

We buy shoes and purses and make-up for the hell of it and sweaters because nothing prepared us for the damp chill of London in March. We take in three silly shows and eat curry in the West End. We charge up to Birmingham on a train for a splash of Rock 'n' Roll: a Tina Turner concert being filmed for MTV with the breath-taking surprise of David Bowie making an appearance, but what I come away with is the national pride of 50,000 people singing "In the Summer of '69" with Bryan Adams, who opened the show.

And the art. The Renoir retrospective at the Hayward. The colour and brushstrokes like feathers against my skin and fireworks in my head. Our last day in London: The Tate. What can I tell you about this experience? I am infused with the great and the divine, the fussy and the sublime, from the visions of William Blake to the incompressible contortions of Francis Bacon. I suck it up; I have been starving all my life. I have toured the world's largest underground powerhouse and watched the top being carved off one of the Rocky Mountains, but none of that has moved me like this breathless visit to The Tate Gallery.

That evening, exhausted from our tromp around City of London, I choose a small Hungarian restaurant from the telephone book to be our last exotic repast. We fall into one of those famous black cabs and abandon our packing chore in a freezing cold room in our hotel near Marble Arch. The restaurant is crowded when we arrive, so we're directed upstairs to the bar to wait. The only other occupants are four young men sitting at a table. We choose a seat at the far end and order pints of beer.

Before coming, I made it clear to Wanda that this trip had to be about us and sightseeing, not about men or looking for men. But there is a kind of pulse coming from that table I can't ignore. I keep sliding my glance to the man facing me. He is cute and dashing in a sort of Beatleish way. When they are called down for their table, I am relieved to have him out of sight. Five minutes later, when we are called down, I am stunned that we are placed at the same table as the young men. They turn out to be Hungarian filmmakers working on a documentary with the BBC. Only one speaks fluent English. The really cute one. They seem charmed by us and we are equally charmed by them. After the meal, they invite us to a disco. Why not? The perfect end to a perfect trip. When we step outside, two of the guys fall away. The other two pair up with us. I am beside myself to find the really cute one, the ringleader, with me.

All kinds of things go through my head, but the main one is *Be cool. Act like you have everything under control.*

The disco is a disappointing cellar in a nondescript building off a side alley. The music was unfamiliar and the lights kind of hokey. But the dancing — this guy turns me on big time. I could have had him right there on the floor. We neck and pet in the booth and I don't care who's looking. I am going to get back my teen years when I should have been out doing this sort of thing.

Wanda, on the other hand, is not having such a great time. Her guy isn't so hot. She wants to go back to the hotel and finish packing. My guy wants me to go back to his hotel with him. The only thing that stops me is my cold hard Canadian sense. I don't know who this guy is or where his room is. I need to get on a plane and go home to my children and husband in about six hours. So I kiss this guy right down to his toes and then I stand up, straighten up my dress, and walk out the door without so much as a glance back.

Before I board the plane, I am already flying. Art and Eros have commandeered my soul. I have taken one giant step across the ocean and I will never, ever, step back into the person I was before I left.

Jamie, with the girls tucked under his arms is watching *Wheel of Fortune* in the den when I walk back into our house.

"Oh. Hi. You're back," Jamie says as if I'd just stepped out to the convenience store to pick up ice cream. "What did you get me?" the girls ask.

But you, Muriel, you are the one who can't wait to hear all about my trip. For we have grown truly affectionate since we moved to Sussex and we've been able to spend time with no agenda. Now you regard me as more than just a listener, you look forward to the youthful pleasure I give you in my stories about our parties and the gossip I bring home from the newspaper. You applaud my independence, and my irreverent behaviour toward Agatha, and you secretly admire my laissez-faire attitude to child rearing. Yes, you love me like a daughter. And I am definitely fond of you, and sympathize with your sorrowful life. I haven't the heart to add grief to it. But still. What about me? Am I to be a sacrificial lamb? Live out my life traipsing after mega-construction projects? I don't think so.

And, if you love me like a daughter, can I ever confide in you like a mother? Will the day come when I say that just like you I too walk the floor at night and moan? That my Jane Fonda body and my Estée Lauder face, my dark curly hair and my silly sales job are only as real as my presentation, and that I have become the object of my own life? That the only thing I know for sure is the fathomless bottomless love for Andrea and Caitlin? But can I tell you that when your son asked if I love him, I didn't have an answer, that somehow in the mish-mash of family loyalty I've ended up regarding him somewhat like a brother?

HERE WE ARE in the only part of Thunder Bay you're going to see. Four corners with four lanes and four lights and four gas stations. A string of fast food joints as far as the eye can see, and the smell of French fry grease and car exhaust permeating the car. I wish you could drive for a while because I'm dead tired. I used to understand your fear about driving, and didn't even question it, but now it seems to me that someone should have handed you the keys and said, you're on your own.

Believe me, it would have done you a world of good; shaken you out of your victimhood. I'm not blaming you. I'm just naming. Victimhood. Back then, a word I wouldn't have even associated with someone as high and mighty as you. From this distance, I see now that while I gave you all the compassion I could muster, it was a sort of idiot compassion, a one-way street. That's why I didn't insist someone take action the day you confessed that Donny drove right through a stop sign. That really scared you, didn't it? But not enough. Not enough to take charge.

"It was only a stop sign. Anyone can go through a stop sign."

I listened to your excuses. I validated them. Like an idiot, I soothed you.

Until the day when you and Donny round a corner on the back road from Alma to Moncton, a road you have travelled all your lives, and meet a passing car, dead on, in your lane. Remember what Donny said?

"What do I do now?"

He let go of the steering wheel for a moment, the other car barrelling down on you. Both helpless, you froze. The speeding car pulled into its own lane at the last minute.

"Can you imagine?" you ask me. "'What do I do now?' It missed us by this much," and you hold up your thumb and index finger to one eye and repeat: "By this much."

Jamie starts to see the light of day after that squeaker. It's clear Donny shouldn't be driving anymore. So what do you do? Cook up a story for Donny: sneak his licence from his wallet in the middle of the night and cut it up, then inform him he can't drive anymore because he's gone and lost his licence. You blame him and he has no choice but to believe you, because he can't come up with a better story himself.

Jamie and I shudder, thinking *He's not going to like this, He's going to put up a fight*, but you only have to tell him a few times before he stops going to the driver's side of the car. We all think it's funny how he remembers he can't drive anymore. My guess is that he's relieved of a terrible burden.

Jamie finally agrees that something has to be done about Donny. Odd how we don't think to phrase the problem what can be done *for* Donny. Like we've already written him off and now we have to do something with him for you. For once, Jamie's the one who has a long talk with you and you are frightened because whatever this means for Donny, it means something terrible for you too. You will have to take over the responsibility of your day-to-day lives. You will have to do more than the driving. You will have to do everything. You're stuck.

When Jamie reluctantly takes charge and books an appointment for Donny to be examined by a geriatric specialist, Alzheimer's is not a familiar word.

"Alzheimer's," we mouth awkwardly.

"Alzheimer's," you whine in such a bewildered fashion it's hard to know whom to feel the most sorry for.

The doctor guesses that although Donny displays all the symptoms of Alzheimer's, his days of binge drinking have something to do with his present state. He explains how chemical changes can occur when the brain is starved for nutrients. "We can only be sure it's Alzheimer's after an autopsy is performed."

You become alarmed at the nutrient-missing theory, and feel guilty. You worry yourself sick about getting enough food into Donny lest he deteriorate more quickly. You worry you may not have fed him well enough in the past. You blame yourself for not having been a good enough wife to stop him from drinking. "Here I always complained that he could eat all the cookies and bananas and ice-cream in the world and still stay skinny."

Now Donny has pretty much lost all interest in even his favourite food; though one thing is easier, he forgets that he doesn't like rice or pizza or anything strange or foreign. He eats anything without complaint, though he still eats his hamburgers with a fork and knife.

In no time, you become as bewildered as Donny. All you can imagine is the present as a never-ending chore of keeping an eye on Donny. You never go anywhere because you have to drive.

I can just imagine the fear that rips through you when by early summer of our second year in Sussex, it becomes apparent that the other big potash mine is not going to be built. World demand for fertilizer is depressed. Potash prices are falling. This project is almost completed and Jamie has worked himself out of a job again. He checked his contacts in the area to see if there is any major construction happening in the Halifax vicinity, but his effort is a bust. Economic activity across the country is at a standstill after the past few years of absurdly high interest rates. We have no choice but to head west again.

BY AUGUST, I have our place all spiffed up and listed on the market. We don't know where we'll be going or what we're going to do. I have nothing to hold on to: no illusions about going back to Halifax, no distractions about a love life with Pozzi. There is just me and my naked anxiety. Will the house sell? Will Jamie get a job? Where are we going to go? A pernicious sensation of weakness seeps into my joints. My genitals and the cavity where my uterus once was attached now feel devoid of energy. I get through this time living each moment as it comes. The only thing that keeps me from going under is that fire that was lit in me in London, and a dire curiosity to find out what will happen when I stick my neck into the unknown.

But at least my unknown has some promise of a future. There is hope. Your unknown is like a bad dream. Although it isn't too likely that Donny will go on a bender again. There doesn't seem to be much hope Donny will get it up again. You walk the floors day and night — there is so much more to moan about.

Jamie and I ease you into your new life, arranging a lawyer to give you Power of Attorney so you can get a grip on all the cheques and financial affairs. A Red Cross worker is hired to give you a hand in the house, at least so you can get out and have your hair done, because, given half a chance, Donny will wander off. He's forced to quit smoking when his cigarettes and matches are taken away. After all, he could burn down the house. As far as we can tell, he doesn't mind; he's forgetting his cravings.

Although he doesn't forget where he belongs and where he doesn't belong. A few days after he's checked into the hospital for further tests and observation, he manages to escape and hitchhike all the way back home. He waltzes into the Harbourside café, where you and Agatha are having lunch. He pulls out a chair and joins you as if he just got back from a haircut. You and Agatha don't say a word. Simply order him a piece of apple pie and ice cream so the locals won't get suspicious, then drive him back up to the hospital. This time, they hide his street clothes.

Later that week, you and I light into Moncton for a farewell day on the town. There's something you want my approval for. "It's my last splurge," as you put it. A full-length wild iris mink coat. Six thousand bucks worth of comfort with a matching hat made like an English riding helmet that makes you look rather silly.

"What do you think?"

"It looks great, Muriel. Agatha will be green with envy."

That cinches the deal.

To tell the truth, I had my eyes on it even then.

"You can wear it when you come visit us this winter."

Jamie has already left New Brunswick to start work building a cat food factory north of Toronto. The construction gang is dispersing. Pozzi takes off on a sailing trip to the Caribbean with a young secretary. I'm left to pack up the house. New people are moving in on Thanksgiving weekend. Wanda transfers down to an affiliate newspaper in Florida. We cry our hearts out when she leaves.

Jamie arranges to rent the house of a colleague in Mississauga who will be working in Sudbury for a year. We figure it should be a cinch for me to find another job selling advertising again. But that's all talk. Inside I think I'd rather die than sell advertising in a strange place.

The girls and I spend the weekend before we leave with you and Donny out in Alma. On Sunday morning, I leave them with you making blanc mange while I walk the big tide out. I stand at the water's edge, at slack tide, dangling my Nike Airs by the first two fingers of my right hand while volatile emotions flow through me. I came back here with such high hopes. Now I realize my hopes were as ill defined as my crazy idea to figure out the exact moment when the tide turns. And all of a sudden I start to laugh when it occurs to me that I was trying to grasp something solid like predictability in something as elusive as water, the nature of which is ungraspable.

Back at the yellow house, you and Donny and the girls and I sit down to an early dinner of over-done chicken and Bisto gravy. Blanc mange for desert. You are still fretting about the loads of books and boxes of ornaments Jamie and I stashed under the bed before he left. The skis and odds and sods of stuff we stored in the basement. What if there's a fire? What if there's a flood? What are you going to do with all the stuff we unloaded on you if something happens? I don't quite get what you're on about, only that this business is too much for you, and I wish you had made your anxieties apparent to Jamie, not just me.

Donny plays with his food, not listening. "Where's the boy?" he asks quite suddenly. His dark blue eyes seem startled by his own question.

"Donny, I told you a hundred times. Jamie's gone up to Toronto."

"Mississauga," I correct.

"Jamie's got a job in Toronto. He's not coming back," you say with cruel exasperation.

"Wellwellwell. Good show for the boy."

Late in the afternoon, when the girls and I are on our way back to Sussex, I stop on the gravel verge to drink in what will be my last view of the salt water for who knows how long. I will miss this place. Yet I can hardly wait to get away from your two old pleading faces. I've got two little girls to settle into a new place, a husband to try and relate to, and a future for myself to come to grips with. Looking out over the bay, all I can think about is the unbearable, daunting task of packing up and clearing out again. On the surface of the water, oily patterns of light blue and dark blue swallow each other whole.

TWENTY

AN INCIDENT WITH the waitress in the diner at Kakabeka Falls this morning has somehow blown the cover off this story I've been telling you.

"I see you're from New Brunswick," she comments innocently enough, nodding toward the car parked out front.

"No I'm not," I snap, the sound of my own voice startling me.

"Oh, the plates," she motions to the car and clears away the bacon rinds and toast crusts I've left.

"I'm from Nova Scotia, but I live in Calgary now," I try in a softer voice. She shuffles away, a red-roughened hand kneading the fat ropes of her hips as she disappears into the kitchen. Oh well, why would she be interested in my attempt to lighten up? I stare out at the licence plates and realize they embarrass me. They're something I want to get rid of. I'd toss them away on the spot, if I could.

A few minutes later, she comes back with hot water to refill the ugly little stainless steel teapot. "Headed east or west?"

"West. I've been on the road five days now. Sorry if I sounded irritated. I'm tired."

And lonely, I want to add.

"No big deal," she says. Then, "You've got a ways to go?"

"At least three days."

"Don't be in a hurry, if you don't have to," she sighs and tucks a strand of dyed black hair behind her ear. "I wouldn't mind a week to myself on the road."

Did I tell her I was alone? Or can she just see it? I find myself wanting to make an excuse, as if being alone on the road is a punishment. I still feel her eyes on me, twenty-five miles away, the sound of longing in her voice. The last couple of weeks have been so weird and I've been so balled up in telling you my side of the story that I haven't stopped to think about how extraordinary my journey is. When do we ever get to see ourselves as others see us? We spend most of our lives going on automatic from one moment into the next, like waves into waves, and life goes on until a rogue wave rises up and slaps us awake. But even then, how often do we take the time to think about who we are and where we've been and where we're going, before we go back to automatic? Without taking that second look not only at how others see us, but how we see ourselves. Like being embarrassed by licence plates. We just want to get rid of those parts we don't like and drive on down the road.

I was in a bad mood this morning because for once and all I was going to tell you how much I hated living in Mississauga. But you know what? I've had a change of heart. I see now that those miserable eleven months might have been the best that ever happened to me.

But in the beginning, I was pissed off. I didn't want to move there and I wasn't even consulted about the new car.

"It's a five-speed," Jamie says. "You're gonna love it."

He's hustling me and the girls through the Toronto airport parkade, suitcases piled high on rickety carts, when he delivers this news.

"Jesus, Jamie," I protest. "I don't know how to drive a five-speed."

"The Spitfire was a five-speed."

"I never got to drive it."

"Really?" he asks over his shoulder. It's clear he has that old picture in his head: if I've done it, you've done it.

"Really, Dahling," I mock.

"Well don't worry. You're gonna love it. A Cavalier. Real sporty. No power steering though. Saved a few bucks there."

I want to mow Jamie down with my cart. He had skedaddled from Sussex a week before to start the new job and I had been left with the heft of packing up and clearing out. We had to make the move on the cheap. The company had offered a flat take-it-or-leave-it rate. The days of big jobs and big money are disappearing into thin air. Heavy industrial construction is in a slump. Jamie's worried about the future; he wanted to economize, which meant no professional movers. Sure, lots of the gang came over to help out, but I was the one responsible for the whole nine yards. I was the one who had to pour Andrea and Caitlin onto a plane when they turned into molasses saying goodbye to all their dear little friends.

(You've been abandoned again, my dear.) (It's not Jamie's fault, he had to start when he had to start.) (We're not that hard up for cash, couldn't something better have been arranged?) (Buck up, it's only a move, nobody died, you'll be tiptop in a week or two.)

I hate the Cavalier on first sight.

I hated everything about Mississauga. The oppressive brick houses clumped cheek by jowl. My heart sinks when we turn off Burnhamthorpe Road and Jamie points to the conglomerate of monstrosities where we will spend the next ten or eleven months. River Mill Way. I can't stand it. Where is the river? Where is the mill? Where is the goddamn Way? And where the hell is my say in all of this?

I get a lesson in driving a five-speed on Thanksgiving Monday afternoon in an empty parking lot. Thunk, grind, thunk. Jamie is exasperated. I am in tears. On the whole, I prefer a great big automatic in the world of wilderness and bears to a five-speed and eight-lane thoroughfares with endless collector lanes.

Tuesday morning I'm supposed to go to the Manpower Office and put in my claim. "Take a cab," are Jamie's last words leaving for work. "So what if it costs fifty bucks." Fifty bucks? I look out at that wine-coloured car in the driveway. Why should I spend fifty bucks when there's a perfectly good car? I grit my teeth and take a map — the Manpower Office is a few miles away, but it's a fairly straight route on Dixon — and get in the car. This is not a making-the-best-of-it deal, Muriel. This is a leaning-into-what scares me deal. With a lot less clunking than the day before, I make my way there and back. I don't think I breathed. It takes me two hours to get the cramps out of my hands.

A few days later, I venture out again for an interview at a stupid little rag. Its sole purpose is to sell advertising. I get all dressed up, but I come on like a real hick. I do not want this job. In fact, I do not want a job at all. I want time. I am thirty-one and I have to think about where my life is going. I want to walk Andrea and Caitlin to school in the morning and pick them up in the afternoon.

I do not understand life in Mississauga. The indifference of neighbours. The rudeness of bank tellers. I have never heard someone complain that cats leave yellow piss-holes in the snow, thus disfiguring the neighbourhood, bringing down property values. Not that there is a house for sale on the street, or anyone to talk to. Nobody is home in these big brick houses. My weekly outing is to the grocery store, which, I have to admit, is chock full of anything I could want or imagine. I could go to the malls but I find them too vacuous.

Every other Friday night, Jamie and I meet with people from work at one of the local pubs. On weekends, we did the sort of thing happy families in big cities do: take our kids to art classes and enjoy coffee and Danishes while we wait; troop off to the zoo, the planetarium, the Royal Ontario Museum, the Art Gallery of Ontario, the McMichael Canadian Collection, and take a good snoop around downtown Toronto. We all hold hands and skate at Nathan Philips Square or Harbourfront. We go to the ballet to see the *Nutcracker* and splurge on *Cats*. It's a razzle-dazzle world after living in Alma or Sussex, let alone Churchill Falls or Tumbler Ridge.

My very favourite place is the McMichael Art Collection in Kleinburg, where in me rouses some deep numinous feeling the minute I step down the strangely lit corridor smelling that climate and humidity control smell I've come to identify with great paintings. There is something I can't name here that is rendered and framed, speaking not so much to me as through me. I see how people have leaned into the mystery of our monstrous Canadian landscape and left for us a mark of trying to know it. And I think how different this is from how I have experienced Churchill Falls and Tumbler Ridge where the land was seen as something to subdue and take from.

As I say this, Muriel, it sounds false to me. This is my trained mind interpreting my experience from back then. Perhaps it's just safer to say that I was in awe, and something in me was stirred, although the word *awesome* has been drained of meaning these days by servers in mediocre restaurants who say "awesome" when you give them your order.

The other significant part of my Mississauga experience is that each morning I sit in the chilly kitchen, wearing a pair of old knit gloves with the fingertips cut off, and read *The Globe and Mail* cover to cover, trying to learn something about the world into which I have been catapulted, and where, if anywhere, I fit into the larger scheme of things, because for the first time in my life I understand that there is a centre, and that for all of my life, I have been living on the fringes.

So when you start calling, wondering what we are going to do at Christmas, Jamie and I freak out a little. We do not like it here, but I am not ready to go back. We're on a city adventure. And it's not just that: we're not ready to face you and Donny and your unending sorrows. Not yet. For a change, we actually have a choice because Wanda calls from Florida and invites us down for Christmas. I figure Jamie is going to say no; but, to my everlasting surprise, he agrees.

"This will probably be the only chance we'll ever get to take the kids to Disney World," we explain to your stony voice on the phone.

Oh why oh why did you have to go all the way down to that darn place when you could have come home? Ten days of this on the phone after New Year, when we get back and we are begging you and Donny to come to Mississauga for a visit.

"How can I leave the cat?"

"Agatha can come in and feed her."

"What about the airport? You know Daddy almost got us lost there when we flew out west. You know what he's like now."

"We'll arrange to have an attendant to meet you as you come off the plane."

"What if nobody shows up?"

"Don't worry, Mom. It'll be a piece of cake."

"Nobody could miss you in that gorgeous coat of yours, Muriel. Wouldn't it be nice to wear it in Toronto?"

There is silence for a moment.

"Okay, if it means that much to you."

So there Jamie and I wait anxiously at arrivals on Saturday morning and our eyes light on Donny towering above your minked fuming ball of a body and we know right away there will be hell to pay.

"There was no one to meet us," you hiss. "I had to find you all by myself."

"But aren't you proud of yourself?" Jamie and I chirp. "You made it all alone!"

"It was an ordeal."

Then you catch Jamie staring at your mink hat for a moment too long.

"Don't you like my hat, sweetheart?"

"It's great Mom. It's just great."

As soon as we get in the house, you corner me. "Robyn, you said this hat looked good on me. Jamie doesn't like it at all. And do you know what Donny had the nerve to say when I put it on this morning? He took one look at me said, 'Wellwellwell, isn't that the genuine article?' How do you think that made me feel?"

I know right then and there that this week is going to be a disaster. To make matters worse, the weather is miserable. Damp, dark, snowy, windy, and bone-chilling cold. Jamie and I hadn't thought about the fact that a January visit would be dreary. We hadn't calculated that the cold brick house we're living in will create a downright clammy crisis for two old people who never seem to be warm enough. We hadn't counted on the accusations rumbling below the surface of every conversation.

You went to Florida without us. There was no one to meet us when the plane landed.

"We didn't have much fun in Florida," I fib, trying to butter you up. "It's one of the coldest winters on record down there. We nearly froze at Disney World and it was awful the day we went to Cape Canaveral. Even now NASA can't get the Shuttle off the ground."

"I'm cold," you respond. "Can't you turn up the heat?"

The place is like a 3500 -square-foot refrigerator. I try to explain it's so cold inside because the floor is concrete and the ceilings are so stylishly high.

"Concrete?"

"Yeah, you know, cement," I whisper.

I don't want Jamie to hear me say *cement* when it's really *concrete*. Cement is just the powder. I've heard it a thousand times. *Concrete. People are so stupid*. I take you down into the unfinished basement and show you the massive excavation under the main floor. I mimic the owner's voice, another engineer who works with Jamie. "Had to dig an extra twenty feet to get good ground for the foundation so thought I might as well put in a pool. Don't want a post in the middle of my pool so figured I'd put in steel girders and a concrete floor. Designed it myself. You could drive a tank into the living room!" Then I draw your attention to the far corner of the "pool" where snow has been billowing in through a hole in the foundation since mid-December, creating that clammy bone-chilling climate we're experiencing. But you don't care about my explanation; you just want the problem fixed.

"Can't you just turn up the heat? Your house was always nice and warm in Churchill Falls, and that was in Labrador."

"I'll try," I say.

I turn up the heat and the cold still permeates our feet and ankles, legs, between the shoulder blades, making our fingers ache and noses drip. I swaddle you in blankets on the couch when we watch TV and bring you steaming hot cups of tea, which make you pee too much.

On Monday, we brave the weather for an expedition to Sherway Gardens to look for a new hat.

The parking lot at Sherway Gardens is chock-a-block. I offer to let you and Donny off by the door. "I'd just as soon wait for you since we've never been here before," you say with alarm.

The still, damp cold descends on us slowly as we creep through the sea of parked cars. Halfway to the mall entrance, you place your hands on your ears. You're having a hard time keeping your balance on the ice-ridged and rutted pavement, so Donny and I hold you under the elbows and guide you along. I wonder to myself if Donny knows where we are going, or if he even knows where we are. We shop all afternoon, but we can't find a hat to suit you. You buy me a sweater to keep warm, but won't get one for yourself.

The next day we try Square One. We find a parking spot handy to the mall, so we don't have to perform the elbow shuffle of the previous day. As we trundle along, pretending to look for hats, we stop in front of an expensive little jewellery store that has a well-mannered sign propped up on a wrought iron easel announcing: SALE NOW IN PROGRESS. In we go to cruise the glass counters. The clerk follows as if attached by a wire. Suddenly you stop in front of a delicate necklace with matching earrings. Your ears twitch.

"White gold, pink gold, yellow gold. Just like my wedding band. How much?" you ask, lifting your eyebrows up to the roots of your hair so you can see over your bifocals.

"Half-price. Four hundred and fifty."

You hiss ever so delicately.

"Why don't you treat yourself," I prompt.

"Well," you fret. "I don't want to use up all my cash."

I figure you've got at least a thousand in your wallet. You always did. It gave you something concrete to worry about.

"You have a Visa card," I remind you.

"Well, it's so long since I used it. It might not be good anymore."

"Let me see." I check the expiry date. "Go ahead, Muriel, use it. It'll keep your account up to date."

"Yes, that's a good idea," you say brightly.

On the way home, we're stopped at a red light listening to *Morningside* when the program is interrupted to announce that the Space Shuttle *Challenger* has just exploded. For a moment I lose all sense of time and space. We had just seen the *Challenger* when we were down in Florida. There's been all the hype about the teacher, Christa McAuliffe, being on board. When the light changes, the car behind blares its horn to nudge me on. I have to concentrate on my driving, because all I can see is the flat Florida landscape and off in the distance, the *Challenger*, as it sat loaded on its ramp, pointing straight to heaven.

I rush into the house and switch on the TV, car keys in hand, boots dripping slush. I don't have to wait long to see the image of the space shuttle exploding. I don't know how many times we watch that horrible forked plume over the next couple of days. Or the faces of Christa McAuliffe's mother and father transform from wonder to disbelief in a few short seconds. It's the mother's parka I focused on when I couldn't stand to watch her face once more, but at the same time, I can't stop watching. The spectacle thrills and sickens me.

At some point, I realize the mother's parka is just like mine and stroke the fur on my hood as if I could somehow stroke the mother's grief. How would it feel, I wonder, to have the world witness that split second change from joy to grief?

"Will you look at that," Donny says every time he watches the explosion.

"Will you look at that."

Every single time is a new experience for him. Not a replay.

Is this why, I wonder, he only remembers what he learned by heart? The faces of Muriel and Jamie and Alexis. The *dead mother, the missed funeral, and The War*. His dog tag number, R148763.

I allow my imagination to ignite as I watch the images of the events leading to the explosion and the immediate following moments.

Finally, I walk away from the television. Dumbfounded how this event has bored into me, leaving me porous and vulnerable.

"A school teacher. A school teacher and a mother," you remark, peering into the screen. Then you shift your focus to the socks you're knitting.

"And I can't believe it's so cold in Florida," you add. "Will you look at the winter coats? It was so hot when we were there a few years ago, I could hardly wait to get back home."

"But Muriel, don't you remember we told you on Christmas Day when we were at Disney World the temperature hovered around zero and we weren't prepared. We had to buy those damned Mickey Mouse sweatshirts and hats to keep warm. That we couldn't even stay for the fireworks that night because we were freezing our butts off."

"Well, we watched the parade on TV to see if we could get a glimpse of you. I said to Donny 'Isn't it a beautiful day down there in Florida for Jamie and his family?' Didn't I, Donny? Donny."

"What?"

"Didn't I say what a fine day Jamie and his family had for the parade on Christmas?"

"Oh yes, yesyesyes."

Happy to please. Miles away. Then his face darkens. He looks apprehensive, then angry. All of a sudden I think I know what Donny wants to say to you when he comes at you threatening *Don't you ... Don't you ... Don't you come here and ...*

Ask me any questions. That's one of the things I realize makes him afraid and vulnerable and angry. Questions he has no hope in hell of answering.

I see now that he has no expectations, no prospects, no hope, and certainly no trust. He can't even trust us to stop asking him questions. And then I understand that along with his memory, Donny has lost his ability to interpret. He can't make meaning out of anything. He has no hope of crossing the abyss of his own mind. I can't think of anything more terrifying. Not even being blown up in a Space Shuttle.

A few days after you and Donny are snug and warm back in Alma, you call to ask if I have seen your new earrings. You can't find them anywhere and are somehow fixed with the idea that they are still in Mississauga.

"I shouldn't have let you talk me into buying them," you moan. "Couldn't you look again?"

I pull back the carpet from the moulding and run my fingers across every fibre of the room you in which you slept. I even sift through the dirt in the vacuum cleaner bag.

"No earrings, Muriel."

You moan again.

I find your preoccupation with the lost earrings obscurely depressing. Surely there are other important things to worry about. But even more distressing is a comment you had made about Christa McAuliffe a couple of days after the *Challenger* disaster. I can't get it out of my mind.

"I don't see what she was doing there. I really can't imagine," you say.

I understand that somewhere in this comment is an accusation. You can't hide your distaste and suspicion of the kind of woman who wants something bigger. You have been brought up to know your place and accept it.

I HAVE JUST passed Ignace, Muriel, and I don't have one interesting thing to tell you about that place. Ignace could be home to the biggest Wooden Indian in the world, planted right along the highway, and I would have missed it. I am so caught up in the story of your hat and the earrings, and the ordeal at the airport. *There was no one there to meet us.*

Jamie was hurt to think that you would think he made a promise and didn't keep it. Of course he called Air Canada and arranged for an escort. The night you arrived we talked about it in bed. I had an idea about what happened and reminded him about the time you and Donny came down to see us in Halifax before Andrea was born. We wanted to go see *Young Winston* at the theatre, but you protested, saying you couldn't take crowds, that all the people took your breath away. We talked you into it and when we arrived in the throng in the lobby the smell of popcorn drove you wild to get some and you pushed your way forward, elbows whirring like a mix-master. We sucked in right behind you, afraid you'd get lost and have a panic attack, and you lined us all up abreast at the counter, shoving other people out of the way. At the time Jamie and I were acutely embarrassed with this performance, but we laughed our asses off that night in Mississauga when I reminded Jamie of the story. This, I suspected, was how you made it to the baggage carousel at the Toronto airport. I'll bet you marched right past your Air Canada escort.

NOW I HEAR my own voice from this morning, the defensiveness in my response to an innocent question. What am I hiding from? What made me so hot about those New Brunswick licence plates? I feel my answer like a spike: I am not from New Brunswick. I am from Nova Scotia, but I live in Calgary. Do I think they are superior places? I must. For all my love of Fundy and the beach and the giant tides, I resist being identified with New Brunswick.

That mink coat, Muriel. I really wanted it. How it felt on my body when you let me try it on, almost weightless. The cool satin lining, like a membrane between me and the fur. The richness of it. The marker between me and the world. Not just warmth but protection.

Would I have traded the coat for the car? I think I would have. But then I wouldn't be here in the hinterland re-thinking our story. I would have been still telling myself and everyone else that Mississauga was the worst place in the world and how I hated every minute of living there. But that's only part of the story, isn't it? In Mississauga, I got what everybody says they want: I got time. Time to read, to think, and to awaken that old longing of mine. I even got half an hour five mornings a weeks to sit with my body in front of the television and practice yoga with the woman on PBS. Just me and my body. No little hands. No big hands. No thoughts of Pozzi's sizzling hands. Just the feel of my body, stretching. The feel of my mind, stretching.

I can imagine wearing the mink coat now, just as I joked about it a few days ago, inside out. The protective fur next to me and the silk membrane exposed to the world. I've got the rest of today and a couple of more days after that to sit with myself just as I sat with myself in the cold house in Mississauga.

There's a big thing that lies hidden or dormant in the debris of our everyday lives. We label it loneliness. It's an elusive feeling that we feed with food or sex or work or the company of complete strangers. I got a glimmer of loneliness in Mississauga. I feel keenly today, that it's not really loneliness, it's something that embodies the desires of loneliness, but it wants more.

Stay with me, Muriel. I think I'm getting somewhere. The landscape is passing by and I feel like time is flowing through me, but mile by mile my thoughts are getting more and more still.

You know it really shocked me to realize that, in the end, you didn't react to the *Challenger* disaster in a more meaningful way than Donny. Now it dawns on me: because you could never put yourself in the shoes of others, you lacked simple human compassion.

Thinking back, I now see that in all the turmoil about Donny's condition, the person you felt sorry for was yourself.

I have an inkling why Christa McAuliffe took a chance for a ride on the shuttle to teach kids from space. Not that I particularly want to do that. But I'm dying to zoom off somewhere, out of my confining world. I want to push up hard against the core of adventure and discovery. I want to test myself, to see what I'm made of.

The morning after one of your calls, when everyone's gone for the day, I wrap up in a green blanket and sink into the couch. I watch a fine drizzle of snowfall disappear into the pavement. An image of Christa McAuliffe turning to smile and wave to the cameras as she boards the *Challenger* is on the TV. I am stricken by that face; the wonder, the joy.

Your voice *Let this be a lesson to you; there is only disappointment* fills my head.

No, I want to shout. Disaster and failure can't be the lesson. There has to be something else.

And then I lurch into a different time altogether. The round, happy face of Mona, my mother's little sister, comes to mind. She's turning to wave us goodbye on the July long weekend. The image solidifies, particle by particle, at the centre of my mind.

"What do you want to do when you grow up, dear?" she had asked me that morning before she and Marjorie drove off.

"I want to be an artist," I answered shyly, knowing already at the age of fourteen what a preposterous idea this was, but still wanting to name it.

"What kind of artist?"

"I want to paint portraits. I draw them all the time in school. Especially during math class."

"Show me some."

"They're not very good," I say, handing Mona a pad of writing paper filled with awkward drawings of my classmates.

"Oh, my. I think they're very good. Do you have any more?"

"Only these." I show Mona another wad of dozens of drawings of the same, idealized face, drawn in three-quarter profile.

"Who is she?" Mona asks.

"No one," I shrug. "I don't know who she is, but I draw her all the time."

"She looks awful lonely," Mona says, and gives me a warm beery hug. She lights up a smoke and winks. "Want a drag? I won't tell."

I inhale the damp concrete smell in the chilly living room in Mississauga and fall flat into the heart of my mother's desolation. There is no give, no bounce, just the hardpan of grief and anger. For the first time since I left home, I feel like a traitor. I had run away from the unbearable and hooked into a family who didn't know anything about me. I realize I've been hiding out. Not even allowing myself to remain faithful to memory.

A long suspended cry perforates the tight walls of my resistance and I let myself be carried away in an effusion of tears. Oh, god, how I miss them, my mother and Marjorie and Mona, the way they were, before the accident. I see their pale, luminous skin and milky sea-blue eyes. Mom and Marjorie with fine black hair teased high, and Mona with her hair dyed red and razor-cut. Their rough laughter. High hopes. Bitter jokes. Cigarette butts. Clinking glasses. Perfume gone sour. The sting of it all.

I rub my puffy eyes and fall further into my own desolation. *I have not been true to myself.*

A rogue wave has crashed into me. If I have not been true to myself, have I been able to be true to those around me?

There's something I couldn't bear to tell you, Muriel, when you were visiting. My mother is living in a boarding house in the town where I was born in Nova Scotia. On welfare. We send her one of my unemployment insurance cheques each month, because she simply can't get by. High interest rates and the slow economy have caught up with those least able to defend themselves: beds are being shut down in the nursing homes where she has worked as a nurse's aide for the last ten years. I find my mother's situation unbearable and

I'm not even the one who has to bear it. In fact, except when I send the money, I try hard not to think about it.

For the rest of the winter, after reading *The Globe and Mail* every morning, or listening to *Morningside*, I draw the faces of the women I knew from the cradle. I start with my mother. At first I try drawing from a black-and-white photograph my stepfather had taken in 1957. Mom was twenty-three. She's displayed in three-quarter profile from the waist up, wearing a heavy dark wool coat with wide lapels opened to show off the contrasting light grey lining. The pleated ruffle of a white blouse peaks through at her neck. In the background are a few patches of crusty snow along a wild grass dune leading to a beach and, off in the distance, just above Mom's eye-line, not far from the horizon, the barely discernable white edge of a rolling breaker. Her lips are full, pressed into a slight smile. Chin-length black hair is caught up in the wind. Her small straight nose is framed by the lovely curving line of her cheeks. Her dark eyebrows feathered and arched over pale eyes held tight against the glare, looking serenely off into the distance. There's no doubt that she's an object of beauty in that photograph. There's no doubt that this was the face of my mother. But this is not a face I know, and I can't make a likeness in my sketchpad. No matter how many times I try, the face is stiff and lifeless. Filled with self-doubt and frustration, I hunt through an old shoebox of photos for pictures of Marjorie and Mona, but the only ones I find are bleached and blurry.

Only when I discard the photographs and remember my mother teasing me when I was little that I summon the courage to draw from my heart. I hold a soft pencil to fine-grained paper and in a concert of short and long overlapping strokes, waltzing back and forth from the centre out; I find my mother's face: handing me a spatula coated in chocolate peaks of cake mix; asking if I know what happened to David's hoarded Easter eggs. I see my mother's face with the cheek of a baby held next to her own. I see my mother's face, split and empty, after the baby was gone. I see my mother's face locked into the faces of her sisters as they sit around the table, raking up the past. I hear my mother's voice torn from the unheavenly space in her soul, when the telephone call comes. *There's been an accident.* I draw that mouth and those eyes with a hard zigzag line. I draw and I draw, but I can't find the face that my stepfather photographed on an early, cold spring day.

Soon the dining room table in the Mississauga house is covered with artless piles of women's faces. Mona, plump and blousy, waving goodbye. Marjorie, with her city shine, skeletal and stylish. Christa McAuliffe's mother searching. You. And me, in three-quarter profile, eyes reaching out for something bigger, something deeper.

The other pile I've accumulated is a tower of books that I've read in the late afternoons. Fifty-four books, I counted when we packed up. These books and *The Globe and Mail* and *Morningside* and the stiff little watercolour paintings and the drawings and the galleries and the planetarium and all the other places and new activities I engage in while living in Mississauga have twined into a rope of hope, a rope of imagination, to get me across the abyss of who I am and who I want to be.

I used to think that living in Mississauga was one of the worst years of my life because I didn't have any friends and my mother was on welfare. But now, from this distance, what I see is the rope.

I have to laugh, thinking back to how I thought you'd be so easy and uncomplicated to love, Muriel, with your one tragedy. You hid behind your old nursing school failure. Both you and my mother ended up the same: cut off by your own pain from the world around you. I had so much fear of ending up like you. I didn't see my own personal journey had begun.

IN MAY AND June, a smudged yellow haze descends upon the metropolis and bricks up a hellish heat that I can't bear. Instead of falling for the trap of feeling stuck, as I did in Tumbler Ridge or Dawson Creek or Churchill Falls, the thought enters my head that I can simply pack up the girls and drive out of this confinement.

"We're coming home for a few weeks," I announce to you on the phone. "I'm going to visit my mother and some cousins in Nova Scotia, but thought we'd stop in with you first, if you don't mind. Jamie's going to join us later."

For a moment you're speechless. "You're going to drive yourself?"

"Yup. Jamie's going to come with me to Kingston for the weekend and take the train back. Then a high school friend from Sussex is going to share the driving with me."

"In that small car?"

"Nope. We traded in the Cavalier for a Jeep Cherokee. Five-speed. I love it. You're high up and it feels safe and sound."

"Oh my goodness. When are you coming?"

"July first. It's so hot here, I can't wait any longer."

"Hot!" you hoot. "Hot! I can't imagine it ever gets hot in Mississauga."

TWENTY-ONE

WE ARE JUST entering the Lake-of-the-Woods. I think we're out of the hinterland now, Muriel. The forest is changing dramatically, it's lush and leafy and airy, soft; a relief after the hard climb around Lake Superior. It's only 3:30. I was so tired and grouchy this morning that I thought we'd spend the night here, or Kenora, but I think we can make it to Brandon. The days are getting longer. I know a good hotel there with a pool. Jamie and I stopped there with the girls when we moved west in '86. Just about seven years ago.

I read somewhere that all of the cells in our bodies are renewed every seven years. I wonder if that's why there's also the idea that our life changes every seven years as well. I often think about that. Twenty-one when I had Andrea. Twenty-eight when I kissed Pozzi. I must have been in transition the afternoon I smacked Jamie on the cheek with a dry one and dropped him off at the train station in Kingston.

THE NEXT MORNING, I set out for home with my high school friend from Sussex. I'll never forget the wide-open feeling of hitting the road. Other than getting home, there's something big on my mind: I am going to go back to school to try something new. Jamie is waiting to hear about a job in Saskatchewan where a new heavy oil upgrader is to be built. If it all turns out right, we'll be living in Regina by the first of September.

Sixteen hours after we started the trip, I drop off my high school friend at her destination, and forty-five minutes after that, I arrive on your doorstep, Muriel. I'm drunk on the cold wet fog and the feeling of power from peeling up the roads between here and Ontario without a man in sight. We only had a few tricky moments merging on one of the bridges while I steered and she navigated. Other than that, we were A-okay.

The following day, the sun is strong and the bay is a satin blue. We all go and, without a performance of prancing around getting used to the water, we dive in, swimming out into the cold, all the while keeping an eye on Donny. He seems happy enough just watching a fishing boat cruise out the channel and circle around the harbour.

At supper that night, while we dig into fresh strawberry shortcake that Agatha brings over, Andrea and Caitlin beg, "Wiggle your ears Grandma!"

Without a word you jump up from the table and run upstairs. Then you gallop back down to perform your trick. Wiggling away on the pillows of your great wrinkled ears are the white, pink, and yellow gold earrings you bought the day the *Challenger* exploded.

"Do you remember how cold it was at your place last winter, so cold I couldn't wiggle my ears," you explain. "Even on the last night. I never got warm in your house. I was so vexed with myself that I held my ears close to my head trying to warm them up. The backs of my new earrings were sticking into my neck so I took them off. After supper you brought them to me and said, 'Don't forget your new earrings, Muriel.' I must have put them in the pocket of my sweater that I haven't worn since. I haven't even thought of that sweater until just now."

"Well it's a good thing I drove all the way down here just to remind you, Muriel," I say, the memory blooming in my head.

"You should have remembered anyway, Robyn," you scold me, somewhat mockingly. "You always remember everything."

Do I? I wonder a few days later when I walk the big tide out. Do I always remember everything? It's been seven years since we've been back when conditions were just right for mud larking. The girls and I wave to you and Donny anxiously perched on car blankets on the Alma beach, not far from where the brook runs into the channel. You're like two dots, but I know you're there. I kick my feet out, now understanding that by this very act I can alter the surface texture and change the pattern forever. But what about underneath, I wonder. How do you change the deeper patterns? What about that legendary memory of mine. It seems to me that memory is like the surface of the bay — I can stir it up here, and stir it up there, but I'd never be able to see, let alone map, the flux of a body in motion. For most of my life, I brood, I've been content to be like the tide, following it in and out, letting myself be carried along, but never really getting anywhere. From now on, I decide, I'm going to be more choosy.

Andrea and Caitlin and I stand ankle-deep in the hot sun at the tide's edge squishing mud up between our toes. Wave by wave, the water creeps up our shins. Time to turn back to shore. I steer us over the patches of sand and gravel to a long flat of mud where we slide and slick ourselves up and wait for the water to steal over us and wash us off.

As my fingers mess around in the mud, a door opens in my mind and I am instantly back to an art afternoon in primary school where we were given free reign with pots of finger paints and large shiny sheets of creamy paper. I don't remember anything about the images I made, just the fathomless joy of my hands and the paint and paper and the doing. As I connect with this doing again, out here on the Alma beach, there occurs within my chest an event I can only describe as seismic. Before I know it, salt water warmed from the sun on the beach begins to inch in and around us as we loll about like a family of well-fed seals.

TWENTY-TWO

AN ENCLOSED TWO-STOREY courtyard of highway hotel rooms surrounds the swimming pool and brown-tipped decorator palms. Boisterous kids lash about in the smelly water while their parents sag in deck chairs, lifting glasses of beer or rum and cola to grim mouths, trying to appear as if they enjoy the spectacle. They've been on the road all day. There is nothing to say. They are contained in the strange sound of children's voices bouncing against concrete and ceramic and chlorinated water. Fluorescent light stabs every surface. There are no shadows. Outside, the prairies, vast and looming, lie incongruent with this manufactured space.

I don't know why I bombed past Winnipeg to make it to Brandon for the night. Jamie and the girls and I stayed here on the last leg of our journey to Regina after we left Mississauga. When you've been on the road by yourself for a week, you'll go for the familiar, even if it's awful.

I'm trying to remember how I felt that night, but all I can summon is a state of exhaustion, a kind of near trembling in a body too tired to tremble. A mind blitzed by the road. I order room service. A Monte Cristo sandwich with fries and coleslaw. Two Extra Old Stock. One for now, one for later — with a zanax. *Do not drink while taking this medication*, the label says. I allow that this could mean *Do not drink too much*. I am beginning to allow certain inconsistencies, trying to make small adjustments as I go along. There are benefits and consequences for every choice I make.

We didn't know it then, but that was the last night Jamie and Andrea and Caitlin and I spent shrouded in the arms of the post-war family dream. The moves had not destroyed us, Jamie's ambition had not destroyed us, Pozzi had not destroyed us, even you and Donny and my mother and their peculiarities had not destroyed us. As long as I had remained intact — untouched by knowledge, unblemished by credit or reward and a sense of belonging and doing well — we had remained contained.

I slept fitfully that night, weaving in and out of the gauzy bandages of hope that had kept me together since the days we left Halifax and ventured out into this great hulking country. I knew without a doubt that Regina, a city that had barely registered on my consciousness until the preceding months, would be my chance to break out of the unbearable familiarity of the daily grind.

I had such a bad cold and sore throat that morning when we left Brandon under overcast skies, driving along on autopilot straight as an arrow toward Regina, not really taking in all the space around me, when all of a sudden the city loomed up out of nowhere. We are accompanied by a magnificent flock of Canada geese; dozens of them in a perfect V. My heart gives a series of little blips. The reality of moving to a prairie city begins to sink in. Suddenly, I feel all the excitement of moving into the house I'd flown out and bought in August.

I have big plans.

But first things first.

Get all our stuff out of the vehicles and into the Sandman Hotel. Settle Andrea and Caitlin into their new school. Meet with the real estate agent and lawyer. Hook up telephone, power, and gas. Open new bank accounts. Get insurance and change the licence plates from

Ontario. I do not want to be identified with that province. Find the best grocery store.

Now it's my turn. With a pair of tweezers I pluck the tiny scales peeling around my red nose and dab on generous amounts of Ponds Dry Skin Cream. Dress up in an outfit I hope looks artsy, and present myself at the University of Regina's Fine Arts Building on College Avenue. It's September 17th. Ten days into classes and I'm here to ask for the moon. Feeling naked, laying bare my new-found desire to earn a Bachelor of Fine Arts degree. As I drive up Albert Street, I wonder how to play it. One look at Roger Lee, department head of Visual Arts, and I know to play it straight. So in one big gush I spill my guts.

"I-just-moved-into-town-and-more-than-anything-else-in-the-world-I-want-to-study-art."

I prop my stiff new Grand and Toy portfolio against my knocking knees praying that I won't have to show my even stiffer watercolour still life paintings or deeply personal portraits. If he laughs, I will bolt.

Roger Lee is a medium-sized balding Asian man with a spacious laugh. He doesn't laugh at all.

"You are serious about this. Aren't you?"

He listens to me in a way no other man has taken me in before. I let go of my attitude.

"With all my heart."

He leans back and stretches his arms behind his head to contemplate me. Scribbles on a piece of paper, while my heart flakes into pieces with excitement. He passes me the note.

Before you can take any studio classes, you'll need Visual Arts 100. You have missed a week. I'm teaching it this semester. Take this note to Admissions. If they give you a hard time, ask them to call me. Make good and sure you're in class at seven sharp, this evening. If you miss tonight, it will be too late to catch up.

"I'll be there!"

I offer to show my portfolio. He waves me away.

"There will be plenty of time for that."

I shake Roger Lee's hand, and float out of the building. Toss my portfolio into the back of the Jeep and check a city map for the main campus. Two hours later, I am admitted, photographed for my student ID, and have bought Lois Fichner-Rathus's textbook *Understanding Art*. Without a doubt, the day will come when I have *something important to say*.

Although when someone has something important to say to me later that evening, I don't know how to respond. Jamie and I are sitting around watching the girls in the pool at the Sandman with Pozzi, who is one of the managers on the new job. He was instrumental in Jamie getting hired on. When Jamie gets up to take a leak, Pozzi leans into me and whispers, "My heart is broken." My heart freezes. I don't know what he means, what he wants. I have no answer, so show him my shiny new U of R student ID card.

"I'm going to be an artist," I announce with more confidence than I feel.

"I didn't know you could paint," he says in amazement.

"I can't," I say. "But I will."

Bet your bottom dollar.

I wonder how things would have turned out, Muriel, if Roger Lee hadn't let me into his class. As I unpack twelve thousand pounds of stuff in our new house, a decade's worth of moving memories gets unpacked also.

Maybe it was too little too late, Muriel. If I'm honest with myself I have to admit that I love my daughters, I've loved our homes, I even love Jamie. I've been addicted to the anxiety of waiting to find out about the jobs and the excitement of meeting new people. So what is it that I want in 1986? What's missing from the picture? I don't know if I could have named it then. But what I want is respect for what I have already accomplished. The truth is, by then I want more. The tide has turned here, on the arid prairie.

No doubt my feelings are more conflicted than ever. That fall, I experience a sense of purpose I have not felt since walking the floors at night with Andrea and Caitlin when they cried a cry I could not decipher. And, though thrilled, I feel the same kind of exhaustion as those walking-the-floor nights. My cold turns into strep throat and I can't shake it. There is so much to be established: find a doctor, a dentist, an orthodontist, an optician, a piano teacher. The best place to buy curtain rods, a new bookcase, wallpaper stripper. Register the girls for swimming lessons. Contact the Brownie and Girl Guide troops. Locate the sheet music store. Memorize the main avenues and streets, the exits for the Ring Road.

And one thing to do for me: find the private art galleries, the civic art gallery, the artist-run centres, and write papers on what is showing. A whole new language has to be learned. It's exciting, but daunting. I'm frantic about these assignments, because they always end up on the very bottom of a very long list of things to do. Each night in the early fall I listen to the constant honking of the Canada geese elbowing their way around Wascana Park after feeding for the day in the grain fields surrounding the city. Soon they will fly south for the winter. Oddly, these geese comfort me as we settle in. Andrea and Caitlin like their new school. Jamie is happier than a pig-in-shit to get back on a big project. It isn't hydro and it isn't mining, this is the oil patch, he's on a steep learning curve, too. Lots of new people to work with, but he's holding his own, he's into it. He appears to be content.

One night while he's in the bathtub, while I sit on the toilet waiting to scrub his back, I watch Jamie blow bubbles until he has expelled all the air in his lungs. When he sits up to inhale he turns to look at me and says rather nonchalantly, "Pozzi was thinking that maybe the three of us should get together on Thursday nights and shoot pool downtown, or something."

Watching Jamie in the tub, I get that paralyzing sensation again. (I want him to butt out of my life.) (I want him to declare himself once and for all.) (I can't let myself get swept away again.) (Maybe it would be fun. Just once a week, I could control myself.) (Are you nuts? You know what will happen.) (What is it with these guys? They haven't got the sense god gave a goose.) I say, "I don't know. I've got a lot to do. I don't know how to play pool."

"We could teach you."

"I don't think so. Tell Pozzi to forget about it."

Someone has to have the sense.

The upgrader project is a union job and the hours are regular, 7:30–4:30 five days a week. Jamie is home to help with supper and get groceries on the weekends. No fast-tracking, not much overtime, just a steady schedule toward completion in two years' time. I can't contemplate that end-date. I live each day as if the end-date doesn't exist. I'm registered in a four-year Fine Arts program and that's how I have to think. *I am going to be here for four years. This time I am going to finish. I am going to be something.* Not just a wife and mother and homemaker. Not that I don't think these are honourable things to do, far from it, but since leaving the cloistered world of company towns it's become clear to me that nobody else does. All those months of reading *The Globe and Mail* I can't help but notice that the way I have spent my life so far sure as hell isn't making any headlines, let alone column inches.

With Visual Arts 100 aced in the fall, I plunge into three classes in January. Drawing Fundamentals, 3-D Fundamentals, and Film 100. I learn about shape, line, texture, presentation, and, most important of all, the edges of things — where they begin, where they end. I draw every night in my sketchbook. What I draw doesn't matter. That I draw does. The thing is to keep going. The point is discovery. The drawing instructor makes this abundantly clear the first time we put drawings up for a critique.

We're all nervous, shuffling. Throats are cleared. Nobody knows how this goes. The instructor throws his hands up in the air. "You might as well all go home," he rants. "Nobody wants you here.

Nobody cares. There's enough art in the world. You're wasting your time. You're wasting my time." With that, he walks out. Nobody knows where to look, but we all show up for the next class, as does the instructor; it's clear he has no interest in us. I keep my nose low to the ground. Work hard in class, work hard on assignments. The instructor is retiring after this semester. There will be somebody new in the fall.

I have to admit this art stuff is harder than I imagined. Not only is the work demanding, the mental adjustments are a killer.

The 3-D instructor is driving me bananas. She's into assemblage and junk sculpture: giant hamburgers, fur-lined cups and saucers. A maniac in her own work, she concocts ceramic furniture painted with a million dots and dashes. She believes in the element of impersonality, making art that has no existence other than as an object in itself. I don't think I'm getting it.

"What has this got to do with fine art?" I ask.

"Nothing," she retorts with a gleam in her eye. "That's just it!"

I don't tell her that when I signed up I thought I'd be modeling Greek and Roman gods or sculpting soapstone. Our first assignment is a killer: make three transitive verbs into 3-D objects. She doesn't mean illustrate, she really wants us to make verbs. Next we have to change the meaning of an object by altering its surface and texture. Good grief. Then we have to get a ball across the room without touching it. The assignment I do sort of get is to make a visual pun. So I make two half moulds of a Ken doll with Ken-doll smiles, set them behind a curved desk of big white waxy teeth and pink gums, dress their torsos in suits and ties from the Sears catalogue and plaster the stage background behind them with images from *Time Magazine*. I call it "Denture." Only the students who don't watch the news on Sunday night don't get it, but they think it's pretty funny anyway.

Not only do we have to make this stuff, we have to write about it and talk about it in our weekly crits. Sometimes all I can do is sing the lyrics to obscure songs in response. I just don't know what to think. I've witnessed the construction of energy megaprojects, but nothing that bends the mind like this stuff.

Finally for our free assignment I take a hunk of clay and sculpt, from the memory of how this feels in my own body, a small female figure in the yoga pose known as the cobra. The instructor examines my little figure top to bottom and asks, "Do you think you learned anything making this object? Do you think if you did it again you'd do it better?"

"Of course," I huff.

"Well good," she says, handing it back to me. "Do it again."

Just about everything I want to learn about making art I learn in this class, it just takes me several years to figure this out. Even the project I bomb the worst on, the change-the-meaning-by-changing-the-texture project. I make a Mr. Potato Head rendition on a butternut squash slathering it with millions of cumin seeds and cloves. Nobody gets it. Nobody knows what to say. I have to do the assignment again. This time I wrap light bulbs and knitting needles in pink and white yarn and place them in a basket à la plastic fruit.

"Now you're getting somewhere! What else do you think you can do to make it better?"

My heart sinks. Why didn't I think of this myself? "Wrap the basket?"

"Bingo!"

It takes me every evening for a full week to turn functional objects into kitsch. The instructor approves. Not because it's kitsch, but because I'm learning to look at edges, turn things upside down and inside out. Developing a critical eye about how things look in the world.

I'm pleased with myself, but I have this nagging feeling that these objects d'art I am making don't hold a lot of credibility with engineers or Baptists. Jamie does his best to support me in my efforts, occasionally pitching in to help with some of the larger and weirder constructions out in the garage. He throws himself into the fine art of cooking chicken with a can of soup in the microwave, battles his way through Superstore with me on the weekends, helps out with vacuuming and mopping the kitchen floor. Most of all, he presses me to stick with it when I get down on myself, reminding me that time is of the essence, that I have to get going while the going is good. My education is costly and we won't be able to keep this up forever. He even takes the last of our savings to buy a second vehicle, a dandy little 4 x 4 pick-up to drive to work so I can drag all my stuff back and forth to the studio in the Jeep.

Each day on my way to the Fine Arts Campus up on College Avenue, I pass Wascana Park, amazed to see gaggles of Canada geese huddled tight together trying to protect themselves from the merciless cold and blowing snow. I wonder what the hell they are doing in Saskatchewan during the winter. Why haven't they migrated south?

"It's an abomination," one of the instructors exclaims at coffee break. "A perfect example of how the system of capitalism has interfered with the natural order of things. It all started with the warm outflow of water from the power generating station. A few geese got hooked on it and stuck around for the winter. It screwed them up all together. Now there are hundreds of them that don't know which way is up." This is when I begin to understand that going to art school is as much about politics as it is about making art.

My take on life is changing, even the way I look at the sky through the kitchen window, watching clouds scud by. The ever-changing soft hues in the early evenings. Turquoise, amethyst, and smoky blue. Candle-yellow opalescence. Pink. On clear days, the blue sky goes on forever until it drains into the night, invisibly leaching light away, encasing the night in quiet black, lit from behind by streetlights. I lie in bed picturing the geese huddled under the moon-globe lamps dotting the park. I begin to admit to myself that all is not as well as I pretend in the daytime. Sexual pleasure is leaching from my life like a sky-blue day into a black starless night. Sex is becoming something that gets added to that long list of things to do. I am guilt-ridden. As if sex is something I should let Jamie do to me because he lets me go to art school.

Hardly a turn on.

There simply isn't enough time for everything that needs to be taken care of. I'm tired all the time, just like when the babies were born. Even though I ache to be aroused, each night I go to bed hoping to put sex off. I simply don't want it and wonder if that part of my life is over for good.

Then Pozzi comes to dinner one Saturday in February with some of the guys from work. Andrea and Caitlin are out on sleepovers. The mood is tense. We all drink too much. Pozzi keeps pouring Jamie large glasses of scotch from the bottle he brought and before long Jamie stumbles into bed and passes out. So there's me and Pozzi, eyeing each other. He perches on the edge of the couch; I sprawl in the love seat, legs dangling over the arm. Here we are again, I think, as the blood starts to move through my body. My brain is pleasantly numb, my limbs tingle. I'm swathed in anticipation. Everything disappears. I don't see him make his move, suddenly he's there beside me, kneeling on the floor, his thumb stroking softly between my index and middle finger. I edge toward him. He bundles me up off the love seat and cradles me into his body as if time and circumstance have not forced us apart the last three years, our lips and tongues sweetly filling in the gaps, all that empty space closing in a rush.

"I can't believe, after all this time, that we still feel like this," I whisper, stroking Pozzi's sleek silver hair.

"Time has nothing to do with it. This will always be the same."

"I need to see you more often."

"You mean like have an affair?"

I nod. Can't get that word on my lips.

"Because it would never work. It would never, ever work."

Before I can ask why, Pozzi kisses me savagely, biting lips, kneading fingers into my backbone. I pull his hair, rake fingernails along his neck as he wrenches up my blouse and bra and latches on to my breast, sucking hard. Over we roll, Pozzi flattening me against the gleaming hardwood floor, working open my zipper. I bite the flesh under his arm through heavy cotton twill. I bite again and again while his fingers work into me. "Pozzi," I shriek. He closes his mouth down on mine, reaching his arms in under and shifts me onto him, clamping tight. Shh, he whispers, the fight gone out of him. We lay there, devastated. The minutes tick by. "I'm going now," Pozzi says, gets up, and leaves.

The next morning at breakfast Jamie casually mentions that things will be a little different around the site now that Pozzi is going to the Vancouver office.

"I guess so," I say, hoping to hide the surprise and bewilderment in my voice while my mind screams, *You pair of gutless wonders. Is this some kind of game?*

"Oh well," Jamie sighs, clearing away the table. "Anyway, I'm going over to the gym to play squash in a couple of hours. What needs doing before I go?"

"There's a mountain of laundry downstairs. Try not to ruin the girls' stuff. And don't touch anything of mine. I'll get round to it this evening. Right now I've got to work in my sketchbook."

I sit at my worktable in the living room and stare at a blank white page. *Shit or go blind* I finally write in the middle. Shit or go blind. My mood plunges and hangs down somewhere around my ankles. I cross and uncross my legs a hundred times. Look around the room and wonder how to fill the pages. Then my eyes light on the wolf skin draped over the back of the couch. I start flicking long angry strokes across the page until I find the rhythm, and draw and draw into the heart of the dead beast's fur. Last of all, I draw the flattened face, the black-rimmed holes, and remembering Pozzi's face turned from me, those undomesticated eyes of his shut tight. I know now that not only is he gone, but that he has never been here to begin with. I wonder how I've been so foolish not to see that he never did have anything to offer, except this: when he looked at me, or held me, I felt new, in the here and now. I think not getting him made me ask for something I could have: this very act of drawing. Is it enough? I don't know. If he walked through the door right at this moment, I would want him. Yet I know that all this wanting is nothing but destruction. Even still, I don't know how to get rid of this desire for him.

But that doesn't ring true, does it, Muriel? There's something going on that I don't know the word for yet: sublimation. I'm learning how to transform my chaotic energy into something else. The drawings. The crazy 3-D objects. I study the narrative structure of film and write a first class paper on *Betrayal*, the film adaptation of Pinter's play.

When the semester ends, and the hard prairie winter softens into spring, I can hardly believe we made it through. My attention turns to our bungalow, which sorely needs sprucing up; I paint my way from Andrea's bedroom in the basement up the stairs into the kitchen and out to the living room and dining room and down the hall. Now the place feels more like ours and I begin to attach to this cozy space we call home, such a relief after the monstrous house in Mississauga. We're on a corner lot with big trees and a shady backyard. The girls' school is practically across the street; they come and go in relative freedom. I don't have to worry about picnicking bears.

I have made two good friends. Beth at school, a soft-spoken, pharmacist with an intuitive feel for making unusual images, and Vivian, a neighbour from a few blocks away whose kids go to school with mine. She studies piano and trains on the Nautilus machines to build upper body strength and introduces me to a whole new world. The first thing I have to get used to is the smell: that feral odour of armpit, feet, and crotch; that unmistakable stink of male power shooting little arrows through my veins. A bunch of Roughriders strut their green-and-white-clad selves around every morning, but I'm not interested in their pumped-up bodies — even the ones who can do the splits. Vivian and I both watch the women: the array of spandex outfits, the size, shape, and movements of their bodies.

Like Vivian, I favour loose t-shirts and stretchy slacks. Gone is my Jane Fonda pink-and-white outfit. Coming to this place is about something more than tight buns and going for the burn. I am intoxicated by the whole scene and the increasing strength in my upper body. The chronic strep throat finally clears up. I'm learning to face myself in the mirrors three times a week, trying to see beyond my pretty face. I'm holding steady to the contract I've made with the machines.

I straddle the narrow bench and strap myself in, bending forward at a forty-five degree angle, inhaling as I pull the bar down behind neck and shoulder blades. Exhale slowly, trying to keep a steady rhythm, concentrate on keeping the bar weights from crashing into one another. The movement should be easy and quiet with only a purr from the chains. After thirty reps, I hang forward, belt cinched tight across waist. Eyes close; clouds of magenta and indigo storm against my lids. I raise my head slowly, opening eyes, catching the reflection of the tall skeletal frame of the black Nautilus machine in the mirror before me. I shift my attention to Vivian strapping herself into the next machine. She sits comfortably in the tilted seat, feet resting on pedals. With arms raised parallel to shoulders, elbows bent, the inside of forearms pushing against pads and hands loosely gripping handlebars, she propels the pads together until they just barely meet, then eases them back almost to the beginning position in a smooth controlled movement. She closes her eyes for the briefest of moments when the pads meet, then steadies her gaze in the mirror before her.

We start our routine with yoga stretches and wide-open, receiving hearts. Our bare feet together — heel-to-toe, heel-to-toe — clasp hands and pull each other slowly forward one vertebra at a time, easing space in scrunched-up spines and cross-stitched hearts. We become each other's diary, with seesaw stories pulling gently back and forth, in and out. There's my need to get Pozzi out of my head and Vivian's need to work out a peace with the biggest story in her life. We need to speak out loud so we can hear what sounds true and what sounds false. I have a deep fascination with her story. I can still hear her voice.

"George and I had sex. We were stupid about it. I thought I was safe in my cycle and he didn't even know me well enough to ask if I was protected. I was seventeen. He was nineteen or twenty. It doesn't matter, we were stupid. I never thought I would get caught like that. Then it started to gnaw away at me. Then the not knowing was worse. Once I had confirmed the pregnancy in my own head, I was lying in bed one morning and it washed over me. I was sick. I was thinking this is not what I was going to do with my life. I had plans.

"I was just sick.

"So I walked over to my mom's bedroom. Dad wasn't home. It was a good thing my dad wasn't home. I stood in the doorway and asked my mother if I could crawl into bed with her and she made room for me. She knew and she put her arms around me and we cried."

We stop our seesaw stretching. Her face is contorted. She pulls on my arms. Pushes my feet. Breaks down and cries.

"These memories just ... never ... go ... away."

We shift back into our smooth motion.

"And now that I am a mother, I don't know who that morning was worse for — me or my mother. All her dreams came crashing down too. How would she tell people?

Then we had to find a doctor. In those days, you only went to a doctor when you were sick. We were never sick. So she called this doctor she knew from fifteen years ago. I was scared. But I was still hanging on to this little thread that it could all be wrong. All wrong. So I went.

"I could kill that man. He said, 'God, you girls are so stupid. Would you walk down Albert Street with a bag over your head?' I looked at him. I didn't know what he meant. I was so caught up in my own drama, and then it hit me. This man was telling me I was stupid because you'd have to be pretty stupid to walk down Albert Street with a bag over your head. I did not need to be called stupid. I should have walked out, but I was seventeen. I was scared of him.

"And then when the time came for him to examine me he did it and walked out. I didn't know what to do. I thought, you can't just stick your fingers up me then walk out and say nothing. So I waited. Then I got down off the cold white table and went home."

This is my mother's story. I am hearing it for the first time. I can hear it a hundred times, and still try to understand it. She has never talked about it and I can't bring myself to ask. What was it like for her before she married my stepfather? I was three when they got together; that's where my mother prefers my biography to start. There is a conspiracy in my mother's family to protect me from the truth. But in reality, I think this conspiracy protects them more than me. I hunger for details and find some edgy comfort in hearing Vivian's story. Her truth gives me necessary satisfaction.

We are thirty-three, Muriel. We have raised our babies. We have safely launched them toward adolescence. We have a certain amount of freedom to think about our lives and the lives of those around us; to question the assumptions we were raised under. When you were thirty-three, you had just left home, married and had your first baby. You were in a different space altogether.

Fifteen months after Vivian and I started going to the gym, I tried fruitlessly to get this down on paper. My big crisis after such surprising success. That winter you came to stay with us and urged me into the third bedroom I used as a home studio, "I'll do up the dishes. You get your homework done." You shoo me in there just like you used to shoo me out the door with Jamie when we were courting. I know you struggled, trying to understand what I am doing. You had no idea about art, other than the landscape paintings you bought for the yellow house. You don't pretend to like what I'm doing, though at some level you connect with the trying.

But the urgency in your voice and your manner conflict with

my purpose. For as much as you understand the trying, in the end I know what matters is success. So I sit in front of my drafting board and try to achieve instead of trying to understand.

ALL THAT WINTER your telephone calls, Muriel, become increasingly alarming. It's apparent you are coming apart at the seams. When you first offered to foot the bill if we'd fly out for a few weeks, Jamie doesn't want to take the money. He already feels guilty about the thousand dollars you sent in the fall so the girls won't have to give up their piano or swimming lessons because I'm going to school. So he hesitates. Until you blurt out, "I have to get into the shower with Daddy. He doesn't know how to wash himself anymore."

At first, I am ecstatic. Beach time! Cool weather. We're getting out of this prairie heat. But, as the departure date draws near, I realize this means leaving Vivian and the gym. I don't want to stop our conversation. Sometimes I even resent having to leave her presence to make lunch for the girls. We have become inseparable — so much so that I didn't miss Pozzi packing his bags and fleeing town.

For the first time, I do not want to leave home; and then comes the bigger realization: this is home. Alma is away.

And yet, a few nights before we leave, when an isolated windstorm blows up just after supper, I'm relieved to be escaping this unfamiliar landscape. Andrea is safe watching TV, but Caitlin is out riding her bike. Jamie and I race to the playground where dirt devils are rising up out of the dry ground. The sky turns green-black, the air howls. We have to take cover in the school doorway, our hearts heavy. In no time, the wind disappears as fast as it came. We jump in the truck and find Caitlin coming out of a neighbour's house. Thank god she'd had the sense to bang on someone's door. We bundle her in with us and drive around the neighbourhood to check out the damage, the most startling being the concrete wall down by the Catholic high school on 25th Avenue, which is blown to smithereens.

When the girls and I arrive in Alma, I don't know where I'd rather be.

At a glance, Donny looks fit as a fiddle, though here's the kicker, not only is he unfamiliar with us, he's unfamiliar with himself. You look downright haggard. Your eyes have gone the colour of skim milk and your mouth is gathered into small sallow pleats. When we drive into Sussex the next day, you warn me over and over *Don't let Donny out of your sight*. I'm thinking *Give it a rest, Muriel.* And what happens? We promptly lose Donny at the mall. He simply vanishes. As you became more worried by the second, I have the queasy feeling that you will slip into one of your silent self-exiles. I don't stop to think that you no longer have that coping mechanism as an option. You can't leave Donny alone for five minutes, let alone five hours, or five days. Since you are in such a turmoil, I take the situation in hand and call the town cops who start looking for Donny immediately and advise us to stay put. Sure enough, twenty minutes later the cruiser pulls up. There's Donny in the front seat, happy as a lark. He'll go for a drive with anybody now. Although he still seems to know who you are, Muriel, at least most of the time.

Over the next couple of days, I see glimmers of recognition in his face, but mostly he watches every move the girls and I make with great suspicion from his rocking chair in the hallway. One morning he leans forward, staring at Andrea for quite some time and says, more as a statement than a question, "Didn't you get married again?" Then he sits back in his funk and claps his hands.

When he isn't rocking or clapping he paces, jingling change in his pockets. Now I understand why you look so haggard. It isn't just watching out for Donny, the whole responsibility of him, it's putting up with all his inane activities.

"Can't you just take the change away from him?"

"He fidgets even worse if he doesn't have a bit of money. He needs to have something in his pocket."

"Have you talked to the people at the Alzheimer's Support Group?"

"I can't go all the way up to Moncton."

The situation is so claustrophobic I almost can't stand it. You worry and complain endlessly, but no matter what I suggest you block and tackle immediately. You are so gripped with fear and worry that all your responses are automatic. I only see this now, Muriel. At the time, even though I feel sorry for you, I just figure you're a real pain in the ass. In fact, what happens to me is that I develop an automatic response to you, a kind of nervous tic, and I hate myself for it.

"Donny wears his pyjamas over his street clothes. I don't know what to do."

"We were in the store one day and he picked up a banana and started eating it right on the spot. I almost died of embarrassment. I don't know what to do."

"One day he disappeared when I was in the bathroom. I nearly went out of my mind thinking he'd get lost up in the woods and die like the man I read about in the paper and it would be my fault."

Each time I answer, "No. Really? Poor you."

Who was thinking *poor Donny*?

There is no escape and we think we will all die from it. Such a tight watch has to be kept. Donny only fools us once, at supper, when he gets up to go to the downstairs bathroom. Then out of the corner of my eye, I spot him sprinting across the front lawn as he disappears down the hill to his sister Jeannie's. As soon as you clue in you jump up from your supper.

"I have to go get him."

"Jeannie can keep an eye on him for a few minutes," I say, trying to get some breathing space in the situation.

"I don't know why he's always running away from home."

"It's not your fault."

"What if he wanders up into the woods and gets lost?"

"I'll call Jeannie. You just relax for few minutes."

"Relax!" You burst into tears. "This is too much for me. It's all too much for me."

It takes a moment for me realize that *all* means us — me, Andrea, Caitlin. We are restless too; we miss our friends. Bringing the girls is not as easy as it used to be. They are twelve and nine and they need something to do. You've already warned me that you have enough things to worry about without them going off to the beach by themselves. Your mother's hysteria is making a comeback. *Don't go near the water.* Not that it matters so much. They've become city kids. They like their water square and deep for diving, surrounded with concrete and a roof overhead; they are squeamish about things in the water.

So you come up with a plan. We'll send them off to horseback camp next week up at Hudson's. You'll pick up the tab. It's only seventeen miles. We can drive them back and forth.

The first day of camp, I offer to keep Donny occupied so you can go to the hairdresser.

"Do you want to go for a drive, Donny?"

"Oh yesyesyes."

We tour the shore road until Donny wedges his hands into his pocket and starts to jingle his change. Back at the yellow house, I sit him in front of the TV and slip into the kitchen to make a snack. Before I know it, Donny is standing right behind me. When I turn to him, he locks me in a tight grip and bangs his pelvis into me. His body is rigid. Hard. Strong. Determined. I try to break away, but he has me imprisoned.

"Donny stop!"

"Aaahaaahaaah," he cries. "Aaahaaahaaa."

Bangbangbang.

He darts his hand up the inside of my shorts and wrenches my hand, placing it on his enormous erection. My mind races for something to distract him. "Bomb!" I holler and stamp my foot on his. "Watch out for the bomb, Donny."

He releases me, looks around blankly, frightened. I lead him by the hand back to the living room. "Stay!" I turn up the volume on Sesame Street. "I'll be back in a few minutes."

Back at the kitchen table, I try to compose my wits. A hard-on. The poor sorry bastard got a hard-on. Could this be his first hard-on in twenty years? Seems unlikely. I get the creeping thought that perhaps some of Muriel's stories weren't always entirely true. Rubbing my welted arms where Donny gripped me, I feel his strength again — the filthy anger in his embrace; his vulnerability. Now I understand that Donny is much more than a nuisance. He's a hazard.

Do you remember when I ask you that night if you're ever frightened of Donny? The way your whole body seems to turn to pudding. You hold your hands to your face. "He comes at me sometimes and thuds his body into mine. I tell him to stop, but he won't. Then he just lets go and wanders off. It makes me feel sick."

"Have you told the doctor about his?"

"How could I?"

"Something has to be done, Muriel. Donny will have to go away."

"I know," you say. I feel a flood of relief that you agree, then you completely confuse me by adding, in a very small voice. "It's all my fault."

Your hands fall into your lap. You look so old.

"Come on up to bed. I'll give you a back rub."

During the night, I'm wakened by Donny's bewildered shouts.

In your room, next door, with the worn and drab hot-pink carpet, you quietly weep.

The next day, after we drop the girls off and tidy the house in the afternoon, you suggest we go to the beach so I can work on my tan before Jamie arrives. We no sooner get comfortable on our towels in our bathing suits when wisps of fog start to blow in, but there is still lots of heat from the sand as it works its way through to my body. A lovely effervescent relaxation starts to seep through me. Everything slows down. I sense that you are somewhat at rest and even Donny seems content in his long pants and heavy jacket. The fog grows thicker, until it encases us like a shroud; the heat of the July sun still permeates it. Such a delicious, unusual sensation. You fall asleep, snoring lightly. I drift in and out of consciousness, wrapped in a ribbon of far away sounds and strange visions. Every once in awhile my eyes flutter open to make sure Donny hasn't strayed, like listening for an infant's breathing the first few weeks after birth. Presently, I hear the water lapping up over the rocks, tumbling them gently. We have been caught in this atmospheric spell for a long time, like no time at all, a blessed relief.

I waken you and Donny; it's time to pick up the girls.

I drive. You sit in the front, Donny in the back. Zipping up the back road, we make plans to go shopping in Moncton the next day if you can talk Agatha into looking after Donny. You remind me that we have changed speed zones. I obediently slow down. Flick on the indicator to turn into the ranch. A screech of metal alerts me that something is happening. A figure in helmet and red leather whoomps across the hood, onto the road, and into the ditch with a motorcycle skidding along right behind him.

The next thing I know the car is stopped. People come running from all directions. I jump out blood pumping, thinking I just killed someone. I run to the ditch.

From somewhere in the background I hear a young voice, "Oh my god, that's my mother."

A man gets to the ditch first and shouts, "He's alright! He's alive!" Then, "Don't move buddy. Don't move."

A bewildered male voice rises from the ditch, "I thought she was going for the horses. I thought she was going for the horses."

The horse stables are on the right side of the road. The farmhouse on the left. I remember seeing a motorcycle far off in the rear view mirror. Just before you warned me to slow down. In a daze, I walk over to the car. The motor is stalled but the indicator light is still flashing. To the left. Thank god. I did signal the right way. The guy tried to overtake me while I was turning and must have been clipping along at one hell of a speed. Then I look at the side mirror: *objects in mirror are closer that they appear*. Shit. Did I check a second time? Was he in my blind spot? Was it too late? Would it have made any difference?

Then I notice that Donny is still sitting in the back seat without an apparent care in the world.

I look around for you. You're over with Andrea and Caitlin, surrounded by dozens of kids, taking in their role in the spectacle.

"Wow. Is that your mother?"

An excitable bunch, I sniff to myself.

You are wringing your hands. "If only," you start. "If only I hadn't told you to slow down. This never would have happened."

I am carried away in a flood of ambulances and the RCMP and highway patrol reports, and most of all, concern for the guy in the ditch.

"A miracle!" one of the ambulance attendants shouts. "The guy landed in a century's worth of maple leaves."

But the car. Oh, dear. Front fender on driver's side shoved down into the wheel. I call a tow truck. You fork out another couple of hundred dollars so the girls can board at the camp the rest of the week.

After we get Donny off to bed that night, you and I sit with a pot of tea in the kitchen, shaken and stunned, recounting the day's events. You alternate between repeating *If only I hadn't warned you to slow down* with *It's all my fault*. Somehow I understand that your mind is trying to grab the moment and alter the outcome and when it can't, you keep insisting it was all your fault, as if taking it all on yourself gives you some ground under your feet. I am tired. I want to go to bed. I want to go home.

"It just happened, Muriel," I say for the umpteenth time. "We can't change it. I was driving."

"Do you want to know what you said when it happened?" you ask me.

"No," I say. "I mean yes. I mean, I didn't know I said anything."

"You said, 'We've been struck.'"

"Isn't that odd."

"Yes, 'We've been struck.' Do you want to know what Donny said?"

"Okay. Tell me."

"He said, 'Wow!"

"Wow?"

"Wow."

We catch a fit of laughing; it's almost hysterical.

"Shhhh," I finally manage to get out. "We don't want Donny down here. He'll think it's morning."

"Yes," you agree. "And he doesn't have his street clothes under his pyjamas. It's a good night."

I lay in bed that night with my own words that I didn't hear track endlessly through my mind. *We've been struck*. There is a gap in my memory. Hard as I try, I can't remember uttering those words or hearing Donny say *Wow*. I have completely missed the moment.

WELCOME TO SASKATCHEWAN. Here we are, Muriel, crossing another border. Moosomin is not far ahead. Odd, isn't it? How when you first cross a boundary, even an invisible one like a provincial border, you can feel it somehow. Something is palpably different, but it's hard to put your finger on just what.

The biggest boundary Jamie has to cross is that summer, when you insist that he call Donny's caseworker at the DVA. A few days later, the caseworker visits to reassess the situation. Sympathetic as she is, the next day she calls back to say there is little she can do because Donny's condition is not the result of a war injury. The best she can suggest are the names of nursing homes.

The Albert County Nursing Home has a long waiting list. The hospital in Sussex offers a respite care program, but is shutting down due to lack of funds. There's a private nursing home in Riverglade. They'll take him for a trial period, but if he acts up, they'll send him home. The cost is prohibitive.

"I'm going to lose my house," you wail. "I'm going to lose my house to pay Donny's bills."

Jamie and I talk over the possibility of having you and Donny move into our basement in Regina. The thought is enough to send me sprinting across the front lawn. It isn't practical anyway; already there is talk of us moving in a year or so when the upgrader is finished.

"Do something, Jamie," you appeal. "Do something for me."

We don't know what to do.

A couple of days go by where we drag ourselves to the beach, listlessly playing happy family.

Then a miracle happens. The DVA caseworker calls to announce that a bed has become available on the Veterans ward of the Georges Dumont Hospital in Moncton.

"How did you manage that?" Jamie asks.

"Just let me say I found a loophole and pleaded your case. The catch is," she continues, "you have to take Donny tomorrow or the bed will go to someone else. There is always someone available to take a bed."

As Jamie repeats this to us, holding his hand over the receiver, we understand that someone has died. That's the only way for a bed to become available on that ward.

"You have to let me know by late this afternoon," the caseworker goes on. "I'm sorry. That's the way it goes."

You look to Jamie to make a decision.

He has two choices. Sacrifice his mother. Sacrifice his father.

That evening, Jamie and I leave you and the girls watching *Lassie, Come Home* and walk down to the wharf. I've had a couple glasses of wine. Jamie's had a lot. The night is quiet. We stop at the edge, enveloped in a thick Bay of Fundy fog. We can't see two feet in any direction.

"You showed a lot of moxie today," I offer.

"Hunh. Moxie," he declares. "You want to talk about moxie. When I was sixteen I picked up my father's government truck and went down to the take-out to pull him away. There was Nellie Parsons with a smirk on her face. Where's my Dad, I asked her. She pointed out back. I rounded him up and said 'Dad, we gotta go home.' He was happy as a lark. But it was embarrassing, okay. Nellie Parsons with her cow grin. I didn't give a shit. I could have shoved her teeth right down her throat. Just like my mother. Thought she was too good for everybody. Well I was friends with Nellie's sons Leonard and Harvey and could have told her they can puke with the best of them. That cow grin ...

"So I got Dad home. Mom was quiet. I put Dad to bed and that was that. I wasn't going to take over as head of the family. Do something, Mom said to me. Do something."

"Why did you have to go get him?"

"He was too drunk."

"How did you find out he was drinking?"

"Because he was missing for the day, and it wasn't the first time. Because I found out from the guys. Leonard and Harvey and Jerry. They said he was down at the take-out."

"If he was happy as a lark, why did you have to go get him?"

"Financial security. He could have lost his job."

"But he was happy as a lark?"

"He was on duty, in full uniform. He was driving a 1966 International. Do you want to know who the fuck bought it? Is there anything you don't fucking want to know? He was my father. And I had to turn him in. And now I'm going to do it again. How the fuck do you think that makes me feel?"

I make no attempt to answer. We walk home in damp, ghostly silence.

I can't sleep that night. Jamie's rant marches back and forth through my mind. In the sixteen years we've been together, I've only heard him talk about his father in adoration, admiration, and respect. Why had I badgered him? What had I wanted him to say? What had got under my skin?

Happy as a lark. That's it. Donny is always described as being *happy as a lark*, but everyone knows that can't possibly be true. That's what gets under my skin: the never-ending grind of silence.

It's not okay for Donny to be anything other than a happy man. It seems that to keep the family intact, this story has to be held up at all costs. You and Alexis and Jamie can't tolerate him any other way. How can anyone have a hope in hell of living up to that?

Only you are allowed to be unhappy. You're the repository of sorrow, the great balancer.

I resist the urge to shake Jamie awake. I'd like to knock your heads together, you and Donny, Jamie and Alexis. I want to scream the house down. Because I finally see now that this is how Jamie sees himself too. *Happy as a lark*. And like you, it's my job to hold and release the family steam. That's the deal. The family package I had bought so willingly so many years before.

So did I really figure all that out that night? No. I got as far as Donny being happy as a lark. Then I just got an inkling of the rest — enough to know that something big and tumescent is lurking under the family packaging just like that big fat something under Donny's pants the week before. Maybe I should have tried to make an equation out of it. It would have gone something like this:

1 impossibly happy-as-a-lark father
+ 1 hormonally unbalanced mother
+ 1 messy daughter
+ 1 neat and tidy son
= a perfect family

Compare this with:

1 driven father
+ 1 pretty though sometimes emotionally unpredictable mother
+ 1 blond daughter
+ 1 brown haired daughter
= a slightly less than perfect family

A FAMILY THAT could be balanced by a happier, more stable mother.

Has Madame calmed down?

Not bloody likely.

We all keep it under wraps the next day. The silence grinds against us, you and Donny, me and Jamie, as we drive Donny to Moncton to deliver him to the Veteran's ward at the Georges Dumont Hospital. Donny's apprehensive, like an old hound dog being taken to the vet. Jamie stashed his suitcase in the trunk when he wasn't looking, but there's no hiding it from him when we arrive.

The floors shine with paste wax and false hope. The smell of dust bane and despair permeates the air. Old broken men are propped up in rocking chairs and wheelchairs in front of the TV in the lounge, or gathered in pairs and foursomes at tables idly playing cards or checkers. Some, those who still have a sliver of curiosity, watch the procession of Donny and family to the main desk; most ignore the goings-on. I peek sidelong into some of the rooms down the corridor, the festive attempts to make the cells look like home, with bookcases and framed family photographs, afghans folded ever so neatly at the bottoms of the beds, bad paintings of sunsets and mountains. When we come to a halt at the reception desk with Donny, a bottom-heavy nurse with a big professional smile comes forward and thuds Donny on the back.

"Well, well," she booms. "You must be Donald. Welcome to the fourth floor. Let me show you around."

She leads Donny off while you and Jamie complete the necessary paperwork. I hang beside you like a damp tea towel. Watching Jamie's face, anxiously, looking for telltale emotion, but like you, he focuses, stone-faced, on the task at hand. You hand back the papers and we are led to Donny's new room. He'll be sharing space with another Alzheimer's patient, a skeletal man who spends most of his time in bed, working his lips wordlessly.

"We didn't know what to bring," you say hesitatingly as you unpack Donny's suitcase, eyeing the remnants of home set out like props around the roommate's bed. "We just brought his clothes and shaving gear."

"Don't worry, don't worry," the nurse assures. "You can bring anything up at any time."

I know by the look on your face that you can't bear to think about coming up for visits. But I also know that you will come, remaining faithful not so much to Donny as to duty. Donny is brought in to the room and shown his belongings hanging in the closet. "We've given him a little something to settle him down," the nurse explains. "You should try to leave as quietly as possible in a few minutes."

TWENTY-THREE

A RIBBON OF highway undulates through bright green fields, far as the eye can see. Your little Buick crests and dips toward Regina. In my mind's eye, I see myself against the landscape, a whir of burgundy, speeding on. No more dingy motel rooms on this journey, tonight I'm staying with Vivian. Tomorrow I will be home.

In a flash, the sky darkens. Geese are heading north, their cry deafening. I wonder about the Wascana geese tending their nests along the shore by the parliament buildings. Do their hearts flutter when they hear their wild cousins? Are they better off staying put, not making the arduous journey?

How can you tell if you're making the right decisions?

I've often wondered if we did the right thing the day after Donny was sentenced to the Georges Dumont. Sending you off with Agatha to Sussex for the day, while Jamie and I do the dirty work. What assumptions we made on your behalf!

Do something! Did we get busy doing something.

Taking his bed apart, storing it in the basement. Emptying his drawers and closet, taking the clothes to the Sally Ann. Dragging the high boy and dresser into the hall. I vacuum and clean the windows while Jamie lugs the grandchildren's furniture into Donny's old room.

Satisfied with our effort, we say that now when you climb the stairs you'll see a cheerful room with toys and colourful quilts. We don't press on with the thought that it will be an empty cheerful room.

We're so sure we're right.

Even the bathroom gets emptied of Donny's shaving gear and toiletries. The pink plastic cup he kept his teeth in.

Downstairs is easy. We cast Donny's favourite rocker into the rec room down in the basement. "He'll be watching Sesame Street from a hospital chair now," I say grimly. His golf clubs haven't been out of storage for years. His tool room is as tidy as Jamie left it the year before. The bits of his war memorabilia and the little bag with the bomb diffusing tools, we store in the highboy in our room. Out back, we leave the shed as is for the handyman. Except for the chainsaw. You know how Donny had become a maniac with the oilcan his last few years at home. How anything he could get the top off he filled with oil. His favourite target: the chainsaw. Jamie packs it up to take back to Saskatchewan. He still can't get the damn thing working properly. Once or twice a year he fights with it for an hour or so. "That was my dad's," Jamie will say with a catch in his throat. "He filled the gas chamber up with oil once too often, I guess. Someday though, someday, I'm going to get it working again."

I should have been paying more attention to that chainsaw. It's a big fat yellow clue to Jamie's devastation over Donny's illness and subsequent hospitalization. But to tell the truth, I had just about had it with the two of you being a monstrous focus in our married life.

Getting back to all that work we did that day. It was a warm-up for how we attack the task four years later. And *attack* is the right word. It must strike even you as aggressive: steamrolling the situation so nobody has to feel the bumps. We endeavour to make transition as smooth as possible. We don't want you to feel anything. Maybe we were too afraid that all your emotion would spill into us. You're a good old gal. You comply. Always assuring us when we call that *I just have to put it out of my mind and go from one day to the next*, which is exactly what we want to hear. But the bumps don't go away, do they? They go underground and pop up in places where you least expect them.

This is how we live from now on. Urgency runs the show. We think we're just an ordinary family living in a bungalow on the prairies. It's only been a year since we arrived by the time school starts again in September, but already I'm running out of time. Jamie pushes me to sign up for a full course load. I'm afraid I won't be able to hold my head above water.

"Look. We don't have much time here. It's not like you're taking rocket science."

"Or engineering," I say under my breath, making sure he doesn't hear. Jamie doesn't appreciate a sarcastic sense of humour. He doesn't appreciate a lot of things. But then again, neither do I. Something fundamental changes between us that fall. He pushes and I shove back with never-ending criticism. He tries and he tries, but nothing suits me. Not the way he does the laundry, picks up the groceries, washes the dishes.

By mid-December, I'm looking in the middle of the list of student IDs posted on the drawing room wall with the end of term marks. I can't find mine. My stomach lurches. The bad things the new instructor has said about my drawings congeal in my stomach into a lump of misery. I look down to the bottom of the list. Not there either. Maybe she forgot me. I'm feeling hopeful. My eyes fly back to the middle, then one-by-one I scan to the top.

My art-buddy Beth is standing beside me. We crept in together when no one was around. I'm at the top. Edward, the competent young Chinese guy I watch jealousy is second and Beth is next. We're so deliriously happy we splurge on cabbage rolls and perogies at a bistro by the commercial galleries.

"I can't believe it," I keep saying. "I thought she didn't like my work at all."

Three months of life drawing, memory drawing, and gesture drawing has gone by in a flash. Whenever I'm solidly with the materials and the subject there is no time, just one long present moment. And then the crits. Pinning my work up next to the others. The fear and dread of getting trashed. Learning how to talk about what we do. Learning how to look. And something else I didn't learn so well.

"You know why you didn't think you were doing so hot," Beth explains. "You only glommed onto bad things. You've got to open your ears and mind to the good things too. You've got to take it all in."

There are things you have to know to look for to take it all in. At the time, Beth's advice just hovers somewhere near my consciousness. It doesn't really sink in. All I know is that I've aced a whole semester and am one step closer to the achievement of a BFA, but it has come with a toll.

Inside, I am trembling with exhaustion, near the edge of something I can't name. Looking back now, Muriel, I have to wonder why I went for the straight As. Why I still had to make two dozen muffins for the girls' lunches every Monday morning. Why the kitchen floor had to be washed. Why didn't I let something go? Why did I think I would have been a lesser mother, a lesser student?

Why couldn't some things just have been good enough?

Why did I think that all the tension in the house came from me?

Why didn't we see that something hard and real, something invisible, was driving Jamie, too?

Why didn't we talk about who we were to each other? Why didn't we make time for us? All our efforts went into the home and the girls and getting me through school, and to worrying about you.

Do you remember that snazzy jumpsuit and jacket you sent me to wear to the company Christmas party that year? When it arrives out of the blue, I am so touched that you are thinking about me. When I call to say thanks, you explain that you'd seen it on display and knew I'd like it.

"I even went to the trouble of getting the salesgirl to try it on," you add. "But I'd sooner see it on you."

Ah, the guilt again. You're spending Christmas alone. Not that we hadn't asked you to fly out, but you can't see your way clear to a decision. In the end all we can do is ask, "What should we send Dad for Christmas, Mom?"

"A teddy bear."

Jamie and I and the girls spend Christmas with our new friends from the upgrader. They're from Northern Ireland, like Donny's family, and Jamie is drawn to them like long lost relatives. Rhonda and David, another engineer, and their son Jason, who's the same age as Caitlin. You must remember them, Muriel, though we never speak of them anymore.

I've made an effort to be friends with Rhonda for Jamie's sake. So we have a couple to socialize with. We'd lunched together a couple of weeks earlier. The thing we have in common is that we've both moved so often for the sake of the men's careers. Which, they never fail to defend anytime the subject is brought up, they are doing for the sake of the family, not themselves. Rhonda tells me about her correspondence courses to become a GPA, although she always wanted to be a rock star. She thinks I'm going to art school to become a star too, so I try to explain that it's not about wanting to be famous. Our conversation comes to a standstill when we both realize we're listless and stuck. I sit back in my chrome chair in the desperately ugly nouveau-eighties restaurant, somewhere in the north end of Regina, and the damnedest thing pops into my head. I blurt it out without even thinking.

"What I'd really like is to have a lover."

"So would I," she counters.

Then she goes on to tell me about a crazy fling she had one night in a hotel in Durban when they were working on a South African job. She and David and a couple who were their best friends had been swimming in the Indian Ocean. They were all having dinner when a rugby team crowded into the restaurant. Everyone was little drunk, especially the rugby guys, having just won a big game. One of the players bumped into their table; he and Rhonda made eye contact for the rest of the evening. Sometime in the wee hours, the rugby player stood by the door and gave her the nod. She went to the washroom with her friend and got her to promise to keep David's attention for a while. "How, the friend asked?" "Sit on his lap," Rhonda suggested, then bolted for the foyer where she met up with the rugby player and they snuck off to his room for a quick fuck.

"It was brilliant," she confesses.

I am seduced by this story: South Africa and the Indian Ocean. A rugby player I assume is gorgeous. I tell her about my night with Pozzi.

"It was like a movie," I gush.

"Hot," she says.

"Absolutely," I say, staking out her lilac eye shadow and bad haircut. Thinking she's too dumpy now to attract a good-looking rugby player.

A great cook though — a treat to help with the Christmas feast.

You have Agatha up for Christmas dinner that year. It's your first Christmas without Donny in forty years. The only consolation is that you don't have to worry about him going on a little holiday toot.

In the fall you told us in a small, mortified voice that Donny is being regularly sedated for the crime of acting out. The most notorious being his talent for sneaking up on fellow inmates in their wheelchairs and pushing them down the hall at break-neck speed. He just won't stop. So they pop him a few pills every couple of hours to keep him calm.

I imagine you so vividly that Christmas sitting at the colonial table in your aqua dining room eating your chicken dinner and Bisto gravy. Two old women, you and Agatha, with her *You made your own bed now you must lie in it* look. One empty chair. I see it all in soft edged detail, a graphite drawing. I render your figures: you and Agatha and Donny on 6″ x 8″ pieces of medium tooth paper using fat #4B to #8B graphite pencils and, with short and wide or, long and narrow, fluid arching strokes, I work from the middle to the outside, refining the images with #2B or #2H pencils, defining not so much what the memory demands, but rather, what the image demands. I practiced these for hours. It doesn't seem to matter that most of the images I draw are imagined, not memories. Somehow, once I draw something, it does become part of my memory bank. From this practice, I discover the most amazing thing — my ability to make memory drawings out of things that never happened is just as good as my ability to make real memory drawings. I can take people, places, and things and mix them up to my heart's desire just as long as I keep the edges soft. Detail to a minimum.

Memory drawing, Muriel, is a dubious, if dangerous, talent.

I put the scenes together but I can't read the deeper meaning yet. I am only beginning to live in my own skin.

I see myself sitting cross-legged on the floor at home in my studio with a large heavy sheet of black Arches paper clipped to my drawing board, propped up in front of me. I tip out a new tray of soft pastels. Where to begin? I play with them for a while. Roll them around. Make squiggles on scrap paper. Imagine magenta on black, cyan on black. Naples yellow. The tooth of the paper. The possibilities of texture.

In an armchair in the corner by my bookcase, Jamie is reading a Len Deighton paperback, his pipe and a large scotch-and-water on a shelf at his elbow. We've barely had time to speak to each other during the week, so I invite him to keep me company while I tackle the last drawing assignment of the semester. For the Monday morning crit, my class is assigned to make a drawing of one of our strongest childhood memories. As I reach for the eyes in the back of my head, I'm comforted by Jamie's presence, waiting for a strong image to surface.

My fingers chose a warm pale yellow that I brush over the centre of the paper in a filmy haze. I contemplate these marks for quite some time, then with a deep ochre, in a flood of quick sure strokes, the image of a bassinet takes shape. The bassinet I helped my mother decorate for the baby sister that died of crib death. Over the next hours, as I bring the bassinet into the present on black paper, I notice that my childhood feelings are overcome by a profound sadness for my mother and her loss. Is this now a kind of hybrid memory — that of a child and an adult who has a deeper, more complex understanding?

"Jamie," I ask, trying this out. "When you remember things about your childhood, do you remember them just the way they were, and how you felt then, or do you remember them the way you are now?"

"What do you mean?"

"Well, if you remember your mother and certain incidents, say, the day she got chocolate cake all over the place, do you remember it exactly the way you did as an eleven-year-old, or do you remember it as a man."

"I don't know. As an eleven-year-old, I guess. Yeah, I guess I try to remain pretty faithful to my memories. Why?"

"Because I'm wondering if it's possible for a person to remain faithful to memory and grow up at the same time. I mean really grow up. So that you understand things better. I mean, isn't it better to be faithful to how you're relating to something now, with the memories sort of informing the situation, not just dictating the present?"

"I don't know what you're getting at."

I recognize the edge in his voice that says *Stop right there*. How many scotch-and-waters has he had? I haven't been paying attention. His face looks rubbery. He's had a lot. No sense trying to have a discussion about memory now.

Later that night, I tiptoe out of bed and hold the scotch bottle up for examination. Just as I figured, more than half is gone from a bottle he just brought home. As I slide back to bed, I'm ashamed for looking, thinking about my stepfather holding my mother's bottles up to the light. She started drinking after the baby died. Then I think about tiptoeing around her, how it had started with the empty bassinet. And how, in so many ways, I've been tiptoeing around ever since.

Over the weekend, I add finishing touches to the drawing — a little extra colour or sharper line; sometimes I rub a bit of the colour out. When I'm not working on the drawing, it seems that every five minutes I pop into the studio to simply take it in. I know the luminous image of the bassinet with its layers of lace and satin rising out of the black paper is a show-stealer.

A big fuss was made over the drawing. "Leave it here after class," my instructor says. "I'm going to put it in the display case." The honour of having a piece of work in a display case is usually reserved for fourth year or graduate students.

I can't shut up about it at the end-of-semester dinner party Rhonda puts on to celebrate my hard work. Jamie and I have been invited over more and more often and usually, we're the last to leave. Rhonda is always seducing us with exotic dishes. We drink a lot of wine, end up in the living room dancing and belting out "White Rabbit" with Grace Slick and Jefferson Airplane so many times I can hardly talk the next day.

"Don't you think it's strange to have dinner with them so many times?" Vivian suggests when we're doing our workout. "Is something funny going on?"

"Can't imagine," I say. "It's just a release, that's all. The guys work hard. I work hard. Rhonda's got lots of time to cook."

"I'd keep an eye out, if I were you. That's all."

That night I dream I'm walking up the flight of stairs in the Visual Arts building to the drawing floor. At some point, I get stuck and can't move. Something is pounding at my heels. I'm terrorized. Finally, I make it to the top only to find that my drawing of the bassinet is missing from the display case.

In the morning, I drive over to the Visual Arts building thinking *It's only a dream.* Take the stairs two at a time, and just like in my dream, the drawing of the bassinet is missing. My heart stands still. Nobody knows where the drawing went. The buzz is that it's been stolen.

Stolen? What does this mean? First the dream, then the fact. Why would somebody steal something from me?

Life is reaching a critical point of complexity, Muriel. Coming at me from all directions and dimensions and yet I can hardly keep up with what is on the surface. The more I open up to my own potential, the crazier things seem to get. I don't have the insight yet, just markers. Signs. I can't put two and two together.

Oh gosh, look out there, Muriel. Can you see it, off in the distance? Plumes of talcum powder soil rising up from the alternating rows of green shoots and beige prairie. Somewhere there's some kind of two-storey tractor with air conditioning and video cameras recording what's happening on the ground, and a stereo tuned to the local FM station, and perhaps even a cappuccino machine. Who knows what's happening out there; a transfusion of fertilizers and pesticides being laid over the eviscerated soil like a blanket of death. We are in the middle of the world's most manipulated landscape; the biggest wound on the planet. What used to be the prairies. The first art installation I ever saw was in a small student gallery, all about what was called the Great Plow-Up. On the walls, a grad student drew and painted a cross-section of what prairie sod and soil used to look like before we ploughed to the Rockies to feed Europe during World War I: perhaps two hundred and fifty perennial species, a massive tangle of cross-haired roots, some shallow and fibrous, others long and tunnelling, supported by clumps of soil alive with microfauna and microflora. An ancient natural system that made the most of light rains or hard rains, years of drought, periods of heavy rainfall. On the gallery floor, wall-to-wall, were empty cardboard beer flats planted with rows of real wheat, sticking out of strips of corrugated cardboard. At first glance, the wheat was simply beautiful, lit by yellow spotlights, creating the illusion of movement. This is what first captured my attention. Then the drawing and painting on the walls beckoned. The tangle of roots in chocolate pudding soil and the seemingly endless variety of stocks and leaves and flowers above, but I couldn't get close enough to have a good look. The wall-to-wall wheat fended me off. I felt like I was missing something — or had lost something, which is exactly what the artist was striving for.

A tad didactic perhaps, but I got the message. What remains in my mind is that unreachable wall of natural prairie grassland.

It's just about all disappeared. Out there, through the windshield, what I see is the same thing I've been looking at for most of my adult life: a pattern industry imposed on the land. We come from such heroic, backbreaking people, now being displaced by the "get big or get out" efficient machine of the farming corporations. How could all of this have happened in a hundred years?

That big tractor is far behind now but the dust is still in the air. Like that little jaunt our second summer in Regina. Jamie and I and Rhonda and David take the kids down to this town just over the border in Montana for a night, just for the hell of it. There's a coupon for gambling in the paper to tempt us. Driving back into Saskatchewan the next day is like being steadily absorbed into a science fiction movie, some kind of Armageddon, as we drive into an all encompassing, strange, thick, drab, brown light. At some point, we look behind and realize we have been surrounded. We slow down. Switch headlights on. The road is eerily empty. We sniff for smoke, but there is no fire. The air is murky and still. It becomes hard to breathe, as if all the oxygen has been used up. Finally, we realize that we're driving into a massive wall of heat and soil particles, unimaginable and almost unbearable. The temperature soars from 23 degrees to 37. We have been ambushed by the first of the heat waves to hit the province that summer. It's only the first week in June.

A few days later, when the mercury climbs to 42, school attendance is declared optional. Not knowing what to do with myself, I strip wallpaper and paint our bedroom. The paint dries in a flash. If I stop moving, I'm afraid I'll spontaneously desiccate.

"Good idea to freshen the place up if we're going to put it on the market," Jamie comments.

I ignore him. I'm not painting the house for the market. I'm painting in prayer for a miracle. I'm painting to stay.

At night, the temperature only dips to 25 or 26. The house doesn't cool down. While the girls flake out in front of the TV in the basement, Jamie and I wander over to Wascana Park at midnight to find scores of people riding their bikes or sitting in the grass near the water trying to find relief.

Back home, I lie in a tub of tepid water feeling fearful. The weather is ominous. I am obsessed by the tornado watches that scroll along the bottom of the local cable news station. The incident of the year before — when the concrete wall down the street was blown to bits — snakes through my mind, like a ghostly twin to the tornado alerts on TV. All night long, I stand guard listening for the warning I've been told about — the sound of a train in the distance — ready to hurl my family into the basement for safety. Trouble is real trains pass through the city at frequent intervals; my heart leaps into overdrive, wearing down with false alarms.

Almost all of June is hotter than the hubs of hell. The girls and I take off for Alma for a month.

This time I'm reluctant when you call with your offer. The summer before had been so awful, but you're desperately lonely. The only way I can cope with the idea is insisting that Beth come along for the two weeks until Jamie arrives. Did you guess at the time why I wanted her there? It was to keep me safe from you. I knew how much you disliked having strangers in your house. You balk, but for once, I have you over a barrel.

I arrive with a mixture of relief and foreboding, but you and Beth take a shine to one another right off the bat. Everything is so much more relaxed without poor old Donny around. And you, you're downright girlish. You have a resplendent youthfulness that somehow makes you seem ageless. You allow the girls to invite their friends from Sussex out for sleepovers without becoming anxious. We have a whale of time every night playing three-handed bridge, drinking gin and tonic, bidding recklessly on the dummy. Sometimes making the bid, most times going down. It doesn't matter. We laugh and hoot.

"Muriel, why don't you join up with the elder hostel?" I suggest one night. "Light out of here in the fall. Have a little adventure."

"Oh, I couldn't," you protest, but your eyes spark up.

"Why not? Donny's never coming back. Jamie wouldn't mind."

"Wouldn't he?" you ask coyly. I can see you have been thinking about something like this.

"Of course not. Why would he?" You've still got a lot of life in you, Muriel.

I know you like the sound of this, because I get you bid up to four spades. The dummy is loaded, and surprise, you make it and then some. I've got a light buzz on and figure you have too and the funniest thing pops into my head.

"Do you remember all those years ago, Muriel, when you read that magazine article about, um, ah, oral sex and, um you sort of, you know, wanted to ah, you wondered what it was, you know, like?"

There's dead silence. Beth is concentrating very hard on her bridge hand. You blush to the roots of your white hair while I remember the night so many years ago when you brought the subject up and I had hotfooted it out of the kitchen, lying that I didn't really know that much about it.

"Do you still want to know?"

"Well, I don't see why not," you manage with a straight face. I let out a laughing snort and have to get a paper towel to wipe her cards off. Beth watches, eyes dancing. You finally laugh and shrug. Before long, we're howling. Caitlin pounds on the floor above and shouts, "Hey, you guys. I'm trying to sleep."

"Just think of yourself as an ice-cream," I start. "A big fat strawberry ice-cream. The man of your dreams takes a little lick and then another little lick, up and down and around the sides. And when it's all nice and pointy he sucks the whole thing in his mouth and pushes down in the centre with his big hot tongue, flattening it out, burrowing in, and then he starts his little licks again, up and down, in and out, shaping a nice little peak ..."

Beth's hand of cards pops and spills to the floor.

I'm looking straight at you, squirming in your chair, and think, I'll bet there's a lot of juice in the old girl yet. I have to give you your due, when you smile a small smile and flick your head to the side, "Yes, well, I figured something like that."

This starts us going again with snorts and titters. Upstairs one of the girls thumps on the floor rattling the light fixture overhead. We've never been so outrageous in your house.

You know what I liked about Beth being there? Seeing my beloved landscape through the eyes of a prairie girl. How she notes the moist air on her skin the moment she gets off the plane. How she is surprised that the landscape is so close up, especially driving on secondary roads like through the park or up to Moncton. The hills and curves beguile her. She's gripped with the sensation there might be nothing to drive over or around, that we might just drive off into space. The smells of salt water and marsh and fir trees tantalize her; walks in the woods cloak her in mystery.

One evening we duck through the railing on the boardwalk and settle on a flat boulder with a good view of the bay and the headlands of Nova Scotia.

We fall silent in contemplation.

"Is that where you're from?" she asks, pointing across the bay.

"Not Nova Scotia's Fundy Shore, the Northumberland shore, though I'm more familiar with the South Shore or the Eastern Shore."

"All these shores."

"Yup. And they're all different."

"And now I know where you get your colours when you paint."

I hadn't thought about that. How this shore influences my colour palette. In a way, her delight almost makes me see Alma and the park as if I've never seen them before.

Just like seeing you without Donny is like being with a new person. You are more visible, touchable. We are less irritated with each other.

DESPITE YOURSELF, YOU liked Beth, didn't you Muriel? We had a lot of fun. But you know what? If I hadn't had Beth's body between us, things would probably have been different those two weeks. You would have demanded all my energy and sympathy and I would have ended up as usual after a protracted visit, feeling depleted.

You know what, Muriel? I just figured something out. That's just exactly what Jamie has been doing with me all these years. Whether consciously or unconsciously, he has been using me, just as I used Beth, body and soul, as protection, as a shield, between himself and you.

TWENTY-FOUR

I WISH YOU'D bought a car with air conditioning, Muriel. The sun is hard on the driver's side. I'm getting a godawful headache. When I get to Vivian's tonight, I want two extra-strength Advil, a large single-malt scotch, and a colder-than-cold beer chaser.

That's what we could use when Jamie arrives in Alma, because our first family chore is to visit Donny. He is gaunt, dull-eyed, and grey. He has a bad buzz-cut. He hasn't been out of doors for over a year. A man who spent the best days of his life as a national park warden, teaching Jamie and Alexis how to swim at Broad River, now drugged and strapped to a chair parked in front of a TV with a dozen similar men. Their eyes clap onto anyone who wanders into their line of vision. I can barely look at these men. I feel like a fake, smiling at them without meeting their eyes. I have no idea how to acknowledge them. It's hard enough to take Donny's hand to say hello.

"Hello Dad," Jamie says in as big a voice as he can muster.

"Hello Grandpa," the girls say shyly.

"Hello Donny," I say fearfully.

"Hello Daddy," you say brightly, striking just the right false note. "Look who's here. We're all here."

"Ahhhhhhh. Yesssss," Donny answers, hollow-eyed, devoid of recognition. He looks away.

We work to bring his attention back to us every time we speak. He always responds with, "Mmnnnnn. Wellllll. Yessssss. Ahhhhhhh."

Then stares at the new sneakers with Velcro tabs they make him wear so he won't untie the laces. He has to wear pullovers so he won't eat the buttons. Pull on pants without belts and buckles because he picks and scratches at any lump or bump on any surface his hands come into contact with. He has nothing left to jingle because he might pop anything into his mouth.

Jamie unstraps Donny from his chair. We walk him down the hall to the empty games room. Donny shuffles along, looking down at his feet, uncertain how they work. We sit him down and babble brightly all the family news. He nods or utters monosyllables. After twenty helpless minutes, we walk him back down the hall to his room for a rest. He stares at us as we say goodbye, leaving one by one. Jamie is last to pass through the door. Quietly Donny utters, "Jamie." Jamie turns back into the room.

You and I and the girls wait by the elevator. Five minutes later, Jamie joins us. He's rigid. Jaw clamped. I silently take in his smarting eyes, nose red and flaring, trying to keep control. He stands enormous in his pain.

Less than an hour later, he ducks outside for a cigarette after he gobbles his last bite of lunch. The girls are restless and join him out in the parking lot of the restaurant in Moncton. As soon as we are alone, you lean toward me and ask, "Is Jamie prepared?"

I'm caught off-guard. I don't know what to say.

"Is he prepared?" you ask again.

"Well, you know. As prepared as can be. He knows every time he sees Donny may be his last."

"No," you interrupt, annoyed. "I mean, does he have a suit."

"A suit?"

"Yes, a suit."

Now I know what you're getting at though neither one of us will say funeral.

"Yes," I answer up smartly. It feels like betrayal. "I made him take home one of Donny's suits last year when we cleaned out his closet."

"Good," you say, satisfied. "I wouldn't want him to be unprepared."

Why is it always the future we're supposed to be prepared for? Not the present? Are any of us prepared for visiting Donny? Are you and I prepared to go outside and approach Jamie in his moment of suffering? I'm not any more prepared to approach him than the old men on the ward.

I feel so set up. If Jamie uses me as a bodyguard, Muriel, you use me as a membrane. Everything you want to say to him passes through me. I'm quite disgusted with you in that restaurant. The hymeneal bargain I struck with you all those years ago is beginning to scum over. Yet I am silent.

Days later, flying home, I look down at the prairies. Golden squares and rectangles with rows of trees or shrubs forming the shelterbelts and the odd irregular patches along the coolies or depressions with the edges all tucked in and stitched up. Looking like a map of itself. Underneath the carpet of wheat, the topsoil is being destroyed and poisoned.

As we approach Regina, I look down to the Ring Road. Already the earth looks scorched and it's only the first of August.

I can no longer ignore the reality: a move is hanging over our heads again. The heavy oil upgrader will be commissioned this fall and start operation by the end of October. Jamie's company doesn't have a lot of work on the books. We were hoping something close to Regina would come up; but, with the drought, Saskatchewan is going through a mini recession. There's talk of a hydrogen peroxide plant in Prince George going ahead and this seems our most likely destination, but it's all conjecture at this point. Pozzi is going to manage the project from Vancouver and will fly in every couple of weeks. Just what I need.

I want to go to Prince George like I want another hole in my head and I'm making no bones about it. How will I finish my degree from there? As much as this prairie landscape stumps me, I am not prepared to leave. Nor are the girls.

As soon as the plane lands, I scuttle back to my bungalow surrounded by trees, my backyard protected by a canopy of green filigree that hides me from the hot sun and dry air. I breathe in the order and spaciousness of my own home after a month of living Muriel's yellow house. I have always worked hard to make each new place look and feel like our place. I stand in Andrea and Caitlin's rooms, filling up with the very being of their things, the posters they plaster on the walls. The little spaces even children and adolescents make for themselves.

This year a big bad surprise awaits us. The weather has been so hot and so dry, the ground around the house has shrunk, shifting the foundation just enough to stress the walls, so that while we were away, long crooked cracks, some as much as a quarter inch wide and deep, have appeared in the plaster throughout the living room, dining area, the kitchen, and the bedroom. My paint job is ruined; all those hours of hard work vanished into thin soil-speckled air.

Work revs up at the upgrader. Jamie is working long shifts, coming home exhausted. When I complain about the heat, he claims it doesn't really bother him.

There is something about the weather and our situation that is making me a little nuts. When I'm not glued to the forecast crawling along the bottom of my television screen, I'm out stalking insects. An outbreak of Maple Bugs plagues the city. At first I watch a crowd of them scamper across the backyard. Then they start to show up in armies — marching up the trees and the side of the house. They squeeze into the bedrooms through the screens and if you swat one of the little buggers they splat red jelly all over the place. At night they hide in trees and descend in the morning. After I figure this out, I stand guard with a bottle of insecticide and spray them as they move in a solid red and black mass down the trunks. Every once in a while the wind shifts, blowing the deadly spray over my bare legs. I don't care, I'm obsessed.

I feel like I'm under siege, and I'm trying to hold my panic at bay. Trying to tell myself that this is my reality and there is nothing I can do about it, everything will work out for the best. Trying not to listen to the part of myself that knows something is about to break, or crash, or get crushed under the weight of so much uncertainty and resistance.

As another big heat wave builds, I keep myself busy by preparing a welcome back dinner for Rhonda and David who've been away too. A cold dinner: gazpacho, tortellini salad, lemon pudding. While I chop vegetables and purée the base for the soup in the food processor, looking out the window across the street to the brown lawn with the odd green dandelion stem here and there, it occurs to me that if Jamie is killed in a car accident on the way home from work, then the girls and I could stay in Regina until we all finish school. I'd get my degree and maybe a master's so I could teach, make a decent living. Not that I want Jamie dead; I just want him in some heavenly place where he won't have so much control over my life. No more worrying about his next job or where we're going to go. No more planning our lives around his schedule. I'm surprised how detached I feel about this idea, chopping vegetables in the heat of my little kitchen.

I drive over to the strip mall to buy fresh pasta at the new Italian Deli, aware of the temperature rising all day, but not prepared for the blast of heat that hits me outside. The wind is blowing a good clip, the air is gritty, and the sky a peculiar, solid, battleship grey. I have the feeling I might get snatched away and end up in Kansas. The Italian guys have closed shop for a coffee break. Back in 15 minutes, the sign states. I wait. The city seems deserted. Leaning against a concrete block wall, waiting for the Italians, I feel strangely abandoned. My throat closes up and my face starts to crack open. I know I'm going to cry so I bite my lips, struggling to stop the tears that are pooling in my eyes, but they spill down anyway, vaporizing almost immediately in the hot dry wind, leaving salty tracks on my cheeks. I catch a sob in the crook of my arm and gulp, pressing hard, trying to keep it back. All of a sudden I become terrified that Jamie really will get killed in a car accident on the way home. The thought sickens me. Fear tears through me. When it comes right down to it, I can't imagine my life without him, or the girls without their father. I damn myself for letting such a devious thought roam in my head.

Back in my sheltered yard, I set the patio table and I wonder if we'll be able to get through the night without a storm. By midnight there's no change. Jamie and I and Rhonda and David are sitting under a giant hairdryer, caught in a gritty spell. We pick at the food. Satisfy ourselves with cold beer and wine instead. Slouch in the hot dark, stewed in booze, brooding about the future. Rhonda and David are returning to their home base in Calgary in a few weeks; but, like me and Jamie, they're stalled. David complains about the money they lost in the stock market the year before.

Jamie says, "We didn't need to worry about that one. All our savings have gone into this house or the truck I needed, or tuition for art classes. Oh well, one thing's for sure, Robyn and I won't be getting a divorce. We can't afford it."

The wind is still blowing. My heart stands still. Who said anything about divorce? What does he mean?

"Of course we can't get divorced," I laugh. "Who would cut your hair?"

"Yeah. Anyway, we've got other things to worry about. Like work for me."

"Why don't you guys make a home base in Calgary?" Rhonda suggests. "All the oil and gas jobs come out of Calgary."

We pour more wine. It's almost two in the morning. Draped across chairs we simmer. Coming to the conclusion that the night is never going to cool down, we drift into the hot little house. Feeling a little loosey-goosey, we stay up all night in the ruins of my freshly painted walls listening to music. We dance.

Does it make you feel queer for me to be telling you this stuff? That the thought arose that my life would be less complicated without Jamie? That sometimes I forget he is your son? Did you ever wish Donny out of the picture? I'm sure you must have. And he must have imagined life with you off the scene too. Obviously, Jamie had such thoughts about me or else the word *divorce* wouldn't have slipped out of his mouth with such ease. And I know you sought refuge, if only in your imagination, in the arms of Dr. Moore, who always remained young and sure of himself.

Is there refuge where you are now? I keep forgetting you're dead. I just chatter along to you as if you'll always be with me. Maybe you will. Maybe the talking is refuge.

There seems to be no escaping bad news that summer, especially for farmers. Crops fail in the sun and heat. My hope of finding a way to stay here sun-dried.

The night before they leave for Calgary, Rhonda and I sit out on the front step when the guys have gone to bed. We'd spent the day in the cool of the downtown mall shopping, me showing Rhonda where I buy my clothes. I'd even cut her hair similar to my own, flattered by her wanting to copy my style.

Earlier, we had wandered through Wascana Park along the lake that did not smell so great. Too much goose poop and god-knows-what else brewing up in the turbid, foul water. Still, it's the only place to wander if wandering is on your mind. Somehow we'd paired off — Jamie and Rhonda, me and David for a little goodbye smooching and petting. I don't take it seriously. It's just a way to crack the tension of the weather, and the impending move, and everything being up in the dusty, hot air.

"I'd really like to have another baby," Rhonda says wistfully. "But David doesn't want more children. I've always wanted to have daughters, but he got a vasectomy. You're so lucky, you know, with your beautiful daughters and getting to go to art school. Doing what you want."

There is something about the use of the word *luck* that bothers me. I sense the shadow side of being told how lucky I am that night and I feel a little guilty because here's this dumpy woman who doesn't think she's had much luck, so I empathize with her to take the heat off me, and that's one of the dumbest things I ever do.

I am still listening for the howl of a tornado when I should have been listening closely to the woman who is sitting next to me. Or better yet, to the woman who is emerging inside of me.

When Rhonda leaves the next day, I think the summer spell is over and am relieved to fall back into what I regard as my real life: my children, my schoolwork, and my best friends, Vivian and Beth. I'm back at the gym again.

When Jamie comes home with the news that the hydrogen peroxide plant in Prince George is a go and he's slotted for it, I panic.

"There's no university in Prince George."

"It would only be for a year. You could take a break."

"I'm afraid of losing my momentum."

"Hey, you could paint all day long. No classes."

"I still need the classes. I need the other people. I'm not ready to wing it alone. Who would I talk to?"

"Some of the old gang will be on this one. Pozzi will be up from Vancouver every couple of weeks. In fact he's coming in next week for big a start-up meeting."

I look at him. Is this the deal I've made? Does he think I'm going to go into the woods and paint dogtooth violets and be happy about it? Is this what I've promised for the luck of going to art school?

I start to think about car accidents again.

And worry about those cracks in the walls and who's going to fix them and who's going to paint these goddamn walls again and I worry about how I'm going to finish what I've started.

The phone rings.

"Hello!" a familiar voice drawls. "How are you doin', Darlin'?"

I'm rocketed right out of worry. The fucker, I think. How dare he call me? Who the hell does he think he is?

"Jamie told me you were coming to town."

"Yep. But only for the night. Sorry I can't get over, too busy. But I guess I'll be seeing you in Prince George."

Do I hear a train in the distance? Am I going to be derailed? Hell no!

"I'm not going to Prince George."

"What do you mean?"

"I'm going to move to Calgary and finish my BFA there. There are lots of oil and gas jobs out of there. Jamie will have to travel back and forth."

"I didn't know anything about this."

No, I'm thinking, you wouldn't, because I just made up my mind. This is how it's going to have to work. This is the only way it will work.

"Well then," I flaunt, "I guess you're behind the times."

"Guess so."

"See ya."

Click.

I repeat my strategy to Jamie.

"I'm not going to Prince George. I'll go as far as Calgary. But that's it. You'll have to get a job with David's company."

"Are you sure this is the best thing to do?"

He seems relieved somehow, excited about trying out for a job with one of the world's biggest construction and procurement companies.

"Absolutely."

"Okay. I'll talk to David. I'll see what's coming up with his company."

"Go for it Jamie. You always get what you're after."

I believe this. Whatever personal grief I've ever had with him, I know I can count on him where work is concerned. Do I think this is because he's *lucky*? Not for a second. He works hard.

By the time the wild geese have abandoned town, in early October, word comes that there is an opening for Jamie in Calgary. I'm a wreck. My painting class is going okay, because I know the instructor and most of the other students. The drawing class is the pits. For some reason the new instructor and I get off on the wrong foot. Somehow he sniffs me out, preys in on my insecurities and seems to take some kind satisfaction in levelling me and my work to the ground in every crit.

"It's obvious you have lots of facility, but you really don't seem to have anything to say," he accuses.

Bull's-eye. He's found my sore spot. I am mortified. Paralyzed. Things go from bad to worse. My hand clamps up. My mind shuts down. I can't draw. I can't come up with any good ideas for the mid-term project. Finally, I decide to do a series of drawings of Vivian and the Nautilus machines in the gym.

"Bad idea," he says with complete disinterest.

"Why? Women's bodies have been the subject of art through the millennia."

"Your friend in the gym is too middle class."

"I'm middle class," I retort.

"It's just too domestic," he sighs.

"I'm domestic," I snap.

"Nobody cares."

This from a guy named by *Chatelaine* as one of the five young collectable artists in Canada. Little Prick. This is how he will forever be identified in my mind: drawing of dog and telephone pole on the lone prairie by the Little Prick from Regina.

After this, I wear my high heels to class.

I spend four weeks on the drawings. They're stiff and illustrative. I can't get heart and soul into them. The Little Prick tears a strip off me. "You're wasting not only your time, but my time."

I am humiliated. In desperation, I try to remake my stolen black drawing. I spend hours closeted in my studio at home, but all I can come up with are bad forgeries of myself. I don't know where to turn.

This is where you come in, Muriel — all the way from New Brunswick on an airplane by yourself. Two big suitcases and that mink coat, hat long gone. Jamie has already started work in Calgary and is bunking in with Rhonda and David. Our bungalow is on the market; you're going to help me keep it spiffy. We've rented a house in Calgary for mid-December. A four-bedroom, because the plan is for you to stay until the spring. Do I think this is a good idea? Bless my optimism indeed I do.

Little do we know that there is no market in Regina, as we're lost in an exodus of 50,000, but we can't see that yet.

I am dutifully grateful for your presence in Regina. We're able to resume the relaxed connection of the summer, despite would-be buyers tramping through the door every few days. I silently forgive you for asking if Jamie's prepared. For the moment, the men are out of the picture, we focus on the domestic end of things. The girls love having you around. With all this instability, you are a comfort to them. And world of wonders, you actually like my paintings. Especially the 4′ x 3′ canvas of the blown glass goblets you gave me when we moved to Sussex. There is good flow and harmony of colours. Something luscious about the cranberry goblets arranged on a teal silk drapery, three right-side up, one upside down, painted against a reflective background. The energy in the painting is sexual. It's my best painting to date. I receive lots of applause at school, though it doesn't help my attempts for the drawing class.

"You'll just have to put your nose to the grindstone," you say to encourage me.

I don't know how to explain that the problem isn't work. The problem is being stuck. I find it doubly hard to get unstuck with you breathing down my neck, all anxious and fretful on the other side of my studio door. I make a lot of bad work, which I have to take to the final crit.

Fifteen students pin their work to the long white wall in the drawing studio. I can't even look at mine; I know they suck. The first hour and a half of the crit I spend in sickening anticipation. When the break comes, I look out the window at the breathtakingly cold day, with the sun dazzling off the snow, and hoarfrost that had developed over night. I wonder what the hell I'm doing waiting around to take shit from a two-bit sessional. So I zip up my parka and walk out of class.

"Hey," the Little Prick shouts, catching me in the hall. "Just where do you think you're going?"

"It's such a beautiful day," I say, with more equanimity than I feel. "I think I'll take my mother-in-law for a drive to look at the hoarfrost before it melts."

I turn and walk slowly down the hall, down the stairs, and out the front doors. I take a deep breath of the frigid crystal clear air that has swept down from the arctic overnight. In Wascana Park, the stupid stay-all-year geese are massed together on the fresh glittering blanket of snow, trying to protect themselves from the merciless cold and blowing wind. Every bush, tree, and clump of long grass poking through the snow is bejewelled in an icy cloak.

What a gorgeous day.

And then it's gone. The hoarfrost disappearing as magically as it appeared. My torment with the drawing class is over. It's time to pack up. Jamie makes a quick trip back from Calgary to pack up the garage and take the wall unit down. I'm so busy finishing up my final painting assignment, I barely acknowledge him. Before he leaves, he uncharacteristically brings me flowers. Kisses my cheek. For days and weeks, I feel that kiss. Like pentimento, it keeps coming through, but I don't know what it means. He says *I love you*. Then he's off. Leaving you — his seventy-four-year-old arthritic mother — and me — his thirty-four-year-old exhausted wife — to pack up the house. Plus all of the moving-in things that have to be done in reverse: switch off the power, the phone, the gas, cancel the insurance. The clean-up. Then there's the Christmas concerts and the brooding, unhappy girls to attend to. All this in a cold snap with bad roads, rutted and icy.

The day before the movers are due, I don't think I'm going to make it. You have gone grey around the gills and I'm worried about your high blood pressure so around 4 pm, in the last light of day, I tell you I've got the situation almost licked and deliver you to our hotel room for supper. Back at the house, I tackle the packing with mind-numbing determination. At nine o'clock I have to deliver a bundle of clothes over to Andrea, where she's staying with a friend. I warm up the Jeep, jump in, and run my errand. On the way back, gripping the steering wheel, without warning, I begin to cry. I drive myself over to Vivian's without really knowing where I am going. I sit in her driveway for a few minutes to calm my breathing and stop the floodgates. I get up my courage and knock on the door for help.

It takes the two of us six hours to shove the rest of my household goods into boxes. Final count: ninety-seven. All that's left is the cleaning.

By the time I get to hotel it's 4 am. I draw a hot bath and hold a cloth to my face to muffle the sounds of my crying. All the moves we have ever made parade through my muscles in the here and now. Under the water I slump and blow bubbles until all the air is out of my lungs and I count: seven moves, seven locations, seven years.

The next morning, while I'm trying to make something of my tired, pudding face with a little make-up before going over to supervise the movers, you scold me by saying, "When you came in this morning you woke the people in the room next to us when you drew your bath."

In the mirror I see an all too familiar look: the look of a woman who has been hard done by.

"Too fucking bad," I reply.

That shuts you up.

TWENTY-FIVE

YOU MUST UNDERSTAND it doesn't make me feel good to curse at an old woman, especially one who has tried her best to help out in a helpless situation. We spend the next day and a half in a rigid silence, while we clean the house and paint my studio walls. As a reward, I treat us to a manicure the afternoon before leaving. An almost beatific look spreads over your old face during the hand and arm massage. How many years, I wonder, has it been since you've been touched for longer than just a moment in a passing hug, or goodbye kiss. This makes me think of my own aching body and how for the first time in a long time I look forward to snuggling up to Jamie the next night.

That's all I give you that day, a passing thought for an old woman, and then I'm onto my own craving. Today, it really strikes me that you were only fifty-seven when you first confessed to me that you ached and moaned and walked the floors at night. Oh god Muriel, how you endured.

I'm beginning to think that endurance is an overrated quality. An insidious moral virtue passed on from generation to generation, like a genetic disorder. Only survival is expected under this precept. Not flourishing. You know, the world will provide us with enough circumstances to endure: drought, flood, economic downturn, loss of life, war. So why do we create further circumstances to endure?

Do I have some kind of hidden agenda taking on that move by myself with you there to witness? Do I have something to prove? My worth? What do you have to prove? Your worth?

It's wrong, Muriel. The whole thing stinks. Why don't we open our mouths? Who are we trying to protect?

All that *luck* of mine getting to go to art school. Where is the liberation? What is *luck* without some kind of liberation?

We have to drive eight hundred kilometres in the winter. Can you see now how absurd this is? It's the 17th of December, for Chrissake. We've got Christmas to think about. Talk about another endurance test coming up. Why don't I bundle you onto a plane? What are we doing? Saving a few dollars. No! We're out-enduring each other. We're proving something. We think all we have to do is get there. Withstand this one more day. And then we'll be safe. But what about the consequences? Does anyone really think we're going to get through this without compromises we can't name at the time? Can't I look at you and know what is going to happen?

There is going to be rage, isn't there, Muriel? And not just from me. There's a thirteen-year-old scrunched into the back seat of the Jeep with a ten-year-old. Rage is going to march down the line. Rage is that insidious twin of endurance.

After the bath that night, I start to see everything with underwater eyes.

But that morning, when we're departing from Regina, I'm just holding onto the thought that everything will be okay once we arrive in Calgary. This is the kind of thought that's not good to hold onto. I should be paying attention to what is real. Like when I stop at the mall to get snacks. As I back out, I hit a patch of ice and we slide into the side of the truck behind me. Without a blink, or a look to see what the damage is, I slip the Jeep into 4-low, step on the gas ever so delicately, and say to you as you let out a good long hiss, "Don't look, Muriel. Don't even peek. I'll just have to be forgiven."

Forgiven for what?

Forgiven because I'm so exhausted. Forgiven because my heart is breaking. Forgiven because I know my daughters' hearts are breaking. Forgiven because I've worked an old woman to the bone. Forgiven because I'm scared of the drive and what lies ahead.

Forgiven because I want more from life than an endurance test.

Filling up with gas, I start to break down again. I can't bear this leaving. I don't know what I could have done about it. My throat constricts and my heart feels like it's been plunged into cold water. I can't even attend to the misery hitting the back of my neck like buckshot from the backseat. The gas jockey doesn't know where to look. I don't give a shit. You pretend not to see when I wipe my snotty nose on the sleeve of the white parka you gave me.

Eight hundred kilometres stretches before us this flat grey day. As I nose the Jeep out onto the ice-patched highway I note a gaggle of geese heading west.

TWENTY-SIX

NO ARMS AROUND me the first night in Calgary, no sex. Exhausted from the long drive, I worry that I'd have to turn him away. But Jamie is not interested. I lay there, bewildered, still alert for patches of black ice, the snow-packed road speeding through my limbs. Crazy images splinter in my head. A renegade tumbleweed the size of a rum barrel lashing across the windshield near Swift Current, where gale-force winds threatened to bring our journey to a halt. Approaching Calgary in the dark, naked fields, a Chinook wind had melted all the snow the day before, the eerie brown desiccated appearance of the hills in the sodium streetlight as I hit the rush of traffic where the Trans-Canada intersects with Deerfoot Trail. Where the hell is everybody going on a Saturday night? The piece of crumpled paper on my lap with the directions to our rented house. Deerfoot Trail dwindling down to a dark single lane. Stumbling back on to MacLeod Trail. Jamie's short temper when I call, lost, having somehow missed the exit onto Southland Drive. The kindness of the strangers in the Mac's convenience store who guide me to the parking lot at K-Mart where Jamie meets us, his annoyance apparent. The homemade lasagna, Caesar salad, and President's Choice cheesecake provided by Rhonda, who had been there all day helping Jamie unpack the kitchen. And, weirdly enough, my studio: books, art supplies, all put in places that don't suit me, feeling more like a stab in the back than a favour. This is something I wanted to do for myself and it has been stolen away. The milk container stored on the fridge door instead of on the middle shelf. Nothing adds up. My back is killing me. I wouldn't mind a rub. I wouldn't mind a bit of attention. I remember the flowers, the kiss. Finally, I fall into a flinty sleep.

TWENTY-SEVEN

SEVEN DAYS TO arrange the household before Christmas. I push through with a perpetual headache. Shoulders cinch up to ears. At least Rhonda has us over for Christmas dinner. What a treat. No bird to stuff. She plays board games with Andrea and Caitlin to cheer them up and keep them out of my hair as I sort things out. Jamie is sluggish. I can't get him to set up the wall-unit. The centrepiece of our home sits unattended until after Christmas when I badger him into assembling it before he leaves for a sour gas construction project in northern Alberta. I hadn't expected him to go away so soon. I thought he was going to work from the office. Isn't that why we rented this place? Didn't I want to look for a place up in the northwest close to the Alberta College of Art? Wasn't I talked out of it by Rhonda, who wanted us to live in the south close to them, and Jamie who wanted to be close to work?

Now I have to beat my way down Southland drive across MacLeod Trail, up Heritage, Glenmore, then Crowchild Trail. All that merging in the aggressive Calgary traffic. Scares me shitless. Though not half as much as my first drawing class.

Because of a mistake on the registration form, I can't find the right room, and walk into the sound of charcoal skithering over newsprint. The class is Gesture Drawings, with a model. I set up at an easel; it feels foreign; I always used a drawing horse in Regina. I fumble the charcoal. Try to get a sense of the model — tall, skinny, long black hair, average penis. I can't see the other students' faces behind their easels. I can't breathe, I can't draw. Wish the floor would crack open and swallow me up. The index finger on my right hand has turned a peculiar blackish-white from clutching the charcoal.

"You must be Robyn Gallagher," the instructor says, ticking my name off on the class list. I should have guessed. Everyone in the class has known each other since first year. I'm out of the comfort zone. They all turn to eyeball me. I hate being new. The drawing instructor looks over my mess of gesture drawings, and gazes at me and my blackish-white index finger. Oh boy, here it comes. I brace for a Little Prick-like comment.

"Why don't you use your left hand? Maybe it'll loosen you up," the instructor suggests carefully.

With my left hand I don't have such a death grip on the charcoal, but my drawings aren't much better after the break. Damn and double damn. Drawing the model has always been my strength.

I drive home longing for bed.

It's Friday night. You've been stuck in the house all week. You and Jamie want to go to a movie. Andrea and Caitlin are out-of-sorts. They were new too, with no friends and nothing to do. I feel guilty. Sorry for myself. Sorry for all of you, but I can't budge from the couch. You all go without me. I turn my back into the stuffing, mumble "Have a good time," as the door closes.

On the weekend, I confess that I don't think I'm up to two studio classes and art history. I need some recovery and recuperation time. You both bear down hard on me. Neither of you took the news well that it will take me two and a half years to graduate as it is, the art college and the U of R not being in sync. Now you won't hear of me dropping a course.

"Just put your mind to it," you say.

"Yeah, get with the program," Jamie tries to be funny.

But none of us is having any fun. Andrea slumps on the couch with her arms crossed. "I hate it here. You have ruined my life."

"You'll get over it," I say, wincing. I sound like you, I'm trying to convince myself.

You and Caitlin retreat to the kitchen to make blanc mange and cookies, even though I have had a little talk with you about feeding the girls too much sugar.

That January the only thing that brightens my day is when Rhonda calls or pops by. Sometimes she takes Andrea and Caitlin shopping, while I finish unpacking the house or work on my assignments. In appreciation, and because Rhonda has lost so much weight since we all lived in Regina, I lavish her with the gift of my red party dress, cut her hair, and fix her make-up for a special event at her son's school. I'm feeling generous; after all, you have just bought me a silk pant outfit, *to keep up my looks*.

"I'd keep an eye on her if I were you," you whisper to me as I'm taking an apple pie out of the oven after Rhonda leaves all a-gush in her get-up, prancing into the living room where Jamie is stoking up his pipe.

"What?" I don't get it. I figure you're just miffed because Jamie and I are going to a party with Rhonda and David the next weekend and we've asked you to babysit all the kids. I know you want to go to the party, too, but Rhonda is becoming adamant that we do some things without you.

To make it up to you, though, she invites us all over for supper the next weekend when she and David drop Jason off and pick us up.

I'm glad to get out, but I experience none of the crazy hot and bothered restlessness of the summer. The party isn't much of a party, just a bunch of people standing around drinking and talking in a rec room. I'm bored. There is not one single person in the room who grabs my attention. There I am, enjoying a great big yawn, when out the corner of my eye I catch Jamie and Rhonda smirk when he grazes her breast while passing her a drink.

It's the smirk, the milk container in the wrong place, the slit of my eye when I'm yawning. There's a lot you can see with one eye closed. In the distance I think I hear a train. Dust devils whip up in my heart. I'm stunned, skewered, stung.

"We're going home, Jamie. Now."

"But I'm having fun," Rhonda protests. Then she too looks at me and sees the jig is up. The four of us hustle out to the car. Rhonda starts to cry. I sit in the back seat listening to her snivel. Freezing my ass off in the thin silk outfit you bought me. I'm cold, hard, and real. It's all going to come out now, I think. I'm sickened by what I know I'm going to hear and what I'll finally have to tell.

At the house Rhonda stays put, while David rushes in to rouse Jason from his sleep and carries him off, never to be seen again by me or my children or my husband. You stir from bed to check out the commotion, but scurry back to the warmth of your covers when you catch me glowering at your son. You know that if I have to, I will huff and I'll puff and I'll blow this house down. And you do not want to be the witness.

In our bedroom, I back Jamie into the space between the closets. His face is like our golden retriever when he was forced to bring back the dummy with a soft mouth, when all he wanted to do was swim away.

"What the hell is going on?"

"It all started when I was staying there. David and I would come home after work and he'd go read the paper and Rhonda and I would have a drink and talk. You know he never talks to her?"

"Perhaps David doesn't think she's got anything important to say."

"What?"

"Never mind. You sound just like your mother. But go on, spit it out."

"So then she started calling me at work. I was flattered. So I started calling her. And then we started, like, making plans."

"What kind of plans?"

"To run away to South America."

"You've got to be kidding."

"No, I'm not. We just sort of got carried away with everything and then I didn't know how to get out of it."

"Are you in love with her?"

"I don't know."

"What did you expect me and the girls to do?"

"Well, we were going to take the kids with us."

"You were going to do what?"

"Take the kids. Rhonda said David wouldn't care and you'd be better off. You'd have more time to do your art. That someday maybe you'd be famous and have this other life." My mind explodes and I think I'm going to puke. Bile rises in my throat. If Rhonda were a bear, I'd have her shot. No, I wouldn't. I'd do it myself. And I'd use the 7mm. One clean shot, right between the eyes.

"Making art is not like being a stupid fucking rock star, you know. You don't do it to get famous. And even if you did hint that you thought that way, the art instructors would wipe the shitty floor with you just so you didn't mistake the idea of making art with the idea of being a superstar."

"I know."

"No, you don't. You don't know anything that isn't directly related to your own little world. You think you live in the real world, but I've got news for you. You live in one stinking corner of the world. It isn't any more real than my world. Get that through your stupid head."

Jamie doesn't say a thing. I sense a shift in power. And I know that Jamie is not going to ask me anything about Pozzi, the chicken shit. In some ways, I'm disappointed. It would have been a relief, but I am not about to hand myself over to him on a platter.

"Did you sleep with Rhonda?"

"No."

The answer comes too fast. All of a sudden I know it's a trade-off. I know why Jamie has never questioned me.

"You call her in the morning and tell her the deal is off."

"Yes," he says. Grateful. Expecting to be protected.

"There will be no South America. And tell her that if she ever comes nosing around here again or ever comes within a mile of my daughters, that I'll kill her. Have you got that?"

He nods.

I know it's a lie. I know he slept with her. But I also knew if he had said *yes* that I would have no choice but to walk out the door and slam it in his face forever, just the way my mother had with my stepfather. I'm not prepared to do that. Not living in a strange place with no support and no one to turn to. If we had still been living in Regina, perhaps I would have tossed him out into the night like an old tomcat. But here in Calgary, I don't feel safe. Andrea and Caitlin are struggling so hard in their new schools. I figure I have to negotiate. I figure I have to let his answer be the truth I could live with to get us through for the time being.

All that night, as I wash in and out of sickness in a half-sleep, I wonder how we got from the kiss that nearly blew the top of my head off to this murderous feeling I hold in my heart. I wonder about the deal I have made. I wonder if I have the will to go forward with your son. There is such an accumulation of good things and bad things. I hear him saying *You're so strong, you're so brave* as I pelt him with questions and accusations. Yet I've been told about his explosive temper at work. I know he got into fistfights in bars before we got married. I know he was the bruiser on the hockey team at private school. That he took knocks on the rugby field. I just didn't know that he doesn't know how to fight with a woman.

The next morning, you don't open your mouth. No one does. To get some breathing space, Jamie and I take a walk around the neighbourhood trying to sort things out. It's a broody day with clouds fighting for position with the sun. A soft warm wind blows. Snow is melting and rivulets are running everywhere on the road and sidewalks. A queer January day. But not for Calgary of the fickle weather. This we can expect in Calgary when the Chinooks blow in over the Rockies. We both agree that keeping the family together is paramount. A vast hurt tenderness hangs between us. A red pulsating hurt that stings like a jellyfish. We each say *I love you.* Although out of fear or truth, I don't know. Yet we yearn to love.

That night, we sleep tucked-up in a ball of ache.

He leaves for the construction site in the dark of the early morning. After the girls bundle off to school you and I get busy with housework.

"I cannot abide filthy windows," you declare, dragging a chair outside to tackle the kitchen windows in the fickle sun. Monday morning at the end of January, 12 degrees.

While I uselessly run a broom across the floor pushing cat hair and crumbs into corners, I wait for the phone to ring. When the call comes, I take it in the bedroom.

"Who was that?" you ask nonchalantly when I reappear in the kitchen.

"Just Jamie," I answer flatly. "He got to the site safe and sound."

You know he doesn't usually call when he's at work, but I won't tell you that has performed his duty and cut it off with Rhonda. No sooner have his words sunk in when the weather suddenly turns. The high wide sky turns a periwinkle grey then flattens to an iron colour as the temperature falls swiftly and big fluffy white snowflakes burst onto the clean windows out of nowhere. As the temperature dives in the afternoon, the clouds turn sooty, lowering over us and now the snow bursts open from this heaviness with tiny white pellets that form a thick dry crust over our suburban world. As evening falls, I am overcome with restlessness. When I announce that I'm going to the store to get chocolate bars, you surprise me with an offer to keep me company.

Our progress along Willow Park Drive is slow and treacherous. Patches of ice lie below the building snowfall. We inch along, making our own path, my dark brown sheepskin arm linked with your mink one so we won't fall. It is now minus twenty and the wind is picking up. I can't get myself up for conversation. You take the opportunity to tell me a story about a woman you knew who went back to school to get her B.Ed., and while she was so busy studying, her husband simply took up with another woman.

"What an asshole," is all I can think to say.

"She put her whole family at risk."

That loosens my tongue.

"Look Muriel, I spent four years of evenings alone while Jamie studied for his degree. I accepted it because I knew it was for our future."

"Well, to tell you the truth dear, I don't see how studying art will be of any benefit for your family."

You just had to sneak that one in there didn't you, you old bag. I'm holding your life in my hands and you're putting me down. With a simple wrench of my torso, I could send you flying and there wouldn't be a witness because everyone else in Willow Park has the good sense to be tucked in behind their drawn drapes on this foul evening. A car doesn't even pass us by. But this day of formidable tension is almost over and I'm not going to be put off my mindset by your hints and innuendoes, so I ignore your comment as best I can.

At 11 pm when the only sounds in the house are those of the walls and pipes contracting in the now -32 temperature, I make my telephone call.

"Hello Rhonda," I say in a voice as black and cold as the night.

"Oh," she returns in a small, tight voice. "It's you. I think I'm going to cry."

"You needn't bother."

"I'm sorry. I didn't know this would hurt so many people."

"How could you not know?"

"I'm sorry. I just don't know. Do you think we can be friends again in ten years?"

It's been five years. The gun is still loaded.

I lay in bed as snow and wind howls around the house and think about the hot nasty night in Regina when we all sat around, restless, itching for a change. I daresay we all had a part to play in this misery, but running off to South America with my husband and children is beyond the pale. No wonder she was always having the girls over or taking them out shopping. How dare she? How dare she plot behind my back with such energy and detail?

And you. I now know that as much as I have thought of you as a mother these last seventeen years, I can no longer look at you this way. You have your son to protect. *Watch her*, you warned. *Watch her.*

A line is drawn. Because when you think about it, what would a mother say to her daughter? She might say *Watch her*, but really, we both know what a mother would then have to say. She'd say *Watch him.*

Watch him.

That's not what you said, is it?

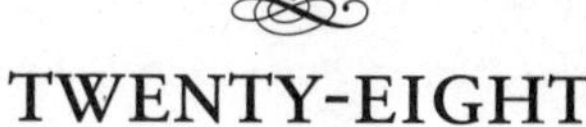

TWENTY-EIGHT

ARCTIC AIR CLAIMS Calgary for the rest of the week. On Thursday night, I brave the Deerfoot, picking Jamie up at the airport instead of letting him come home in a taxi. The four days apart has done us good. We are shy with each other, and make love in the rawness of injury, seeking each other out. I feel more alive to him than I have for years.

At breakfast, you watch us like a hawk. I have refused to tell you anything all week because I will not have you accuse me of being so selfish. I will not have you tell me that I must sacrifice the rest of my life for my family. When Jamie goes out to shovel a wider path in the driveway, you fold your arms across your chest in the draft of the door closing, briskly rubbing your shoulders and say slyly. "I thought we going over to Rhonda and David's for supper Friday night."

"No."

I walk to the dishwasher with our bowls and cups.

"Well, in that case I think I'll go up to Edmonton for a week and visit Alexis and the kids. You don't need me here anymore."

"Suit yourself."

We are all relieved when you get on that bus, Muriel. Even more relieved when you book a flight and leave us for the rest of the winter. Somehow we have all failed each other and none of us has the strength to keep up appearances. We have not been taking care.

And to hide the truth from Andrea and Caitlin we tell them, *Mummy and Mrs. McGratten had a fight.* They have a hard time taking it in. We confuse our daughters to protect your son.

I feel so disoriented.

HERE WE ARE coming up to Moose Jaw, home of CFB Moose Jaw and 15 Wing, the largest jet-training base in Canada. Sometimes I almost forget where we are. I get so balled up in that story. It is always so present to me. I was completely back in time, if that makes any sense. I have to remind myself that almost three-quarters of this country is behind me now and by tonight I will be back in Calgary safe and sound with Andrea and Caitlin and can go to sleep in my own bed for the first time in three weeks.

There is this big question hanging over me.

The same one that hangs over me that week you leave us.

Do I have the will to go forward with Jamie?

Have we taken enough care to make our marriage work for the rest of our lives? I don't know, Muriel. I have just turned thirty-nine. I am just beginning to know not only what I want, but who I am. From here, the rest of my life appears as vast as the landscape around me.

You leave us that winter because we have failed you. You go back home to take care of the appearance of things, especially your respectability.

Up in the Georges Dumont Hospital, Donny can no longer take care of his handsomeness and his Irishness and his name, his blessed name.

Agatha is taking care of herself and her virtue. She gives to the community. She will not offer a warm ear to your newest sorrow.

Alexis is up in Edmonton, taking care of her independence by getting her PhD in genetics.

Jamie leaves home each week for a sour gas plant, so he can take care of providing for us.

I am slowly going out of the business of taking care of the sorrows of others. I am taking care of the children as best I can, hoping it is good enough. I am taking care of my own needs, trying to live my life to the full extent of my capabilities.

When you head east again, you do so with a heavy heart. In your eyes, I have failed. I have failed to keep your son from harm's way. That is what is implicit in *Watch her*. I have neglected duty, exposed my children, and pulled the rug out from under your legacy of respectability. So now you are a complete failure. With an alcoholic, demented, institutionalized husband, a divorced daughter who was pregnant the second time she got married, a son who's been having an affair, and a daughter-in-law incapable of keeping order. I finally understand that underwater smile of yours, Muriel. It's as if you've been walking on the bottom of the sea and could never open your mouth because you'd drown. Even learning how to swim has not enabled you to make your way to the surface. And there we are — Donny, Alexis, and Jamie and I — rocks in your pockets.

TWENTY-NINE

I HAVE NO sense of how many kilometres I've gone since Moose Jaw.

Watch him is drilling a hole in my head.

There's something I'm forgetting. Some little thing I can almost grasp and then it's gone. Something about your face before you leave. You are trying to draw me in. Find out what happened. Or perhaps you've been triggered. You're telling me about parties and Donny and how he used to bother other women. Your face is all sunk in like an apple doll, dried out and brown. You're standing by the love seat with weak late afternoon sun lighting you from behind. Your thin white hair is askew. Arms limp by your bulging hips and round tummy and, yet, you somehow appear caved in.

I am standing near the wall unit across the room. I don't know what I'm doing there. Perhaps I'm about to put some music on. I don't know how we got started. I don't trust you. I don't want to tell you anything. You sense this and yet you can't help yourself from speaking and I am rooted to the spot. You say it again. Donny bothering other women. I don't want to hear this. I start to feel mean. And then I let you have it, because I think that Jamie's lie when I had him pinned to the wall isn't the only lie.

"Like father, like son," I say, watching you collapse further into yourself. "And the drinking too," I add just in case you haven't heard enough.

"I thought something like that," you confess. "Oh why, after all the trouble ..." you falter. Then your voice trails off because I walk out on you. I know you can't figure out how to end the sentence. *Oh why after all the trouble his father caused* or *Why oh why after all the trouble I went to hide what his father did from him.*

All these years you have represented Donny as dead as a doornail in ye olde sex department and I never questioned you. Not even when he grabbed me in the kitchen a couple of years earlier. I thought his big hard-on was an aberration. And here you're trying to tell me that Donny wasn't so inert as I'd been led to believe. You're trying to give me a new version and I don't want to hear it. I've got enough to get my mind around without you changing the foundation of my beliefs in how your family operated. I needed more time if you were going to change your tune.

Now something I heard last week is starting to make sense. I walked in on Jamie and Alexis when they were going through the insurance policies you kept stashed in the drawer of your hutch. Something was being said about Donny and ladies of the night up in Moncton. Jamie was tight-lipped when I questioned him about it later. All I could gather is that either together or alone they were sent on missions to bring him home. There was so much going on with the funerals that this tidbit completely slipped my mind.

Now I have an idea what that was all about. You spent two summers down at Mount Allison getting your B.Ed. a couple of years before I met you. You hated every minute of those courses, but getting them gave you a much better salary as a teacher. In fact, it was so worthwhile that you were finally in a position to make more money than Donny. I'll bet that didn't go down well, did it?

So now I get it. The story you told me the evening we walked to the store in the blizzard was about you, wasn't it? You were the woman in the story. But you couldn't bring yourself to tell me.

Who were you trying to protect? Or should I say what were you trying to protect?

Although I guess I could ask myself the same question, couldn't I?

THIRTY

WE DEVELOP THESE versions of ourselves that we stick to, as if they're something solid that we can hold onto if the boat tips over. You know what? I think the boat just tipped over. I was geared up to tell you my sob story about the rest of the winter in Calgary: a stranger in a strange land, betrayed, shamed, broken-hearted, no gym, no Vivian, no Beth. An empty bed half the week. Two miserable kids who hate their new schools. The week they both came down with the chicken pox. Finding a new way to get to ACA the morning after a snowstorm when I watch a van back down the steep exit I'm supposed to take. All of this I have to negotiate. Yet in this struggle, somehow I connect to a part of myself that is not involved in our crisis. I find the quiet centre of my heart, where moment by moment I truly calm down and restore the sense of myself as separate and real, uninvolved with the chaos that surrounds me.

Every evening after settling Andrea and Caitlin into their homework, I disappear into my studio. The drawing instructor figures nobody in the class is really into drawing the model so she devises a project to keep us busy for a few weeks, assigning the following: make three drawings of your workspace, one more or less realistic, one emotional, and one conceptual. We will meet in three weeks for the crit. I start with the realistic. What do I see? Bookcases and books, a drafting table, art supplies: pencils, charcoal, paper, paint, brushes. A clear glass piggybank crammed with pennies I've had since I was fourteen. There is variety of shapes and textures, lines, forms, grey values. Couldn't be simpler, right?

I clip a sheet of white paper to my drawing board. Now I must choose a point of view. Nothing starts without a point of view. I place myself just inside the door looking into a corner. One-point perspective. Corners provide plenty of visual interest. I begin plotting out the space for a fairly conventional drawing. I'm going to play it straight. I don't question. I draw exactly what I see with graphite pencils and graphite sticks. There is something so soothing about drawing with graphite, the sound of a pencil connecting with good paper, the translation of colour into black and white and all the values in between. The image begins to take shape. The flow starts. I'm as much in the drawing as in the world. The space between collapses.

The image of Jamie's hand grazing Rhonda's breast blooms in my head and I'm swallowed by the intensity of what I understood in that split second. I am afraid that I'm doomed to be stuck with this image, like Donny in Mississauga, reacting anew to the Challenger explosion each time he sees it.

I bring my attention back to the drawing. I do this over and over. After a week, the realistic drawing of my studio space takes on a life of its own. There is order and some weight. Something of me and not just my space lives on the paper.

I stand back to admire my work. Reach for my cheek without knowing. The faint imprint of Jamie's kiss that last time in Regina. The unexpected bouquet of flowers. The unprompted declaration of love. *The flowers, the kiss, the stab in the back*. How he had unpacked my art supplies and shelved my books the night I arrived, then turned a cold shoulder. *Seven moves, seven locations, seven years*. The lie I had accepted. The hands that had been on Rhonda had sorted through my stuff. The stuff that defined the world I had chosen. Yet I don't want these hard scared feelings that piggyback on that image of Rhonda and Jamie; what good do they do? I feel so much pressure to draw back into my body and roll into a round, happy woman, a good woman. But I am not a bad woman. I am unwilling to accept that old polarity. Jamie's not the bad guy. He always wanted to do the right thing. In fact, he always believed he would do the right thing. So there is this space, this void he doesn't know he has to fill; it will take some effort on his part to be a good man.

When he comes home on Thursday nights, I am happy to see him. Not *happy as a lark*; happy like someone who has escaped a burning house.

With good will after good sex — the kind of sex you have when you're afraid you're going to lose everything — we try to talk. Jamie confesses that he's deeply afraid of not being able to provide. Our bungalow on the prairies sits empty. There are no buyers. He's paying the mortgage there and the rent here. We're flat broke.

"I don't think I can afford you, Robyn," he sighs one night as we walk hand-in-hand around the block.

A warm Chinook wind blows like buckshot through my heart. What does it mean to be unaffordable?

Back in my studio, I prepare to make drawing number two. Conceptual space. Blank paper on a white drafting table. I sit for a while with my eyes closed, focusing on my breath and the psychedelic swirl of red and blue and purple that pulsates under my eyelids. An afterimage of the white paper hovers in the swirl. The *smirk* pops up. Dirt devils whip my heart. *Off with their heads*. I let that thought come and go. Refocus on the project at hand. The afterimage has disappeared into the chaos. I summon it back. It's hovering, floating. For the briefest moment, I manage to make it stay still. I realize I have not been breathing. I breathe. Open my eyes.

My heart is quiet. I am in control.

I reach for a red oil pastel and lay a ground of colour, white showing through the tooth of the paper. I add a ground of blue.

With a drawing stump, I patiently blend the red and blue together, merging the two colours into a pulsing cover of purple with blips of red and blue breaking through. This is what I do for several nights until the sheet of paper is transformed. Every time my thoughts stray, threatening heart and breath, I let them pass without grabbing on. Again and again I gently bring my focus back to the sea of colour. Again and again, ugly thoughts pass through.

JAMIE AND I try to figure out where to go from here. This is where we make our big mistake — trying to get a hold on the future. We feel like we don't belong in Alberta. That to make things right again we need to go home, to the Maritimes. We long for the familiar, even though we have been through this before. We re-concoct the spell of the magical kingdom and locate it in Halifax. Jamie convinces himself that if he tries hard enough, he can get work there and all our problems will be solved. We will leave this mess behind. Back home, everything will be okay.

After we make love to seal our resolve, we cocoon in the living room with cigarettes and brandy. Jamie breaks into the enchantment with five little words.

"I'm not having any fun."

His confession strikes an odd note with me. Fun? I don't understand.

"I work so hard and don't get anywhere," he goes on pensively, grinding a butt into the ashtray, lighting another smoke. "There's no reward. And worst of all, Dad is on my mind all the time. I'm so scared I'll end up just like him."

He scares me, opening up like this. We are so raw.

"I want you to promise me something."

"Okay," I say tentatively, snakes darting in my tummy.

"If I ever get like Dad. Before I get really bad. Before I'd have to go into a home or something, I want you to promise me you will find a way ..." Jamie falters, squeezes my hand. Looks me in the eye. "I want you to find a way to put me out of my misery. For good. I can't stand the idea of ending up like Dad."

The snakes writhe up into my throat. "I'm not sure how ..."

"Will you find a way?"

"Yes. I'll find a way."

I promise, believing this pact will bind us back together. Not even thinking that he's still looking for protection. Not really questioning whether this is something I can truly provide. I'm eager to make things right.

BACK IN MY studio, I confront the pulsating paper on my drafting board. Over the top of it, I lay a ground of gold oil pastel and let it dry for a day or two. From memory of the drawing I have already done, into this ground I make a line drawing of my studio with a scratch tool, working into the layers of colour, depositing the excess, like overburden, onto the hardwood floor. Next, I scratch in the dimensions of an empty stretcher frame two inches inside the edges of the paper. All three images: the coloured ground, line drawing of the studio, and stretcher frame exist non-hierarchically within the context of the whole. The eye can pull either of these images forward, independently of the others, or the viewer can see the image as a whole. I don't really know if this is conceptual or not but at least I'm not stuck.

All over the house I track tiny balls of oil pastel. Smears of red and blue and gold appear on doorknobs, the kettle, the microwave. The carpet looks bruised.

I keep wondering what Jamie means by *fun*. I mean, is anybody having any fun?

Certainly not the girls. First Caitlin, then Andrea comes down with chicken pox. I spend many hours, day and night, sponging them in tepid baths to take down their high fevers. I drench them in calamine lotion. Warn them not to scratch or they'll be scarred. Their illness exhausts me, irritates me. I can barely stand to be near them, their misery and pain so great. Almost as if I'm covered in a lumpy rash too, only mine is on the inside and it can't be soothed with lotion. Between trips to the bathroom, where they soak, or their bedrooms, where they moan, I paint a still life of African Violets in an orange enamel pot for my watercolour class. It is somewhat less than successful.

You call on Sunday. You're glad to be home.

I'm relieved to escape to the concrete hulking mass of ACA and the Art Since '45 art history class that directs me toward the present in art practice. Three blessed hours a week in a dark room with the most beautiful, crazy, provocative images projected onto the wall and the quiet, informed commentary of the instructor. I'm really getting this stuff. I love it. And I'm going it alone. There is no Beth. No Vivian. This solitariness bothers me, it's something I want to get rid of, I'm lonely, but, looking back, I see now how being solitary was the best thing for me. With no distractions, I'm forced to internalize my experiences. I have a lot of time to confront myself. Not so much to judge, but to be curious. More open. Or perhaps I should say that in my solitariness I allow room for the possibility of cracks that lead to openness.

Number three of the drawing assignment: emotional space.

At the Regina art school there was a popular idea that emotion is the property of expressionism, a surrender to the unconscious. Marks born of boldness or frenzy, whether lyrical or violent, fluid or nervous are the act of self-purification. The canvas as priest. The gesture as release. The paint nothing more than the medium of the soul. Anything less is marking time. This is such an appealing notion that it's hard to dispel. Expressionism as surrender. Authenticity of expression. The discovery of the self. Transcendence. Purity.

What about control? Intentionality? How about historical analysis?

Even when we're told in art history class that Jackson Pollock knew exactly what he was doing when he stood over his canvas draped on the floor and dribbled paint off the end of a brush, that he was good at it, in fact that he could dribble with incredible accuracy, even if it was reacting with one dribble to the dribble that came before it. Even after all that telling, there are students who will flee the dark classroom and run as fast as they can into the arms of authentic expression.

So, as I approach the emotional depiction of my studio space, it is not just the fear of my emotions that stop me from jumping right in, it is the expectation of what this drawing should look like. I have absolutely no intention of abandoning myself to fury and mayhem. I will not act out. Not now. The time isn't right. As I ponder the blank sheet of drawing paper the thought comes up that all of my life I have been blowing with the wind. Reacting to this situation or that. One person or another. Tagging along with hormones. And, the past few years, abandoning myself to alcohol in social situations. Understanding that we know ahead of time we'll do weird things when we're drinking. This is part of the appeal. I think there must be another way. I'm tired of knocking around. I want to be more observant about what I do.

In the first drawing, the realistic rendition, the viewer is placed within the space. In the conceptual drawing, the ground of viewer shifts within the piece. Approaching the emotional space, I do something counter-intuitive; I place the viewer outside the frame looking in. In the foreground, on either side, is a sort of opalescent puss-coloured wall. The background is a corner depicted in a dark menstrual blood pulsating colour. In the middle ground is a drafting table. There are no other objects. I try various colours for the drafting table but find nothing that works. Finally, I scrape off all the colour with a razor blade, right down to the bare paper. In fact, into the paper. Hundreds of slice and scrape marks add a surprising texture. There, I've got it, the rendering of emotional space with nary a slap-dashing heroic stroke — just small, precise movements. This drawing looks scared and lonely. If the first drawing has some weight, this one possesses gravitas.

This is the beginning, an emergence of sorts; me standing outside myself, looking in. Asking, in a very small voice, but asking nonetheless, *Who am I*?

The crit goes well. My confidence beefs up. I ride the swell to the end, acing the drawing class and Art Since '45. The watercolour class is hit or miss, almost a throwaway, but I get through my first semester at ACA feeling pretty good about my work.

But at home, things are dodgy. Nothing ever comes from Jamie's attempts to find work back in the Maritimes. We finally manage to sell our house in Regina for less than the mortgage is worth and this throws us into a slump. *I don't think I can afford you* and *I'm not having any fun* sit in the back of my mind like congealed egg yolk. I make a half-assed stab at selling encyclopedias but it's grim work and only pays commission. I turn instead to the prospect of selling a line of women's clothes at home parties, which brings in some extra cash for art supplies and odds and sods.

From you, Muriel, there is mostly silence. We are not offered a free ride home this summer. There will be no beaches, salt water, and swimming. Calgary is hard on the eyes for a family of Maritimers. Jamie likes to head out on the bike trails in the city parks, but often I send him off on his own. I'm tired and enervated.

We are still trying to be tender with one another. We say *I love you* hoping it's for real and not from fear. I promise to find a fulltime job if worse comes to worse. At heart, I don't really mean it. At heart, I plan to finish art school no matter what. I don't intend to make room in my old age for the sob story *I quit my dream* to please someone else. Not that Jamie doesn't want me to finish, he carries that old dread in his bones too. But he feels the pressure to provide and it is wearing him down.

We try and we try, Muriel. Something is missing. The marriage has been assaulted and shamed. We have not treated it well. We can't seem to get it all together.

We're still thinking about ourselves.

Banff and Kananaskis beckon, but we can't seem to get the hang of what to do here in the summer until one Saturday when we head out to Barrier Lake. I am mesmerized by the turquoise jewel colour of the water. The mountain air is clear. Wildflower sweet. We drag the hampers and coolers and blankets to a secluded spot with a bit of beach and no sooner get settled and have some lunch when Jamie wants to pack up and go. The girls and I grumble, but we know it's useless to argue when he gets fidgety so we tramp off to another spot. The water is so inviting.

"I'm going to jump in," I announce.

"Are you nuts?" Jamie hoots. "That water can't be much above freezing."

I take a deep breath and hurl myself into the lake. It wraps its icy arms around me as I sink into a wondrous, clear, turquoise world. There are no fish. No plants. No visible signs of life. Just shock waves billowing out from my startled body and the crisp rocks on the bottom in every imaginable shade of brown. For a moment, I am suspended in time, place, and intention. Anger and frustration leech out of me. I become pure in the pure cold water. If I could breathe underwater, I would've stayed there for a long, long time.

My heart lurches with joy when Andrea and Caitlin come cannonballing toward me. The three of us grab hands and break the surface bellowing.

"Come on in, Dad."

"Come on, Jamie."

"No way, José. And don't stay in there too long. You'll get hypothermia."

I ignore his Muriel-like concern and stay in the water until I'm damn good and ready to get out. Millions of needle-like points shoot, exquisitely, through my skin. I rub the girls with terry towels, the misery burning out of me.

For the rest of the afternoon, we dawdle through Kananaskis country, taking the long way home, driving south in the evening.

The mountains reflect the sunset, shimmering gold and red as if an exotic fabric has been draped over the hard surface for the night. Cattle roam the road here and there. Andrea and Caitlin fall asleep. Jamie and I rest easy in the ebb of the quieting day, our Jeep like a big rocking chair holding us together, up and down and in and around the mountains. Somewhere below skin and muscle remains the trace of each kiss and caress we have shared, an anatomy of desire and promise and trust. In the back seat snooze the tangible existence. One child conceived in excess and abandon, another with purpose and intent. Both loved beyond language. In Andrea and Caitlin, there is still an *us* and always will be; the product of our love could never be denied or forgotten.

Humming along the highway in candle-yellow light, touched with orange and red, I remember my slim young body offered up completely and wondrously. This is the body I still feel from time-to-time, my body before the children and fatigued muscles and tired bones. The body before I became wary and mistrustful. As the mountains smooth out in favour of rolling pasture as we enter the Turner Valley, flattening into prairie as we head east to Black Diamond, then north into Calgary, I wonder if Jamie will ever have that special touch again, the one that brought me, whole and aroused, completely to the surface.

THIRTY-ONE

NOW WHAT. THE car sounds funny. Wisps of steam are escaping from around the hood. Shit. The red temperature light is on. I'm pulling over. Shutting down. What do I do? Open the hood. What a smell. Crackling and popping, violent little bursts of the remnants of something. Coolant? I don't know. It's like listening to a kettle on a woodstove. What do you think, Muriel? It's your car — was your car.

I think we're in trouble.

There's nothing out here but the highway disappearing into a shimmer. I sure as hell hope help materializes out of this mirage. I can't be that far from Maple Creek. We're in ranch country. Perhaps some cowboy will come by and get us out of this. Here comes a dusty red pick-up. He's stopping.

"Hey lady, I can give you a ride into town."

The radio is tuned to a local AM country station. The young man drives with his deeply tanned elbow out the window. A plume of dust explodes behind the truck as we turn off into Maple Creek.

I WAIT IN the grimy corner of the service station, oil, grease, and gas fumes almost overpower me. I don't know if I can cope. So close to home. I thought I'd eat in my own kitchen tonight with the girls. A deep lethargy spreads through the tissues in my back and neck. My tailbone aches. I feel dull and disoriented.

A tall thin man in greasy overalls and a John Deere cap looks under the hood, looks at the plates. I still wince. He raises the little Buick Skylark up on the hoist. Clanks and prods. Opens the door and comes up to me as he wipes his hands on a rag. It's questionable whether the dirt is going from the hands to the rag or the rag to the hands.

"I'm surprised you got this far," he says.

"What do you mean?"

"I don't think anybody's had a real good look under the hood for a long time. Your car here is time-hardened. Looks good on the outside, but it's been neglected on the inside. You're lucky you just blew a hose. All the hoses and belts are brittle and cracked. Going to have to replace the CV joints sometime soon, too. How far're you goin'?"

"Calgary."

"Suspension's badly rusted and the struts aren't lookin' too good. She can't take much abuse, but if you stay on the highway and don't get off on the dirt roads she should get you there."

"I don't understand. This was a little old lady's car."

"Well this here little old lady's car suffers from the Maritimes. It's not worth much," he pulls his lips in and shakes his head. "Rust never sleeps, ma'am. It never sleeps."

I look at his fingers, rounded tips with black etched into the grains of skin, a thin line of black rimming what remains of his fingernails. Under his ball cap, stringy sandy hair skims his collar. Like the rag in his pocket, he looks well-used and a little past his prime. I'll have to trust he knows what he's talking about.

"What can you do for me today?"

"Well, to get you going, I can make a call and order the hoses in on the bus from Medicine Hat that comes in later this afternoon. Maybe get you on the road in the morning. I'll take you over to a

B&B in Maple Creek that's pretty good. You aren't going anywhere tonight, that's for sure."

Time-hardened, Muriel. That's a good one, isn't it?

Your hairdresser offered to buy this car because it's in such good shape and we almost took her up on it. Jamie and I talked it over. In the end we figured because Andrea has her licence now, another vehicle would be a good idea. Oh well, nothing to do but kick up my feet for the night. Think I'll go for a walk first.

It's pretty here, you know. Sort of like Alma, gateway to a park. The Cypress Hills. Jamie and I and the girls camped here one weekend with Vivian and her family the first year we lived in Regina. We arrived in the dark and set up just before a hard rainfall. The next morning smelled so good out under the lodge pole pine and white spruce. We hung the sleeping bags out to dry and fried up bacon and eggs. I was happy. The sun came out and we went for a swim in the small lake. Drove up into the hills in the evening.

The Cypress Hills form the highest point of mainland between Labrador and the Rocky Mountains. High enough so that points were not covered over by glaciers in the last ice age. It's a strange place. You can feel it. I loved being here and we told ourselves we'd come back often, but we never did. You have to wonder why. Partly because Jamie hated camping, partly because I never wanted to face the heat in the four-hour drive. Partly because of inertia, I guess.

That and the fact that Jamie was never comfortable around men who weren't related to his work. This made it hard for us to socialize with my crowd. Truth be told, I was finding it harder and harder to hang out with his crowd.

The next time we went camping, after Cypress Hills, was not long after I hurled myself into Barrier Lake in Alberta. I had such a desperate urge to do something and talked Jamie into taking a few days off work. We headed off for Invermere through Radium, but it was so hot when we got there we simply kept going until we ended up at Moyie Lake in the cool of the evening. A couple of days later, we drove over to Creston and up to Crawford Bay to take the ferry over to Balfour. Set up on Kootenay Lake at Woodbury Resort, poked around Nelson one afternoon. I laughed my head off at the men's neckties tied around trees and poles along the west shore from Nelson back to the campsite. I fell in love with the great swooping branches of the cedar trees, the long deep lake. Something stirred in my heart.

"I could live here," I said to Jamie sitting by our campfire the evening before we left.

"Not me," he said firmly, gesturing to the mountains that seemed to rise up out of the lake. "Too closed-in. I'd feel trapped."

I was disappointed. For the first time ever I thought I'd found a place other than Nova Scotia where I could live out my life.

Now here I've been walking around this place thinking old thoughts, hardly taking it in. Could I live here? I don't think so. Easy on the eyes, but doesn't touch me where it counts.

I'm looking at a map of Saskatchewan I found in the night table spread out on the floor of my room in the B&B. I have only travelled across this thin skein of highway where the Trans-Canada runs through. The southern half of the province looks like the grid of a big city, highways and roads crisscrossing everywhere, but north of Prince Albert, everything changes abruptly. There are hundreds of square miles of what looks like nothing, littered with lakes, large and small. All this unexplored space I am about to leave behind in the morning.

Five years ago, we owned a house here. We held on to it, not seeing that the price, though reasonable at the time we put it on the market, was much too high. But we held on and we held on and in the end got so much less. Odd to think we let that loss press down on us so. It shaped our lives. What was it we couldn't see?

Why is it we hold on so tightly when the price is too high?

THIRTY-TWO

OKAY YOU OLD rust bucket, let's get going, there are 400 kilometres left.

Last night when I talked to Andrea and Caitlin, I got another surprise for the day. Jamie's flying in tonight. My hackles went up, but I kept my mouth shut because they sounded so pleased. I wasn't expecting him until next week.

At least the girls sound good. There was minimal squabbling on the line. Maybe they've taken this time to sort out some things between them. They've been awful to live with the past couple of years. Not that I've been the Queen of Hearts.

There's a roll of film Jamie took one Sunday out at Elbow Falls a couple of weeks before we got the moving-again news. We got there early enough to set up on our favourite picnic table, close to the fast-moving Elbow River just before it spills over into the canyon. Cool, green, clear, then the white roar of it. Yellow leaves fluttering lazily against a deep blue sky. Smiling faces. A beautiful day.

The first hour or so I am seething. I have my hand up to the camera, pushing Jamie away. Something under my skin sizzling away like the bacon in the orange cast-iron frying pan on the Coleman stove. Stay out of my hair until everything's ready. Scrambled eggs, buttermilk pancakes, a pot of tea. The perfect outdoor breakfast. Okay, now you can come to me. All of you.

Already, before I think I'll break, I am pushing everyone away. What I put between us is perfectionism and academic achievement. Two studio classes. The core third-year painting and figure painting taught by Mr. Authentic Expression himself. We don't get along. I wouldn't put myself through it, except it's a required course. Apparently the upstairs of ACA doesn't know what's going on in the downstairs. In the dark classroom, I struggle through Contemporary Art Theory: Post-modernism and Deconstructionism, where I've been informed that painting is dead. This is news to me, because it sure seemed alive and kicking in the spring. According to the theorists, it seems that ever since Jackson Pollock took the canvas off the stretcher and laid it on the floor and Morris Louis managed to get rid of all sculptural effects and any references to drawing with his veil paintings (thus banishing literature for once and for all, and scouring itself of figure, contour, and chiaroscuro and any hints of the psychological and expressive), apparently painting has come to its historical conclusion.

I try to integrate these lofty ideas in my head while at the same time running around to house parties, selling clothes to women. And driving to music lessons or swimming lessons and picking up kids and dropping them off. Nobody walks in Calgary. I'm strung out, keeping everything together. Then Pozzi comes to town on business. There we are on a Friday night sitting next to each other on the love seat when Jamie pops out to pick up Caitlin at her friend's place and Pozzi slides his arm around me and says *I miss you.* For a moment, I wonder what he'd say if I told him about how close Jamie and I came to breaking apart, and an opportunity arose for me to come running into his arms, along with two little girls. I know what he'd say. Nothing. He'd run. I've always known this, that's what makes us so safe from each other. So I shrug and murmur, "I miss you too." Contenting myself with a little smooch in retribution for *the flowers, the kiss, the stab in the back.* A little sad that Pozzi has become an ordinary obsession.

Is anyone having fun?

Not on the 30th of October when I get a call from the rental management company informing me that the people who own our house are coming back from Saudi Arabia a year early. We have to be out by December 31st. I don't even get off the phone before the tears start to gush. I call Jamie at work.

"Calm down," he says. "We'll figure something out. I'll be home Thursday night and we can take it from there."

Calm down! I need him here right now. Not Thursday night. I need him to hold me. I need him to talk to. I need him to make love to me. I don't need him to tell me to calm down.

Madame has finally flipped her lid.

The lid keeps flapping open, hissing and venting at every opportunity. For the next few years, no one will quite know what sets me off. I become unpredictable. Jamie will just look at me and I know he is thinking something like *Surely to god she's much too young to be going through The Change.*

In the meantime, we have a crisis to solve. I'm desperate to find a house in the same neighbourhood so we don't have to move the girls into another school. One of my great false assumptions: for once, the girls would have been glad to move — they hate their Calgary schools. I don't know why this didn't get through to me.

When we can't find another place to rent close by, Jamie gets his cap in hand and calls you for money. Thirteen years since he graduated and what does he have to show for it? All our savings are down the tubes of a bad real estate deal and my education. What a blow. You fork out, but you're reluctant. When he asks for a bit more you say no. I hit up my stepfather for a healthy lump sum, too. We put together enough to buy a house a few blocks away.

This, I declare, is where I'm staying put for a good long time.

My final painting crit for the semester is three days before the big move. I take in all the drawings I'd done the winter before, because they were integral to my paintings. Back home that night, when I'm washing up the dishes, I suddenly feel like I've been struck. I know deep in my bones that I don't have my drawings anymore. I search the house, top to bottom. Check the Jeep a hundred times. Slow down, I tell myself. When did you last have them? Think. I close my eyes. See myself rolling them up and standing them in a corner in the big painting studio while I load the Jeep up with the paintings. Then I go back and put on my coat and tuck the drawings under my arm. I walk to the parkade. Put the drawings on the roof, open the door, get in, start the Jeep, and close the door. Wait. Back up. I put the drawings on the roof, open the door, start the Jeep, close the door, and drive away.

I can't believe it. I've lost my best drawings again.

This is too much. The crit was hard enough today. I want Jamie. Now. He's never here when I need him. When the girls go to bed, I pop myself a beer — and another and another. The one thing I have never done is drink alone.

Around midnight, I haul myself into my home studio to do my last assignment for the figure painting class. We're supposed to do a nude on a large canvas. I have to admit I've been slow getting to this one. I hunt up a little 8″ x 10″ canvas on a stretcher I bought at an art supply store in Mississauga. In about 10 minutes, I slap out a self-portrait of my head looming out of the blues, greens, and yellows of the Nova Scotia tartan, holding a paintbrush close to my cheek. Not bad. It captures the moment exactly: me, bleary-eyed and pissed off.

THIRTY-THREE

I WAS GOING to stop and get another coffee in Medicine Hat, not change course. When I descended into the first coulee, I thought I'd stop, and started looking for a place. But I kept going. I have become one with the steering wheel, as rigid and unyielding as the moulded plastic, past the college and a park, down into the next coulee, past the world's tallest teepee and down, into grand coulee and the motel village, straight across the bridge and up the hill where extra engines are attached to make it over the longest train climb in Canada. Before I know it, I am out on the open plain again, with tumbleweeds drifting across the desert-like terrain. Then, without a second thought, I get onto the Number 3. The Crowsnest Highway. This is uncharted territory for me. It's about time I stop second-guessing. I'm just going to go.

So why didn't I get out?

The landscape was unfamiliar. I didn't see anything.

How we hold dear to the familiar. Too bad you never took this drive for yourself. It might have changed: the way you thought, the way you lived, the way you judged. But you were never a mover-on-er. To change would have implied that you hadn't got it right in the first place, wouldn't it?

So where am I going? I don't know. A bit south for now. I'm not ready to go home and find Jamie in my house.

My house. Listen to me. We've lived there three-and-a-half years and I call it my house. I've painted its interior. I've planted the gardens. I've talked Jamie into helping with some renovations. In the last year, he has taken to muttering, "I hate this fucking house." There you are. He hates the house I love. The house I care for and maintain. And he's going to be in it when I get back. Why is it I am constantly adjusting myself to his schedule? Like about this time last year, when he was working up in Caroline; ten days away, four home.

"Hello, I'm home!" he bellows one afternoon as he comes through the door.

"What the hell are you doing here?" I yell, switching off the vacuum cleaner. He's three hours early. I'm not ready. I have not adjusted. His face falls. "I just wanted to surprise you."

"Some surprise."

I wap him with the hose and resume vacuuming. The weekend doesn't go well.

I can't walk into that same situation tonight. I won't put either of us through it again.

What is he doing there? Just before I left Alma, he said he'd come back and we'd talk, but it never occurred to me that I wouldn't have some warning. I feel set up. I feel like the twelve thousand pounds of stuff we've been dragging around for years is sitting right on my lap.

AFTER MOVING ON December 17th for the second year in a row, before I know it, I'm back at school, three studio classes with three instructors who all have different strategies to keep tripping the students up. Mad Maud's credo is that you never have to explain anything to anyone; she always wears red vinyl lipstick and a heavy line of black kohl rimming her lower eyelid, giving the impression she's got her make-up on upside down. She's good. I'm left with the impression she's just said something profound. The Bearded Wonder is English and lets the last five or six words in his sentences sink into a low mumble. He also gives the impression he's just said something profound. Professor Never-Shut-Up, well, sometimes he actually is saying something profound, but it's simply that I tend to tune out so I miss it.

The best thing I've figured out so far is that Modernism isn't really over, it's just been usurped by the theorists so they can have a go at being the tail that wags the dog. Now art has to serve theory and criticism rather than feed it. Subversion is the name of the game. So what I have to do is wave my hands a lot and spout a lot of rhetoric while I figure out what to do. This may sound dishonest, but in art school you can choose to go down the drain or down their funnel. If you're going to go down their funnel, you might just as well give them a few elbows on the way down.

What's a girl supposed to do?

My final frontier is video. I have found my medium. No more staying up until three in the morning washing dirty brushes. I'm out of the business of static images and into time-based art. Nobody else in my class is doing it. I rent a video camera and away I go. A whole winter of new lessons. Lesson number one: I quickly learn video is far more than image; it is sound too. Lesson number two: this might be easier than I think.

Lesson number three: merging at 120 kilometres an hour on the Deerfoot in the morning when I haven't even had a cup of tea yet. This is how I jolt myself awake. The rush. In no time, I'm an addict. The thrill of speed on the highway, cutting in and out of lanes. Always trying to make up time, precious time. I learn to do my best thinking when I'm driving. Everywhere and in everything, I begin to see possibilities for making art — or kitsch, all the better if it's ironic.

The only site I trust that is available to me as subject is my own body, my own story. Video in real time.

I set up a video camera just outside my bathroom door. The camera is reflected in the mirrors and is captured on tape. With methodical precision, I cut my hair from a medium length bob to a short shag. I can't decide if the inclusion of the camera is too intrusive or not. At best, it exposes any Modernist notions of self-referentiality. At worst it looks just plain dumb. A conundrum. The instructors can't decide either.

"Do one without the camera," Mad Maude suggests.

"We'll have to wait until my hair grows a bit," I deadpan.

Deadpan becomes my style. For my next video, I mock the shtick of selling clothes at home parties. It's a hit at school. But I have mixed feelings about the tape. I wonder if I have betrayed the women who came and bought clothes at my shows. Sad as it may be, sometimes the only way a woman feels she can change her life is to change her clothes.

Lesson number four: exposing yourself to make meaning out of the personal will usually involve taking someone down with you. No woman is an island.

All winter I make video tapes, take Polaroid pictures, make audio tapes about my aunts, write poems about growing up. I can't separate what I'm doing for each class. It doesn't matter. What's important is that I'm learning how to talk about this stuff. The Modernist notion of progress is taboo these days, but you can have a work-in-progress. You're not an artist in the old heroic sense but you can have an art practice. Everything is shifting. Whenever I come to a lull during the crits, my instructors suggest a book to read and give the following advice: "If you can't think of anything to make, read a book." Mad Maude not only suggests books, she brings them to us, often badly photocopied articles on theoretical feminism. I try to read these articles, but can't make head nor tail. Maybe it's the print. Who knows?

And then I experience a profound conversion. I go away for three days at the beginning of April with four classmates to a literary and art conference at the University of Alberta in Edmonton. There I dream and awaken.

We're booked into an apartment on campus. The first night after driving up is like a pyjama party for matrons. We're all in our thirties or forties and married. Three of us have children. We're all tired. We order pizza. Drink beer and scotch. Argue. Tell secrets. Divide loyalties. Take photographs and videotape the whole she-bang. One thing we've learned at art school is to document, document, document.

The theory in the speeches and papers delivered at the conference is so out of my league I can't begin to understand what is being said. It's like listening to a foreign language. The academic jargon is beyond me. I am out of my element, but fascinated. The lectures exhaust me. By the end of the second day, I excuse myself from dinner to take a nap, arranging to meet my friends later for the literary readings.

I arrive early in the auditorium. The room is empty. I'm grateful for the silence. After a few minutes, a woman joins me. We chat. She seems nervous. Then I discover she is one of the readers and has never read in front of such a distinguished crowd. She's First Nations. I didn't realize. I just knew she was nervous. But she reads well. All the writers read well. I am overwhelmed by their power and presence.

That night I dream that I shape a sheet of glass into a cube with my bare hands. Into this cube, I place a word. To me it is the most important word in the whole world. I say the word over and over and over again with orgasmic release. This is the most pleasurable dream I have ever experienced. I don't want to wake up. I just want to repeat the word. The beautiful, perfect word protected in my clear glass box.

When I awake, the word is lost. My feeling of loss is profound. I can imagine the box and the attendant pleasure but I can't find the word. I recite the alphabet, searching for a clue to my word, but there is nothing.

My attention is so diverted by the lost word that half an hour into the wrangling of closing session at the conference I seek shelter in an adjoining room. There sits the writer from the night before, flipping through a glossy magazine. She smiles in recognition and we start to chat. We both have mixed feelings about the conference. It's important to recognize difference, she says, but the feeling is foreign to her, authoritative. She tells me a little story about herself, how when she went to university she would walk into the cafeteria full of white people, look around, leave. She felt there was nobody there. No First Nations people to talk to.

I tell her about my dream, demonstrating how I shaped a sheet of glass into a glass cube.

"Oh I know what that is," she says. "That's a bentbox. Bent-boxes are used in special ceremonies, but they can also hold ordinary things like food. They're usually made of cedar wood, but there's no reason one couldn't be made of glass. Theoretically!"

We laugh and share more stories.

"Ask the dream to come back, she suggests. Maybe it will send you the word again."

On the drive home, my classmates and I make a list of all the words we heard that are used in a new or unusual way: agency, autoeroticism, in-narrability, imperfection, stasis, fragmentation, phallic discourse, isomorphism, specula risible, morphology, and on and on. But the word that continues to haunt me is the lost word from the glass box — that and the writer saying, *Nobody there.*

How many times have I stood in video stores looking at the covers of adventure movies, war movies, you name it, and thought, "Nobody there." Or snapped a book shut: nobody there. Walked into a room: nobody there. Only men. A woman can read bad photocopies of feminist literature until the cows come home, but until it hits you somewhere you recognize, it's just a bunch of cows grazing. But it's getting better, right? Not fast enough. All of a sudden I have a context for what I have been experiencing all of my life. I have something to declare. Something Important to Say: I am a feminist.

And I'll bet you, Muriel, that Jamie can tell you the exact minute, hour, and day of my discovery. Because when I walked through the door when I got home he knew I was a bigger woman than the day I left. He can hardly stand it.

The timing couldn't have been worse. He's just been turfed off the site he's been working on up north. He and his boss do not see eye-to-eye. He sure as hell did not expect to come home and find me decked out in an emerging identity. Right after "How was the conference?" and "Just fine thanks," we spend hours discussing his nemesis and whether or not he should take legal action. I offer sympathetic murmurs, but I can't bridge the gap of his torment. I can only offer comfort and a sympathetic ear. Something I'm good at — offering myself. But it's not enough.

At ACA, I am a research assistant for the summer, working on an outreach project in my little corner of the Extensions Services Office, a walk-in closet, dark and gloomy. There's hardly a person around; it's perfect for soul-searching and reading feminist texts at lunchtime, coffee breaks — whenever nobody is looking. I read about anger and rage, depression and madness. I let down my old fear of *women's libbers*. It's not just about women being angry with men. It's about women being angry with women, their children, and if they have a God, with God. It's about being angry with the social structures that have been built to ensure women keep their lids on and provide happy homes and circumstances for the men going out into the *real world*.

Where does all this anger go? I wonder.

Anger steeps and simmers like tea. If it boils over, it's ruined.

I haven't boiled over yet. I still haven't admitted to myself how angry I am. No, I stew and simmer, thickening into a dark brown sludge at the bottom of my own teapot. Devouring the pages of feminist texts, I understand it's time to take up a new challenge — this is the end of my fantasy of happy domestic life, as I know it. Now it's time for me to get to real work. Swivelling in my steno's chair in the cave of ACA, I put together the idea for a video installation. I am about to begin my work. Two little words stick in my mind: body and writing. I have come to art school in search of making beautiful objects and instead am surprised to find that my task is to make meaning of personal experience.

SOME SURPRISES ARE better than others. That's the last summer we all fly back to the Maritimes as a family. The summer you are such a sourpuss and my mother spikes her tomato juice with vodka in order to medicate her way through our visit. The summer you lure Jamie into the living room to warn him to make sure I graduate from art school no matter what because Agatha is predicting that I'll drop out. The summer I am slammed with the thought that *I can't do this anymore* when I walk through your door.

Yesterday, I learned that this car suffers from the Maritimes. *Rust never sleeps*. The appearance of this car may be tip top, but the insides are time-hardened. I am driving in a metaphor, Muriel. Imagine that.

THIRTY-FOUR

I SHOULD HAVE set the clock ahead when we crossed the border between Saskatchewan and Alberta. No wait, I got that wrong. I mean set the clock back. Are we gaining time or losing time? Weird isn't it? What does time mean after all these kilometres? It's not like flying, when you leap from time zone to time zone. Driving like this you get to adjust as you go. It's not so disorienting.

Today, if we look out there, at this strange Southern Alberta landscape — those ancient rolling hills covered in that warm green grass like corduroy, the way the soft blue sky meets the sculpted ridge in the distance, with not a vertical landmark in sight — you can almost see the wind shaping the land as we sweep by. You can feel time.

Sometimes we mark time by events. Stop it in its tracks. Or hurry it on. Whatever time is, we don't feel neutral about it. When I told you about Jamie surprising me when I was vacuuming that day, one of the things that bothers me about his coming and going is that he always acts as if the girls and I have remained frozen in time while he's gone. All he has to do is wave his magic wand when he walks in the door and we will be just where he left us. As if we don't have lives of our own. Perhaps it wouldn't seem that way if we had kept daily communication and stayed up-to-date on events, little as they often are.

Jamie doesn't know us in our details, only the picture in his head.

There's a lot you can miss without the details. Perhaps that's one place where time is found — in the details. Whether they just become static or flow like a river. Sometimes distance is the only way we can get to the story.

Entering my fourth and final year at ACA, things finally seem to come together. At last I am in sync with all my courses: five for the fall and five for the winter. Then I graduate. First of all, I have to convince my four studio instructors to all come on board for my one big idea. I've already booked the student gallery for the second week in December for a video installation. The amount of research I did over the summer impresses them. Plus the video-making skills I have picked up through the scholarship I got in the spring from EM/Media, an artist-run audio and video centre in town. Last, but not least, the scope of my project and the passion I've developed for it is the clincher. They're so willing to give me a chance.

Armed with video and sound equipment, I fly out to Regina to look failure in the eye: my old school, my old gym, my bad drawings. When I meet with my old painting instructor to arrange times for shooting in the freshly whitewashed painting studio, she asks me a surprising question.

"Did you leave your husband? You're different. You're like, so sure of yourself. You were such a wife-and-mother before."

At the time I don't have an answer for her. She sees something before I do. She sees me beginning to know myself as separate from Jamie.

A student I knew from the Little Prick's class comes by to offer support.

"It was so shocking how he treated you," she says. "I've had time to think about it. He was abusive. That's the word. You should have filed a complaint."

"I didn't know enough to do that then."

"Are you going to confront him now?"

"I can't be bothered," I retort. "I've got work to do."

But now I know I don't understand my own power yet. I'm still afraid of the outside world. I prefer to vent my rage at home. Though prefer is a word of choice and I haven't got my choices sorted out yet either.

I spend two-and-a-half days shooting Vivian at the studio, in the gym and locker room, and playing the piano. Back home on my regular VHS machine I review the tapes and log them with a stopwatch. Six hours to narrow down. When I feel like I know these tapes, I'm ready to book time in the editing studio at EM/Media, dump the VHS onto three-quarter-inch professional tape, add time code, and make a new log. I'm going to make three separate tapes for the installation so the next step is to make the rough copies. To start, I lay down the music track of Vivian playing the piano. Now it's time to lay down the images one frame at a time. Thirty-two frames per second from which to choose. I am mesmerized by the process of matching image with sound. Ordinary time simply vanishes when I am in the editing suite. I am locked into time-code; shunting images back and forth, punching numbers into the computer. When technical glitches crop up — ones I can't figure out myself — Jim, the technical coordinator at the centre, comes to my rescue. This is not really his job, but he never says no. He's as fascinated by the tape as I am.

This is the part of the process that outsiders never get. Once the preliminaries of making a piece are decided and the work has begun, the artist's ego simply vanishes. The work takes over. Time unfolds in a different way. Jim and I both fall in love with the tape that is taking shape; we slave to get it done.

Meanwhile, back at home, Jamie is off: Brampton, Belleville, Sudbury. I'm juggling my time driving Andrea up to Mount Royal College for clarinet lessons or heading southwest of the city where Caitlin takes horseback riding lessons. I cram in reading for my last academic class, Postmodern Literature, while waiting for them.

The usual domestic stuff never gets caught up. Like sex. I try to keep Jamie somewhat serviced because his attitude toward my activities is a lot more favourable if I put out.

At ACA, I meet with my instructors and keep them up to speed with my progress on the tapes. I design the structures that will hold the equipment for the installation, drop into the Extension Services Office where I still work ten hours a week, and meet with my compadres, the women I went to the conference with. We discuss things like our interest in a *feminist epistemology that derives from women's lived experience which rejects traditional theories as being too rationalist or too empiricist*. Like any new convert, I am a mouthpiece for feminism.

This does not go unnoticed at home. I am not the seventeen-year-old who drove along the coast with Jamie on a foggy night and declared *I am not a women's libber*. Oh no. I have become something a lot more powerful than that. Jamie is scrambling to keep up. When he's in town, he does what he can. He pays my tuition. What more do I want? A good question because, after all, whether consciously or unconsciously, Jamie has become my artful target for all the injustices against the female sex I perceive in the world.

One thing I want is to be able to work at the kitchen sink without Jamie coming up from behind and latching on to my breasts, saying *Honk honk* or *I'm just testing the plumbing*. Fiddle with the breasts. Fiddle with the crotch.

Is Jamie having *fun*?

I'm not.

Who knows if Andrea and Caitlin are? They are largely left to their own devices. Andrea has fallen hard for a boy in the school band. At least I know where she is most of the time — wrapped in the gangly arms of Bradley Hughes, either at home or his place. This looks serious. I must have one of those mother-daughter talks with her soon.

Two notes I find coming in late from EM/Media one night makes me laugh at first:

Dear Mom,

I am really sorry that I did not do the dishes, but Andrea told me that she threw up in the hamburger bowl. Please don't be mad. Because I did not do the dishes I will wash your walls where they are dirty. Come up to tuck me in when you get home. Again I am very sorry. I went to Kims and we did study believe it or not. Andrea and Sherry studied almost the whole time she was here. I love you and please come tuck me in.

Love,
Caitlin

PS I love you. Bye the way the number one is missing on the typewriter

Andrea made the hamburgers.

I need to talk to you about my loan agreement forms for band. Will you be home tomorrow when it's about 3:30?

Love Caitlin

Mom,
Hey!

Caitlin did not do the dishes, but she, however, found time to stay at Kim's house until 9:15.

The house almost got hit by lightning — it was about 10 m away — Chere and I felt it. It was scary. I called Mrs. Hughes right after it happened, and she was going to come and get us but had no car. Anyway ...

I have an exam tomorrow at 10:45 (Social) and at 1:00 (Math)

Love,
Andrea

LAUGHTER THEN WEEPING. Where was I? What was so important I wasn't home when my daughters were frightened? Despite all my bravado at school, some days I find it hard to cope. Since moving to Calgary, Jamie has been on the ten days away, four days home routine. Our combined schedules are brutal. When he's away, I miss something, but it's getting harder to identify what exactly I miss. When he does come home, we have to fit him in. He's becoming a "nowhere man."

This is when he starts to hate our *fucking* house. He won't say *life*. He hates our *fucking life*. Our fast-tracking life.

Designer runners and piles of books are strewn in the entranceway. Coats piled up. Alternative music blaring from the downstairs rec room. I rant as I pick my way through schoolbags draped over the stairs. Poke my head through the rail. "Doesn't anybody around here know what a hanger is? For god's sake, girls! Can you turn that damn thing down? I can't hear myself think. What are you up to anyway?"

"Nothing. Just watching *Much*. Dad called and said if you're too busy, he'll take a cab home from the airport tonight."

"Okay," I say absent-mindedly, then, "By the way, where's Andrea?"

"She's over at numb-nuts."

"Don't call him that."

"You do."

"It was once. Just that once."

I wonder if anyone adult is home over at numb-nuts. Lately I have tried to talk to Andrea about sex. Mostly suggesting she wait a bit longer to have sex. That sex changes everything. That her relationship with her boyfriend will change in ways she couldn't imagine. Oh god, who am I trying to kid, I finally ask myself. Call our family doctor. "If Andrea asks for birth control, give her all the options."

"And if she doesn't?"

"I'm not pushing it on her. I don't want to force a play she may not be ready for. I just want her to be prepared."

I pray that Caitlin will stick to horses for the next couple of years. Even if it means driving her south of the city three times a week.

I get busy with my sketchbook that's due for class tomorrow. Not that I'm sketching, I'm writing to support my project with the theory that's driving me. I don't make it out to the airport.

This is a mistake. What Jamie wants is for me to come and pick him up. I can see that now. But how the hell, in all the jumble of what was going on at home and school, how was I supposed to figure out that what he really meant when he left the message, was that he hoped he was still important enough that I'd make time to pick him up. Why couldn't he have been clearer about it? Maybe we wouldn't have driven each other crazy all weekend and the rest of the fall. The house is always such a mess. Dirty dishes all over the place, handprints on the walls, dust balls like tumbleweed. He tries. Digs out the vacuum cleaner and picks up the slack. But it's never good enough for me, is it? I cringe now to think how I criticized the way he did everything. But you have to understand, Muriel, it was never about the vacuuming or washing dishes or picking up the wrong groceries.

Nothing is good enough for me. A scribbler left on the coffee table sets me off. I scream at Andrea. Andrea fights with Caitlin. Jamie comes home to the cold shoulder.

You are invited for Christmas. Just fucking wonderful. I can hardly wait.

The editing suite at EM/Media is my refuge. Frame by frame, I polish up the three videos. There is no past. There is no future. Just the now of the frames, each one forever unchanging. And yet, as I edit, I impose order, a kind of narrative, that is then viewed in time. I give the frames flow, invent meaning.

At the time, I can't explain why I am so mesmerized with the process of editing. But looking back now, I see that partly it's an effort to find a rhythm in my life that is not imposed by the outside world. Given the choice, I would have spent most of my life there.

I have one weekend to set up the installation in the student gallery. The three large structures I had built are absurdly heavy, made from particleboard because I was trying to save money. It's all one of my classmates and I can do to get them in place. I've painted each white, made of a four-by-eight centre panel, with a hole cut out in the middle for the monitor and a smaller hole in the bottom for the VCR. Hinged to each side is another four-by-eight panel. They're set up back-to-back in a way so that each monitor is in its own space and the viewer must walk around them to get the whole effect. At three o'clock on Monday afternoon, one of my instructors is still helping me with all the wiring. Vivian arrives from Regina in time to view the tapes before the opening at 5 pm. I've promised to call the whole thing off if she is not okay with what I've done. Two and a half months earlier, she had said *I trust you.* Thank god she still feels that way, if a little overwhelmed at seeing herself displayed for the world to see. I hand her a paintbrush to touch up the scuffmarks on the structures.

Jamie flies in from Toronto with you and picks up the girls. You're all there when the tapes roll. This is it, my big debut. The tapes simultaneously start, play, stop, rewind, and start all over again without a hitch. The magic has begun.

Tape number one is Vivian going through her stretching routine as she warms up for weightlifting. The soundtrack is low, intimate, barely audible fragments of confidential conversations mostly about pregnancy, childbirth, sex, our husbands, and the need for deeper connections with them and our desire for intense sexual arousal. Not intercourse, but arousal. A speaker for each track is hung in the corners. If the viewer wants to walk into our space and hear more closely, they can.

In tape number two, Vivian is seated on a grey pedestal in an empty white room wearing a tight pink tank top and navy blue stretch pants to the calf. The music for this tape is my recording of Vivian playing Debussy's "Reverie" on piano. Sitting on the grey pedestal, she performs her entire Nautilus routine as if the machines are present, but they're not. Her face and body are in perfect focus and control. Her muscles flex, contract, push. The machines are imagined through her, then forgotten. Every thirty seconds or so there is a cut to the cams on the back of the machines, moving up and down like lungs.

Tape number three is Vivian sitting nude in the whirlpool, her shapely long arms stretched out across the back wall, the foamy water veiling and unveiling her body, as she tells the story about expecting to get flowers from her husband when their second child, a boy was born: *this was the baby we wanted, this was the baby we planned.* Cut into this sequence is Vivian showering, shaving her legs, and cutting her toenails. Echoing water sounds fill in the background.

I am frazzled. But I know I have pulled it off.

The atmosphere at my crit the next day is more celebration than critique.

At the end of the week, when I am tearing the whole thing down, Mad Maude walks by and sticks her nose in with a passing comment, "By the way. We asked if we could give you a mark higher than an A. It's too bad, but I'm sorry, we can't."

Deep down I know what this means. I have done better than student work. One semester to go and I am out of here, ahead of schedule and under budget.

In the meantime, Christmas.

Jamie is off to work in Sudbury and you're anxious to get the tree up before he comes home. I could care less, but you're right on my tail. *You old douche bag*, I say under my breath. Then wonder from what un-feminist part of my archaic brain that came from.

"And while you're at it you could do something to brighten up this living room," you add and I call you a douche bag again. In my head, of course. We never say anything out loud.

I forgive you a few days later when we're at the Glenbow Museum watching a series of art videos and you sit through them sighing then finally shrug and say, "I don't know what to make of it all, but you know what, I think yours was better."

Christmas comes and goes as it always insists. We eat too much and complain about distended bellies. You are having a big problem with diarrhea. I try to get you to go to the doctor, but you say it's too embarrassing. Just a little left over flu from the fall and upset from the holidays. You're worried about your bus ride to Edmonton to visit Alexis. I finally ask a pharmacist who suggests Imodium, warning that if it persists, you have to see a doctor. You come back from Edmonton saying everything is dandy. A few days later, you fly home. The next time we see you you're looking as girlish as a kitten while I'm looking like something the cat dragged in.

THIRTY-FIVE

LETHBRIDGE IS COMING up soon. What am I doing here? Buying time? If I turn north, I'll still only be a couple of hours from home.

The image of the Nautilus cams in my video opening and closing, opening and closing keeps playing in my head. The fragment of "Reverie." At the time, I thought the opening and closing of the cams was just like breathing, but now I see it's also like the heart opening and closing.

The next time you visit with us in Calgary is when you parade your paramour, Charlie Dixon, out for our approval. *Gentleman caller* as you called him. Gentleman caller, my ass, I think when I get a look at the goods.

"Twice divorced. He's out to feather his nest," I say to Jamie.

"What difference does it make? As long as he treats her well and she's happy. What are you so worried about?"

"Your mother is lonely and vulnerable. I think she should be careful."

I can't put my finger on it. I simply sense that no good will come of your relationship with this retired telephone man who showed up in Alma when his sister bought the take-out on the Millpond

Road. You sense my reservation and try to fix things up by taking me to lunch.

"Guess what?" you say. "I saved $1000 for shopping." Opening the pink wallet I gave you for your birthday and flashing an envelope you take out to show me. By god, there it is: $1000 in cash, separated from your other heap of cash for the trip. I can't help but wonder if Charlie has paid for his way.

I am still miffed at you from the night before when we are watching TV with Caitlin and a commercial comes on for hair dye. Caitlin pipes up with, "Mom was so stressed her last year in art school that her hair started to turn grey." And you say, "I don't know what she had to be so stressed out about. She was only doing what she wanted to."

She? I'm sitting right beside you, you old douche bag.

After lunch, when you clear your throat and practise a couple of "a-hems," I should see what's coming. I should be able to duck, but I never learned that trick with you. You wipe the corners of your mouth with the chintz napkin, fold it beside your plate, tidy up your cutlery, and lean toward me. By the time I recognize the tilt of your head and the coy look on your face — a peculiar look for a seventy-seven-year-old short fat woman — I know a question or a confession will come tumbling toward me.

"I suppose you and Jamie have been wondering about me and Charlie."

"Nope. Not at all." I clear my throat hoping to force some phlegm up into my ears so I won't have to hear what you're going to say next.

"We've had sex."

Oh, Muriel; you take my mind where it doesn't want to go: the two of you, lumpy old bodies humping away in your antique spool bed. Your nightie hiked up around your hips. Charlie's big ass pumping up and down.

"My gracious. Good for you. How brave."

"Do you think so?"

I have surprised myself with, what? Specks of revulsion, flecks of disgust? Vestiges of hypocrisy. Flinty morality. Are we wading into the scrap heap of questionable behaviour here?

Is this a confession or a quest for permission? Have the tables turned? Are you calling in the old favour for letting Jamie and me have sex in your house before we got married? I figure I've paid for that one. We both have.

And then you tell me the bicycle story. Donny's dead nephew. *She's better off he's dead you know.* My sudden realization that you do not know me at all or else you wouldn't have said that to me. I close down on you in an instant. Here you are hanging on to your old judgements, while coyly asking for permission to take on a lover while Donny lingers up at the Georges Dumont. The situation leaves a bad taste in my mouth.

Or is that really it? You don't know me at all. Maybe the old me wouldn't have blinked at your heartlessness. Maybe the old me wouldn't have understood you simply don't have the ability to put yourself in someone else's shoes. Maybe the old me would have just gone along with you, simply to curry favour.

But the old me is seeing through all the tricks now, even if she can't get her mouth open yet. Maybe I'm understanding about collusion.

The new me isn't sure where her next step is going, but she has had it with the old dynamic. When you hustle back to Calgary with your lover, I say good riddance. I've had it with you. Half-heartedly I wish I hadn't let you buy me those black suede Bally shoes.

This is the year everything falls apart and I shut down, not just on you, but everybody. When Andrea's boyfriend dumps her, her pain is intolerable. I finally tell her not to bring her tears into the house. In a rage, she practically brings the house down around us. She and Caitlin are continuously at each other's throats. I can't deal with them. Jamie's company wants to send him to a job in northern

Manitoba with a one-month-in one-week-home turnaround. I put my foot down. I cannot handle all of this by myself. When he refuses the position, the company lays him off.

"You have ruined my career," he rages.

I am anxious, but refuse to feel guilty. Look who's on unemployment insurance now. We spend two uptight months until he gets work with another company. The part-time contract I land at the Glenbow Museum in the contemporary art department offsets some of our financial problems.

I keep my head down in my home studio, turning out small pieces of image-text work and work on the poetry-writing workshop I'm taking at the University of Calgary. In May, I land an exhibition at the Muttart Gallery, the civic gallery in Calgary. This is my big break! Five years of work coming together.

Then the news: you've got cancer. The call from Charlie because you can't speak the words: the cancer is inoperable. I feel a kind of terror for you, and for all of us. Because I also know, in a flash, that everything is going to change. That with you out of the way, either Jamie or I will cut and run for good.

The morning after Charlie's call, I am trying to get to work at the Glenbow on Eighth Avenue and get caught up in the Calgary Stampede Parade. A bagpipe band approaches as I try to elbow my way through the throng on the sidewalk on Ninth Avenue. People think I'm merely pushing through to the front and won't budge. The bagpipes remind me of home, crossing the border between New Brunswick and Nova Scotia in the summer, a piper always playing in the gardens to entertain the tourists. Even in the winter when the piper isn't there and the soil in the flower gardens is mounded over, something of the piper lingers. I struggle through the crowd enough to get a peep of the dark kilts swishing past and, on their heels, decorated horses with cowboys in big white hats clip-clop past. A few gaudy floats and a military band bring up the rear. Colours and sounds waft up behind them offering no end in sight. I am crushed by bodies. Noise and the smells of sweet cotton candy mingled with dense people odours and horseshit overwhelm me. I get my elbows and "excuse-mes" going again and then I am swamped by memories of you and your beminked elbows and this godawful sob lurches through me. I cry because I can't imagine you dying. I can't imagine how you're coping. I can't imagine who will guide you safely through.

THIRTY-SIX

I'M ON THE double-lane highway now. Lethbridge seems to be bearing down on me rather than me bearing down on it.

WE ARE SUMMONED home to Alma, though we want to run for cover. Jamie grows a brittle mantle. I watch him weep inside out, staring straight ahead, swallowing with each deep breath. The muscles of his jaw working hard as we stand beneath the *Passengers Without Tickets* sign at the Calgary Airport. We hop the red-eye to Toronto where we meet up with Alexis, then fly together east. Moncton is hot and muggy. Agatha picks us up. We stop at Sobeys in Riverview for groceries on the way down to Alma. Food? I can't imagine.

"How's Mom?" Jamie asks.

"Your mother is in a great deal of pain," Agatha answers in her slow deliberate voice. "The doctor has given her two kinds of morphine. One dose every four hours and the other for breakthrough pain at night."

The closer we drive to you, the more I'm able to imagine your pain, as if there is a direct ratio of how much you can understand a person's suffering by how far apart or close you are. My stomach goes wormy. I don't know what I'm going to say. As I watch the landscape whiz by, I wonder how everything can look so familiar when I feel so peculiar.

"Your mother is in such distress that she can't be left home alone."

"Who's with her now?"

There was a deep pause for a moment then Agatha answers like a brick is caught in her throat. "Charlie." It's clear that Agatha's agenda is to get him out of your life for once and for all.

I've had my doubts about Charlie, but Agatha has absolutely no tolerance for him. Don't you think it's odd how she struck a pose of outrage on Donny's behalf? Now there's irony for you.

The yellow house smells the same, like firewood and lemon oil, but instead of a whiff of baked cookies, I detect a strange smell. Sharp, medicinal. As we open the doors, I realize it's the smell of helplessness. I brace myself, afraid to look at you. Afraid to look at Jamie. I wonder how we will manage the next few days. This silent family. A wall of late afternoon stuffiness hits us as we enter. You are propped up on the couch with flannel sheets and a blanket, wearing a nightgown. You look bewildered and terrified of this moment — perhaps hoping we will be able to do something to halt the horror — but you know at first glance that we're just as helpless as you are.

We bend over, dispensing little pats, half hugs. Afraid to touch. We have come all this way and there is nothing we can do to save you. Oddly enough, Charlie's the one to ease us into conversation. He asks the normal questions. How was the flight? How are the children? You must be tired. Agatha retreats to the kitchen to make tea.

"How long are you staying?" you ask.

"A week," Jamie answers.

"Oh."

"I've brought you presents," I say.

You flush with pleasure then struggle to hold your face. I know immediately I've done the wrong thing. Brought a satin robe lined with soft terry cloth, a roomy nightgown, a pair of pretty slippers. "They look comfortable. Thank you," you say in your little voice. I'm wishing I'd brought something more hopeful. "I've got a bottle of massage oil from *The Body Shop* in my suitcase. Would you like me to give you a back rub?" I ask lamely.

Everyone leaves the room.

I am afraid to touch this body so near to death.

An act of faith in the living is required. My hands clench and unclench. Fingers flex. I lay my hands upon your back. In an instant, I give up all hard thoughts about you. My heart opens up as I gently stroke from top to bottom, up and down and press my thumbs into the muscles on either side of your spine and push up, mounding your flesh into soft rolls. You relax. I squeeze your shoulders, pause, and squeeze again. You expel a deep, long breath as the rolls of flesh flow smoothly into place. I slide my hands down your back and start again, watching your back fold and ripple like ridged sand flats after a heavy sea has made its way out. Near the right side, where you said the pain is almost unbearable, I simply let my hand hover. Then, hand over hand, from underarm to waist, waist to underarm, I try to stroke out the pain until you fall into an exhausted sleep.

The house is quiet. Charlie and Agatha are nowhere to be seen. In the backyard, I find Jamie and Alexis drinking scotch. I pop a beer. Fog is pushing its way into the yard. Judgement is working its way out of my heart. When we hear you stir, Jamie slips into the living room and closes the doors.

All those years you waited for love and affection and when it finally comes to you, you send it away. Jamie takes your hand into his and cries. He wants to tell you how much he loves you, how much he will miss you. He sits with you, Muriel, longing to be drawn in, but you couldn't save him any more than he can save you. You tell him to hush.

Later that evening, you ask me to tell him not to cry.

THIRTY-SEVEN

LETHBRIDGE IS SURPRISINGLY attractive, given the arid surrounding countryside, built on the Oldman River, the steep coolies gouging their way through the city, lending a strong sculptural dignity. I stop on one of the tree-shaded streets and call home. The answering machine takes my message, as I know it will; the girls still being in school. All I can say is this for now: "I'm not coming home today. You'll be fine with your father for a while. I'll call back later tonight. Don't worry."

Don't worry. As if. But I can't save people from worry.

Just as I can't do what you ask of me. I can't tell Jamie not to cry. We're back to our old drama. Thinking about it now, I see that when he goes through the doors it's too late. Why should you bother to get to know him at this stage of the game? All you ever did was indulge him when it suited you. Well, here I am, back to my judgements already. But that week in August I give my best shot at simply being there for you.

During the rest of the week, the brittle mantle Jamie erected is fired to a rock hard shell that I can't breach. We don't push our twin beds together. We don't make love. Each night I wash down Zanax with a bottle of beer and fall into a hard dreamless sleep. There is a long rigid pole between us — we're attached but we can't touch each other. As the months pass, the pole will lengthen and harden. The points of attachment fester and crack.

WE CAN'T REACH each other, but we can talk about you. A few days later, when it appears your pain is under control, Jamie and Charlie take you on your favourite drive through the Maple Grove. It's warm and sunny. Jamie tells me how strange it is, the three of you chattering happily about past events before Charlie ever knew you, but he plays along. Your face and voice are light, like you forget for a short time that your drive through the park is just an interval. Jamie is pierced to watch you like your old self — the self that keeps death on the other side of a thin membrane of reality. You are in balance. The morphine is working with your body, not too much or too little, and you've had enough rest and attention to let go of your prognosis for a few hours.

To celebrate the good day, we put on a festive supper. Charlie's invited and Agatha is persuaded to hold her tongue. We dress up like Christmas and dish out a feast of scallops, lobster, and shad. You nibble, take a sip of wine. We are jolly. In fact, Jamie and Alexis and I are pissed to the gills in the house where Donny was not allowed to drink. When I announce that I'm going out for a skinny dip in the bay, you egg me on. "Don't be skittish!" you exclaim. "Don't be skittish!"

Agatha ignores you. Jamie and Charlie and Alexis bet I won't do it.

It's almost dark when I wade in. The tide is full up, the water fabulously cold. I keep my stride — no dancing, prancing, and squealing — until I dive under and pop up chest high, bathing suit in hand. Jamie wades out to meet me and fetch my suit as I swim to shore. Stripped, and momentarily unfettered, I dive back down into the black water and swim out, released from those on shore. Stinging head to toe, I break the surface, wave, and make my way farther out, rising and falling in the easy swell, the salt water so cold that I'm conscious of nothing but my body and the sea. When I flip under, to return to shore, I am suddenly aware of a powerful feeling: the tide has just turned. I'm flooded with a blissful urge to surrender as it falls away. To just go with the tide, wherever it's going, though ultimately I know the tide is simply coming back to shore. There is no escape from here. Then before I know it, I surface, my cells needing me to breathe. My head caught in the beacon that marks the channel for safe entry. The spell is broken. I swim for shore.

Later, when I tiptoe into your room for the nightly back rub, you do not respond. My body is cramped, fingers ache, arms a dead weight. Your flesh sucks up all my strength. *More*, it demands. *Don't stop; don't stop — save me. Save me*. My hands resting on your right side, I concentrate on the mass of cells multiplying, riddling unsuspecting organs. I knead and palpitate: short strokes, long strokes, light pressure and deeper pressure, trying every combination. Focusing so deeply that at some point, I realize that the boundary between us has collapsed. I have allowed myself to become too porous. I am afraid you will leak into me and that neither of us will get out of the room alive, yet I can't leave you. At great length I become aware that you're pretending to be asleep, releasing us both. Sapped and wobbly, I leave your side. The hall light blurs my vision. My tissues feel like sponge. I have lost my edge.

DOWNSTAIRS, I CAPITULATE to scotch, straight up. In the kitchen, Jamie and Alexis and I sip away at the better part of a bottle. There is business to be discussed and not much time left. We need to find out about nursing care, contact the lawyer, check with the insurance company about benefits. And, last but not least, we have to persuade Agatha to lighten up on Charlie.

Upstairs your door opens. A little voice calls down, "Can I have another pill, please?"

Agatha would never budge from the medication schedule, but

Jamie and Alexis and I, self-medicated ourselves, shrug. Jamie takes you up another breakthrough pill. The good day is over. The next day we have to bite the bullet and go up to the Georges Dumont.

THIRTY-EIGHT

FORT MACLEOD IS where the #2 north to Calgary meets the #3. It is my last chance to change my mind.

I feel the wind picking up.

Alone in our thoughts, we ride the elevator to the fourth floor of the Georges Dumont. If we touched one another, we would have created a small storm. The hospital is old. Its floors polished in that horrible shine of false hope. The smell almost palpable — disinfectant mingled with spiritual subjugation and the kindness of the caregivers.

We find Donny strapped to a chair in the lounge. The staff know we're coming and have kept him up after lunch. It's clear that his torment is over and he has crossed to oblivion. His head lurches toward us, mouth opening, his face stares with a gap of empty toothless thoughts, eyes widen with no consolation in our presence. Donny's days of endless shuffling, clapping, and jingling are over. His brain is so thoroughly riddled by disease that we don't even have to be afraid that he'll have a breakthrough moment where his former self tunnels through and speaks one of our names. We watch Donny pitch his head and jerk his hands in response to physical touch, the sound of our voices, a scarecrow tilting in the wind.

I don't know what's worse: looking at Donny, or watching Jamie and Alexis witness the destruction that is their father.

You're in a bad state when we get back; the breakthrough pain conquering your fear of death.

"I want it to be over," you plead as we get ready for your nightly rub. "But I can't believe I won't live long enough. Long enough to go to Andrea's wedding. Long enough to see Caitlin graduate from high school. Long enough to out-live Donny. And especially, long enough to marry Charlie and make good. I should never have listened to you, Robyn. I'm going to die for my sins. And please, please, please don't leave me all alone with Agatha."

I have nothing to offer, nothing but my hands. I will not offer guilt.

Did you feel that? The wind has come up. Big gusts broadside the car as we roll up and down and over these dry stippled grasslands. Pincher Creek is not far off. I've only been there once before, on our way down to Waterton National Park. We set up camp at Twin Butte on a quarter section that a friend of mine from art school and her husband had recently bought. This was about a year and a half ago, on the Labour Day weekend. I think that must have been one of the last times Jamie and the girls and I did something as a family, and it ended in fiasco the last night when we were sitting around a campfire having a few beers. My friend made some kind of comment about Jamie's indulgence of Andrea and he blew up. I guess he'd had more than a few beers; in fact, I know he had; they were going down fast. He got nasty pretty fast, nasty and defensive. When we left the next day, I was drowning in shame and disappointment.

When we got home, Jamie took me out for dinner at our favourite Indian restaurant. It was our nineteenth anniversary. We went out so rarely together, so I tried to pretend I was enjoying myself. The food was wonderful, but we hardly had a thing to say to each other. What was said was forced. I couldn't bring myself to mention what had happened. I couldn't risk another public display. I didn't trust him not to blow up again. So I squelched my feelings. Curry and swallowed pride are not great for the digestion.

Sometimes we swallow too much, don't we? Or we make up a story to cover our tracks. Do you remember the morning you tried to teach me how to make hospital corners when we were changing the bed and you told me the story of your nursing school failure, how you got sick and couldn't go back because your father wouldn't let you? Then you gave me the six Hudson Bay silver teaspoons nestled in the slim dark green box. Well, about two weeks ago when I was going through your cedar chest that story came back to me in full force, like there wasn't a breath between you telling me and me unfolding the yellowed letters bound with a piece of two-inch gauze, stiff and crumbling. *Dear Mother, the work is too hard. Dear Mother, the girls make fun of my accent. Dear Mother, I am in love with a doctor but he doesn't even know my name. Dear Mother, In our own little village I know my place and who I am; up here in Montreal I don't know who I am supposed to be.*

I wasn't the only one to write letters to my mother I never intended to send.

You could have had more compassion for me, Muriel. You could have given me more than clothes and jewellery. You could have given me the truth. The whole truth. I would have loved you anyway — probably even more.

You could have given me love. My face was upturned for it. What did you say to me in the sun porch when we tried to find some final, lasting words for one another? *You have been a good daughter-in-law*. You praised my role. Not who I am. Though I guess that would have been a tall order to ask from someone who didn't have love to give to herself.

You asked me to make sure you got a nice, tasteful coffin, meaning not a cheap one. You did not trust Alexis's frugality or Jamie's sense of decorum. You asked me to make sure three hymns were sung for you. "In the Garden," "Amazing Grace," and the third, funny I can't remember today. Another well-known one.

We did ask Agatha to lighten up. The three of us, Alexis, Jamie, and

I, paid her a call to ask if there was any way she could accommodate Charlie into what remained of your life.

"Either Charlie goes or I go."

Good old Agatha, up on her goddamn Baptist high horse. Riding into good and bad, right or wrong. Why did we expect her to make an exception? After all, she has her principles to hold on to while you've only got a few weeks. She has the upper hand. We need her and she knows it. We have to get back to Alberta and our families and jobs. I've got my art show coming up. The only concession we're able to get from her is that she's willing to countenance Charlie looking after the yardwork. She will occasionally let him into your house as long as she doesn't have to be there.

Can you feel the energy of that wind? This corner of Alberta has everything: coal, natural gas, and now experiments have begun to harness the energy of the wind with huge turbines. Even in this era of fossil fuels, the future is upon us: tall white turbines, stark against the sky. Glossy muscular horses, dark against the grass.

I watch Jamie's shoulders cure like concrete. First he has to abandon his father to the care of strangers; then he has to abandon his mother to the care of Agatha. And how could we judge her? She has lived her life with such a purity of purpose, without a speck or smudge. She is a woman who never gave into the moment and would be there, day in and day out, to look after you and remind you just how far you have gone astray.

Where is the mercy for you, Muriel?

At least you took some for yourself the night before we left. Your last act of defiance against Agatha is to hold a screening of super-eight home movies in the rec room with the grey wallboard and cold asbestos tiles. Charlie holds your hand. Agatha is not invited. You encounter the golden moments when Jamie and Alexis are little: learning to skate on McLaren Pond, Donny teaching them to swim back at Broad River, winter picnics while out snowmobiling. An idyllic family captured on film.

I had never seen all these movies; usually the projector frigs up or the film snaps, but on this night everything goes smoothly. You are mesmerized. I watch you closely through the dust in the projector's beam as the reels fly by and the sweet moments in your life are spun before you; the best and the beautiful, the tender and untouchable, frame after frame of undeniable goodness — two sunny children, a take-charge dad, a smiling happy supportive mother — all that had been worked so hard for and achieved. With only the sound of the film clicking through the sprockets and the whir of the motor, you are completely enraptured with the truth of the silent film. Your happiness plotted through mechanical reproduction and the gold dust of happy 1950s motherhood.

While Alexis helps you up to bed, I stay with Jamie to put away the projector and films. Moments later, Alexis runs back down. "Mom says to leave everything just the way it is. She wants to see them again." Relieved of the chore of storing away old memories into little orange and black boxes, Jamie is just as well pleased.

"That went great didn't it?" he says, smiling. "First time nothing broke down. Slick as shit."

Or straw into gold, I'm thinking at the time. But now, with all these miles behind me, what else could I expect? Whoever thought to get the movie camera out for *the curtains, the cake, the kick in the ass*? Much less *the dead mother, the missed funeral, and the war*. Jamie will tell anyone straight to his face that he had the most perfect, the happiest of childhoods. Except for the times when his mother was going through *The Change*, life for him was always a super-eight movie. But both you and I know damn well that Alexis would have something different to say.

It wasn't the change, though, was it Muriel? It was the fact that nothing ever changed. Like Agatha, you could never bring yourself to see another way through things. Time did not flow through your life. You lived a set of stacked moments, each perfect and unchanging. The way you thought about them, the way you told them. Like the frames of a movie, you viewed them one by one. You never gave them awareness, you never gave them time.

All of our moments exist for us, Muriel, but if we are to have any freedom in this life at all we must animate them, make meaning out of them. Time does not exist out there somewhere. It exists in here. In the deepest part of us. Like the hills of this weather-beaten landscape, we can show time to itself.

After you settle for the night, Jamie and I take a nightcap in the living room. While Jamie gazes at all the furniture and objects in the room — that jam-packed room — his face gets all flabby and bleary. He turns to me.

"I'm going to keep everything just the way it is."

I hear a great whoosh of fluids in my ears and the plonk of my heart pushing up against my throat. There isn't an inch of space in that sentiment for me. I know I should say something. Right that instant.

I should have told him I had lost the will to carry on.

There is too much distance pooling between us. But with you lying upstairs on your deathbed and the super-eight memories of his childhood in the magical kingdom still dancing on the walls, I fall completely silent.

I can't compete with you, Muriel. I can't make the world safe and cozy for Jamie as you did. And I had absolutely no intention of ever coming back to your big yellow house to give it a try. After all these years, I felt like the third hand; useful, but bracketed somewhere between Jamie's perfect past and his perfect future.

THIRTY-NINE

UNLESS I TURN around, that was my last chance to head north to Calgary. *Last chance.* Didn't I say that before, at Fort MacLeod? That's because I forgot about Highway 22 that runs down along the foothills past Longview and Black Diamond and joins the #3 here just past Lundbreck. Really, when it comes right down to it, there are almost endless ways to get to Calgary from here if you take the dirt roads along the sections and quarter sections of farm and ranch land.

How do we know when a story is over? How do we know where to begin and where to end? Just think, if I had set off on my journey straight from the cemetery after we buried you, I might have remembered everything differently. After all, it's not unreasonable to suppose that a person's story is over by the time a fistful of earth marks the shiny new casket's lid. Yes, it was the cheapest, but I gave it the once over and it looked as good as the more expensive ones. You'll just have to live with our decision.

He must have known. He must have known.

The murmur that built rhythm and speed while we were all stuffing our faces with funeral food, a loop against which everything's been playing in my head all across this continent.

I must have known.

How about that one?

There's something I'm not facing yet, isn't there?

I'm wondering if you have a privileged view of things now. Could help me out a little here? Would I still be making a run for it if the girls hadn't told me Jamie is coming home a week early?

What am I running from?

The way Jamie always privileges his reality over mine, his time over mine, his schedule over mine.

Like the way you always privileged Donny's story over yours. My god, right up to the end, even past the end. Donny's story gets privileged over yours.

He must have known.

Jesus Muriel, at least your own funeral should be all about you.

Not that you don't hold court over everyone after we leave you that awful week in August when we came to say goodbye. For once you're practically the only thing we can think about. Donny recedes into the background like old news. *A few weeks at the most* we're told.

Deathwatch is unbearable.

You hold and hold.

Every time the phone rings I wonder *Is this it*?

We have to lose ourselves in something, anything to keep on going. I've got the girls, the house, my part-time job, a new writing class at the university, and, most of all, I've got my artwork to absorb me. My show is coming up fast, so night after night I prepare paper with an electric sander, layer on oil pastel, scratch in verse I've been writing about my legless grandmother and poor dead aunts, the dead baby and my scary mother. Bit by bit, I sew these fragments together until my piece is sixty-four feet long and fifteen inches wide. All that feeling about you goes into my work.

Jamie has his engineering work and he has his domestic work. On weekends he takes the cars through the carwash. Cycles the bike paths in and around the city. I don't think any of this measures up to the fun he thinks he's missing. Out of the blue one weekend, he comes home with the strangest habit. For some reason, he scoops his three hard boiled eggs out of the shells, as usual, then mashes them up, so unlike him, in a cup not a bowl, and uses a wedge of toast, not a fork, to chow down. For someone who is going to keep everything just the way it is, his new egg eating habit leaves me feeling like the shells are in my mouth.

On the night of my opening, he stands in the background, watching me get all the attention. He doesn't understand what I've made, but he knows it's making a good impression on all the right people. At home he looks at me flatly, briefly, somewhere around my chin and says, "I'm glad it went well for you tonight."

The sixty-four feet of my stitched-up show stands as a great divide between us. He's out of the picture. We both know from here on in we will each move further and further from this mark, but we're not acknowledging any of it. We're waiting for you to die.

Despite all the best predictions to the contrary, you reach a sort of stasis. You don't get worse. You don't get better. You just get little. Cancer and morphine are the weight-loss program you've been looking for for years.

"As long as I can remember," you tell us on the phone, "I've wanted to be thin. Now look at me. What good does it do?" Meaning there is no man to admire you.

YOU ARE A prisoner in your own house, Agatha has placed herself in the upstairs bedroom, across the hall from your hot pink bedroom. Your lover is denied entrance. The phone calls are racking.

"Can't you help me?" you whisper. "Agatha won't let Charlie into the house. I miss him so much. And he's so nice. He still goes up to see Daddy every week."

And he comes faithfully to cut the acre of grass.

You send us a photo of yourself taken on Remembrance Day. It's the warmest fall anyone can remember. You're standing out in your garden, skinny and bent, your clothes hanging off you, holding a big red dahlia in your upturned palm. Feeling helpless, I rush off to The Bay and buy you some new clothes, petite, size extra small. *Thank you for thinking about me in that way*, you write.

You mean the alive way.

I search my heart for something encouraging to write back, but come up blank.

After the desperate Sunday calls, Jamie and I drive around the countryside south of Calgary while Caitlin grooms her horse after her lessons. I love the rolling foothills, the stands of aspen, clumps of willow, the undulating fields and meadows, the horses and cattle and sheep. Estate houses and tidy barns. White fences. A rural paradise. We find ourselves looking at houses for sale and both fall in love with a two-storey with a garden conservatory on a two-acre lot set into a bit of a ridge and surrounded by trees. I imagine us all bunked in during a blizzard, fireplace roaring, Jamie and I reading together peacefully. The girls tucked into bed upstairs. A dog asleep at our feet. Cats sphinx-like on the hearth. I can also imagine wet firewood, Jamie conked out, me pacing back and forth because Andrea is out on a tear in the truck. But still, I want it. The girls want it.

One more chance at the magical kingdom.

Jamie argues that living out here wouldn't be practical. Too much driving. We can't afford it.

"Well not now but when your mother dies ..."

Jamie will not talk about inheritance.

When his contract is up in early December, he flies out to spend a week with you and comes home with nothing much to say except that now you're just a little stoned woman that he doesn't know anymore.

Most nights he comes to the dinner table tanked. I can't stand it. When he opens his mouth about anything, I'm right down his throat, even if it's something he has read in *The Globe and Mail.*

"You can't believe anything you read in *The Globe and Mail*," I say. "They're just a bunch of Bay Street yes-men."

"Well, what would I know? I'm just an engineer, a dumb-fucker, one of the great unwashed," he nods to Andrea and Caitlin. "Your mother here. She knows everything. She's got that first class education I paid for. And she's always on to the next greatest thing. I can never keep up to her. Never could."

"Our problem," I seethe, "is that we have no dialogue. We can never talk about anything because you can't express your feelings."

"Jesus H. Christ. Who the hell has the chance to say anything while you have all the right answers flying out of your mouth at the speed of fucking light? Why bother starting something you can't possibly win?"

"Is it about winning, Jamie?"

"See, there you go. I haven't got a hope in fucking hell."

He retreats to his corner in the living room with a tumbler of scotch and plugs into his earphones, cranking up Howlin' Wolf. The tinny music escaping from the earphones gets on my nerves. I sneak a peek from the kitchen every once in awhile. Finally, his eyes close. His head bobs back and forth. I tiptoe up to him and give the earphones a gentle rap. He turns down the sound and faces me smiling expectantly, as if nothing has happened. I squat so we are face to face and pull the earphones away from his head.

"Has Monsieur calmed down?"

Christmas comes and goes. Minus forty weather sets in. Jamie still isn't working and is bored beyond distraction. "Why don't we renovate?" I suggest. To my everlasting surprise, Jamie gets with the plan of cutting a seven-foot opening between the living room and kitchen-dining area.

"Are you sure this is going to work?" he asks, skill saw in hand.

"Positive," I say, shitting myself.

We're both desperate for a way out, a way into the future. The change in the house is dramatic, as if it has been gasping for air and now there is flow. Jamie gets so caught up in the renovation, and me at work, that we don't notice that you don't ask us for help to get

Charlie into the house anymore, until Agatha drops her bombshell when Jamie thinks to ask about him.

"Muriel has had a change of heart about Charlie," she says when you're napping. "Now she finally understands the error of her ways."

What has made her understand is that Charlie has taken up with your cousin Eileen Black. Agatha has won the day.

"This isn't right," Jamie says sadly. "None of it is right and never has been."

This news throws us each into our own corners again. Later in the afternoon, Caitlin asks Jamie if he's going to come out to her horseback riding lessons.

"No."

"Why not?"

"No reason. Your mother will take you."

He sounds calm but his body is tense, wired. He's sending signals Caitlin doesn't understand. She pushes.

"Don't you like horses, Dad?"

Jamie pounds his fist on the kitchen table. His face is squashy. White.

"No," he thunders. "I don't like horses. I hate horses. Mom and Dad gave me and Alexis Shetland ponies. Mine threw me off. I hit the ground. Real hard. I never wanted a pony. They never asked me. They weren't even watching me!"

Caitlin and I are too stunned to speak.

He pounds the table again. "They should have been taking better care of me."

Caitlin bursts into tears and rushes from the room. I'm left gawping at him.

"Well, you're always telling me to express my feelings," he roars.

"Not like this, Jamie," I yell. "Not like this."

That evening I suggest to Jamie that he take that job in northern Manitoba that has been offered to him again.

"We'll sort this out after your mother dies. We don't have to tell anyone back home right now. I'll talk to the girls."

He doesn't look at me.

This is the great rift that comes between us. The rift in his head between the super-eight childhood and the reality.

Although we exchange short calls about you and the girls, I don't see Jamie again until three months later at the airport when he and Alexis and I converge in Toronto.

We missed you, Muriel. I am so sorry about that. We should have come sooner. We hedged our bets against the quantifiable and measurable world; the doctor's prediction of how much longer you had, and left it too late. In my mind's eye, though, I have followed Agatha up your staircase to sit with you for the last time.

The pain in Agatha's back is almost intolerable; she's spent too many nights on the hard narrow bed across the hall from you. She has practised all her life to ignore the clamouring of her body, but today is aware, more than ever, of the hip implants. They grind with each step, plastic against bone. Halfway up, Agatha holds the rail; she hears your rasping breath echo between the walls of the long narrow staircase. Pain shoots like a double-headed arrow up her back, down her legs. Two more steps. She can't stop the terrible noise of your fight for air from filtering into her own body, splintering the cold silence of a Tuesday morning. On the whatnot she places a photograph of two little girls. One with dark hair, the other fair, dressed identically: big white bows, shiny shoes, silver bracelets, golden lockets. Two little girls; one sitting, one standing.

Agatha is wrapped in a thick fog of stench. She fingers the gold chain in her pocket. Eases into a chair beside the bed. Refuses to wince or cry out loud. She will not betray herself or you. She places her hand on your caved-in chest. The terrible rattling of your gasps vibrates through her fingers, up her arm, into her lonely heart. She peers into your shrunken face and sees that you are taking death by the hand with the same look of defiance as when you gripped her hand when you were little and led her to the forbidden brook. *Mother, I have done my duty. I have tried to keep my sister from harm's way.*

Seventy-eight years resonate between you. Like highly polished metals sticking together quite firmly, Agatha cannot release her life from yours. They are cold-welded. The process of becoming unstuck is almost more than Agatha can bear. She feels life ebb from your body, the vertical fall into a measureless place. A breath, no breath. The interval unrecorded. Gradual shutting down. Agatha cannot name the instant when the stream of life stops its flow through you. She can only feel the knowledge seep into her.

Agatha releases her body into a silent howl, placing the locket she has hidden for seventy-five years on the dry rough surface of her tongue. Salt tears slide down her face into the gully of her mouth, creating a foul metallic taste.

For my yoke is easy, and my burden is ...

Not much comfort. Here I am again, riveted to that moment after your funeral. The funeral food and hot tea is a welcome, unexpected relief at the senior citizens' hall. Except for Charlie, most of the village is in attendance. Agatha's whispering refrain *circulate, circulate* to Jamie and Alexis and me. Jamie flees the room to go outside for a cigarette. Alexis stays put. I take an empty seat next to Donny's sister, Jeannie.

Jeannie clutches my hand. "Does Donny know?"

"The nurses have told him."

"Have you seen him yet?"

"No. We're going up in the morning. With all the arrangements ..."

Jeannie nods. "He doesn't look the same."

"No. I'm sure he doesn't." I'm thinking. That prisoner of war look of his flashing when an awful chill branches up the back of my neck. Jeannie looks puzzled. She's heard something too. Her face puckers.

"Whose brother just died?" she asks, letting go of my hand.

Everyone looks at Alexis. Stunned, she glances over at me and Jeannie.

"What on earth could they mean?" Jeannie asks. "Jamie just went outside. I don't understand." She realizes people are staring at her. Her face unpuckers. From over in the corner a flinty laugh is cut off on a high note. Jeannie strikes her fist to her chest. "Oh Donny, not Donny."

I look back to Alexis and the same kind of look that was smeared across Christa McAuliffe's mother is smeared across hers.

The air is thick with murmuring. A gasp ricochets as people begin to understand what has happened. I look around the room: tables and chairs, crumbs and paper napkins, forks dangling off the edges of plates and half-empty cups perched to the side, everything in complete disarray. The shocked villagers have gone blurry around the edges; a big cold fog has just blown in, swallowing the words right out of their mouths.

He must have known.

I run outside. There is Charlie twisting his foot in the dirt, his hand on Jamie's shoulder. All the friendly village there to witness. He had tried hard to stay out of our way since he had abandoned you and taken up with your cousin Eileen Black, but fate has tapped him on the shoulder.

"The hospital called. They tried your place, but there was no answer. They didn't remember about the funeral and they had my number from before, you know, in case of an emergency. I'm so sorry Jamie, your father passed away at two forty-five."

Just as the United Church minister spread open his arms and opened his mouth to say *Today we are gathered to remember Muriel.*

I know the talk will jump like fire from rooftop to rooftop. A great myth of marriage will build that the bond between you and Donny had been so strong that he must have sensed the exact moment when you were being buried, and chose to follow you into the hereafter.

I don't believe this for a minute.

Back at the yellow house, Jamie and I are standing by the fireplace in utter silence. I touch his arm and, without warning, he turns and collapses into me with a great sob. He is cored. *This is where it hurts*. Finally I can kiss him. Hold him. He holds on to me.

Alexis and Agatha enter the room. Jamie stands back. Straightens out. Wipes his face with the back of his hand. Grabs the keys to your car.

This will be our final trip up to the Georges Dumont Hospital.

The silence during the drive is heavy and grotesque. The four of us separate and ponderous. There will be papers to be signed. A funeral to arrange. Everything we have done only four days earlier.

Our footsteps are alarmingly loud as we walk down the hall on the veterans ward. There are sharp looks of *You're too late, Where have you been*, from the nurses and orderlies. If only they knew. The second time we'd been too late in four days.

"Do you want to see your father's body?"

"No," Alexis says.

Jamie shakes his head.

As Agatha and I make our way to wait in the kitchenette, I try to smile at the spotted and patchy old men without actually looking at them. She can't meet them in the eye, because once a man arrives on the fourth floor of the Georges Dumont, he is on his last legs, he never gets out except for an occasional airing in the hospital van. Donny was so safe there that you were finally able to relieve your guilt from time-to-time.

"Let's take Daddy a beer," you'd say.

You stay there and be good, Donny. We'll be back soon.

Agatha sits straight-backed looking at a kitchen cupboard. She seems papery, but strong. Without taking her eyes from the cupboard, she tells me about the two of you when you were little. The brook. The locket. Her voice turns bitter and she claims, "It was Donny's father, James Gallagher, who was burning slash the day a spark jumped the millpond and burned down half the village. He was an ambitious man and he would not listen to his neighbours when they pleaded with him not to burn that day. Donny never had his father's ambition. But he had his look about him."

I remain silent. Trying to make sense of what she is saying.

"Don't tell Jamie and Alexis. They don't need to know that about their father."

"It was their grandfather."

Agatha presses her lips together. She has said too much.

I understand. What a life.

While we wait, Jamie and Alexis instruct the nurse to give Donny's clothes to anyone who needs them.

Jamie reaches down and through the body bag, gives his father's hand a quick squeeze. He only tells me this the night before we leave.

FORTY

THERE IS SOMETHING very human about wanting to say *I should have seen it coming* when catastrophe strikes. There's something very human about thinking *I should have been able to get out of the way; I should have been able to help someone else.* You never know what nature, or your own nature for that matter, might throw at you. This is when we start with the *If Onlys*. If only we had got there sooner. If only I hadn't done this, said that.

I've been driving for over a week now and I did not see these mountains — the Rocky Mountains for heaven's sake — descend upon me. I say that as if I haven't been ascending to them for more than 3000 miles. In my mind's eye, I have been visiting the past. I could tell you how the mountains stand up out of nowhere when driving from Calgary to Banff. I can tell you how they press on your right shoulder, while the rest of the world falls away to the left when driving south from Calgary. But I can't tell you how these mountains have surrounded me here in the Crowsnest Valley as I'm passing Bellevue.

I still feel the impact in my body of Jamie collapsing into me in front of the fireplace, that moment when he opened. I could say

If only Alexis and Agatha hadn't walked in on us and spoiled it. But this is like saying if only the family hadn't behaved as it always behaves.

That sob cut off when Alexis and Agatha entered the room. I thought it was about me, that Jamie was collapsing into me because I was the only one he could collapse into. That moment gave me such hope. But there's this image I have of him standing on a mountain with his weight on his right leg, toe in, waiting for Donny to acknowledge that he had finally built a big road, and Donny didn't give him the time of day. That's what he collapsed into. The knowledge that Donny would never, ever, give him what he really needed. That sob. He was collapsing into himself. Then he cut it off.

In the end, I don't know if Donny knew at some level that you were gone. All I can do is prevent that moment from becoming a defining moment in the lives of my daughters. I need to set them straight before I set them up. The moment when Donny died as you were being buried is only a moment out of time. All moments are out of time. It's what we make of them, how we set them back down into time that matters. It's up to us.

At some point in your life, you have to figure out what is inert and what is moving.

Look at the rubble. Boulders strewn as far as you can see on either side of the road, some the size of a house. There are places where the rock is 100 feet deep. Nothing is growing here. This is the Frank Slide, I was here on a writing retreat just about a year ago, and even though I've seen it before there's something so powerful about driving through the middle of a disaster. Eerie, isn't it? What is it they say about the Frank Slide? Ninety million tonnes came whistling down Turtle Mountain in ninety seconds, sometime in the middle of the night covering a small portion of the town, killing at least seventy people, most of them still buried beneath, in the early part of the century. Even the water and sediment of the Crowsnest River was shifted, making a dam and creating Frank Lake. Immediately following the slide there was fear that the backed-up water might flood the town, but the water spilled over the rocks and resumed its flow eastward to the prairies.

I'm going to stop at a coffee shop I like in Crowsnest that makes cinnamon buns in the shape of bear's paws. A little sustenance, as Donny would say, to get me through the woods before dark. Although this is not like the woods back east. Here the mountains with their white peaks tower above me on either side. As do the trees.

When I took your pink leather wallet out of my purse to pay for the cinnamon buns, I saw Jamie's face and heard his voice *That's garbage*. And my own, hard and mocking *No it's not*. Well it might be a little late, but I've decided to give up on that one. For a moment, I thought about driving back to the Frank slide and heaving it into the rubble but that seems like a melodramatic gesture. Instead I hold the bag of cinnamon buns under my arm and empty the wallet of its contents, except for a penny for good luck, and toss it into the trashcan outside the coffee shop. A magpie hops up to see what I've done before I walk away.

I feel kind of light now; the sugar's perked me up. I shouldn't be drinking coffee so late in the afternoon, but right now I think I could drive forever.

I'm climbing into British Columbia now. The mountain peaks to the south are jagged. Red dogwoods grow along the side of the road. The valley is behind me. There's a sour gas processing plant with slabs of yellow sulphur four stories high waiting to be shipped off to Vancouver. Now a sawmill. Compressor station. Seams of coal twist through the blasted rock on either side of the road. The railroad twins the river here and there. The water is so pretty, clean, and bubbly.

Look at that! Isn't it strange? The water is flowing west.

Oh my, I have come a long way.

FORTY-ONE

LAND FALLS AWAY as I lean back onto the cool sloping bridge of the Queen of Oak Bay departing from Horseshoe Bay for Vancouver Island. Vibration from the big diesel engines that turn the prop and churns the dark green water into foam and froth penetrates my body while the hiss of the wake spreading out wide fills my head with relief. The sun is beginning its buttery descent. Everything around me is deeply saturated in early evening colour, like the pages of a glossy magazine. I am seized by the beauty. The cliffs sprouting evergreens tower to my left, above the marina with the shiny white boats sporting cobalt blue sail covers, and to my right, the quiet wealth of well-designed homes nestle on blasted-out ledges. The air is soft and moist, sweetly scented with the over-abundance of flowering trees and shrubs.

I could live here, I think, without a touch of irony. Now I see it. Now I smell it. Feel it on my skin. I am not distracted by romance. I'm just here and alive and taking it all in.

Last night, as I lay in bed at the hotel in Nelson, the sensation of driving on the road kept accelerating through me. It wouldn't stop. Especially that long last push up the endless climb to Kootenay Pass, the highest mountain pass in Canada. The road was dark, the mountains were dark. No moon, just stars way up in the fathomless sky. I thought the ascent would never end. I wondered if there was anything on the other side.

When I couldn't get the sensation to stop, I gave up the idea of the car and the highway altogether. I gave up everything to experience the ride. The car was gone. The highway gone. Even the story was gone. There was just me on a journey across a great continent.

Sometime before I lost consciousness, a voice came through to me, soft and clear. *Ask the dream to come back*. And then I went big. All of me. Bigger and bigger as I spread out into the night in a kind of web, and just before I contracted back into myself I became a sheet of glass, smooth, clear, transparent, and I bent into the shape of a perfect cube — the glass box — and fell through space that was black.

I thought I'd stay in Nelson, spend a few days poking around to see if perhaps it really is a place for me, a place I choose. Then this morning when I woke up I was aware of the call of the coast, urging me on. I felt like a blob of concrete. I didn't want to go anywhere. But something bigger than me broke down my resistance and I threw myself back into the Buick Skylark trusting that if that poor old neglected car had got me this far, it would see me to the end.

My bottom moulds to the seat and my hands take to the steering wheel like an old lover. Off we go again, as if we could both smell the sea.

I am still sleepy as we follow the deep flowing water of the Columbia River with its swirls and eddies into Castlegar and across the bridge and up the steep hill into the forest. Then a half hour later, hitting the rarefied air of Nancy Greene Provincial Park, where everything is covered in a fresh light snow, I begin to wake up. Evergreen buds poke through the glittering blanket with cheerful resilience. The world looks new. There is not another car on the road.

As I plunge toward Lake Christina, the snow disappears as if it had never been here, and I am greeted by blazing blue water unsettled by a little wind. In Grand Forks, I slow to a crawl as I make my way through this solid, placid town entrenched in the Kettle Valley. Here I think *a good place to raise a family*. But this is not the kind of place I am looking for. I stop at Tim Hortons for low-fat muffins and a large coffee, then press on through Midway and Greenwood and Rock Creek, then up and up the mountains until it seems like I am on top of the world before I begin the long descent along the desert switchbacks of sage and pine to Osoyoos and the wide-open vista of the long lazy lakes shimmering in the valley below. As I approach the town, swathes of fruit orchards mark the way. Early afternoon heat engulfs me. I roll down the windows and breathe in the dry sweet air. All the little aches and pains in my body dissolve. Sunshine blasts off every surface. I enjoy the heat while it lasts, but make my way steadily to the long climb out of town before the car ignites. A logging truck is in front of me, but I manage to charge past it before the road narrows to two lanes up in the mountains again.

I have crossed the Rocky Mountains, the Purcell Mountains, the Selkirk Mountains, the Valhalla Range, and now the Midway Range as I thunder across the ranchland of the Similkameen Valley like a Palomino with the wind in its face. I stop at an organic fruit stand in Keremeos and load up with goodies to get me through the Cascade Mountains, where I begin to tire, the claustrophobic crawl up and around the forested road wearing on my nerves and reserve. All I want is to get to Hope and crash for the night.

But when I arrive in Hope and stop for gas, I get a whiff of the sea in the damp grey air. Perhaps it's only a phantom whiff, but I am stirred in my very cells and for the first time in a long time, know where I am going.

"What's the easiest ferry to get to?" I ask in the convenience store.

"If you just stay on the Trans-Canada it'll take you right to Horseshoe Bay."

So down I head out of Hope onto the Trans-Canada Highway like a skier on a victory run past Chilliwack and Sardis into the electric green of the Fraser Valley, following the twinned highway divided by a lush carpet of wildflowers and long grasses and a canopy of mixed trees in full vigour. The air settles on my face. I am engulfed in moisture and fragrance.

Traffic picks up as I pass through Abbotsford and Aldergrove. I'm in the thick of it, jockeying for position like everyone else and by the time I hit the Second Narrows Bridge I'm buzzing in a solid groove of cars, breathing shallowly as I clutch the wheel and hold my place, teeth on edge, nerves on fire. Traffic thins out somewhat as I pass Taylor Way and I can finally look around again to see where I am. And there, all of a sudden, a view of English Bay awash in sparkle, punctuated by the dark hulks of anchored freighters. And before I know it, I'm on the last steep decline of this journey as I enter the ferry terminal of Horseshoe Bay just in time to purchase a ticket and spill into the dank, diesel mouth of a B.C. Ferry.

We've cruised past Bowen Island now and are heading across the Strait of Georgia. The forest-covered Coastal Mountains rise straight up out of the water into the clouds in ever-receding waves of height and shape, creating such a layered vista that I am in genuine awe of what lies before me. The word *illusion* forms itself in my consciousness and I know without a doubt that *illusion* is the word from the glass box of my dream.

Oh dear, I think, so much of my life has been built on illusion. This will have to change now.

Looking out, I am struck by how ordinary it is to be travelling on a ferry in British Columbia before all this extraordinary beauty, and that this is a good place to be, suspended somewhere between the ordinary and extraordinary. Making my life up as I go along.

ACKNOWLEDGEMENTS

The writing and thinking about this book took over a decade. A lot of people supported me in the journey within a journey. Some would come and go; they all helped immeasurably. Thank you to my early readers Suzanne Sarioglu, Mary Lou Riordan, and Betty Jane Hegerat for your insight; Dianne Swanson and Mary Anne Cherney who shared so much more than their stories with me; Judy LeBlanc, Sheryl Dunn, and Marilyn Bowering who cheered me through the first draft; Shirley Naylor who tidied up that draft.

Thank you to Joanne Whittaker who provided information about nursing school in the 1930s, and the staff at Fundy National Park who guided me through the park archives and the Devil's Half Acre.

When my own memory or imagination failed me, I contemplated the text and images of the following: *FUNDY Bay of the Giant Tides*, and *Fundy National Park* by Michael Burzynski; *Tidal Life, A Natural History of the Bay of Fundy* by Harry Thurston with photographs by Stephen Homer (where I found the marvelous mud larking!); and *Fundy National Park* by Mary Majka.

Diane Martin and Bethany Gibson provided editorial guidance in the early stages. Ann McDermid told me to never give up.

Thank you to Jean Cardno, Cynthia Rome, and Sue Goldswain, members of our writing workshop who kept me on my toes, and asked the hard questions about one of the middle drafts.

Many people helped with information. Thank you:

To John McLaughlin who could always be counted on to provide technical clarity about mega-construction projects.

To Paul Deacon who helped with technical information about cars, car mechanics, aircraft, and hung bombs

To the late Elizabeth Clark and Desmond Clark who guided my character through Montreal. William Coombes got her through Medicine Hat.

To Lee Maracle who told me about bentboxes.

Thank you to Cathy Yeomans who patiently proofread the last draft, and kept all its secrets.

Special thanks to Joan Caplan who drove me through the Crowsnest Pass and all the way to Horseshoe Bay so I could imagine a new ending, which turned out to be a new beginning.

Big hugs to Reesa Steinman Brotherton, my "oldest friend" who always provided laughter when I wanted to cry.

Very special thanks to Marie-Andrée Laberge who was always present on the journey and read hundreds of pages, answered thousands of emails, came and kept me company through the bleak times, and stayed with me throughout the writing rollercoaster.

My next-door neighbour for ten years, Jean Tannahill, provided me with unfailing emotional support, and taught me how to ask all the tough questions. Thank you from the depths.

Heartfelt thanks to Marc Côté, my editor, who understood the story from the beginning. He pointed me in the right direction and said *Go*! His understanding helped me keep faith with what I had begun.

All along the journey there was a guardian angel with me in Terry Rigelhof. Chapter by chapter he read the first draft and always said *keep going, keep going*, the words I needed to hear. For more than a decade, Terry was my constant, my champion. To him I am most humbly thankful.

ENVIRONMENTAL BENEFITS STATEMENT

Cormorant Books saved the following resources by printing the pages of this book on chlorine free paper made with 100% post-consumer waste.

TREES	WATER	SOLID WASTE	GREENHOUSE GASES
19	8,696	528	1,806
FULLY GROWN	GALLONS	POUNDS	POUNDS

Calculations based on research by Environmental Defense and the Paper Task Force.
Manufactured at Friesens Corporation